MW01489888

Copyright © 2024 by Kamich Aelk

All rights reserved.

No part of this publication may be reproduced, distributed, or transmitted in any form or by any means, including photocopying, recording, or other electronic or mechanical methods, without the prior written permission of the publisher, except as permitted by U.S. copyright law. For permission requests, contact www.halfgatebooks.com.

The story, all names, characters, and incidents portrayed in this production are fictitious. No identification with actual persons (living or deceased), places, buildings, and products is intended or should be inferred.

Cover and title page design by Karolina Matsiuk

Cover art by MathsTown https://www.maths.town Used by permission.

Biographic courtesy of D/C-Gorney Pty. Ltd., Melbourne. Used with impunity.

First edition 2024

ISBN

Hardcover: 979-8-9910115-2-5

paperback: 979-8-9910115-0-1

ePub: 979-8-9910115-1-8

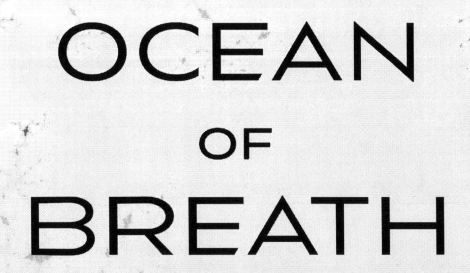

OCEAN

OF

BREATH

heart center

a novel

KAMICH AELK

For ours and theirs.

A story for you.

Freedom brings vulnerability.

Vulnerability leads to strength.

A new kind of warrior:

One who is fierce, and brave, and strong-

But who does not destroy.

The war is within.

CONTENTS

1

ENTRELACEMOS

D espite tactical training, Lieutenant Commander Jonas Porter, following
his heart, leaped through the exploding panes of glass and rappelled to
the sidewalk 50 feet below. Multiple concussive explosions choked him with a
white blinding dust. His strong jawline tensed as his respect for Captain Dylan
was cruelly reversed. The faces and souls of the six men under his command,
certainly dead, hundreds of feet above, drove into his core.

Porter had come a long way quickly. He graduated UC San Diego's class of
1998, a four-year ROTC naval cadet, with degrees in electrical engineering and
military science. Now a commissioned officer with the United States Navy,
Porter was anxious to serve. He'd been assigned to the firing control detachment
of the Naval School of Explosive Ordnance Disposal (NAVSCOLEOD) at
Eglin Air Force Base. His electronics training allowed him to excel in tactical
methods and gave him the freedom to experiment with waveform and frequency combinations. Porter had advanced the Navy's bomb disposal capabilities
and caught his command's attention. He'd been granted discretionary access
to the electromagnetic radiation lab and had developed instruments that could
be deployed in the field with explosive ordnance disposal squads. Among them
was a system, much like the sonar arrays used in submarines, that allowed him
to listen to a mission target's real-time landscape. With a headset and a laptop,
a commander could direct his squad, determine ordnance location and status,
and adjust firing control triggers, timers, and sequencers.

Unlike many information-driven military operations where the commander is
hidden in a bunker, before oversized computer screens, Porter's operation was
mobile.

Porter and his squad were in top physical shape, but not in typical military fashion. Porter insisted that his men were not only strong but also flexible and aware of their balance, enabling them to climb confidently within confined spaces. His squad spent as much time in advanced yoga classes as they did on the climbing walls and rappelling ranges at Eglin. Porter and his squad were lean, light, defined, and centered. Porter himself was not imposing, but his 5-foot-10-inch compact and well-toned body reflected a quiet confidence.

They could safely bring an enemy structure to the ground while performing complex climbing maneuvers that seldom challenged their poise and confidence.

The squad's capability had become so noteworthy that the Pentagon had assigned them to cooperate with counterintelligence operations focused on infiltrating and destroying enemy military infrastructure, which required an almost surgical limit of scope and collateral damage. Porter's team could enter an aircraft manufacturing facility undetected and render the building and its footprint useless without disturbing any adjoining buildings' structural integrity. The Pentagon recognized the value of a discreet, even graceful, asset whose work could easily be attributed to another nation's negligence.

Porter's squad, code named 2703, had established a reputation with a successful string of missions. No one was authorized to have contact with 2703 while they were active, including the flight crews and contracted ground transportation that supported them. Missions often required that 2703 remain uninformed about the location and be given access to the target schematics only hours before arrival. Consequently, Porter soon became an expert at understanding the hierarchy of structural vulnerabilities in any building while studying engineering schematics en route.

The current mission began as did most. The team met at 07:00 Zulu in the logistics barracks at Eglin. The similarities ended there as Porter was introduced to code 2705's lieutenant commander. The permanent furrow on his brow deepened.

This was the moment when Porter realized that the Navy had duplicated his squad. 2705 had been modeled on 2703 to a level of detail that seemed eerily unnecessary. Every piece of equipment had been duplicated, and the personnel were matched one-for-one in size, height, and build. Porter began walking over to Sanchez to question him but stopped short as Captain Dylan's stocky frame strode quickly into the barracks.

Dylan was a clean-cut Navy man, his only physical flaw being a slightly crooked nose, the result of a combat injury. "Porter, I don't believe you've been introduced to Lt. Commander Thomas. He'll be leading code 2705."

Porter turned to Thomas and extended his hand: "Lt. Commander Thomas."

Captain Dylan addressed them. "I'm sure you've both noticed that your teams are closely matched."

As the two men shook hands, they both felt unnerved. Porter realized that Thomas was as surprised as he was. *Were they their own duplicates? What else was the same? Training? Skills? Attitude?*

Dylan continued, "It's due to this mission's nature. We've developed your teams separately but modeled 2705 after 2703. Porter, your technical and tactical augmentations have been invaluable. We elected to explore ways to expand this capability. Lt. Commander Thomas, here are the answers to your questions regarding the atypical specificity of 2705's training syllabus. Each pair of men is as strong, as flexible, and as physically capable as each other. The intention was to develop each pair as physically similar and tactically capable as possible."

"Sir—" Thomas started.

"Let me tell you why, officers." continued Dylan, ignoring Thomas. "Our intelligence suggests that a significant number of possible enemy targets that fit the 2703 approach are paired facilities, nuclear cooling towers being one of many examples. We need to be able to simultaneously infiltrate and destroy both targets. The mission we are executing this morning is our dress rehearsal, and the Chiefs at NavOps are watching us closely. We'll be acting in concert with live wartime simulations, so stay focused, gentlemen. Lieutenant Commanders, you'll be working in tandem on a paired target with live ordnance materiel. Porter, you'll be leading 2703, but in effect, you'll be leading both squads. Your com system has been configured to duplicate commands to 2705's corresponding team member and firing control sequencer. Only you will be in two-way com with 2703. Lt. Commander Thomas will accompany his team to the target, monitor the com on 2705, make minor adjustments if necessary, and be ready to assume command and control if the teams lose sync. Any questions, gentlemen?"

"No, Sir." Thomas acknowledged with a salute.

Porter hesitated, processing the situation. He wrestled between a gnawing feeling of uncertainty and Dylan's bullish command style. *Why all the secrecy?* Duplicate target deployment was a simple matter of scaling the system he had already developed. The potential for uncoordinated error was significant. How could he ensure his own squad's success if another loosely coordinated but strategically linked mission was being executed simultaneously?

"You have a problem with this, Porter?" Dylan stepped closer, regarding Porter with his steel gray eyes. His voice was ten decibels too high for Porter's comfort.

Porter faced forward and straightened to attention. "Sir, No Sir!"

"Good. Transport is wheels up at 08:00 Zulu. I suggest you both get moving. Dismissed." Dylan turned and left the room as quickly as he had entered.

Andreana Brighde Stewart celebrated her nineteenth birthday two weeks before her first time working at the waulking table. That June of 1897, the first shearings had already been spun into woolens and woven into bolts of tweed. Andreana woke early, bathed, braided her long red hair, and tied it with a white ribbon into a loop. She wrapped and tied a full-length, soft worsted wool skirt around her waist and adjusted her blouse. She ran her palms across the skirt top to remove the last wrinkles, then regarded herself in the mirror.

Her mother was already waiting by the kitchen door when Andreana entered and stood before her. Neither spoke, but the light in her mother's eyes reflected their mutual love and respect. Her mother stood tall and straight, pulled her shoulders back, and faced Andreana squarely. Andreana mirrored her mother's confidence and smiled. The walk from her family's cottage to Stornoway would take almost an hour. Early morning fog, typical of the Scottish Hebrides, would make the walk a bit brisk, but they both knew it would lift by mid-morning.

The waulking table sat near a stone wall that supported a basin used to wash the tweed bolts. Ten other women from villages surrounding Stornoway had already gathered around the table and were conversing. The table was three meters long with benches on either side, the thick, alder planked top was deeply oiled and worn buttery smooth from the years of rough wool drawn across its surface. Three bolts sat in a large basket on the ground at one end of the table, and a matching empty basket sat at the other. The women took their places, from eldest to youngest, Andreana sitting at the end across from Mrs. MacLaren. Although well into her eighties, Mrs. MacLaren, who organized the waulking, showed few signs of age behind her bright eyes and well-toned shoulders and hands. She reached across the table and took Andreana's hands in hers as the others fell into a respectful silence. Without a word, Mrs. MacLaren and Andreana reached down to the basket next to the table and grabbed the tweed's corners, the bolt rolling against the basket's side as the tweed payed onto the table.

Within the hour, code 2703 was seated on the windowless C-141 Starlifter's floor, leaning against their gear packs. Porter looked up. Dylan had ordered the arrays fully deployed within 90 minutes after arrival. Porter considered the time constraint irritating given limited intel, but feasible. Two hours into the flight, the Starlifter crew pulled back engine power and began their descent. Porter checked his watch—09:58. They could be anywhere in the east, Midwest, or southwest. They could also be in Mexico, Central America, or the Caribbean.

Dylan had reassured him that the target intel was good, and what did it matter where they were? Get in, set it up, and get out before it drops. *Easier said than done*, thought Porter.

His team was readied for deployment. Each team member had been fitted with wireless earpieces with mission-specific, encrypted com chips.

Windowless ground transport pulled up next to the aircraft. Porter caught a brief glimpse of a clear early morning sky as he loaded into the transport. The truck was rolling before he was seated. The squad settled in. They were accustomed to this routine, never knowing how long it would take to arrive, where they would be, or what they might encounter. Thirty-five minutes later, the transport sergeants opened the rear doors, and Porter stood to exit. They were parked in an underground garage, empty save for a few scattered service vehicles. Porter checked his watch: 11:14.

Now that Porter was in his element, he commanded his squad with precision and speed. "Austin, the elevator control panel is behind these doors. Get tapped in now and wait for my instructions. Sanchez, I'll establish command and control in the third-level tech room. Austin will put you on the 38th floor to start the array. Lateral air plenums are accessible from the east and west elevator shafts. You'll have two sixty-foot runs, each with two ninety-degree bends. Use the remote-control trucks and snug half kilos of plastic up to the exterior secondary air handlers."

Porter checked their attention and continued. "Interior structure is four principal load-bearing vertical steel columns you'll be able to access from the elevator shafts. Ten-millimeter extrusions applied diagonally will take care of those. Bringing down the top six floors will give the punch to pancake the lowers. Set your triggers in pairs, inside to out, com band 387, sequence pattern Hotel. Go."

Trusting Porter's capable leadership, his squad followed his command without hesitation. Sanchez, dressed in black and carrying 60 meters of climbing rope, turned toward the elevator as the doors opened to a dark shaft. As the car's top appeared, Sanchez stepped on, ascending before the doors closed behind him.

Porter continued with his commands. "Nice timing, Austin. Put Sanchez at the 38th floor and hold. Ascend eastside shaft number four now. Drive by the 23rd, stop at floor 31. Bram and Funk—ditto level 38 array at 31 and 23. Sequence pattern Juliet. Go."

Macy and Gilbert bounded up the stairway. Porter checked in with Austin, confirming that the elevators and security systems were now completely under their control.

Porter opened his laptop and started the command and control program. After downloading the encryption algorithm onto his laptop, he pocketed the earpiece in favor of a pair of noise-canceling headphones. Sanchez ran his RC truck's payload down the lateral air plenum. Seconds later, 12 quick tones in Porter's headphone confirmed that the RC truck had arrived at the secondary air handler.

Porter adjusted his mic. "Sanchez, I'm showing one toy in the garage. Signal when you have the second. Slow and easy on the thermex extrusions. I want them perfect."

Porter heard four quick tones: Sanchez's call sign, acknowledging his com. A few moments later, it was followed by a beacon repeating every five seconds on frequency 387 containing Sanchez's call sign, another for the RC truck, one for the transceiver firing trigger identifier, a firing code entered by Sanchez during deployment, and his identifying sequence pattern. Porter confirmed the signal, then muted the beacon's audible representation.

Gilbert entered elevator shaft number six after Austin moved the car to the 12th floor, temporarily disabling it. He loaded a tube into an extruder, attached his climbing rope and harness to the elevator rail, and squeezed a line of thermex across a vertical steel beam. Once it was detonated, it would quickly heat the steel past its melting point. This, combined with the massive load and momentum from the floors above, would accelerate the collapse while restricting the debris' envelope to the building's footprint. Gilbert applied the same extrusion to the beam on shaft six's opposite side, then released his harness and moved across to shaft four. Once again, he applied the thermex, but this time, attached a compacted five-kilo thermex brick with a ruggedized time delay fuse to the elevator shaft wall. The fuse was timed to ignite after the building had collapsed so that the detonated brick would create a core heat under the rubble that would last for weeks and destroy any evidence of their infiltration. Searching for survivors would be nearly impossible. Gilbert sent an all-ready signal to Porter.

Porter confirmed the signal. Macy and Funk performed flawlessly. Bram checked in last. Dust in the air plenum and a misplaced duct fastener had caused Bram's truck to lose traction and prevented it from reaching the secondary air handler. Porter reassessed and determined that the truck was close enough, then ordered Bram to arm the device and report back. Porter checked the time: 12:26. Four minutes ahead of schedule. He signaled to Dylan that the array was in place and that his squad awaited further orders.

The wool fibers tingled in Andreana's palms. The tweed was damp from washing, but the waxy lanolin coated her hands. An earthy pungence of wet heather and lamb's dung wafted from the tweed.

Mrs. MacLaren was a woman of few words. She slowly squeezed and scrunched a section, demonstrating to Andreana the techniques that had, over decades, infused themselves into Mrs. Mac- Laren's hands, arms, and shoulders. She encouraged Andreana to do the same. Andreana alternately watched Mrs. MacLaren and then her own work, growing, learning, and binding with each observation.

Mrs. MacLaren lifted her arm and came down on the tweed with a slap that shook the table. She paused, her open palm still pressing into the cloth, and gazed directly into Andreana's eyes, making the moment ever so clear. Andreana raised her arm and came down onto the cloth with her open palm. She felt the tweed's lull and the deep earthy resistance from the tabletop travel up her arm, warming her shoulder. Mrs. MacLaren embraced Andreana's vigorous strike as a downbeat and fell into a joyous rhythm of drawing, pulling, squeezing, and pounding. The tweed drew across the table's length as the women joined in the waulking rhythm. Mrs. MacLaren began to hum a tune, and the women joined in.

Soon the entire table vibrated with the group's synchronicity, Mrs. MacLaren's Gaelic verses weaving among the warp of the group's choral response. As they worked, the fibers wrapped around one another, binding into a strong, warm, soft, and weather-repellent cloth. Each woman's touch was distinct. Every movement increased the probability of a homogenous waulking. The group's unity lifted each woman's heart. The connective energy bound and infused the tweed's fibers. The fabric would wrap the men's shoulders while fishing the rough waters of the Hebrides and warm the newborn children's delicate bodies. Green-eyed boys with freckles and long tousled cowlicks would tumble across rock and grass-covered knolls in sturdy sweaters. Young women would turn away from boyish things as the wool enhanced their maturing beauty. The deep and joyous nature pulsing in the women's hearts surrounded the bodies and intertwined the community's souls.

Thirty-seven minutes later, a shuddering thud rippled through the building. Porter checked his laptop. Every signal was still in place and pinging as expected. He checked in with the squad.

Sanchez replied. "Something's happened, Lieutenant Commander, but I'm not sure yet. All my systems are intact. I saw flames but it seemed like it was more than 70 meters above me. It also feels like the building is moving. Do you feel that, sir?"

Porter sensed the edge in his voice and answered, "Bram. Can you confirm Sanchez's report?"

Bram came back. "No flames, sir. Can't confirm any swaying, but something's not right. I thought this target's top was only a few levels above Sanchez. How could the flames be that far above him?"

"Agreed," replied Porter. He couldn't shake the feeling that something was off. "Doesn't look like we got the whole story on this one. Everyone maintain positions while I check with command."

"Roger that, Lieutenant Commander." Sanchez shifted to a more comfortable position.

Porter sent an encrypted digital message to Dylan explaining the new situation. Almost immediately, Dylan replied, "Hold all positions. Expect further instruction by 14:00."

"Perfect," Porter muttered in frustration. Why was he being deliberately kept in the dark?

He switched back to the radio. "All personnel hold positions. Looks like we're going to be here for a while."

Porter reviewed the ordnance placements and firing system's readiness on his laptop. The visual indicators all showed ready-to-arm. He switched the mutes off the audible signals, then re-muted them one by one to ensure he was tracking every device. When he finished, he turned to check his com systems, but noticed a faint signal in his headset. He amplified the signal. It was definitely encrypted military. He was probably picking up the repeated commands, he thought, being sent to 2705. If they were going to make him sit here, he would at least try to find out what was going on. Part of him wanted to know if Thomas was as good as he was; the other part knew this was his ego speaking. *Remember to breathe, Jonas.*

He ran the signals through his laptop's decryption software. Nothing came completely clear but repeated patterns did emerge. He fed the signals from his squad's setup into the software for pattern comparison. About a fourth of the new signal was compatible with his current deployment. Another fourth carried slightly different codes. "That must be 2705," he concluded, "but what about the other half?"

Porter checked his watch: 13:55 Zulu. The decryption program showed the related elements changing sequentially and in a regular pattern. There was something familiar about the timing. Porter switched back to the current deployment's active display. Nothing had changed. In fact, too little had changed. He switched to the utility screen and discovered that the last update he had received was over four minutes old. He reset the software's transceiver and queried the system again but received only errors.

"Sanchez, I'm not receiving signals from your gear. What do you show for transceiver status?"

Sanchez did not respond. Before he could check in with Bram or Gilbert, Porter felt a sharp pain in his right thigh. *What the*—Before Porter could finish his thought, smoke wafted through his pants pocket, but there was no tear or rip. Porter instinctively patted his thigh. A sharp electric pulse shot along his leg all the way to his ankle. He reached into his pocket and felt only the earpiece that Captain Dylan had issued him. He tried to remove it, but something was lodged in his pocket. Porter cut open the pocket with his utility knife and exposed the earpiece. As he pulled it straight up, a three-inch curved piece of blood-soaked wire attached to the earpiece exited his thigh. *Bad intel. Crappy gear. Mission delays.* He pulled the headphone mic back to his mouth.

"Sanchez, Bram. Report." No response. "Gilbert. Macy. Funk. Report in! Austin!" No response. 13:58 Zulu. *What the hell is going on?* wondered Porter.

Porter switched back to the decryption software and saw that half of the patterns were now pulsing in unison. He recognized the similarities to his own control system. Both his deployment and 2705's were now armed and ready for a firing sequence, but he had never issued that command.

With mounting terror, Porter addressed the entire team. "2703 abort mission. Return to the third floor for immediate evac." No response. He feared the worst as sweat beaded his brow. Fear was quickly replaced by anger and frustration when he realized that he and his team had been betrayed.

Porter exited the hallway, moved toward an outside wall window, and placed a small C4 charge to break it. In the periphery he saw other buildings close by and emergency vehicle lights reflected in the nearby windows. "What was going on?" He removed a rappelling rope from his pack and secured it to a standing fire sprinkler pipe. He checked the laptop. The pulsing pattern had stopped in the decryption window. The half pattern that had been similar to his remained solidly lit. Then, one by one, the patterns began to change. Porter recognized the active firing sequence coinciding precisely with a deep, low, rumbling vibration that permeated everything around him. He paused with the detonator in hand. The thought of saving his skin while his team was in jeopardy gnawed at Porter, and for a split second, he debated whether he was doing the right thing by abandoning his team. Porter realized with frustration that nothing could be done for his team in the precious little time left. He ducked around a corner and detonated the C4. Adrenalin kicked in, and all he knew was that he had to act as if there was less time than he needed. Porter snapped the rope into his harness's carabiner and dove through the shattered window.

The 12 women worked well into the afternoon. As the bolt's end passed by, Mrs. MacLaren once again took Andreana's hands in hers. Mrs. MacLaren now became aware of something budding in Andreana, but she kept it to herself. Andreana rose from the table, untied the white apron from her waist, and slipped it over her head. Her hands were pruned and raw. Her shoulders ached. She felt exhausted, energized, peaceful, present, and clear.

Throughout the season, Andreana worked regularly at the waulking table, growing closer and more familiar with the weaving women. It was not coincidental that Mrs. MacLaren asked her grandson, Gille Anndrais MacLaren, to help move and tenter the bolts on a day that Andreana was working the table.

Gille struggled at first to accomplish the tentering by himself.

Gille and Andreana courted through the fall and were married the following spring. A year later, the great-granddaughter Mrs. MacLaren saw in Andreana's eyes on the first day came into the world. Andreana handed their daughter to Gille and whispered in his ear. Gille walked over to his grandmother and gently laid the newborn child in her arms. Mrs. MacLaren's eyes welled with tears as she looked up at Gille and then at her great-granddaughter, Keiti Jocelyn MacLaren.

2

CAIGAMOS

After Lillian Mills finished her freshman year at the University of Minnesota, instead of returning home to Boston, she accepted an invitation from Steph Marston to join her for the summer at her parents' house near Lake Minnetonka. Lilli and Steph had become friends as JV members of the Minnesota short-track speed skating team. Lilli celebrated her 19th birthday sunbathing on Lake Minnetonka in July 1975. It was there that she met Andrew Porter.

Long curly black hair, deeply tanned, wearing swim trunks and Vuarnets, Andrew hopped off the ski boat and tied it to the cleat at the dock's end. Lilli leaned over and asked Steph if she knew him.

"Not wasting any time, I see," teased Steph.

"He's adorable," drooled Lilli in a low voice. Her flawless porcelain skin baked in the sun.

"That's my cousin Andrew."

"And why, pray tell, haven't you told me about cousin Andrew?" she whispered, her oval face with its delicate features, never leaving the water-worn paperback novel.

Andrew was directing two other young men in the boat to coil the tow rope and hang the skis on the rack. One handed Andrew a heavy cooler, which he set on the dock. He pulled a six-pack from the ice, laughed, and turned to walk toward the girls.

"Andrew's mom is my Aunt Louisa. That's her boat." Steph continued in a hushed tone with a hint of mischief. "I told Andrew you'd be out here today and to come see if you wanted to go skiing."

"You said what?" blurted out Lilli, inadvertently raising her voice. "Nevermind," she said hastily, realizing Andrew was almost within earshot. She shifted her weight to her elbow and rolled to the side, her blond ringlets spilling over her shoulders. Lilli was struck by his buff physique as Andrew crouched beside them, cold beers in hand.

"Could I interest you ladies in a cold beverage?" he asked, flashing the most charming smile.

"Andrew, this is Lilli, my best friend from school... we're on the skate team together."

Andrew extended his hand to Lilli as she sat up. In her excitement, she dropped her sunglasses onto the towel, and before she could reach, Andrew retrieved them. Lilli took his hand and thanked him, trying to conceal her embarrassment. Andrew renewed his beer offer, which both girls happily accepted.

"You guys up for a ski?" asked Andrew, taking a swig from his beer.

"Lilli is one of the best skaters at UM. She'll pick up waterskiing easily enough," said Steph with a wink while Lilli glared in response.

"What? Lilli? You haven't waterskied? Please." Andrew extended his hand. It was strong, square, and lifted her effortlessly. He pushed his glasses into his hair, holding her hand while taking in her deep hazel eyes.

"You ready?" he asked quietly. Her attraction to him was so unsettling that she could only nod and follow him to the boat.

Steph was right about how quickly Lilli would embrace waterskiing. Assimilating the crossover aspects of speed skating to water skiing, she quickly surpassed Andrew's skills and endurance with effortless grace.

Their bond grew stronger as Andrew listened to Lilli intently. He knew her childhood. He knew the events in her life that instilled seminal changes in her being. He knew and felt the present challenges. He knew her heart, and that laid out her future—her intention. The more he learned, the more he saw, the more he wanted to be himself interleaved with her.

Early in August, Aunt Louisa held a party for Andrew's twenty-first birthday. The night was still and warm, and the crickets had started their late summer pulse. Louisa insisted that the party wind down at 11. Steph expected to give Lilli a ride back to her house, but Andrew offered to take her back on the boat. Lilli bit her lip lightly and nodded almost imperceptibly at Steph, who left with an impish smile playing on her lips.

Halfway across the lake, Lilli laid her hand on Andrew's, pulled the throttle to idle, and turned off the engine. Andrew held her slight figure on his lap, his gray eyes searching the depths of her soul as their passions intertwined. Lilli had never felt so strongly about a man or that the time was right. *It's not just the chemistry*, she mused as the boat rocked gently under the Milky Way. She realized then that they were meant to be.

Lilli knew she was pregnant when she was throwing up over Labor Day weekend. She dreaded the thought of leaving Andrew to go back to school. Somehow, school seemed like it had done all it was intended to do. Andrew's eyes welled up with tears when she told him. He confessed that he couldn't bear being without her either, and this gave them what they truly wanted. Louisa offered them her basement apartment until they could get on their feet. An afternoon visit to the justice of the peace followed by a romantic weekend at a resort took care of the legalities.

Andrew worked on his helicopter mechanic's certificate at the local community college. He waited tables at night to save for the baby and pay for school. Lilli worked at the florist shop in Wayzata until she was two weeks from delivery. Jonas Mills Porter was born in Minneapolis at 6:52 a.m. on May 14, 1976.

3

ESCAPEMOS

Porter stopped the rope from slipping through the carabiner, accelerated toward the building and slammed into a large glass panel, which, amazingly, did not shatter but did absorb some momentum. He could see the sidewalk below and slipped the rope to allow him to descend. He could barely hear people screaming over the increasingly loud concussions coming from above. He knew the building was coming down and that his only hope was to get as far away as possible. Panicked people ran with him.

Within seconds, he was enveloped by a choking, ashen dust cloud carried by a fierce wind blast that knocked him to the ground. He looked up and saw only white. He got up, started to run again, then tripped over a pressurized fire hose. He followed the hose close to the ground, a woman stumbled over him, fell, and quickly scrambled to her feet to continue running. The hose connected to a hydrant. He was able to find a building's outer wall and ran alongside it. The sidewalk heaved and cracked under him as the falling structure's full weight shook the earth. He rounded the corner and found the visibility slightly better. He was now able to see the trees lining the street. He crossed and ran until he came to a graveyard with a church surrounded by an iron fence. The dust was settling onto the trees, giving everything an eerie black and white patina. The concussions had stopped, replaced by the screams of sirens and survivors. Porter started to run again but stopped—only now noticing that his lower leg was cut and he had been limping against the pain. The dust was far enough behind that he could see sunshine. He looked up and saw that the sky was blue and the day bright. He turned toward the towering buildings. One was missing. With mounting anger, he realized where he was.

The guilt of being an, albeit unwitting, accessory to such a heinous crime gripped him like a vice. *All those people!* Porter tried to push the thought from his mind, telling himself: *Remember to breathe.* This was no time to be emotional. His gray eyes shone with dogged determination. Porter was supposed to be dead, and right now, that was his greatest asset. The longer he could maintain this, the better. If they knew he was alive, they would stop at nothing to protect their secrets. That meant leaving, completely shedding Jonas Porter's semblance. He understood. His mind was in overdrive. *A new place. A new life. No driver's license. No bank accounts. No military ID. No social security number. No passport. No job that required an identity. A new life history. Short and sweet. Nothing special. Grow a beard. Longer hair. Different clothes.*

He ran his fingers through his short-cropped brown hair, releasing a cloud of fine dust. *Where to go?* He found ripped pants and a flannel shirt in a garbage bag near a subway entrance. They both smelled of bourbon and vomit. He sat down in an abandoned car and quickly stripped his mission blacks. He kept his boots, pulled the pants over them, and donned the shirt. He removed the cash from his wallet, wrapped his dog tags and wallet with the blacks, and stuffed them into the garbage bag.

He sat for a moment, watching the dust settle on the car's windshield, leaned out the door, and looked up. The morning light was still visible, but the dust cloud was thickening. He wrapped the garbage bag's neck around his wrist, got out, and closed the door behind him. As much as he wanted to leave, there was one more thing he had to do. Porter went back the way he came. As he rounded the corner by the fire hydrant, he was met with suffocating dust and heat. He pulled the shirt's collar over his face and continued toward the building. He could barely see the red emergency lights on the fire trucks as he passed by. He shielded his face with the coat and slowly moved toward the heat. He found himself standing next to a steep pile of girders, tempered glass shards, cement, rebar, and desks. Near the pile's bottom was a garage-door-sized hole—clearly the heat source. Porter dropped to the sidewalk and edged closer, avoiding the heat waves as they lifted the dust cloud up and away.

Through the distortion, Porter could see flames thirty feet down. Chunks of concrete and twisted rebar fused into cars were piled high. Black smoke from burning tires wafted up from the opening. Porter stepped back and tossed the garbage bag into the cavern. The plastic wilted, vaporizing even before the flaming bundle dropped below the sidewalk. *The best way to get far from here is to head west,* thought Porter.

The trains were canceled, and traffic was gridlocked. *Walking is the only option,* reasoned Porter. He headed back past the graveyard and continued north on Church Street. In the offices above a deli on the corner of Church and Vesey, he saw lawyers and secretaries casually sipping coffee, looking up at the smoke and dust. Having long surrendered to the delusion of "justice for all," it had left them all but immune to further impression. He figured there had to be a bridge or tunnel crossing over to New Jersey; he had to find it. His leg hurt, but he found he could endure the pain if he kept a steady pace. He turned left on Chambers and continued north on Hudson. After crossing Canal, he saw the entrance to the Holland tunnel. Traffic was at a complete standstill. *I'm not the only one anxious to get out of town,* realized Porter.

Porter ran past the cars and into the tunnel. There was a narrow sidewalk with a handrail. He estimated the tunnel's length to be about two miles. As long as his leg held up, he could be across in twenty minutes. As soon as he reached the ramp's top on the Jersey side, he doubled back and ran two more blocks to the waterfront. Lower Manhattan was engulfed in a haze of white dust. The other building was still standing, but black smoke billowed from a fire near the top. The building started to collapse in on itself, reminiscent of the controlled demolition training films he had studied. Now he understood the decrypted pattern's other half. *Not two duplicated codes, there were four,* Porter realized. He looked at his watch. 14:28 Zulu. He unbuckled the watch, threw it into the river, and turned back, walking west.

4

APUREMOS

That summer Andrew finished school and started work with a maintenance facility at Anoka County airfield. He worked the swing shift so that he could spend more time during the day with Lilli and Jonas.

Lilli reconnected with Melody Eres, an Asian history professor who taught her at U of M. Melody had studied at an ashram in Kerala during the summer. She was developing a yoga and meditation studio in the West as part of a cultural research project funded by the U of M in conjunction with the recently budding MIU Fairfield. She invited Lilli to work with her. Melody offered to teach her to be a yoga instructor if she would agree to teach classes in the studio. Lilli completed the training course and began teaching three mornings a week in Minneapolis.

They stayed in Louisa's apartment for two more years. After Andrew was promoted to lead mechanic, they bought a small house on 5th Avenue in Wayzata.

Lilli started a co-ed winter speed skating day camp for elementary through high school kids. Andrew set up an ice fishing tent on Lake Minnetonka, complete with a generator and propane heaters, as the office and meeting place for the camp.

Jonas started skating inside the tent not long after he began to walk. Soon, Jonas was out on the ice every afternoon, bundled up in as many thermal onesies and Patagonia shells as Lilli and Louisa could put on him, skating alongside Lilli as she called out times and critiques to the skaters.

Andrew left the camp at three-thirty each afternoon to get to work in Blaine by four. One afternoon as he was getting his coat on to go, Lilli poked her head through the tent door, flushed and breathless.

"Sweetie. I want to run a new drill with the kids tomorrow. But I need the practice area to be bigger."

Jonas pulled back the tent door flap. His flushed and impish grinning face appeared level with Lilli's knee. He had his father's gray eyes and a hint of his strong jawline. "Weedie! Weedie Daddy!"

Andrew turned the page of his technical reference manual and peered around the lamp on the desk. "How much bigger do you want it? You already have a full-size rink and then some."

"Can we try three times as big?"

"I'll tell you what. I've got that timer working again on the resurfacing pump. I'll set it to run for twenty minutes tonight, and we'll see what we get in the morning."

Lilli wrapped her hair into a loop with an elastic and swung a mat bag over her shoulder. She pulled Jonas close to her leg and hugged him as he tried to squirm away. "Oh, and I'm going to stay with Steph tonight after class. Could you pick up this little goofball from your mom's on the way back from work?"

"No problem. So, we'll see you in the morning?"

"Bright and early," smiled Lilli.

5

OPRIMAMOS

"Very impressive, Mr. Hine. Do we have a secure line? May we speak freely?" Hine recognized the drawl on the line and knew he was on a speakerphone. This was the only way he had ever communicated with the man whose code name was Cowboy. He was always on speaker. He assumed others were listening, but Cowboy was the only person who spoke during these conversations.

Hine replied as he looked across his office. "This line is secure, sir. As always, your men from the Service have done a stellar job."

"As we've discussed, Mr. Hine, this is only the start of many great things."

"I understand, sir."

"Were there complications we need to be aware of?" asked Cowboy.

"I did have some resistance from a major at NORAD, but that has been resolved. I was under the impression that the key personnel would be on-message."

"The Service does its best, Mr. Hine, but it is not infallible. We count on you to fill in those gaps. Are we comfortable that this major is now strictly under command?"

"Yes, sir. Under command."

"Building Seven was sloppy, Mr. Hine. We were quite disappointed, particularly with the media coverage. Do we know what happened there yet?"

Cowboy was a force to be reckoned with, and Hine could already sense his usual quiet authority slip away. "It was a separate black op, sir." Hine dropped his glasses on the desk blotter and massaged his nose bridge. I'm meeting with State tomorrow to find out what happened and to get the coverage we need. I've already shut the developer up. It's unfortunate, but we will handle it sir." Hine walked a fine line, avoiding saying anything that might be construed as an excuse.

"No other loose ends, Mr. Hine?"

"General Rappar met with me this afternoon. He confirmed all executory assets are terminated. Drone controllers, Naval EOD, NORAD, and FAA are busy taking the heat for their errors." Hine's tone and demeanor remained objective.

"We don't need that much detail, Mr. Hine. What we want to know is, have you done your job?"

Fine beads of sweat glistened on Hine's balding head. "I have, sir." Hine paused and added thoughtfully, "I have."

Cowboy's tone mellowed to a soothing breeze of hospitality. "Well, that's good, Mr. Hine. Very good. We wish to thank you for the fine service you have rendered today to this great nation. You have opened the door to strengthening this land's security and sanctity for decades to come."

"Thank you, sir. I'm glad to be of service." Hine rolled his chair closer to the desk and adjusted a pen in its stand.

"Well, Mr. Hine. You are going to be very busy."

The line disconnected, but Hine replied anyway. "Thank you, sir," he said, holding the receiver at an angle.

"This is the dawn of a new America. Hell, a new world!" Fischer had been seated next to a table lamp on Hine's leather office couch during the conversation with Cowboy. He had helped himself to a crystal tumbler with scotch and ice. Hine deeply resented him. Fischer was the Secret Service's deputy director and reported directly to Cowboy. He seldom missed an opportunity to remind Hine of the chain of command. The Service wasn't subject to election cycles. Their solidarity with Cowboy and his associates enjoyed a long and loyal history. "You look like shit," said Fischer, rubbing it in. "You sure you don't want a drink?"

"I'm fine. I've got a lot on my mind. And I'm tired. It's been a very long day," Hine answered dismissively, not wanting to give Fischer the satisfaction of sensing the edge in his voice.

"Get some rest Mr. Vice President. Tomorrow, we start reaping the rewards of our efforts." Fischer sipped his drink and settled a little more comfortably into the couch.

"I'm meeting with Rappar at six-thirty tomorrow morning to go over the details. What time do we meet with the Energy Development Group?" asked Hine.

"Eight."

"And State?"

"Nine-thirty. Have you got the "Commander" occupied for us?" asked Fischer.

"He got back from Florida a few hours ago. The press office has him lined up all morning. Your boy Hannefin is coaching him through the message. He won't bother us."

"Excellent."

Hine opened the office door. His fingers rested on the knob as he turned to look through the window at the lights of D.C. Just shy of six feet, Hine used to cut a commanding figure. But not today. Today, he was exhausted. His shoulders slumped from the weight of his role in this elaborate scheme to reinstate the United States as the global superpower. *God help us,* he thought, and to Fischer said, "Let yourself out. I'm going home."

Fischer said nothing. He stared thoughtfully at the finely stained bookshelves across the room. The ice cubes clinked melodically as he finished his scotch.

6

DESLICEMOS

Andrew pulled his Subaru wagon into the driveway and walked into his mom's house at about half past midnight. Louisa was knitting under the light of a floor lamp. A rosy-cheeked Jonas was fast asleep, sprawled across a couch cushion on the floor, with his skates still on. Andrew quietly admired his sleeping son and then walked over to his mom.

"He barely let me take his snowsuit off," she whispered as she set her knitting aside and retracted the footrest. "The skates were non-negotiable. He would not let me take them off. What can I say?" Louisa shrugged. "The kid loves to skate."

Andrew laid the snowsuit out on the floor next to Jonas and rolled him gently into it. He pushed his hands into the little mittens and zipped him up into the onesie. Jonas never cracked an eye.

"Thanks, mom. You're the best."

"I know baby. Give your mama a hug."

Andrew put Jonas over his shoulder and hugged her with his free arm. "Thanks again, mom. Goodnight."

"Best little guy ever." Louisa reached up on her toes and kissed Jonas on the forehead.

Andrew parked the car by the lot near the pump. He left the car heater running with Jonas asleep in the back seat. He switched on the pump timer and set it to run for twenty minutes. The night was cold, and the breeze made the chill even sharper. Andrew watched as the pump began gushing three hundred gallons of water per minute onto the ice. He waited ten minutes, trying to gauge whether the twenty minutes would be enough. *She said she wanted it big.* He reset the timer for thirty minutes and turned back to get into the car. The Subaru's back door was open. Andrew ran to the car, but Jonas was missing. With mounting panic, he turned back to the lake and saw a small dark figure toddling onto the ice. *Jonas!* His blood ran cold. He called to him, breaking into a run, but his hood and the breeze made it difficult to hear over the pump's whine. Jonas began skating with his typical fervor, skimming through the water's thickening layer covering the pond. Unthinking, Andrew ran past the pump and onto the wet ice. He slipped almost immediately, hitting his head on the pump's intake pipe. His limp body lay downstream of the pump's discharge pipe, the rushing water pushing him further from the shore. Blood streamed from his head, mixing with the water. He lay flat, arms by his side, eyes open to the cold night, his jeans, sweater, and hat wicking the water from the ice surface as blood pooled around him.

Jonas continued skating and stopped at his father's feet. He stood still for a moment, his skate blades holding him just above the creeping layer of water.

"Weedie daddy?" he said quietly, his breath condensing in the frigid air. Jonas climbed onto his father's chest and patted it with his small, gloved hand as he looked into his face. "Weedie daddy?"

7

ATRAGANTEMOS

P orter found a discount clothing store near Newark. Despite the disgusted looks from the clerk, who turned away gagging at the smell, he was able to purchase two black t-shirts, underwear, a sweatshirt, and a pair of jeans. He made his way to the station in Newark and purchased a bus ticket to Salt Lake. *Hide out among the Mormons. Perfect,* thought Porter without much conviction. He had an hour before departure. Porter locked the door in a Starbucks men's room and did his best to clean up with the pathetic dribble from the tap, hand soap, and paper towels. The bourbon and vomit ensemble went in the trash, and he put on the new clothes.

The only busses Porter had ridden were around campus in San Diego and on base at Eglin. Long-distance bus travel had never been a consideration because the travel time was always a deal killer. Anonymity was the only pro on this list. After the third late-night stop somewhere in Pennsylvania, some loud boys in their early twenties got on board and sat behind him. Soon, the whiskey fifths came out, and their voices got even louder. Porter picked his bag up, leaned his head against the window using his second t-shirt as a pillow, and watched the cars and trucks slowly passing by in the next lane.

At the next stop, a woman got off the bus and left her evening paper on the seat. Porter picked it up and turned to the front page, which had a picture of the two World Trade Center towers belching smoke. He turned the page to the article and saw a photograph of the smoldering building wreckage. One of the still intact vertical steel columns stood out among the rest, clearly showing a clean forty-five-degree severance at its top. Porter read about the planes and the crashes in Pennsylvania and at the Pentagon. The words fell on his eyes, but he knew it was all a lie. *They are pinning it on Al-Qaeda? Bastards!* thought Porter as his fist tightened on the newspaper. *They have the balls to call it a terrorist attack!* The journalists were too credulous; they actually believed this story. *Who feeds them this stuff? What in the hell was going on? Who stands to gain?*

Porter folded the paper up, and it crumpled in his grip. He looked out and saw his own reflection in the glass of the window. He could hardly recognize himself. *The man responsible for the deaths of thousands,* he thought ruefully. He tried to brush aside the thought of Sanchez, Bram, and the rest of his squad. He had kept a detached air of command with them, but he knew their hearts were good. He shuddered at the thought that his striving for excellence as a Naval officer had contributed to this atrocity. He had done all he could to excel as the squad's leader and in the eyes of his commanding officers. Now he felt completely naïve.

Porter knew that he had to stay hidden and quiet, create a new life in a place where no one knew him, and do nothing to attract attention. As much as he wanted to know more, his training told him to lie low. He was very likely the only person outside the conspiracy who knew the real story. *Time to disappear,* thought Porter.

8

TEMBLEMOS

Lilli's heart began to pound when she saw the Subaru parked by the lake—door open. She pulled up next to it and heard the engine running as soon as she opened her door. She looked out toward the lake and saw the sun sparkling on a frosty bundle within the triple-sized rink. Her mind reeled, and her legs collapsed as she realized what she was seeing. She scrambled to her feet and ran out onto the ice. As she approached, she could see Andrew's body half-engulfed and frozen solid. She fell to her knees, panting, and slid until she reached the ice fillet surrounding Andrew's legs. Lilli began to convulse and sob uncontrollably upon noticing Jonas' snowsuit lying on Andrew's chest. She gently rolled Jonas's body into her arms. She could see he was breathing, but it was very shallow and he was cold to the touch. Seeing Andrew, she wanted to scream, to fall apart, but in the back of her mind, she knew that Jonas had precious little time. She had to get him to a doctor. It took her all her strength to stand up with Jonas in her trembling arms. She looked through her tears at her husband's lifeless body. The man she snuggled up to every night, in whose arms she found such comfort, now lay frost-covered, conjoined with the lake.

9

DISCREPEMOS

"Good morning, General. Have a seat." Hine had been home to shower and change into a different suit, but he was clearly having trouble covering his stress and exhaustion.

US Air Force General Lyle Rappar unbuttoned his uniform jacket and stood by the window. "You hit the hornets' nest with a big stick yesterday, Mr. Hine." Rappar's blue eyes scanned the immaculately maintained lawn below. "I hope you're ready for the aftermath."

"We have things under control here, general. Why don't you fill me in on Shanksville and the Pentagon? How did that go?"

Rappar turned to Hine. "You know I don't like any of this," he said, knitting his bushy brows. The arch of the left was bisected by an abrupt scar.

"It's not your job to enjoy anything, Rappar. It's your job to follow orders." Hine could remain deeply threatening even when he was upset. It was like his face was the sharpened stone on the end of a spear, but someone else was throwing it.

Assuming a cold military stance, Rappar reported, "With minor exceptions, the mission was executed as planned. The Unmanned Airborne Vehicle modifications we installed on the commercial airliners transferred control to UAV command as soon as Langley's foreign trainees made their moves. Once the onboard pilots were incapacitated, UAV pilots in Creech took over via satellite link. For the towers, it was simply a matter of lighting the targets with laser guidance and setting up the approaches."

"And what about the other two, General? There isn't any wreckage at either site. How am I supposed to cover that?" asked Hine, removing his glasses and tossing them onto the desk blotter. He leaned back in his chair and glared at Rappar. "There were passengers on those planes talking to family on their cell phones while they were being rerouted."

"That was my call, Mr. Hine," Rappar deflected, standing to his six-foot-two height. With muscles honed by years of military discipline, broad shoulders, and a robust frame, the General was an imposing figure. "There was too much at stake getting that close to the Capitol or the Pentagon. You may be calling the shots, sir, but you know as well as I that there is still resistance within the Staff."

"So where did those two aircraft go, General?"

Rappar's square jaw tensed as he bit back a cutting riposte. He stuck to the facts. "They became part of Operation Vigilant Warrior. The passengers and trainees were chemically subdued as UAV Command flew them 15 miles out over the Atlantic. You know we had F-16s deployed. We ordered one to destroy them. Part and parcel to the war game simulations we had running yesterday."

"And the explosions? How did you put a crater in Shanksville and a blackened hole in your campground across the river?"

Rappar paused to contain himself. "Two sidewinder missiles out in an empty field in Pennsylvania will do more damage than you'd expect. I had ordnance placed in a construction area at the Pentagon. It was unoccupied at blast time. I'm sure you'll find a way around insufficient wreckage," spat Rappar, almost mockingly. "Putting my command... My colleagues... Damn it, Hine! Our nation's Capital! In harm's way. It wasn't going to happen. Not on my watch," said Rappar, vigorously shaking his bald head.

Hine sifted through some paperwork on his desk. "We've released some photos to the media, but we're not letting them in. We're going to have to work with what we got from the towers and spin the other two sites away from scrutiny."

10
AFLUYAMOS

Louisa's husband, Glenn Porter, owned a communications consulting firm, which kept him busy fulfilling government contracts around the globe. He and Louisa let Lilli know that they would always provide for her and Jonas. Glenn paid off the mortgage on her house on 5th Avenue and set up a college fund for Jonas. Lilli continued teaching yoga and running her skate camps. Jonas started at the Wayzata Montessori school. Later, he grew accustomed to working beside Lilli in the afternoons. He often went with Lilli into Minneapolis and became well-practiced at yoga.

It wasn't until December of 1984 that Lilli felt whole enough to expand the practice area for the drill she wanted to run with the kids. She asked Louisa to spend the night on 5th Avenue with Jonas and asked Glenn to accompany her to the lake that night to help with the pump. Glenn held her close while they stood silently in the moonlight, watching the water expand across the ice.

Lilli started the flocking drill by asking Jonas, one other boy, and two girls from the camp to come out to the practice area early on a Saturday morning. Lilli explained that the drill is designed to promote close team coordination and keen awareness of position relative to the other skaters and the flock as a whole. She asked them to stand facing in one direction, two pairs side-by-side, one arm's length apart, and equally distant from the pair in front. Jonas and Mindy stood alongside each other behind Jordan and Taylor.

Lilli asked them to maintain their placement relative to each other and skate slowly forward. With practice, they were able to stay in formation in a straight line. She then worked with them on shallow turns to the left and right. As they progressed through and became more adept at maintaining formation, she introduced the cycle pattern. The pair in front retreated to the back row and shifted to the opposite column. It required the skaters to cross each other's path as they slowed and entered the following rank. After a brief interval, the other front pair would fall behind and repeat the cycle. The skaters became frustrated trying to figure out who should cross behind first to avoid collision.

"We should decide before we start who is going to go first every time. Then there won't be any more problems," Jonas announced to his mother after the group broke in frustration for the third time.

Lilli stopped them and asked them to listen carefully. "I know this is an unusual practice, and I know how challenging it is. But that's why we're doing it." Lilli turned directly to Jonas but lowered her voice as she addressed the group. "I want you to stay quiet. No talking at all. I want you to feel each other's motions. Try to anticipate what the other skater is going to do. Try to feel all four of you moving as a single unit. We could make a bunch of rules on how it should be done, but that would be too mechanical. The four-skater flock is the simplest formation we'll be practicing. If you're following too many rules, the flock won't be able to adapt when it needs to," her forehead creased with concern. She needed them to get this right. "I know it sounds a little weird right now, but I want you guys to give it your best shot."

The skaters nodded and tried the drill again. There were occasional mishaps and collisions, but the kids worked around them and slowly became more fluid. Once comfortable skating in the cycling formation, Lilli introduced sharper and quicker turns. At first, Lilli told them to skate straight across the rink, turn sharply left at the end, and come back. They moved on to sharp right turns at the other end, alternating directions at each end of the course.

After weeks of practicing, Lilli gathered the four skaters midway through training. "I want to try something new today," she said tucking a stray blond ringlet under her beanie. "Do you remember when we first started flocking?" The kids nodded and laughed at each other. "Yeah. You thought it was weird and hard right?" They nodded again. "But now you guys are stars. The way you flock is amazing even to me. It's time we took this to the next level. I want you to skate in the cycling formation, but instead of doing ovals or eights, I want you to go where the flock wants to go."

"Wait, what do you mean, Ms. Porter?" Taylor asked. "We have to know where to go."

"Taylor, I know this is a stretch, but that's why we're out here. To make ourselves and our team better every day, right?" Taylor nodded. "You all know the flock should stay within the rink, right? Well, there are only so many things you could do inside that boundary. Do what feels right. There are only two guidelines. Stay in the rink and keep cycling."

"But what if Jonas wants to go one way, and I want to go another?" Mindy pleaded. "What if I start turning left, and then Jordan comes to the front and wants to turn right?"

"See what happens. If the formation breaks, come back together and try it again. It's okay if the formation breaks as long as everyone regroups gracefully," reassured Lilli, interlacing her fingers with a smile. "Remember when we talked about competing with grace? Doing your personal best while intending the same for everyone around you? That way, everyone has the greatest opportunity to improve. Gracefully regrouping is as much a part of flocking as is doing your best to sense the direction the flock is pulling. Now let's try it. Start out slowly. Try to feel where the flock wants to go and compete with grace."

Within days, the group was cycling smoothly. Formation breaks were common, particularly when they attempted more challenging transitions. The fluidity they exhibited as they regrouped was as beautiful as their well-executed turns. Lilli rejoiced, seeing their exuberant faces and excited banter.

"You guys did great today. It's fun when it works, isn't it?" Lilli beamed.

Taylor pulled her hat off. A steam wisp rose from her disheveled braids. "In the beginning, I was trying to figure out what I wanted to do and then figure out if everybody else was going to do it too. I know what you mean now about which way the flock wants to go, Ms. Porter," said Taylor animatedly. "It's hard to explain, but it works so much better when I try to feel the whole group at one time."

The group nodded in agreement.

"That is exactly what I've been trying to teach you. Thank you so much for saying that, Taylor. Tomorrow, at the beginning of regular practice, I want you guys to show everybody what we've been working on. Are you ready for that?"

"What if we mess up? I don't want to look like an idiot in front of the whole team." Jordan asked.

"You will only mess up if you forget to compete with grace, Jordan. You guys all know what to do if the formation breaks. That's one of the most important parts of what I want you to demonstrate to the team tomorrow."

The next morning, the team's younger members weren't impressed at first. But the older skaters immediately saw the intricacy of what the flock was doing. As soon as the younger skaters realized that the high schoolers were amazed at what some of the second graders could do, they sat up and paid attention.

"No way. That is so cool. I can't believe what I'm seeing. Ms. Porter, you taught them to do that?" marveled Jeremy, a senior at Wayzata High and one of the fastest and most respected skaters on the team.

"Yeah, Jeremy. I taught them the basics. But they figured out how to do what they're doing now on their own," said Lilli, beaming with pride. You guys want to give it a try?"

Lilli assembled the skaters into groups of four with similar skill sets and gave them the same instruction she had given the initial flock. The older skaters skated out in formation and watched the first flock to pick up on what they were doing.

Rachel, a junior on the team, spoke up after Lilli had reassembled the group by the tent to wrap up the practice. "Ms. Porter. There's more going on here. I understand the formation cycle they follow, but how do they know where to go? There's no lead skater; nobody tells them how to turn, but they move so fluidly like it's all choreographed. But it couldn't be because they were skating around the other groups that were out there practicing. How do they do that?" A puzzled Rachel flung up her arms.

"Why don't you ask them, Rachel?"

Rachel, sixteen years old, turned toward Jonas, Mindy, Taylor, and Jordan.

The high schoolers didn't seem so big and intimidating anymore. Taylor lifted her head and addressed Rachel with confident admiration. "We compete with grace."

11

DESAYUNEMOS

Four days and too many bus station birdbaths later, Porter arrived in Salt Lake. Maybe it was the odd liquor laws, but for a town of this size, there should be a lot more happening on a Saturday in September. *Wasn't there a non-Mormon university in this town?* wondered Porter. He couldn't remember. Still, the downtown was bigger than he expected, and he wanted less scrutiny. He went back to the ticket window in the bus station and asked, "What's the next stop west?" The clerk held out a corner-worn schedule and pointed to the next stop: Tooele. Porter bought a ticket.

Early the next morning, Porter left the Tooele bus station with the plastic bag from the discount clothing store in Jersey City and a little less than three hundred dollars. He pulled his sweatshirt hood up against the chill morning air. The sky was becoming lighter, but the shadow from the steep mountains to the east kept the sun from burning the mist off the valley floor. Porter walked along Main Street, trying to get a feel for downtown Tooele. Traffic was almost non-existent. *Sleepy little place,* Porter decided. He looked for a restaurant where he could get some breakfast, but everything was closed. *Sunday morning in Mormonland.*

He kept walking north along State Route 36 and passed what looked like the town's end. A double-stacked freight train rolled south along the foothills. The shadow from the eastern ridge was beginning to descend to the west, and Porter became more aware of the size of the valley he was walking through. The thoughts of the past four days came flowing back, and the juxtaposition added to the feeling that he had been spat out into another life. After all the time on the bus, it felt good to stretch his legs. Many miles to the north, he could barely make out another mountain range. It seemed like there must be a vast expanse of low-lying terrain before him. He wasn't scaling these mountain ranges anytime soon, and walking felt good, so he kept heading north.

He found an open restaurant across from a drive-in and ordered breakfast at the counter. The newspapers were still in a frenzy about terrorist attacks. *If the journalists only knew how close the real threat was,* he thought as he tossed aside the front page and looked for something else to read. *Sports? No harbor.* All the football had been canceled. Sports writers, the chroniclers of vicarious war games, were eating this up and feeding it back to their readers. "It was time to mourn," they wrote. "Time to reflect on how offensive it is to have another team come in to throw down the gauntlet on your home field." Porter was unfolding US foreign policy, page by page, through the local paper's sports section.

Porter realized that this was exactly what they were looking for in Washington. No protests in Berkeley or Columbus this time. This administration had acquired carte blanche to attack pretty much anywhere in the Middle East. The whole country would stand behind them. Anyone who protested would be labeled unpatriotic. It was as brilliant as it was immoral. Follow the money back to an administration born, raised, and put into office by big oil's home states and the picture came fully into view.

"Can I get you anything else?" The waitress jarred him from his thoughts. Her name tag read, "TwylaDawn," and she refilled his coffee cup, chewing her gum a bit too fast.

"No thanks, I'm fine. Breakfast was great, thank you," replied Porter.

"I'll get the check for you, hon."

Porter looked back up at the waitress as she filed through the tickets in her apron pocket. "There is one thing you might help me with. I'm looking for a job. Do you need any help here?"

"Here? Oh, my heck fer heenie, you do not want to work here." She leaned in a little closer. "Between you and me, unless you're family, they won't hire you."

"Okay. Just thought I'd ask."

"Tell you what, though," said TwylaDawn, momentarily forgetting to chew her gum. "There's a skydive place out at the airport, a mile or so west. I heard from Fairlene—her nephew works there—that they're looking for packers all the time. You might give that a try."

"Thank you, TwylaDawn." Porter braved his way through the pronunciation. "Which way is the airport?"

"Follow this road right chere," one arm waved back and forth while the other held the sloshing coffee pot, "'bout a mile down through Erda, and it's on the right. You won't miss it. They got a big white bubbly thing out there you can see all the way from Route 138. I think Tuesdee's the only day they take off, so they should be out there. They been grounded all week, but I seen parachutes in the sky out there yesterdee. Usually start up around ten or eleven. Well, durn the summer anyways."

Porter left enough cash on the counter to cover the breakfast and a decent tip. "Thank you very much."

"Oh, you betcha. Have fun out there."

12

TRASLADEMOS

The team practiced flocking every day after that. Many arrived early and practiced in groups of their own. Lilli taught them advanced rotation patterns with six, twelve, and eighteen skaters. She taught them how to split flocks in half, maneuver separately, and regroup. The skaters saw it as a fun exercise at the end of each practice.

Jeremy's father pulled Lilli aside after he posted his personal best in the 5,000 meter at the state championship in Roseville. "You don't know how much you've done for him. For our family," emphasized the burly man, his eyes almost welling up with tears.

"Thank you. I'm not sure what I did to help your family, but I sure am proud of him today." Lilli glanced at the scoreboard displaying Jeremy's best time.

"Did you know he used to get so upset before races that he would become physically ill? There were some races we almost didn't make," he shared, shaking his head as if it was a time better forgotten.

"I didn't know that. I'm sorry that happened," comforted Lilli, with concern.

"We found a sports psychologist for him to try everything we could to get him past it. It wasn't until you started the flocking exercises that he got better."

"Really. Wow! That's more than I ever expected," said Lilli, pleasantly surprised. She hadn't intended for it to have that effect on the kids. "Thanks for sharing that." Lilli put her hands in her coat pocket and turned to watch the flocking.

"You know what that sports psych told us? The cooperative focus in the flocking got him past what was upsetting him. He was too focused on who he was trying to beat. As soon as he began focusing on doing his best and relaxing about the competition, his times started coming down. And he hasn't been sick since. You're a miracle worker, Lilli. You really are." The candid gratitude in the man's gray eyes was enough to move Lilli almost to tears, and for the hundredth time since Andrew's passing, she wished that he was here to witness what a difference she had made.

When the teams with skaters who attended the camp improved their competition standings and wins, the camp fell into the spotlight. Lilli had a waiting list before the next season.

Jonas progressed with the camp over the years, which led him through high school. As Jeremy had, Jonas led his team and took first place in the Minnesota State Championships in February 1995.

On the occasions when Glenn was home, he and Jonas hobbied together in Glenn's basement, developing and repairing communications units for his firm. Glenn recognized Jonas' potential to understand electronics and math and encouraged him to pursue an education in engineering. He gave Jonas free run of his technical library and had his administrative staff send books, testing equipment, and experimental prototypes from his R&D department to the house. Glenn also taught him Basic, FORTRAN, and C. By the time Jonas had been accepted early to UC San Diego's electronic engineering program, he was already qualified to excel. A Naval ROTC scholarship completed the package.

Glenn laid the ROTC acceptance letter on the kitchen table after admiring it. "I'm so proud of you, Jonas. You've leveraged the skills we've been working on and set yourself up for success."

"Thanks, Papa. I couldn't have done it without your support." Jonas set a smoking soldering iron down next to his current project and blew lightly on the connection he just made.

In March 1995, Jonas' last season with the skate team was coming to an end. To fulfill what had been a longtime request, Lilli organized what would be the first thirty-two-way skate flock as a tribute to Jonas.

The thirty-two-way is a particularly challenging formation. It is constructed with two crossovers, one in front and one at the rear. The result is two independent but interwoven cycles that must be synchronized.

As with all new formations, they began slowly. Lilli devised a color scheme to ensure success. The two skaters starting in front wore red hats while all the rest wore black. If the red hats met simultaneously at the starting point, the flock knew they were synchronized.

Spring knocked off the chilled sterility that had overstayed its welcome. Life's subtleties, aching to bloom, were evident in the smells, humidity, and angle of the rising sun. Patches of advection fog hung low over the lake, indicating the ice was thinning over the deeper center.

"Jordan. Drop in left a bit more to straighten up the middle wing line. Taylor, a bit faster on your outside turn, please. Better! That looks good!" Lilli called out as she skated close to the flock to keep her directions within earshot." Jonas, fall back on the inside line a bit faster." Jonas glanced at his mother to acknowledge her as she disappeared in and out of the fog. "Jonas. Lead the weave. Feel the whole flock." Jonas glanced to his right to acknowledge her, but the fog was too thick to see. He heard her clearly say, "I love you, Jonas." but her voice was soft and soothing like she was holding him close before bedtime. He looked at the skaters' faces around him to gauge their reactions, but they remained focused on the flock's rotation and movement. Jordan glanced back questioningly at Jonas, puzzled at his distraction. The flock was approaching the edge of the safe ice and began a wide arc to the left. Jonas came to point as his counterpart arrived on the left, and they continued the arc. "Remember, Jonas. I will always love you. It's time for you to find Grandma Keiti."

"Who is Grandma Katie?" Jonas called to her aloud into the fog. An unsettling feeling that something was wrong gnawed at Jonas. "Why are you telling me this now?" Taylor gave him a bewildered glance that said stay focused.

The Hennepin County sheriff's search and rescue team gave up searching for Lilli three days later. They couldn't find any evidence of broken ice near the practice area. Still, they broke through some of the thinner ice nearby. The dive team did their best in the thirty-foot waters but came up with nothing. Sheriff Cunningham put out a missing person report and closed the case a few months later.

13

VOMITEMOS

"How much are jump tickets, baby doll?" said the guy who was easily twice as old as the "baby doll" he was addressing. He was muscular, mustached, over-tanned, and wore a really stupid earring—considering what he planned to do. It was easy to pick out the jumpers who came up from Texas. They were all about showing themselves, like they did on the ski slopes. No one there would jump with them. There was no place for "lone stars" at a drop zone.

Amber put down the radio and walked over to the counter by the cash register. The lace on her tank top straps more than balanced out the biohazard tattoo around her bicep and the packing pin necklace dangling between her breasts. "Twenty-five bucks, and I'm not your baby doll. How many do you want?"

The Texan peered over his Ray Bans toward the tarmac. "Not near as hot here as it is in Plano. Yesterday was wet. Glad it cleared up today so I can jump."

Amber posted the winds aloft report on the whiteboard. "Would you like to purchase jump tickets, sir?"

"I'll take ten, baby doll. And who can I get to pack my rig around here?"

Amber glared at him. Porter stood up on the packing table behind the Texan, giving her a wide-eyed look. Amber hoped he'd take this Texan to the cleaners with packing fees. "Why, of course, sir. Badger here is our best packer. I'm sure he'll take good care of you."

The Texan turned around. "How long you been packing, son?"

"Well, sir," Porter replied, "I've been packing tandem rigs for about..."

Amber interrupted, "Badger's been packing for as long as I can remember! He's the best. And if you ask real nice, I'll bet he'll only charge you forty bucks a pack!"

Porter had to hold the soda can to his mouth to keep from spitting it onto the packing table. Sport rig pack jobs were never more than ten dollars, and that was for the newer zero-P canopies.

"We'll, that's mighty kind of you, son. I'll give one of your packs a try, and we'll see how it goes. Might even get you a tip at the end of the day if it all works out." The Texan picked up a big, brightly colored nylon sack with embroidered initials and dumped a container tangled with a main canopy onto the packing table. Easily a ten-thousand-dollar rig. *All show. No go,* decided Porter. The Texan turned back to Amber and threw three hundreds on the counter, and said, "Looks like I'll take twelve tickets, baby doll. Can you get me on that first load?"

Amber handed him the tickets. "Take one of these over to Jimmy. Thank you for jumping at Skydive West!" she recited, flashing her all-business, no-nonsense smile.

"Well, thank you kindly, baby doll!" said the Texan with a wink.

Porter caught Amber making a gagging gesture as soon as the Texan turned his back on her. Porter was lying on a tandem main pushing the air out of the canopy, and she could see the big, white-toothed grin on his face despite the beard and long hair.

"You better hurry up and finish that tandem. He wants that rig openin' smooth and flyin' straight!'" Amber puffed out her chest and shoved her thumbs under her belt loops in her best obnoxious Texan imitation.

"Am, you know I've only been packing tandem rigs since I came on last fall. What are you trying to do?" Porter stretched out the lines of the Texan's rig and hung the nylon canopy on a bicycle hook.

"Badge, it's simple. It's like the tandems, only smaller, and there's one pull pud instead of two. After you get it folded into the d-bag, I'll show you how to close the container." She turned to leave and added as an afterthought, "And you owe me dinner! You're going to be flush with cash after you pack for that tea bagger all day!"

"Yeah, and what about when he finds out I'm charging him four times the going rate? What then?"

Amber pulled her bra strap onto her shoulder with her thumb, and it fell right back down. "Dude, you worry about stuff way too much," she chided, shaking her head in disapproval. "Justin is the only other packer here today, and he won't even look up, let alone entertain doing a sport rig for some Neanderthal. Relax and enjoy the ride."

Jimmy's voice came over the PA with a manifest announcement, "Load two, this is your now call, head on out to the plane. Load three, you're on a fifteen-minute call. Fifteen-minute call for load three."

"Besides, Badge, you're in for some fun."

"What do you mean?"

"Well, I heard from Pascal that the old man is really happy with all the remodeling you've been doing during the evenings. And so's his wife! Case you didn't figure that out yet, she's the one you have to please around here. He told me they're going to get you all set up with your "A" license and get you a rig you can use as much as you want."

"Skydiving?"

Amber lowered her voice and leaned in closer. "Yeah, dude! Most people have to drop about five grand to get to where they want to take you. Plus, they like you around here, and they want to get you jumping so they can make better use of you."

"You hear that son? That's me on load three. You goin' have that rig o'mine ready in time?"

Porter turned straight into the Texan's chest and looked up into his Ray Bans. "Absolutely, sir."

"Well now that's fine, son. Fine indeed!"

14

TRANSMITAMOS

Porter surprised even himself at how naturally he took to skydiving. He was off student status in two days and earned his "A" license by the following weekend. The freefall coaches were so impressed with his stability and speed control that they invited him to join them in larger formations: four ways, six ways, multi-grip sequences, and sit flying. Porter had a spatial and bodily awareness that few at Skydive West had seen in such a low-time jumper.

Gary Bantam had owned Skydive West for over 30 years. He learned to jump in the army but had no love for other people telling him what or how to do things. He celebrated his 60th birthday by making his 15,000th skydive.

His favorite landing involved wearing slick bowling shoes to skid down the dirt road next to the hangar while finishing a swoop. His birthday jump was no exception. The staff had a love/hate relationship with "Bants." His skydiving record demanded respect, and he was without question the foremost expert on skydiving in the Mountain West. At the same time, he was obsessive-compulsive about certain procedures and never predictable about what would send him into an angry tirade. The staff did their best to follow his rules so they could turn tandems, pack rigs, and get in a few fun jumps each day. As long as everything went smoothly, Bants would stay happy, and the staff could jump. But a drop zone is constantly in flux, and something always requires attention.

Bantam had offered Porter an RV trailer parked by the hangar. It worked well for Porter to have a free place to stay, and Bants felt better about having someone at the DZ at night. On occasions during the summer, out-of-town jumpers would camp in tents on the lawn. For the most part, though, the evenings were quiet, and Porter was alone.

Amelia taxied the King Air to a stop and shut down the engines. The next load had already started walking out to the plane but stopped on the tarmac when they heard the engines winding down. Bantam grabbed the step ladder and jumped onto the plane before Amelia could get out of the pilot seat.

"I thought you had enough fuel for two more loads? What's going on?" Bantam's face was ruddy, pulsing from jumping into the plane.

Amelia hung her headphones on the control yoke and turned around in the chair. "It's the radio, Bants. It's shot. Approach was trying to reach me on jump run. I could hear them, but they couldn't hear me. The transmitter must be out. I couldn't even raise local traffic," huffed Amelia, shaking her head, her red beach curls pulled into a ponytail tossing in sync. "We could run some hop and pops, but you know I can't go to altitude without contacting approach control."

"What about the other radio in the shed? Can we swap it out?"

"This *is* the other radio. Jimmy and I swapped it on Thursday."

"Damn!" Bantam kicked the step ladder away from the plane and jumped to the tarmac. He walked over to the manifest counter. "Jimmy, the radio in the plane is out. You're going to have to call the tandems and cancel for today."

Porter walked up to the manifest counter after Bants had stomped away. "Jimmy, do you mind if I look at the radio? I might be able to fix it."

Jimmy looked up. "Dude, Amelia and I worked on that radio all Thursday afternoon. It's done. But thanks anyway."

"Let me look at it."

"Okay, fine, give it a go. But work with Amelia. You know how Bants gets if somebody's in the plane without her."

"No problem. I'll let you know how it goes."

Porter found Amelia in the parts shed. Within 15 minutes, Porter had the radio up and running. Amelia made a successful check with approach control.

She turned to Porter, her blue eyes wide. "Wow. This is beautiful!"

Porter climbed down the step ladder and let Amelia get back in the pilot seat. Bants stood arms crossed at the bottom of the ladder. Porter gathered his tools from the aircraft deck and turned cautiously toward Bants.

"I could look at the other radios in the shed too, if you like."

"Mr. Badger, you saved my Saturday. Anything you want." Bantam backstepped twice before finishing with Porter, then turned and walked back to the manifest counter.

15

QUEMEMOS

Porter wasted no time taking Bantam up on his offer to fix the other radios. Bantam wasn't kidding about the amount of stuff that he'd collected over the years. Beyond radios and other electronics, there was a wide assortment of aircraft parts: flight instruments, engines, accessories and tools spread throughout the shed. Porter spent almost a month of quiet evenings building a brightly lit workbench, sorting through and organizing the old parts, and cleaning the shed's corners. The workbench was now nested within carefully organized sets of boxes and drawers holding the tools and small electronic parts. When Bants saw what Porter had done, he was so happy that he issued a new DZ rule that only he or Porter were allowed in the shed. Even so, Bantam never did much in the shed beyond the occasional small repair. More often, he would come in and stand peacefully at the entrance.

The last Saturday of August had been a very busy day at Skydive West. Unseasonably warm weather and 85 tandems meant every tandem master and packer was working nonstop for almost ten hours. Amelia had flown 27 loads, including the sunset fun load she agreed to give to the staff—even though she was more than spent. There had been plans for a bonfire dinner that night, but everybody backed out. By eight thirty, everyone was gone, and Porter had his first chance to sit down on the workbench stool and eat dinner. He had packed 28 tandem rigs during the day—a personal record.

Three aircraft radios sat open on the workbench. Porter had been working on them to test the transmitters and receivers in each. He finished his sandwich and turned the radios on. One at a time, he set the radios to transmit and checked the reception on the other two. He used a small screwdriver to fine-tune the frequency generators and, after a while, decided that he had accomplished his task.

Porter normally worked on one radio at a time, but because he was sharing and swapping parts, he had all three running at once. Perhaps it was his curiosity—or maybe something more—that made him wonder what would happen if, in close proximity, they were all set to transmit at the same time. He placed jumper wires across the push-to-talk switches, made an adjustment with his screwdriver, set it down on the workbench, and climbed off the stool.

Porter stood outside the doorway long enough to let his eyes adjust to the night. The sky was clear, the twilight barely visible on the horizon, and the stars bright. The wooden pallet stack the staff had planned to use for the bonfire silhouetted the tarmac. Porter took a can filled with Jet A fuel and a lighter and walked to the pallets. He opened the can, set it upside down on the top, and let the can run dry. He removed the can and held the lighter near a pallet until the kerosene slowly began to burn. The tarmac glowed with the fire's illumination. The flames accelerated across the pallets and grew to almost twenty feet. Porter stepped back from the heat and watched the smoke and sparks rise. He stood watching the sparks mingle with the stars and felt a release from the anguish held in his memories. He felt a door open to his soul, one that beckoned him to renewal, joy, and true freedom. Real freedom to blossom, the essence of what made him *him*. At that moment, his identity was so much less about what name he carried than the connection he felt with the sky.

Porter gazed through the distorted heat waves into the black and orange coals and watched the fire burn to embers, pulling him closer as the cool night braced his back. Sanchez's and Bram's spirits briefly came to mind, long enough to comfort him, each in their own way. For the first time since his squad was killed almost a year ago, Jonas Porter let the burden of their unaccounted deaths and the weight of what he knew rise to the surface. They had families. They took an oath to defend the United States. They lived and honored the unwritten code within the armed services. But the enemy of the state was the state itself. He and they had been betrayed. Three other squads were similarly eliminated. Porter felt a welling rage. What was he doing hiding? Time was wasting. But he stood alone against the awesome power of the US government. There and then, he committed himself to finding a way to make things right—but not simply for himself, or even for the squads that perished. If they are capable of a betrayal of such magnitude, what would stop them from doing more damage? The embers were dim and smoking. He crossed his arms against the night chill and turned back to the storage shed, guided by the light from the workbench.

As he approached the shed, he could hear a faint voice coming over the radio. He was puzzled, having left all three radios in transmit, on how that could happen. It was a baritone voice, although Porter was sure it was female. It was faint, yet clear, reciting what sounded like greetings alternating through about 20 different languages. The fact that the voice wasn't coming from any of the three radios should have gripped Porter's full attention, but it didn't. He became aware of something more bizarre when he came through the door. He slowly sat down on the stool and watched in awe as the small screwdriver he had left there effortlessly floated and slowly tumbled above the workbench between the radios.

The screwdriver moved as things do in a weightless environment, tumbling as if in slow motion. It was as mind-boggling as it was unnerving. He picked up a ratchet socket, carefully held it next to the screwdriver, and let go. It too floated and tumbled. The screwdriver bounced off the socket and reversed its direction. The socket's motion changed too, but not as quickly. *What the hell is going on?* wondered Porter as he tapped the screwdriver on the handle end and watched it tumble faster. His tap also caused it to move slowly away from where it had been tumbling. When it passed one of the radios, it suddenly changed direction, fell to the table, and rolled off onto the floor. Porter watched the screwdriver for a moment, half expecting it to start floating again, but it remained still. The socket was still slowly rotating between the radios.

He pressed a momentary switch on his testing panel to disconnect the power from one radio, and the socket fell to the benchtop. He let go of the switch to reconnect the power, but nothing happened. The socket didn't move. His heart sank for a moment. He slowly increased the gain on each of the radios and noticed the slightest movement in the socket. It was then he realized that it wasn't actually touching the benchtop anymore. He blew on the socket lightly, and it slowly moved away. It continued to retreat until it came close to one of the radios. It seemed to fall for a fraction of a second, then rocked back toward the middle, where it continued to tumble slowly about eight inches above the workbench surface. *Extraordinary!* thought Porter. But he still couldn't wrap his head around it.

Porter was watching the socket so raptly that he hadn't noticed the female voice had begun reciting again. "Hello. Hola. Bonjour. Bom Dia. Ni Hao. Hej pa dig. Guten tag..." He pressed the power switch again. The socket, as before, fell to the surface. A ten-pound radar altimeter transformer unit, no longer neatly stowed on a shelf directly above, dropped with a sickening thud onto Porter's head. He slumped forward onto the workbench. His thumb relaxed, and again the switch closed. The socket and transformer began hovering once again over Porter's limp body.

Andrew pulled the car up to the emergency room entrance of Metro West Hospital and ran around to open the door. Jonas sat fascinated in the front passenger seat, wondering what had got his dad so worked up. A nurse and two staff moved quickly through the automatic sliding doors, one pushing a wheelchair. Andrew reached in and put his arm around Jonas. "We're here sweetie. Everything's going to be alright. Are you still having contractions?"

Jonas was happy to see his dad again. He looked just the same. "What do you mean, dad?"

Andrew burst out laughing. "Did you just call me dad? Are you feeling okay? Let's get you into the wheelchair." Andrew lifted Jonas' legs onto the sidewalk and helped him up. Jonas was bewildered struggling to see anything over a tight, round, swollen belly. The nurse held the wheelchair, ready to receive. Jonas struggled to make sense of what was happening while Andrew helped him into the wheelchair. *What's going on?* thought Jonas. He felt bloated, heavy, and strangely out of balance. His back was sore. He struggled to bring his knees together. The nurse pushed the wheelchair toward the entrance to the hospital.

"Still have momentum and inertia," Porter muttered to himself as he stared into the space between the radios. He wavered between processing the concussion-induced dream and deciding among some challenging states of reality.

"English. English works. Hello. Can you hear me?" Porter heard the eager voice. "I heard you say, 'still have momentum and inertia.'" The female voice was louder now and seemed to penetrate the room and vibrate his body from within. *What the hell*... thought Porter, bracing himself against the workbench.

"Who is that? How did you hear what I said?" Porter looked around, panic-stricken. He was instantly sorry and winced, his head throbbing from the sudden movement. He gingerly fingered the bump on his head. The transformer unit that knocked him out hovered in front of him.

"You can hear me. Excellent! Please continue generating the magnetic harmonics near you. We will not be able to communicate without it." The sense of relief in her voice was unmistakable, but it did little to relieve Porter's own uneasiness. Did they know he was alive? Was his cover blown? Was this some kind of black op to pinpoint his location? *I'm being paranoid,* Porter told himself.

He turned his full attention to the voice. "Who are you? How are you doing that? How am I hearing your voice?"

"First of all, thank you for listening to my transmission. My name is Sariah. I'm an explorer, a research scientist, a patient observer. I've been scanning for anomalies such as yours and attempting communication when I discover them. Please understand how exciting it is that I have made this connection with you," said Sariah earnestly. "What may I call you?"

"Badger," replied Porter dismissively. He had more significant questions. "Anomalies" and "attempting communication" all sounded a bit too cryptic for his liking. *What the hell is she talking about?* thought Porter. "Where are you?" he asked.

"Where I am may require some explanation."

"I have all night." He scooped the transformer unit from its hovering position above the workbench and stored it away.

"Badger, I intend to answer your questions as best as I can. May I take a moment to let you know how grateful I am to you for making this connection. My search has been extensive and difficult. I have failed many times." She sounded desperate and grateful at the same time.

The sincerity in her voice was disarming. *She's obviously not military,* concluded Porter. *I* am *paranoid.* "Sariah, you seem pleasant enough, but this is more than a little strange."

"I understand. This is new for you. Please, tell me, are you experiencing anything that seems to be quite different or extraordinary?"

Porter's gaze returned to the tumbling socket. "There is most definitely something different going on."

"Please describe what you are experiencing," urged Sariah expectantly.

"First, I can't tell where your voice is coming from. I hear your voice as though you're inside me. My whole body vibrates when you speak. It's more than a little weird," said Porter, uncomfortably shifting on the stool.

"I understand, Badger. I'll be able to adjust my communication link, but I have to know more. What else is different?"

"Well, there's a socket floating over my workbench. That's different. It's hovering in the air and tumbling over the workbench like there's no gravity pulling it down." Porter tapped the socket, and it tumbled even faster.

"That's exactly what I'm asking about!" There was a hint of excitement in her voice. "How long has the socket been hovering over the workbench?"

"It began a few minutes before we started talking."

"There must be something flattening your spacetime curvature," Sariah conjectured. "Is there anything near you that generates electromagnetic radiation?"

"There are three radios on the workbench, all set to transmit. Is that it?" asked Porter.

"Yes. They must be generating an electromagnetic harmonic that is creating this anomaly. It's what makes the socket float, and it's also how I know where to contact you. Please continue generating the anomaly if you're able to. If it stops, even for a short time, we may not be able to regain contact." Her low-pitched, deep voice gave Porter the impression that Sariah always got her way.

"I think everything should be fine for a while." Porter got up from the stool, still admiring the socket's movements. Soon, curiosity got the better of his panic and paranoia. "So, can I ask you some questions? Where are you?"

"That's a very good question. One I hope I can answer," said Sariah in her full-toned voice. "Where I am is very much like where you are. Depending on the observer's perspective, we could be considered very close together or very far apart. It's really a matter of scale. When you observe very small things, even with the best equipment available, what's the smallest thing you can sense or experience?"

"I'd have to say research scientists breaking down subatomic particles," ventured Porter. "I think they can only see the paths they follow and offer probabilities about where they might be found."

"I understand. And what about very large things? What's the largest thing or expanse you can experience?"

"Well, the most powerful telescope has measured light from billions of light years away. I don't think you can really call that a thing, but it is definitely a vast expanse of space." Porter realized that he might need some ice for the bump on his head, but the conversation was getting too interesting for him to excuse himself.

"Yes, to an extent, I agree. Can you tell me Badger, in either of the explorations of scale that you have described, has anyone ever determined if there is a limit?"

Porter thought for a moment. "I can't say I'm an expert on the topic, but I believe Planck theorized that the smallest length possible is a ratio of gravity and the speed of light."

"He did, Badger. I'm impressed. His definition of length has the gravitational constant in the numerator. Do you think he might have a different opinion if he could see your workbench right now?"

"Reduced gravity would reduce the Planck length."

"Exactly! And from a relativity perspective, there are some fascinating effects on a black hole when gravity is reduced as well. Badger, my research shows that the vastness you have described is only a sliver of the range of scale in which our universe exists."

Porter mulled this over. "So, what you're saying is that we're generally in the same place, but one of us is much larger than the other."

"Precisely!" replied Sariah.

"Suddenly, the question I asked seems insignificant. Where you are isn't nearly as interesting as how you found me and how we're communicating."

"Yes. You're beginning to understand," said Sariah approvingly. "We're separated not only by physical scale but also relative to one another in terms of location, time, and space expanding around us. The spacetime flattening created by your three radios shows me your path because that signal is coincident with a fold that creates a brief intersection between your scale and mine."

"Brief?" asked Porter.

"Duration is a fickle and relative aspect of our connection. To you, it may seem to intermittently last for hours or even months. We may go for years without a connection and then reestablish it. And that same experience may only last an hour in total for me. Or it could be the reverse. As our conversation progresses, each of our experiences will continue, so we should not necessarily expect our communications to follow a sequential line."

This changes everything, thought Porter. "I have so many questions..." he said, almost mesmerized by the tumbling socket. "How do you speak English?"

"I've studied many languages. Communication is my research field. But what you probably mean is, how do I speak any language you may be familiar with. Because this communication link is new to you, it's natural for you to assume that we're very different beings. Our scales are far more similar than you may imagine. Even more amazing is the countless number of scales that are similar to ours. My scans are designed to alert me when an anomaly occurs, but they also pick up background ambient radiation. I have learned a great deal about your scale's cultures through the transmissions sent to satellites."

"I'm not sure watching our television channels would give you the best idea about life here," quipped Porter.

"I understand that much of your media is designed for entertainment. It offers social insight but isn't necessarily a reliable information source. I learn the most from satellite uplinks that come from government sources. The US, European, and Chinese diplomatic and military communiqués are a great source of current information. I use the financial market transactions to generate an economic schematic of your scale's commerce."

"But how can you decipher the transmissions? Our military encryptions are particularly strong," asked Porter.

"The encryption algorithms I've encountered in your scale are actually quite rudimentary. They're easy to crack," replied Sariah.

"Well then. We *do* have a lot to talk about." Porter turned out the workbench lights, walked over to the doorway, and looked up at the stars.

"More than you even realize, Badger. I must ask for your help." Her tone was almost pleading. "This link we've stumbled upon is vulnerable, weak, temporary. I would like to establish a stable conduit between us that will allow our scales to share our knowledge and talents. There is much we still need to learn, to experience, and for me to share with you."

"Sariah, if you've been reading our military and diplomatic transmissions, you know there is much about this world that should never be duplicated or shared with anyone," warned Porter, something of the old bitterness creeping into his voice.

"And at the same time, there are wonderful, beautiful, and life-enhancing creations in science and art that would bring joy to many people and cultures."

"Who decides what should and shouldn't pass through the conduit?" asked Porter.

"I told you I need your help," said Sariah evasively. Her voice was less penetrating now.

"Me? You want me to be the information gatekeeper between two scales?" Porter walked back to the bench and flipped the light back on. The socket was still tumbling slowly between the radios. He felt overwhelmed and strangely inadequate. He wasn't sure he wanted to be an ambassador between scales.

"You can't do it on your own. I was hoping we could work on it together. I watch my side, you watch yours. We decide together what benefits both."

"An hour ago, I was trying to repair a radio, and now you're asking me to help you play God between two scales."

"I understand how overwhelming this may seem to you, Badger, but know this. The link between us is open because both scales need it to be. It's suffused with reason, intelligence and, most of all, purpose. In varying degrees, people strive continuously to improve themselves and the lives of others. That passion for compassion is energy no different than other forms you have studied and measured. No different than the transmissions from your radios. No different than the confluence of energies that has created the flattened spacetime altering the gravity where your socket is tumbling. The energy in each of our scales has come to levels that allow the exploration of compassion between us.

Despite our personal levels of comfort, you and I are part of the fulfillment of that purpose. We are part of a whole that binds us together. Why do we leave, travel, and find new connections? It's because the larger whole is taking shape, Badger. A larger, stronger, resplendent tapestry that is as powerful as it is beautiful. Have you noticed how ocean waves, when they are gentle, sound like breathing?"

"I do, but not only one person. Lots of them," said Porter.

"Exactly, even on beaches with much larger waves that crash toward the shore. It's much louder, and the sound takes a while to dissipate as the water spreads out across the sand."

"It still sounds like breath. My mother taught me to pay attention to my breath. She said it could tell me where I was," remembered Porter wistfully. "I didn't really understand what she meant until I was older. She taught me to pay attention to other people's breathing in the same way. She said you could tell how people are by how they breathe."

"What else did she teach you Badger?"

"She told me it's one ocean. We all share the same breath," Porter sighed. If Sariah was trying to convince him to help her open a window between scales with metaphors of a larger whole, it was working. He realized that, somehow, his mother had prepared him for this very moment. "Fine, I'll help you, but can we please take it one step at a time? Start off slow and see how things go? I can only imagine the consequences." Porter stepped back to the bench and sat down on the stool.

"I wouldn't have it any other way," replied Sariah.

"Where do you suggest we start?" asked Porter, hoping he wouldn't regret it.

"Without question, the most important step is to maintain close communication with each other. Did you say you have three radios on your workbench that are creating the spacetime anomaly?"

"Yes," replied Porter.

"Let me show you a better way."

16

CONTRAVENGAMOS

I t had been a week since he first made contact with Sariah. Even more than
its increased range and power, the device's simplicity impressed him the
most. Once he understood the design, he was amazed that it hadn't already been
discovered in his scale. Housed in a plastic box about the size of a deck of playing
cards, Porter placed what Sariah called a gondol in a pocketed waistband to
hold it close to his center of gravity. A simple on/off switch and a volume knob
were the only controls. A transmission antenna was sewn into the waistband to
create a circle around his torso. Sariah cautioned him about testing the gondol
anywhere he might injure himself if it failed or was inadvertently turned off.
They both appreciated the importance of keeping the gondol secret, at least for
the time being.

The "white bubbly thing" TwylaDawn had referred to was a free standing
tension fabric aluminum structure. Bants needed a place to pack parachutes
out of the weather and hangar his King Air. The fact that it was relocatable got
him around the county's arcane building codes. Porter turned on the overhead
lights in the hangar. The hangar door was closed, and the King Air loomed
inside. Porter stood up on the packing table behind the aircraft and turned
on the gondol. He slowly turned the volume knob, and although he remained
standing on the table, he felt the lightness in his body. He slowly rose to his
toes and was surprised at not only how easy it was to accomplish but also
how effortless balancing was. Porter stopped turning the volume knob and
experimented with different body positions. Standing tall with his hands by his
sides, he felt the lift but remained on the table. If he raised his arms, he could
feel the additional weight in his feet. The gondol put out a spherical field that
expanded in size as the volume was increased. Body parts outside the sphere

would not be affected. He reasoned that if he could get his entire body inside the sphere, he would be completely weightless. He turned the volume up slowly and continued to stand on his toes and then back down again. He continued increasing the volume until he lifted off the table. As a skydiver, he was used to the sensation of freefall, but weightlessness was something else entirely. It was more exhilarating than he had expected.

He turned the volume knob back down and dropped back to the table. He tried bending his knees into a squat and immediately came up off the table and started rotating. He extended his legs outside the sphere, and his feet dropped slowly to the table. He slowly reduced the volume, and his body lay down on the table. He turned the volume all the way down and felt his body weight return as the table pressed up into him from below. He stood back up, increased the volume, jumped gently with his legs extended, lifted about six feet above the table, and then slowly came back down. The gravitational attraction between the earth and his feet, all that protruded from the sphere, was balancing out the momentum of his body that remained inside. He jumped up again and tucked his legs close to his chest. At first, he noticed how easy it was to hold his legs up without having to overcome gravity.

He quickly realized that while every body part was encompassed by the gondol's sphere, the momentum he had gained from jumping from the table was carrying him up to the top of the hangar. The hangar ceiling was at least twenty feet from the packing table top. He held his legs close to his body and continued up to the top of the hangar. He could feel the heat from the sodium lamp hanging from the ceiling and slowly extended one leg to push away from it. As soon as his toe extended past the sphere's limit, it fell toward the packing table, causing his body to rotate. He kept his leg extended, and his body slowly floated back to the packing table. With practice and experimentation, he soon became adept at landing gently and upright, initiating and stopping rotations across single and multiple axes while adrift. He also mastered speed control. He honed this skill until he was able to approach the packing table so slowly that he could land gently on the top of his head.

17

ABATAMOS

Porter decided practicing in the hangar was not nearly as much fun as trying it while in freefall. If the device failed, he would deploy his parachute. As long as he exited last and solo, he could spend a minute or two testing the anti-gravity effects. The only difficulty was having to explain to the delayed landing to the skydivers on the ground.

It's difficult to spot a skydiver from the ground when he exits a jump plane two miles above. Porter counted on that for the privacy he needed. He loosened his canopy rig's leg and chest straps enough to be comfortable but not enough to be unsafe in case the gondol failed.

Porter asked to be put on the next jump load like any other skydiver. He wanted to be in the mix with the tandems, videographers, and fun jumpers. The request was nothing special except that he planned on informing Amelia and the tandem masters that he would be pulling high. He hoped that he could get away with saying he had spent 20 to 25 minutes under canopy without attracting too much attention from the jump staff below. He was prepared to explain that warm lifting currents kept him aloft.

High pullers always left the aircraft last, which gave Porter the opportunity to sit up front next to Amelia. Porter gathered with the ten jumpers at the taxiway. Amelia had landed and taxied the King Air up to the group for loading. She feathered the left prop as she came to a stop. Porter climbed on board. The familiar Jet A exhaust smell mixed with the stripped-down aircraft interior always triggered a reaction. Even after 450 jumps, his mouth still went dry, and a subtle sweat coated his palms when he climbed into the King Air. Porter ducked slightly as he made his way to the front of the plane, straddled the bench, and nodded at Amelia, who was busy running through her preflight checklist.

After the last tandem had jumped, Porter moved to the door with one hand on the doorframe and the other on the gondol switch. He didn't want to engage it inside the plane. The runway was visible below, and he could see that he was drifting south of the field. After giving the last tandem a few seconds to fall away, he gently rolled through the door. On clearing the plane, he flipped the gondol's switch. Normally, an exit would combine an acceleration from zero to 120 knots earthward while dissipating 90 to 100 knots of the plane's forward airspeed. Porter was surprised at how quickly the wind rush began to subside. What felt like a gentle breeze continued for about twenty seconds, followed by complete stillness. Porter had anticipated the slowing and eventually becoming one with the parcel of air around him. Even if the winds were strong, he imagined he would feel stillness since he would be moving with them. He was right. The sensation was more thrilling than anything he had ever experienced. Suspended in the air, thousands of feet above ground, he felt like a bird gliding on the zephyrs. What was especially uncanny was the silence. Except for the soft sigh of the light breeze, the world was quiet.

"Have you moved?" Sariah's clear voice jolted Porter out of his trance. "I can read your signal very clearly now. The interference is gone. Can you stay where you are?"

"No. I can't stay here for very long without attracting attention," replied Porter.

"Why, where are you?"

"I'm about eleven thousand feet above the ground."

"Badger, you understand that the gondol does draw down its batteries, and if the signal is lost or disrupted, you'll fall. "The concern and urgency in her voice was evident.

"I'm wearing a parachute. I jumped out of an airplane. I'll be okay even if it fails," he reassured.

"Something is odd about your signal, Badger. It's changing very rapidly."

Porter heard a low hum and turned to see the King Air coming toward him, flying straight and level slightly below his altitude. He hesitated for a moment, wondering if he should stay where he was or drop away below it. Dropping away meant crossing directly in front of it, but at least he wouldn't be the sitting target he was now. He couldn't let Amelia see him, but he also couldn't take the chance that she might change altitude and climb up toward him. The plane continued to close, and he saw Amelia's figure in the cockpit window.

Porter reached for the gondol and switched it off. He began to fall immediately but was uncomfortably close to the front of the aircraft. The downdraft from the wings flipped his legs over his head. During this inverted moment, he watched as the King Air banked steeply away and dove toward the west. The plane's abrupt maneuver left no question Amelia had seen everything. *I'm gonna have some explaining to do when I get back,* thought Porter.

Porter had drifted even further over the farmer's field south of the airport. Having been one with the wind meant that he'd been moving right along with it. He couldn't see any canopies below, which meant the rest of the load was already on the ground.

He could talk to Amelia. She might even understand. But explaining his delayed arrival from a skydive to a whole group of people was going to be difficult. Porter checked his wrist altimeter as he passed through three thousand feet. The lowest he'd ever deployed his parachute was twenty-five hundred.

The choice between landing in the corral with the horses or in the orchard with the trees flashed through his mind. He was still in freefall. At one thousand feet, he pulled his main ripcord and watched his canopy begin to deploy. He was only five hundred feet from the ground when his canopy fully inflated. The canopy's pop and shadow startled the horses in the corral, who scattered at the sound. He turned sharply toward the orchard, losing about two hundred feet of altitude. It was too late to turn back into the corral and take his chances with the horses. He started flaring to slow his forward speed and adjusted his flight path. The horses stomped and whinnied at the sounds of snapping branches and ripping nylon.

His canopy and lines tangled with the trees, and Porter abruptly swung forward in his harness. As he came back through the next swing, he pulled his cutaway handle, releasing his harness from the parachute lines. As he began to drop, he switched on the gondol. The swing's momentum still propelled him forward, but the gondol kept him from falling. Now about six feet above the ground, Porter floated at a fast running pace between two rows of trees. As he neared the row's end, Porter slowly reduced the volume on the gondol until his feet dragged lightly in the dirt. His foot caught on a tree root. The jolt bounced his hand against the gondol, switching it off. Porter rolled and tumbled across the moistened soil for about eight feet and came to rest, miraculously unhurt, with a huge muddy grin on his face.

He stood up and looked back down the aisle between the trees to his canopy, still draped across them, with lines and risers dangling below. The countless lectures from Bants about staying out of the farmers' fields echoed through his head. They had complained more than once to the FAA's field office, and the drop zone's longevity depended on good neighbor relations. He had an idea about how to get the canopy out of the trees but stopped short when he heard voices behind him.

"He's walking around. That's a good sign." The farmer addressed Porter as he and his wife walked down toward him. "How'd you get out of that mess without busting yourself up? Are you okay?"

"Yes, sir. I'm a little shaky still, but I'm sure I'm unharmed. I'm sorry about your trees. I'll pay for whatever damage I've caused." Porter was brushing the dirt from his jumpsuit as he walked toward the farmers.

"I called Bantam when I saw you land. He's sending someone over to pick you up." The farmer's wife was looking up at the trees. "I'll bring the picker out after a while and pull your parachute out of the trees. It doesn't look like you're going to be using it again. You're lucky to be in one piece."

"I am. Thank you."

A blue Honda Element pulled up next to the corral. Amelia got out and walked over to Porter, looking him up and down. Scrunching her freckled nose, she squinted up at the canopy strung across the trees, then back at Porter. "I can't believe you're okay," Amelia nodded at the farmers in greeting. "Kyle, Mary. Good to see you. Sorry about this. Bants would have come himself, but he's out on a fuel run. He said he'd cover you for any damages to your farm."

"We're glad this guy's okay. What's your name?" Kyle asked.

"My name is Robert Badger, sir. Thank you for your concern."

"Well, Mr. Badger, you're one lucky man. Please be more careful before it runs out on you."

"Thank you, sir, I will," replied Porter.

Porter and Amelia walked back to the Element. When the doors were closed, Amelia turned to Porter and said, "I know that was all you, and I want to know how you did that."

"You deserve an explanation."

18
ENGAÑEMOS

Porter had explained the gondol to Amelia but stopped short of telling her about Sariah.

"I'm sure you realize what this kind of technology would do for the aviation industry." Amelia's questions and insights unfolded rapidly. "And it's not just a little bit awesome that you discovered this thing in a parts shed in the back end of a drop zone."

"I'd like to do some experiments," started Porter tentatively. "I'm wondering if you'd be willing to help me."

Amelia's eyes lit up. "You want to use it in the King Air."

"I do, but I think we really need to be careful. I'm not a pilot. I don't know everything that could go wrong, but I'm sure it's going to mess with the plane's weight and balance. I have no idea what it'll do to the engines."

Amelia was accustomed to the often-edgy conditions that came with flying skydivers. Open doors. Premature deployments. Hot days, hard climbs, and fast descents. They were all hard on the plane and even worse on a pilot's imagination. "You're right. I don't know what would happen if it's completely weightless," she confessed.

"I think we're going to find that we need at least some weight to keep the plane balanced," said Porter.

"Well, we know for sure that a plane can fly with or without a payload. If we kept the volume on the gondol at a setting that neutralizes the payload, it would be like flying an empty plane."

After a trial run with the gondol in the airplane, Porter exited with his jump gear. It was quiet. A few wispy clouds hung about two miles away over the Oquirrh mountain range. The trucks and cars on I-80 seemed to inch along in both directions, and the stillness conflicted with his memory of the wind, the flying gravel, and the Doppler effect that accompanied a semi-passing by on the freeway.

The Wasatch range ran across the east side of the Salt Lake Valley. The Great Salt Lake stretched out beyond Antelope Island into the haze in the north. The Army weapons disposal facilities and missile silos lay in grids to the south, with Rush Valley's expanse as a hazy backdrop. The pink and green evaporation ponds gave way to the Bonneville Salt Flats and the setting sun. A starling murmuration gracefully undulated beneath him, collecting their evening meals. The sky boasted amber and tangerine clouds set upon blues, fading from pale turquoise to the depth of midnight, aching to burst with the vastness of space behind it. Sariah continued speaking as if their conversation had never paused. The relativity of their respective time passages was becoming more evident.

"The energy that makes up beings like us is very powerful. Once people understand this power, they soon see past material and money. The power of human energy—the thoughts, emotions, and passions of others—naturally affects every being in its field beneficially and otherwise. It can also be channeled and redirected to satisfy selfish needs. It's more than energy. In Sanskrit, *prana* means life force, breath, or vital principle. The Greeks call it *dunamis*. The best English translation is *virtue*. Beings who first recognized prana collected it physically. It could be a passing brush on a sidewalk or subway, a quick glance with eye contact and a polite 'excuse me,' or the casual touch of a boot tip to another's shoe on a bus ride across town. The collector was beginning to understand the benefits. Very often, the victim was only numbly aware of why she felt less productive or in a poor mood that day."

"But what can you do with that kind of power?" Porter flipped off the gondol and dropped into a tracking dive. He held his body rigid as he re-engaged it and arced upwards to a slow stop. "If the only awareness that the giver feels is a little less productivity or a little moodiness, how can that even make a difference? I mean, why even bother collecting it if it is such a small amount?"

"Collect enough, and it's exactly the same energy that's keeping you from falling back to earth right now."

"The gondol is what keeps me up here," argued Porter. "I've got an antigravity sphere surrounding me, and it wouldn't be there unless I had this transmitter operating. Plain and simple electromagnetic science mixed with a little harmonic wave theory."

"All of which happens to be a product of your own prana field. You've removed yourself from energy-collecting distractions such as television, news media sources, and cell phones and given yourself the space to allow your prana to grow and develop. The television was invented with good intentions by a fellow not far from where you are right now. It was its implementation that created the consequences. Advertising is based on the principle that if a mind or collection of minds is influenced to think in a certain way about a product or service, prana flows from those influenced toward that product or service. It manifests itself as corporate revenues. Physical contact is no longer necessary. Television ads have evolved into the internet, which not only allows a more efficiently targeted collection method but also provides a probe into people's thoughts and emotions, broken down geographically, by age, race, interests, and gender."

"Wow! Never thought of advertising that way," interjected Porter.

"And since DARPA funded the initial research into the internet, they, like any government-funded program, retained the rights and privileges to its products. What that means is that the US government has full and unfettered access to all data that flows across the World Wide Web; all information flows through DARPA's servers. Every second you carry your mobile phone, they know where you are. Information flowing across the World Wide Web through the DARPA servers changed from people searching for knowledge to people sharing their innermost feelings under the pretense of controlled privacy. Privacy, now, only exists in the minds of those naïve enough to believe in it. For all intents and purposes, it died with the advent of the World Wide Web in 1995."

"So, who is 'They'? Who is it that wants to gather up all this energy? And why do they care?" asked Porter.

"Imagine a tower, if you will, and these people inside who believe they have worked and studied to gain this place and perspective over humanity. They look out their windows and witness the people below them who want to gain the same privileged position. It generates fear—fear of losing what they have. It consumes their hearts and minds, and they do everything they can to maintain what they have because they've come to believe that who they are is reflected only in what surrounds them. They do everything they can to stay separated from the masses while using them as resources. This naturally breeds more fear and a desire to better defend oneself. When these people became aware of the power available through human energy manipulation, the frenzy began. Not only were they able to collect energy to feed their separation anxieties, but they also gained relief knowing that they had weakened the masses vying for their material protection. They reasoned that the more they could control, the more likely they are to maintain their separated existence. Money, fuel, education, healthcare, security, mass communication, transportation—they controlled them all, but it wasn't enough. They wanted to control the very essence of human motivation: the desire for joy. Once you understand that harvesting joy from humanity is the primary objective of the people in power, much of what has been happening becomes much easier to understand. The lessons learned about central intelligence during World War II and the Cold War are very much still in play. The problem with having accurate information is that if you act on it directly, your enemy knows you have interceded, and they change their behavior.

Massive propaganda efforts were developed as countermeasures. Anyone who challenges what has been touted as the 'accepted norms' is immediately labeled. It is a surprisingly effective technique for keeping people in their place. That man is a 'liberal,' for example. He does not support the ways that keep us safe and comfortable. Shun him, disregard him. Here, listen to this man instead. He will keep you safe from the many harmful people who surround you. Or, 'do not listen to that woman! She is a "conspiracy theorist" and her ideas are "crazy"'. This is, without question, the best countermeasure against someone who sheds light on a perverse policy or action. Too often, people have such inherent faith in their leadership that the possibility that their leaders are insane induces a set of feelings they can't resolve internally, so they simply dismiss it. The irony is that it is this very denial and complacency that gives an elitist corporation or government license to continue to act out with impunity against those they consider to be their lessers."

"I don't know if anyone here could accept this," Porter said skeptically.

"Let me ask you, how would you approach a person who you perceived as being self-destructive?"

"Well, I'm not a psychiatrist, but I imagine I would do what I could to make them feel better about themselves."

"I agree. You would teach them peace. What I'm telling you is that your scale is on a self-destructive path."

"How can you say that?"

"Badger, a significant percentage of people in your scale believe that learning how to kill other people is not only critical to their and their loved ones' freedom and survival but actually believe it's honorable. The only behavior more culturally destructive than going to war is the insane derivative of honoring the people who have already done so. The endless veterans' rallies and memorials do nothing more than perpetuate the self-destructive path from generation to generation. This is the core of your world's insanity. The administration and propagation of it are insidious. American football is a case in point."

"Football? It's a game. It's not war," said Porter, incredulous.

"You still don't understand, Badger, and that's within reason because the mentality of self-destruction has been so deeply ingrained in your minds and hearts that it seems normal to you. But I assure you it is not. American football is taught to young men from an early age. They are taught to prepare themselves for battle. They strengthen their bodies, sharpen their minds, and study rudimentary military strategies, all with the intention of defeating other beings physically, emotionally, and intellectually. They line up and invoke conflict in a brutal manner that evokes basic animalistic behavior in them and all who view it. These young men are taught that this practice will bring them success, and then they can't understand why they fail at making loving relationships with their mates, friends, children, and co-workers.

In the military, they are built up along the same lines, but now, instead of pads and muscles and pigskins, they use lethal weapons. They are instructed specifically about how to kill other beings efficiently. Destroy families. Orphan children. And in doing so, they create anguish, sadness, anger, and lust for revenge in those they attack. You think football is a game, Badger? It's the gateway drug to global annihilation."

"That's a bit extreme, don't you think, Sariah?"

"The most insidious part of this is that you and an astounding majority of your scale still perceive it that way. Everything your governments and the powers that finance them do to perpetuate this insane mentality focuses on keeping those they control *sick, stupid, and scared*. These are the people who will join football teams. These are the people who will populate the militaries. These are the families that will blindly honor those who have killed others because it covers the anguish they feel in their hearts. These are the people who wear wounds, dismemberments, emotional trauma, and deaths as false badges of honor. They brandish their artificial limbs, wheelchairs, and flags with pride when they should be mortified that they went to such lengths to kill others of their own species. These are the people who will deepen the enmity between cultures. This is the energy that will tangle into self-destruction.

19

ENTREGUEMOS

C loudy, overcast days were typically quiet at the drop zone. Low visibility pretty much stopped all the regular activity. So, the sound of a turboprop taxiing in from the runway attracted Porter's immediate attention. Turbine or not, this weather was below minimums even for the best-equipped instrument aircraft.

Porter stood next to the hangar and listened as the whine grew louder. He couldn't see the taxiway on the other end of the tarmac through the fog. The gray gave way to a black outline of an airplane taxiing purposefully. It turned gracefully past the Cessnas, Pipers, and Mooneys parked in the tarmac's center. Porter was curious who would be so bold as to land in these conditions. His curiosity was sidetracked as he listened to the feathering prop and the turbine's spin down, realizing that the airplane was a heavily modified Cessna Caravan. They were reliable, had a high load-carrying capacity, and were easy to fly. The doors opened, and four passengers emerged. The craft was matte black, with no identifying numbers or marks, except one green emblem below the exhaust port.

The airplane's doors had been modified to allow for a much wider opening. Porter withdrew as a tall man with tightly curled dark hair rolled out of the doorway and walked toward him. Even in the foggy light, Porter could see the man's dark complexion and the heavy shadow of a beard. The airplane didn't have the seats typically found in a Caravan. All but the pilot's and copilot's had been removed. The tall man strolled up to Porter. He was thick and muscular, particularly in his shoulders, and wore a red flannel shirt with hastily rolled sleeves, black jeans, and high-top Keds sneakers. Tattoos of women in flowing gowns and random smudges of engine grease adorned his forearms.

He pointed at the King Air and said, "If I am not mistaken, monsieur, this aircraft she uses the jet-ah fuel. We, my friends, are in need. Our desire, monsieur, is the purchase from you. You can help, no?"

The man's accent was thick and carried a timbre connoting one of France's non-European territories. The interspersed English was broken and difficult to understand, but Porter got the gist. Before he could answer, a slender Indian woman in her mid-twenties swaggered past the tall man, pushing a black cubic cargo container. Her onyx hair was slicked back in a bun, and a magenta bindi adorned her forehead. The dark makeup around her large brown eyes made her somewhat intimidating, but she was nonetheless attractive. Her dark pants hugged her wide hips, and a bright fuchsia scarf bloomed from the zipper opening at the top of her lightweight, black leather jacket. She walked behind Porter and set the container down on the tarmac. Porter felt the ground tremble with its weight. "Shmi'naha!" the tall man scolded. "I tell you a-easy with that one, no?"

"I'm giving it my best. This thing is bloody heavy." The woman looked Porter over from top to bottom dismissively, then made her way back toward the plane. Despite the bindi and her sassy presentation, her English was clear, with a well-educated British flair.

Porter, though still collecting his thoughts, spoke for the first time since their arrival. "We have Jet A in that trailer, but it's for the King Air. For the jump plane."

He casually leaned his knee into the cargo container. It did not budge.

"Don't hurt yourself, Porter. That thing is heavy, and you're not moving it without some help." The deep, orotund voice was new and came from directly behind him.

Porter swung around to face the speaker. "How do you know my name? Who are you?" Porter glanced back to the plane suspiciously and saw someone with light hair still rooting around through the cargo. The Indian woman was standing at the edge of the tarmac holding a device about the size of a cell phone. She seemed to be gazing into the fog, not really looking for anything. *This guy must be the pilot,* thought Porter. His t-shirt, chaps, and ankle-high boots—all black—barely contrasted with his jeans. An engraved pewter pendant, resembling the aircraft's emblem, hung around his neck on a rough length of twine. A scuffed pair of black-framed aviation goggles, secured with an elastic band around his head, was pushed up into his hair. He was fit and lean, not excessively muscular, but the veins on his biceps were distinct. His dark, graying hair was closely trimmed. His pale blue eyes contrasted sharply with his bronze complexion. The man extended his hand. Porter took it after a moment's hesitation. He could hear him say, "You doing okay, Porter?"

His voice was clear yet overwhelming. Porter could understand what the man was saying, but it was as if it was so loud and penetrating that the volume overcame his ability to comprehend the words. The man maintained his grip on Porter's hand as though they were shaking hands, helping Porter steady his balance. An intense, focused wave of awareness washed over Porter as the man leaned into him. Through this stranger, he experienced a connection to a sea of faces and voices, a multitude of beings, each individually aware of him and he of them, but at the same time, all united as one single being.

"I know a lot more about you than your name, Lieutenant Commander Jonas Mills Porter. My name is Bahn Waclire. He released his grip on Porter's hand, and Porter slowly lowered into a squat, touching his fingertips to the tarmac. He felt drained, yet the connected experience faded almost instantly. Moments later, Porter stood back up unsteadily to face Bahn. This man knew who he was, and that by itself was a very dangerous thing.

"I'll reimburse you for the fuel we load, but we are taking it." Bahn's commanding presence was persuasive, particularly after the communion he shared with Porter.

"Are you guys military? Some kind of special ops?" asked Porter warily.

Bahn snorted. "Do we look military to you, Porter?"

Bahn looked across the tarmac to the Caravan and waved. The fourth passenger moved toward the edge of the aircraft and lowered himself down. He was short of four feet and wore a black patch with an elastic band over his left eye. His hair was bright blonde, almost white, about one inch long, and stuck out from his head like a stiff brush. Bahn called out to him, pointing to the fuel trailer, "Blue, there's a ladder on the other side of the fuel trailer; top her off and ask Yves to check the oil." "Blue" stopped to listen to Bahn and alternated his gaze between the tarmac and the fuel trailer, never looking at Bahn directly. As soon as Bahn finished the order, he continued, walking with purpose, seeming to slightly favor one leg.

"This ship is the Kartikeya, and I am her captain. Jackson Blueye is first officer and co-pilot." Bahn jerked his head towards Blueye, balancing on top of the stepladder, one hand holding the fuel nozzle, his head angled awkwardly to watch the rising fuel level. He wore a bright royal blue satin waistcoat, embroidered in fine detail with a peacock across the back. His green cotton pants fit loosely around the short section of legs not covered by the waistcoat and were tied around his ankles. Porter noted that black Vans with Velcro closures do come in a child's size five.

Bahn continued, "Yves Muladet, the guy checking the landing gear, is ship's engineer. Lakshmi Anand, who delivered your cargo, is our navigation officer."

Blueye stopped the fuel flow and waited for the dripping to cease, shifted his weight nervously, glanced quickly toward Porter, then settled back to his task. Yves, lying on his back under the Kartikeya, sat halfway up and gently touched the wrench, darkened rag in hand, to his forehead in an informal salute. Lakshmi kept her back to Porter and Bahn but looked up from the device and over her shoulder in acknowledgment.

Bahn continued, "I found the Kartikeya in 1985 in an airport outside of Calcutta. She'd been taken there in the late '70s by a British mining magnate who used it to move engineers and equipment into remote mining sites. Maintenance being almost impossible to obtain, she was soon replaced by helicopters. By the time I found her, she was all but abandoned. I had the spars and control surfaces replaced with composite and Kevlar and refitted her with a more powerful turbine and a five-blade prop." Bahn beamed proudly. "The main fuselage structure has been completely reinforced with titanium tubing and refitted with retractable gear. Yves is still working out the bugs in that."

"What do you guys do? What's all this for?" asked Porter.

Porter knew he had hit a nerve when Bahn hesitated and looked away briefly before continuing, "One day I'd like to get home, but I'm not sure that will ever happen. Today, we're refueling and delivering this package from our mutual friend."

Bahn looked up at the sky. The fog was gradually lifting. Blueye had finished refueling and was seated on a cargo box in the co-pilot's position. Lakshmi was rearranging equipment in the rear and checking that the doors would close. Bahn made a circle above his head with his fingers as he looked at Blueye, and the Kartikeya began to spin up. Yves wiped his wrench with the rag and conducted a walk-around. Porter followed Bahn around the Kartikeya's tail. The wind from the prop was strong, and the smell of warm jet fuel exhaust engulfed both men. Bahn leaned in so Porter could hear him. "I'll be glad when we can both feel more comfortable speaking about the obvious. Good to meet you, Porter." Bahn turned and climbed into the pilot's seat, pulled the door closed, and strapped himself in. Blueye turned to check that Porter was clear of the craft and eased the throttle forward. The ship slipped into the fog, disappearing as the turbine's whine faded slowly with distance.

Porter walked back to the black cargo container. A money clip engraved with a peacock holding five one-hundred-dollar bills sat on top of the container. Porter turned the clip over, ran his fingers across the engraving, and put the bills in his pocket. There were structural indentations running around the entire box. It had no visible latches or buttons—no obvious way to open it. He grabbed the container with both hands and shifted his entire body weight to try to move it. He figured it had to weigh at least five hundred pounds. The Kartikeya's engine sound had faded. The quiet solitude before their arrival had returned. He turned back to glance at the container. That part was real, and there was only one way he was going to move it into the shed.

20

ENTENDAMOS

Porter slowly maneuvered the black crate into the radio shack. The gondol he taped to its top made it possible to lift, once he had pried it from the deformed asphalt. He soon realized that any momentum, whether directional or rotational, would have to be counteracted with the same energy he put into it when he wanted it to stop. He slowed its movement well before it entered the shack, feeling the gondol's effect on his arms and upper body as he entered the sphere. He slowly turned down the volume on the gondol. The plywood decking in the shack immediately began to splinter and crack. He retrieved the gondol, and the crate fell through the plywood floor, twisting and flattening the floor joists into the earth. Porter backed away from the door and waved the dust from his face. It was clear he had grossly underestimated its weight. At least it was out of plain view, despite the damage it had caused.

"So, you met Bahn and his crew." Porter almost jumped out of his skin. It was Sariah. "What did you think?" Her voice, strong and clear, was more like a loud voice in his head than something his ears perceived and manufactured a startling experience. He noticed that he still had the gondol in his hand, and it continued running at a low volume.

"I'm not really surprised you know those guys. Who are they?"

"I've known Bahn for a long time. We were once..." she paused, "closer than we are now." Was that regret he heard in her voice? Porter couldn't be sure. "He changed after he made the jump to your scale. The energy of a different scale can feel..." Porter could tell that she was fishing for the right word. "...isolating," added Sariah. "I think he's lonely."

"What do you mean by jump?" asked Porter, furrowing his brow. "Did Bahn travel from your scale to mine? Is that possible?"

"Bahn isn't from my scale exactly."

"What do you mean not exactly? Where is he from then?"

"I need to give you some more background first. For now, please accept that he is a neighbor but not family." Her evasive response hinted at a more complex relationship than she cared to admit. "Making the jump he did is a huge commitment. It can only be done while many physical and energetic conditions are aligned, and there's no guarantee that they will realign to allow him to go back. I think he may regret that decision. He's been in your scale for a very long time." The weight in her voice underscored more than the gravity of Bahn's sacrifice. *What was it, a lovers' quarrel?* mused Porter, but decided to let it slide.

"What does he want with me? What is this impossibly heavy box he delivered?" asked Porter, casually kicking the crate.

"He did that for me. I am very grateful for his efforts. He hasn't always been so cooperative. After what happened in New York, I think he has begun to understand the urgency of what I've been trying to accomplish." Porter did a double take on hearing the words "New York." The possibility that Sariah knew his part in it was not wholly unexpected. She never broached the subject, but Porter had no doubt that she, and even Bahn, who called him by his rank and full name, were privy to classified information concerning his last mission.

"I have a confession." Porter, winced. "My name's not Badger, it's Jonas Porter, but I have a feeling you already knew that."

"Yes, I did, but that's not important," said Sariah. There was a note of urgency in her voice. "Jonas, your scale is passing through a shift. Relative to your perspective, it is far larger than you can imagine. It does, however, affect even the smallest objects and, more importantly, the beings who love and hold energy. It can be deeply unsettling for many people and can cause widespread fear and distrust. I am not the only one who believes that certain powerful people in your scale's governments have set in motion events that they truly believe will protect them." This confirmed Porter's suspicions. *So, she does know what went down in New York.*

"Their reaction to the fear only appears irrational if you understand the shift, but it is nonetheless irrational. Their fear has driven them to slaughter innocent people within their own country with the hope of garnering support for their misguided campaigns in search of an illusive security. They rationalize their fears by identifying a source, usually another group of beings, deemed as a threat. It's a sadly unsustainable course of action that always leads to greater pain and insecurity."

Fear is often the cause of most wars, Porter observed bitterly.

Sariah continued, "The only way to find peace is to embrace the connectivity and unity of all beings. When you look at it that way, it becomes obvious that your government's actions in destroying those structures and killing those people in New York and surrounding areas were short-sighted. I have seen it in many scales and across many eras. It is a pattern that repeats itself despite the fact that it never brings the security they seek."

Porter realized that Sariah was spot on when she explained that, typically, a very small group of materially or physically endowed beings lose sight of the importance of human connectivity because of the misguided belief that lifeless materials they've accumulated offer security.

"That small yet immensely powerful group causes a shift in the thought and energy patterns of beings within their scope of influence into adopting the group's beliefs. It is a tremendous waste of light," quavered Sariah, her voice heavy with emotion.

"Who are these people? How do you know all this?"

"I'm sure you have your suspicions," answered Sariah, but Porter detected no hint of irony in her voice. "The concentrated wealthy associated with the petroleum industry currently control the United States government. The executor of their will is the Vice President himself. The phone conversations he has with a man named Cowboy are transmitted via satellite link. I've studied them carefully for the months leading up to their destructive work in New York."

For once, Porter was glad that Sariah couldn't see his face as he flushed with anger. But his outrage was soon replaced by despair when he realized what, or more accurately, *who* he was up against. *The Vice President!*

"Changing anything at that level isn't something I can help you with Sariah." Porter hoped that she wouldn't catch the dejection in his voice. "I hope you have a better plan."

"I do and it is one of the most difficult discussions you and I are going to have."

Porter decided to cut to the chase. "What's in the box?"

"More importantly, what does it do?" Sariah paused. "There are more technical names, but most commonly, it's called a halfgate. You can think of it as a portal to a scale that is either much smaller or much larger than yours but one that never gets you there. Everything that passes into it is rescaled in the way it would be prepared to pass into another scale, but nothing more."

"What's the point then?"

"Think of it like a suitcase, or a storage container, or even a warehouse—you can put things and people inside it."

"This thing opens?" Porter ran his hands along the sides of the cube. "I've tried to find a lid or a door. There isn't even a seam on it."

"The halfgate's six faces are intention panels. You can pass almost anything through the panels as long as it fits within the dimensions. Try it. Put something inside," she encouraged.

"Sariah, I've leaned on this box, stacked stuff on top of it, I've even crushed the radio shed's floor into a dusty mess. I've never seen an opening."

"Yes, but have you ever *intended* to put something inside? The panels react based on the intention of the user."

"You mean it can read my mind?" Porter was incredulous.

"It isn't your mind as much as your energy. When you lean on it, transport it with the gondol, or stack something on it, your intention is to do those things. Since your understanding was based on your experience, it remained as you perceived it: hard, heavy, and mysterious. Now, put something inside."

Porter picked up a screwdriver from the workbench and tossed it onto the halfgate's top panel. It skipped right off and onto the floor. "FYI, it didn't work," said Porter nonchalantly.

"Judging by the clatter, I assume you threw something at it," chuckled Sariah. "Pick up an object and *put* it inside this time. Imagine that there is no top to the cube. Intend to put the object inside the box. You don't have to let go if you don't want to."

"You mean I can put my arm inside? I'm not sure I'm ready to change my arm's scale," said Porter hesitantly.

"I may have made this more complicated than I needed to. It's quite simple. You can put your arm into the box and remove it again as you would from a cardboard box. The only difference is you'll not feel the box's bottom or sides while your arm's inside. Go ahead. Try it," coaxed Sariah.

Porter slowly held his hand over the halfgate and pressed his fingers into the surface as if trying to push it open. "It won't open."

"Jonas, it's always as open as you intend it to be. It's you that is open or closed."

"It sounds very zen," scoffed Porter, frustrated. "But I don't know what you want me to do."

"Try this. Sit next to the box with your eyes closed. Imagine you are sitting next to a box of about the same size and that there's an apple inside. Feel around in the box for the apple until you find it."

Porter did as asked and opened his eyes, thinking that the halfgate had moved. His arm was definitely inside the halfgate, and the box was right where it was before he closed his eyes. He could feel the top edge of the side of the halfgate pressing into his armpit, but he couldn't see the rest of his arm.

"Whoa!" exclaimed Porter, quickly pulling his arm up and out.

"So, it worked," said Sariah. It was more a statement than a question.

Porter had no doubt that his arm was still intact but stared at it as if seeing it for the first time, squeezing it with his other hand. Satisfied it was in no way maimed, he lightly pounded on the top of the halfgate with his fist; it felt solid. Then, with fingers pointing into the box, he reached down and through the top.

"That's so weird." He tried it repeatedly, dipping into the halfgate all the way up to his shoulder, reaching down and sideways. "I can't feel the sides from the inside. It's like I can reach around back into where I'm sitting, and I should run into the side of the box or even my own body, but nothing's there. Can I put my head in and look inside?"

"You can and you will, but please wait until Bahn or his crew is here to go in with you. It can be a bit disorienting."

"So, what do you want me to do with this?" asked Porter, pulling his arm out.

"I need to explain a bit more before we proceed."

"Okay."

"The work I do to explore new communication methods, especially between scales, is not exactly condoned by the elder women here."

Porter sensed the hesitation in her voice. *So, she's a radical*, Porter smirked openly, confident that Sariah could not see him.

"In fact, I could get into trouble if they find out what I've been doing."

"Let me guess, they don't look kindly on you sharing things like gondols and halfgates?" ventured Porter.

"They don't. Not at all," Sariah admitted reluctantly. "The elders have seen too many failures and lives lost in past attempts to bring symmetric intelligence to your world. They would consider what I'm doing to be a dangerous breach of trust."

"What do you mean by symmetric intelligence?"

"Up to now, we have been discussing two scales. The one in which you reside and the one where I am. I alluded to the fact that Bahn comes from a third and different scale. In fact, I've discovered many, and the range of scales may be infinite. These scales appear to be arranged as nested spheres much like electron shell configurations."

"It makes sense that the universe is structured using similar patterns across scales," replied Porter.

"It turns out that those pattern similarities apply to biological entities as well. In the same sense that each electron shell is limited by the number of electrons it can hold, scales have certain biological limitations."

"What, like dogs can't exist in your scale, but they can in mine?" Porter was fascinated by the other scales.

"It's more fundamental than that. It has to do with chromosomes. So far, my research has been limited to the scales adjacent to mine, but it appears that asymmetric chromosomes only exist in every other scale while symmetric ones exist in all of them."

This intrigued Porter. "You're referring to the sex gene, the asymmetry of the x-y chromosome. What you're saying is that women are everywhere, but men can only be in every other scale."

"More precisely, females may be anywhere, but males are limited to every other scale," corrected Sariah.

"Not to be trite, but if there are only women in those scales how did they get there?"

"Not trite at all, Jonas. Actually, quite an astute observation." In her voice, Porter could almost sense her smile with approval. "Men are always an essential part of procreation. Women who reside there choose to do so knowing that limitation. If they choose to have a child, they must transfer to an asymmetric scale before they can become pregnant."

"You make it sound so clinical." Porter was surprised by Sariah's impersonal tone but then realized that what was unorthodox for him was only natural to Sariah. "Do they transfer back as soon as they are?"

"It's not that simple. If the child she carries is male, that child, and almost always the mother, die in transit. When she knows the added burdens of having to live and raise a child in an asymmetric scale and the distinct possibility that she may not be emotionally able to leave her son and return, the choice to have a child is especially difficult."

"And if she carries a daughter? What then?"

"That, Jonas, is something I wrestle with every day. A woman pregnant with a girl can transfer back. But once she does, neither she nor her daughter is able to transfer again from the symmetric scale."

"Why?" Porter was finding it increasingly difficult to wrap his head around it.

"The universe abhors a vacuum. It's the balance to the equation. The father gives an X to make his daughter. The male-sourced X chromosome becomes lethal to further transfer only after it has transferred once."

"That's what happened to you?" asked Porter cautiously. He felt like he was walking on eggshells. Sariah was not exactly forthcoming about her family in her conversations with him.

"Yes. My mother was pregnant with me and brought me here. I may never be able to meet a man in person. It's unlikely I'll ever know my father." said Sariah solemnly. Her resonant voice implied that she was not easily moved, but Porter now realized that he had judged incorrectly. *She is just guarded.*

"Couldn't she have waited until after you were born?"

"Yes, she could have, and I wish she had."

"So, why didn't she?"

"I've tried talking with her about it, but she won't open herself to me in that way. I do know that she wanted a child so much but was too afraid to live or raise me in an asymmetric scale."

"Afraid of what?"

"Men and their chaos."

A vision of the collapsing World Trade Center flashed through his mind. Porter was all too familiar with "men and their chaos." "Are we really that bad, Sariah?"

"Neither are bad, Jonas. Both are essential to life's beauty as long as they're in balance."

"But your mother didn't see it like that?"

"Life in a symmetric scale is rich in its own way. Educational opportunities are virtually without limit. Science and art flourish. Emotions, intuition, empathy and feelings are treated with the same respect as logic, mathematics, and scientific rigor. The gondol and halfgate were developed and manifested by women. Social structures among women tend to be cooperative, nurturing, and uplifting. And there are many opportunities for love. My mother didn't want to risk losing that."

"Maybe your mother wanted the best for you."

"Some people imagine paradise as a place that is perfect. Somewhere that has everything in order, where there is no uncertainty. But that's not how I see it. The symmetric scale is like a loom without the weft. All the threads are aligned, and their creative potential is tremendous. But they're all the same and predictable. The integrity—and truly, the textile itself—exist only with a balanced interweaving between the weft and warp. True beauty arises when the weft's chaotic, unpredictable mix is supported by the warp's symmetric structure."

"So, men aren't so bad after all?"

"The scale you live in is severely unbalanced, Jonas. Having too much chaos and not enough structure eventually leads to no structure at all. Your scale has not even begun to resolve the most elemental energy difference: masculine and feminine. The male dominance in your scale has become so toxic and widespread that even most women have come to accept it as inevitable."

"It sounds pretty bleak," said Porter, dejected. *Like the whole loom has come undone.*

"I'm not making an overall judgment. The majority of women in your scale follow their intuition despite the obstacles. There are men who love and respect femininity. Most of them are artists and artisans. They add humor, ingenuity, and impetuousness to a fine tapestry's integrity. They are heroic in their ability to so behave among toxicity. Unfortunately, they are too few and far between."

"Okay, that's one way my scale is unbalanced, what else?"

"Alright," Sariah paused to think. "Let's start with something close to home. How about defense? The concept that it is essential to hinder, cripple, and destroy other human beings to pursue one's own perception of happiness. Worse than killing with false justification is honoring those who have because it perpetuates the idea to another generation. People wearing war wounds and prosthetics as badges of pride romanticize their self-importance by piggy-back-ing on bloated defense budgets rather than looking within, doing the work, and making meaningful contributions here and now."

She has a point. "I'll say that if I heard that anytime before those towers fell in New York, I would've been deeply offended. But I can see it's a solid argument. Your point is well taken. I'm going to have to let that sink in, though. Give me another one."

"The combination of emotional energy, intuition, discipline, and intellect are symmetric scale cornerstones. We attribute our progress to respecting that balance. In your scale, patriarchal religion co-opts intuition and turns it into something that can be used to dictate policy and control the masses. Credit for treating people with love is usurped by ideas that come from an outside source, such as the Holy Ghost. Worse yet, it undermines and erodes women's presence with their intuitive powers because their struggle to adhere to doctrine puts them in conflict with their own feelings. You can see this clearly whenever a man imposes his decisions and opinions upon a woman and enforces them physically. Look at how the Christian stories have been twisted to serve those in power."

"You'll have to explain that to me," interjected Porter. "I'm not too well-versed in church stuff."

"The stories of Jesus tell of a man who taught compassion, forgiveness, long suffering, and love. He sacrificed himself for others after being abandoned by his father in Gethsemane. He lived to serve others. And yet the message that's passed down through generations is that he died for them. Steeples, altars and breastbones are adorned with a symbol of ancient Roman torture. The extension of that message is that dying or suffering for a nation demonstrates loyalty to the Christian tradition. It's a remarkably effective psychological manipulation that reverses his teachings from love to war."

Porter had never thought of Christian doctrine that way, and now he could not unhear it. "We're going to have a hard time changing that cultural mindset, Sariah. What would be the point anyway?"

"Gondols and halfgates are a small sample of symmetric technology. What if I told you ways that could help your scale heal from the atrocities you experienced in New York?"

"Like what? It's all I can do to contain my anger," seethed Porter, balling his hands into fists.

"Combustion rate limiters are a great place to start. Burning fuel for localized heating is under the limit. Guns, explosives, missiles, even the bonfire you just built are not. It means radical cultural changes, but like the effects of the gondol, the affected geography is selectable."

"Are you serious?" asked Porter, incredulous. "There are ways to do that?" *It could render all incendiary weapons useless; it would revolutionize defense!*

"Peaceful defense systems are only a starting point. They protect cultures from most outside attacks without having to maintain an offensive posture. The most advanced that I've studied resembles the Nahua. Their systems work on the principle embedded in the halfgate. Unless each individual's intention is peace, self-reliance, and giving freely within the rights of others, any number of non-combustible things can be used as weapons. Intention filters manage that quite nicely."

Porter knew that the Nahua were an indigenous population in Central Mexico but had no idea they had such a pragmatic conflict resolution method.

Sariah continued, "It is also evident when a mother teaches her children from her heart but is then chastised because her teachings do not conform with religion. This pattern is patently unsustainable and leads to destruction."

"Somehow, that example is easier for me to understand. I feel the same way about my own intuitive sense. Still, I wonder what motivates empowered men to put impediments in place to begin with. Could I be so naïve that I can't recognize what scares them?"

"Perhaps you're beginning to understand why the elders don't support my work. They think it's impetuous and premature." Sariah chuckled wryly. "What my colleagues and I know is that progress only happens when we outgrow the need to protect ourselves from our own ignorance. It seems counterintuitive at first glance, but it is not technological progress that brings power, it is the metered dissemination to the masses."

"So, what you are suggesting is we take advantage of this opportunity to slip through a crack in the power flow." Porter placed a screwdriver on the halfgate with his right hand while his left arm was still inside. He brought the fingers of his left hand up through the intention panel, gently pinched the screwdriver between his thumb and forefinger, and merged it into the halfgate.

"I see it more as a fold, but I understand what you mean. It offers a wide range of opportunity."

"And a commensurate responsibility level. What we choose to do will affect generations," said Porter warningly. For the second time since he met Sariah, he wondered if he was up to the task.

"Everyone's actions affect the entire scale system. What's different now is you and I are holding back the power dissemination until we can set up a consequence cascade that will activate our intentions."

"So, the elders take issue with your qualification to control that much influence. Is that it?"

"Yes. Their intentions are honorable, but their ability to execute is hindered."

"They don't have someone like me." Porter gently returned the screwdriver back to its place on the workbench.

"Exactly," replied Sariah. "What we know and how we're able to communicate presents an opportunity few ever have a chance to pursue. Your government would use it to gain power. My elders would consider it too volatile and intrusive. I'm not willing to let it pass.

"We have the opportunity to do anything. How can we act in good conscience unless we know the consequences and their extent?"

"Research. We study and plan. Then we execute." Sariah was firm.

"That works for me. Where do you suggest we begin?"

"Can we agree for now how critical it is that you safeguard the gondols and halfgates from falling into the wrong hands?" pleaded Sariah earnestly. "Particularly the military."

"I do understand that. What I'm still struggling with is why your elders are unsupportive. Don't they want to find a way to develop a balance here as much as you do?"

"It's not that they don't support the balance. They haven't settled on which scale they believe is next to combine."

"What do you mean which scale?" .

"Consider your scale, which one could perceive as smaller or bigger, negative or positive, this way or that way, as compared to another. Perception is a relative matter. There is a scale that represents your opposite. That scale, relative to mine, is opposite yours. It is a continuous process of change and combination. Our challenge is to prepare ourselves to combine with one or the other and there are differences between the two."

"I thought you said the scales alternate. If two combine into what must be a new asymmetric scale, the result is two asymmetric scales without a symmetric in between."

"From the symmetric perspective, all energies combine. The filtering happens on the asymmetric scale. Those who embrace nurture, intelligence, and love remain and combine. Those who thrive on illness, ignorance, and fear also receive their chosen path. They are free to create and engage in conflict, but only with one another. In their ignorance, they transfer to the newly unoccupied scale, which was the symmetric, like my present scale. There, without the risk of any love being lost, they war themselves into non-existence. Their energy is transformed into a new, blank, neutralized symmetric scale."

What Sariah described was baffling. Porter was all for love and nurture, but people, albeit intrinsically evil ones, warring themselves into annihilation was too morbid. "And the process begins again." Porter sat down on the halfgate, his feet hovering above the splintered wood on the floor. "So, what you're proposing is we gather all the smart, life-loving people so they don't get warred from existence."

"There's no need to gather them. We only need to open the door." Sariah's voice was quieter now.

"How is a really heavy box that shrinks stuff going to help with that?"

"Jonas, I have already given you a risky amount of information," said Sariah, faltering. "The only way we can proceed from here is for you to act on your own intuition. You have to come up with a plan on your own, or my involvement will become far too evident."

"Alright, I understand," promised Porter, launching himself off the halfgate. "My intuition says I should ask if you know where I can find Grandma Keiti."

"I don't, Jonas. But I know where you can start looking."

21

INVESTIGEMOS

The genealogy library in Salt Lake was indeed a good start. Sariah realized it was there but was unable to access the records because they were rarely broadcast or transmitted by satellite. Jonas knew Lilli's parents' names and figured Grandma Keiti was on her side. He knew his grandpa Mills had passed away. He felt following the maternal line was going to get him where he needed to go. He found a marriage certificate for Julian Sergeant Mills and Lilli's mother, Grace McNeil Appleton, dated June 13, 1955, and issued by Barnstable County, Massachusetts. There were two witness signatures on the certificate. One was illegible, the other clearly read "Murielle Jocelin Rose." He searched for Murielle and found her birth certificate dated September 8, 1921. Birthplace was Marston's Mills, Massachusetts. Her parents were Matthew Michael Rose and Keiti Jocelin MacLaren. A search for "Keiti" revealed nothing further. He did find a Matthew M. Rose, age 11 on a 1910 Barnstable County census form, which listed his birthplace as Stornoway, Outer Hebrides, Scotland, UK. He couldn't make a clear connection between Lilli and Keiti MacLaren. The only commonality was one place: Barnstable County.

22

PILOTEMOS

"Amelia. I need to go to Massachusetts," urged Porter, just as Amelia stepped off the King Air. "And I'm in a hurry."

"Bants would lend you an Element for a few days."

"I was hoping for something a bit faster." Porter hesitated. "I have some cargo to carry, but I can offset the weight with the gondol."

"Would the *cargo* fit in the 182?"

Porter nodded, glad she didn't pry about the cargo's contents. *It would take a lot of explaining.*

"It's coming due for an avionics inspection. I could tell Bants I took it to Salt Lake for the inspection," smiled Amelia. "He won't miss it."

"I couldn't ask you to take time off and fly me to Massachusetts."

"You're right. You couldn't. But you could fly it yourself," she shrugged. "You're a quick study, Badge. I'll show you how. The 182 has an autopilot. Landing is a lot the same as landing a parachute once you get used to the controls."

23

ATERRIZEMOS

"How's the piloting going, Jonas?" Sariah inquired.

"It's actually pretty straightforward. We'll see how things go when I get to the Cape." Amelia was right, flying the 182 was a breeze.

"Are you tired?"

Porter was touched by the concern in her voice. "Not really. But I do need to use the bathroom. I think I'm going to have to find someplace to land soon."

"You could, but considering the time you'll need to slow down and the chance you'll be taking, given your limited experience and the halfgate's added mass, landing is time-consuming and risky," Sariah hesitated. "There is another option."

"I'm all ears," said Porter.

"Are you ready to go inside?"

"Inside the halfgate?" asked Porter, surprised.

"Yes, I asked Bahn to set up a place for you before he delivered it. The halfgate face, with the green emblem on it, enters a limited space with a clear path back to your scale. It's reserved for you to rest and take time for yourself while traveling. Think of it as an apartment with a door that transforms you from one scale to another as you pass through it."

"So, what you're saying is that you'll keep an eye on the plane while I go take a shower and a nap?" asked Porter, with a hint of humor.

"Precisely," Sariah's response was deadpan. "The halfgate has a very clear signal point. I'll let you know if you're needed in the cockpit. There's some weather south of Chicago, but we'll stay north. You'll be flying another eleven hours or so. Get some rest."

Looks like she's got all the bases covered, thought Porter. *Might as well get some rest.* "So how do I get inside?"

"It's simple. Crawl through the forward-facing panel while you intend to go inside."

Jonas checked the GPS and autopilot one more time. He unlatched his seatbelt and got down on the floor. Bants had removed all but the pilot's seat and carpeted the floor to keep the tandem masters' knees happy. The halfgate still looked imposingly solid, and the thought of passing through it remained unsettling. He crawled over to the box and passed his hand through the front panel. He moved a little closer and let his head follow his arm. The plane went through some light turbulence, and Jonas found himself tumbling through the halfgate onto a large leather couch, which was pressed against the wall of a tasteful yet comfortable living room. The aroma of meat stew with onions and garlic wafted from a small, black granite countertopped kitchen. Until then, he had not realized he was hungry. He stood up and walked around the apartment. Art hung on the walls; some were familiar, some foreign and stunningly intriguing. The windows faced a beautiful sunset over a blue mountain lake. A short pier extended from a deck off the back of the house, and a small rowboat was tethered to the end, floating lazily in the almost-still water. Sariah's calm voice came to him deeply, but this time far more clearly.

"I hope you like it."

"It's beautiful, Sariah, thank you," expressed Porter gratefully. "I'm certain I've never flown more comfortably, particularly in a 182."

"Feel free to relax, have something to eat, take a shower, and rest," urged Sariah graciously. "I'll let you know when you are close to the Mills."

Porter couldn't find a halfgate anywhere in the apartment. "How do I get back into the plane?"

"The picture hanging over the brown leather couch is an intention panel. It'll take you back."

Porter stepped onto the couch and put his head through the frame. He was immediately assaulted by loud engine noise and the rush of the wind. He could see the twilit sky through the windows. The autopilot was adjusting the elevator trim and the yoke was gently moving to maintain course. He pulled his head back inside and the noise immediately ceased. "Sariah, why can't I feel the plane's motion while I'm in here?"

"The halfgate has altered your scale by a factor of about ten to the minus 256. Relative to the plane and your scale, you are many times smaller than the smallest subatomic particle. Even though it seems to you that you are still inside it, you and the plane's scale are so vastly different that it no longer meaningfully affects you. Any changes in the plane's scale that take place in your absence you'll discover only after you return."

After he showered, Porter ladled some stew into a bowl and sat down on the couch. He didn't realize how tired he was until he finished his meal. The past few weeks had been an emotional rollercoaster. Things were moving too fast for him to process. Everything that happened seemed surreal: first Sariah, the gondol, Bahn and his team, and then the halfgate. Now he was tracing his ancestry to his great-great-grandmother. *I hope I'm not on a wild goose chase,* thought Porter, with a sigh. He had yet to see what Grandma Keiti had to do with saving his scale. He was simply following his instinct, as Sariah suggested. He had not stopped to consider the ramifications of what he was doing, either for himself or the world at large. But now, as he lay on the couch looking out the window at the sun setting over the placid lake, he was overwhelmed by a strangely gratifying weariness, as if he had finally stopped running and hiding and was doing what he was always meant to do.

Porter didn't realize he had fallen asleep until Sariah's voice awakened him a few hours later. "Jonas, you are getting close. It's time for you to return to the plane." Porter stretched and enjoyed the silence for a moment longer.

"What's going on?"

"You are passing southeast of Hartford and are about to enter Providence airspace," reported Sariah. "You will have to contact them on the radio unless you make a course change. It's also time to start descending."

Porter crawled back through the painting into the plane. The cockpit was much colder than the apartment. He pulled on a sweatshirt and lowered the headset over his ears as he slipped back into the pilot's seat. The GPS showed 35 minutes remaining to 2B1, and the airspace around Providence appeared on the GPS as a dashed ring that his plane was about to enter. He tuned his radio to Providence approach and listened.

"Cair one seven. VFR traffic, two o'clock and one mile, same altitude, unverified."

"Cair one seven. I have the traffic. Looks like a small Cessna." Porter scanned the horizon looking for any other aircraft but could not see any.

"Cair one seven maintain visual separation from that traffic. Cleared to land runway two three."

"Cleared to land runway two three, Cair one seven."

Porter knew they were talking about him. He was still high enough to technically not be inside Providence airspace, but he didn't like the attention he was attracting. Time to put his training to the test. *It's now or never*, thought Porter, disengaging the autopilot and gently bleeding off airspeed. The engine quieted, and the sound of rushing air became more pronounced. He was still flying at 140 knots, and when he extended the flaps one notch, the plane pitched forward slightly and began to shudder. He retracted the flaps and pitched the plane's nose up with the trim wheel. His altitude increased by 500 feet, then began to settle back down. When the airspeed had slowed some more, he again extended the flaps, and the shudder did not return. With a sigh of relief, he turned north to avoid the Falmouth Coast Guard airspace and instead headed out across Cape Cod Bay. He continued to reduce airspeed and altitude until he could maintain enough speed to allow his altitude to remain constant at 1,500 feet. Amelia had coached him on 2B1. The longest runway was only 2,700 feet long; it was turf and surrounded by trees. She told him that his altitude and airspeeds were critical, especially with the additional cargo.

Porter put the plane in a long, slow descending turn out across the bay and lined up with runway two seven, almost five miles away. He slowed the plane and adjusted the gondol to create the drag he needed to slow the plane. A white church steeple stood out above the trees as the grass strip came into view. Porter held the plane above the treetops ready to cut the power completely as soon as he could see clearly to the runway. He reduced the gondol volume until he had a steady descent rate toward the airfield.

The plane dropped far more quickly than expected. He increased the gondol volume, gripped the yoke with clammy hands, and pulled back. He was still almost 30 feet above the airfield. A quick glance at the airspeed indicator showed he was flying at only 45 knots. As the airplane pitched up and continued to slow, the stall horn began blaring. "No pressure," Porter cursed under his breath.

"What was that?" It was Sariah.

"Never mind," said Porter through gritted teeth.

"Is everything alright Porter?" She sounded concerned and was no doubt tracking his movements, but she was probably oblivious to the minor technicalities of landing.

"Just peachy," said Porter, trying to keep the edge off his voice. He saw no point in worrying her with aeronautics.

The plane continued to slow, but it was still almost six feet from the turf. Fine beads of sweat broke out on Porter's brow. The tree line loomed beyond the runway ominously. He had little control over the plane as it slowed to thirty knots. Porter decreased the gondol volume in the smallest possible increment, and the plane slowly descended to the grass. Porter found himself holding his breath. One wing began to drop faster than the other, and the aircraft yawed slightly to the left. He shut the engine off, and the plane touched down on one main wheel, yawed back in the runway's direction, and then mercifully, the other two wheels touched down as well. The landing was not pretty, but the plane was intact. He was more concerned about how he was going to explain how the landing looked like to the people in the golf cart driving out to meet him. Porter glanced back at his cargo and remembered the comfortable apartment inside.

The man swung from the golf cart before it came to a stop. His already sparse hair was tousled. Machine grease in the cracks of his hands and an acrid whiff of Jet A indicated that this was the airport mechanic. "That was about the strangest landing I've ever seen," the man professed breathlessly. "I can't believe how slow you were going before you touched down. You must have some serious STOL package on this baby. Are you okay?"

Before Porter could come up with a response, the passenger door opened, and the woman with him stuck her head through.

"You need any help with this cargo, Porter?"

Surprised to hear his name, Porter turned to see Lakshmi already loosening the tie-downs for the halfgate.

"Lakshmi, I can't say I was expecting you, but I'm not entirely surprised," grinned Porter. "Yeah, I could definitely use some help with that." Lakshmi already had the halfgate and gondol unloaded from the plane and strapped to the golf cart. She called to him over her shoulder as the cart's engine started.

"Come to the northwest corner after you've parked. We're camped there. Bahn wants to meet." Porter could see the Kartikeya in the distance.

"Thanks, Lakshmi. I'll be there soon. Tell Bahn I have to find someone in town first."

24

DISTORSIONEMOS

Colonel Michael Fowler looked older than he should. His amber brown hair was noticeably receded, thanks to the stress that came with the territory of being the commander of the 388th Fighter Wing. He sat at the head of the conference table, his blue-gray eyes scanning his command, and stopped at Major Rice.

"Major Rice, I want you to brief the staff on the anomaly your controllers have been recording in the west desert."

"Yes sir. We initially received reports of radar interference from F-16 pilots on sorties into the Wendover MOA."

Fowler was lanky and cut a sorry figure beside the stocky major. But what he lacked in physique, he more than made up for in charisma. "Describe the interference, Major," he insisted.

"At first, we thought it was a maintenance issue with the avionics upgrades, but their radar screens got bent."

"Explain that." Fowler was a man of few words, and his slit of a mouth parted only to dispense such curt commands and blunt questions.

"It's strange, sir. The equipment wasn't damaged, but the displays were distorted. Target practice bogeys were evading us even when missile lock was engaged with the firing systems. We had wingmen fly preprogrammed trajectories, so we knew exactly where they were supposed to be. Both the radars at Hill and the systems onboard the F-16s showed modest distortion of the actual location but enough to render our firing systems ineffective. They are failing in the field, but in the labs here at Hill they have demonstrated perfect compliance."

"Where does it happen, Major?"

"Most recently it has been happening during our sorties into Gandy MOA, it's most prominent when we are flying across the lake, and it appears to be stronger from the south."

"So, you've determined that this is outside interference? Have we checked with Dugway?"

"We have sir," nodded Rice. "They aren't using any equipment that would create this disturbance."

"What about civilian?" ventured Fowler. "Have we checked with the FCC? Anything new there?"

"We checked with them, sir, and they report no new installations over the period we have been experiencing the anomaly."

Fowler ruffled through a report in front of him and gave up. "When did you start receiving the reports, Major?"

"The first report from an F-16 sortie came in last week. But when I briefed the pilots, they informed me that they had been experiencing the distortions as early as late August. They thought they were experiencing bugs in the Mark VII systems. Now I have them all reporting anything unusual."

"What about the base radars at Hill? What do they pick up?"

"It's never as prevalent, sir," explained Rice. "It seems to be a localized phenomenon, but we have seen it on base radar."

"Can you pinpoint it?" asked Fowler.

"No sir. The source as far as we can determine does not come from one location. It keeps moving."

"Can we see an image of incident scatter plot overlaid on a satellite image?"

"I have that for you now sir," said Rice as an image appeared on the monitors. "The points all tend to center around TVY sir."

"TVY?" Fowler knitted his thin brows.

"TVY is a civilian municipal airport south of us. Tooele Bolinder Field."

"Get the FAA on the phone. Find out what they are doing at TVY. What about these two indications here and here, Major?" He motioned to two isolated points on the monitor. "Why do they appear to be coming from the east instead of the south?"

"Those happened yesterday, sir. We have never seen them from that direction before."

"Are there any other bases reporting similar distortions?"

"Yesterday, after I saw those two blips to the east, I called one of my instructors out at the Springs and asked him what he thought. He told me they had been experiencing the same phenomenon across northern Colorado."

Fowler was a rationalist and was known to relentlessly attack a problem until it was resolved. An anomaly that defied logic made him uneasy. "Major, I want a clear description of what the anomaly does and how it affects our systems distributed to base commanders across the network, and I want to be advised immediately if any further indications are found."

"Yes sir, Colonel."

25

GOLPEEMOS

If Murielle was Grace's mother and Keiti's daughter as Porter suspected, she would have to be about eighty, making Keiti at least a hundred years old. A young cashier at the local grocery store was kind enough to dig up a phone book for him to begin his search. Within its aging pages, he found a no-address listing for George Appleton in Marston's Mills. He called the number, but there was no answer. Jonas looked at a map of Marston's Mills. The place was tiny. It couldn't be too hard to find someone, especially if they had lived there for so long. He found the library at the town's center, but it was closed. From there, he continued on to a market in the middle of the intersection of Route 149 and River Street.

A heavy, middle-aged woman behind the counter wore a white apron, horn-rimmed glasses, and a yellow bandana in her hair. She had been ladling chowder into a container for the prior customer and was wiping the excess from her hands onto her apron front when Jonas approached.

"What can I do for you, young man?" she said in a Boston accent, mellowed by years on the Cape.

Porter explained the particulars of his search.

"Let me see the list." Porter handed it to her. "I don't know any Keiti MacLaren. But I do know Julian Mills. He and his wife moved back to Boston years ago. It was sudden. Folks were talking, but I never got the whole story. And George Appleton. He died about eleven years ago. Can't remember his wife's name. She always kept to herself. As far as I know she still lives out in George's old farmhouse."

Porter had to follow a dirt access road through tall trees for about three miles to reach Appleton's place. A lattice archway entwined with roses, long wild from neglect, marked the entrance. The modest single-level house was almost obscured by overgrown fitzers, crabapple trees, and ivy and he could see that the roof shingles were in deep disrepair.

The front porch was dark. Dust and cobweb-covered cushions adorned two Adirondack chairs. A pair of gardening gloves and a small trowel were equally time encrusted. The oak-framed screen door sagged ajar onto the slate porch floor. Yellowed, water-stained curtains covered the windows from the inside. There was no evidence that anyone still lived here. If someone did, they hadn't come through the front door in a very long time.

Porter tugged on the screen door which torqued around its sunken bottom corner. He reached in between the frame and knocked on the front door. After knocking a second time, an elderly woman parted the ragged curtains behind the porch chairs. It was difficult to see her through the dusty glass, but Porter could hear her call to go around back.

Porter waited for about five minutes by the back door without knocking. The same elderly woman, hunched over and struggling to lift her head, opened the door and smiled. Her silk dress slipped around her cane as she walked. She silently stepped aside, holding the door open in invitation. Porter hesitated only for a moment. The ceilings were open to the rafters and uninsulated. The house was filled with eclectic trinkets and art. The woman slowly sat down at a metal folding kitchen table and invited Porter to join her.

"What's your name?" she asked.

Considering what he was trying to accomplish, he dropped his alias. "Jonas Porter."

"Jonas Mills Porter. Lillian's son. We've been waiting for you." She chided him playfully, "What took you so long?"

"How do you know who I am?" asked Porter, surprised.

"Unlike some of our relatives, I pay attention to who's who and where they are." Her voice was weak and raspy, but her azure eyes twinkled through her wry smile.

"You must be Murielle. My great-grandmother?" Murielle bobbed her sparsely-haired head in response; Porter grinned in relief.

"You could start by giving me a little hug," she cooed, spreading her arms wide. Porter got up, put his arm around her, and squeezed her frail body close to his chest. He stayed crouched next to her chair.

"Why didn't my mom tell me anything about you?" Porter held her hand as they talked.

"I'll venture she didn't tell you much about Gracie either. It's easier that way. It doesn't hurt so much when you're making the choices Lillian did," sighed Murielle listlessly, looking into the distance.

"Gracie?"

"Grace was our only daughter," said Murielle fondly. "She had Lillian when she was eighteen."

"Grace—my grandmother. Did she die?"

"Not any more than your mother did."

"She's still alive, then." It was more a statement than a question.

"You've known that, haven't you, Jonas? And you knew she had a good reason for leaving." Murielle tapped Jonas's shoe with her cane.

"It never made any sense to me that she fell through the ice." It was Porter's turn to gaze into the distance. "She knew the hazards on that lake better than anyone. Especially in the spring." He turned to Murielle. "What choices? Why would it hurt her to tell me about my relatives?"

"It's hard enough to love and raise a child." Murielle let out a wheezy sigh. "It's even harder when you know from the beginning that you will have to leave him without even saying goodbye. The leaving is easier for everyone if there are fewer attachments."

The conversation with Sariah about the symmetric scale flashed through Porter's mind. "So, where is my mom? Is she with Grace?"

"I think so."

"So, if I'm going to find my mom, I should be looking for Grace?"

"Why are you here, really, Jonas?" countered Murielle earnestly, peering into his eyes.

"The last thing my mom told me before she left was to find Grandma Keiti. But I think it's too late."

"Actually, you're a wee bit early." Murielle's eyes crinkled as she flashed him a yellow-toothed smile. "Mim'll be up from her nap in about an hour. Would you like some tea?"

26

VISTAMOS

"We're at the cusp of a paradigm shift," said Murielle over tea, sounding quite eloquent for her advanced age. "If history is any indication, space and time are a chain of paradigm shifts, ebbing and flowing like the tide."

She was convinced that the border separating these is not so much a threshold as a hazy boundary, where the old paradigm slowly subsides and the new emerges. Right now, they were shifting from a materialist paradigm to one of consciousness.

"But there are precursors," continued Murielle, placing a bony finger on her thin lips. She pointed out that the period from 1780 through 2002 was characterized by materialism, and the 1960s resurgence of art and music was a high tide foreshadowing the change to come.

"But the fall of the Twin Towers marked the beginning of the actual forty-year transition, the midpoint being 2022. The transition should be complete by say..." Murielle paused to calculate. "2044."

Full circle from materialism to consciousness, thought Porter, admiring Murielle's power of deduction.

She believed that transition periods are marked by chaos, plunging the world into disarray, rife with conflict, plagued by fear and anxiety.

"Make no mistake, the change is potent and fast approaching," she cautioned. "Yet it ebbs and flows, toying with those who pine for the materialism of a bygone age as well as those who ache for the humanism, compassion, and cooperative progress that generate heightened consciousness.

Murielle's point of view made Porter realize the significance of opening a portal between the scales. He had no plan. All he knew was that on the road to full consciousness, things would get worse before they got better.

The thick Scottish brogue was a fanfare announcing her advance from the bedroom. "'Sset thins streat right off, shall we? W'donna have much time. Laddie, yer 'bout'a git th'shite kicked right outta ye." Keiti, 102 years and three months old, took an immediate and astonishing command. "Doncha go underestimatin' wassa 'bouta happen cuss ye ken emsum feeblo' lass."

Porter backed away from her walker and sat in the kitchen chair. He looked over at Murielle, who nodded at him knowingly.

"Yer skeel 'sabout hava sec fro' been leh goah. I'm steel 'ere, dammit. 'M steel 'eere 'cussa believen ye. Ee meeda premise t'th' likesa ye mum."

Porter had never felt so helpless. He was accustomed to being in control and commanding the people around him. He didn't even know how to respectfully address this woman, with scanty white hair and pallid skin, hobbling before him.

"Wh'achee goin' do, lad? Ye fahn me, yea, but's ye t'hasta ac'. Tell me, Jona'. Wha's ye plen?"

Porter looked at her as a child would. "I... I'm not sure I have a... plan," he muttered. "I was hoping finding you would help me know what to do."

"Och! Tha's whacha call fallin' yern twishen, is't? Thas th'bess ye ken? Ye ca' brinna bildn' ooh's knees b'chu kent fig'r how t'address th' prob'm? Howda gi' min'a respe' th'lassies? Howda gi' min'a respe' thr'own keen? Thr'own species?"

Her gaunt form trembled as she jabbered passionately. "Howda gi'thm pess kenin they betr'in others? S'their grea's flah. Grea's stopper th'progress?" Keiti turned sharply to Murielle. "A bheil seo mar a dh'fheumas sinn obrachadh, mo nighean?" *Is this how we must work, my daughter?*

"Hold on, Grandma Keiti," said Porter raising his palms in defense. "May I call you that? I do have a plan."

Keiti looked at Murielle and then back at Porter. Her voice and body relaxed. She stood taller, slackening her bony grasp on the walker. "Weel then, Jona'. Less 'ear't."

"You said you're still here because you made a promise to my mom," said Porter tentatively. "She's still alive, and I want to find her. You know where she is, and you'd like to be there too."

"Thasa good starr'. Wha'els ye gi'?" pushed Keiti, critically regarding Porter with foggy, gray eyes.

"Why should we stop there? What about everybody else?" Porter looked at her expectantly.

"Laddie, fallvm go, why doot atall? There's many who'd ne'er goah. Wouldn't want it," she said with a dismissive shake of her head that shook her frail body. "Nay, an twuddn't be worth a ha'penny t'narne."

"I want to open a door that lets people be the way they want to be."

"An what o'those who tak't frem othrs jus t'serve themselves?"

"That's the beauty of having another choice than this scale. The lovers can be as long as they continue to love. If they don't, they can always come back here to be with those who choose to fight."

"Ay, enteel there's no one left to fight wi'. So, Jona'. 'Veard the whay. Steel 'vent heart th' 'ow."

Porter felt pinned. He knew his plan would involve the gondol and halfgate, but he wasn't sure he should reveal that to Keiti and Murielle. "I'm still working on that part. This is going to take some time. But it has to get started now."

"Braw! Nah'ye kanny! Muri, be alove an' fetch th'seacaid. Ye ken th'un."

Murielle struggled to get up from the chair. Porter hopped up and offered his hand to her. She took it, stood, gained her balance, and walked out of the room with her cane. He turned back to Keiti. They stood facing one another in the kitchen.

"Gotcha wee prize, la'. 'Ll hep'ye figge' howt'luv th'aerth. Ye shaw th'aerth ye love, ye shaw th'min." Her old eyes grew large, and it was as if the fog of senility lifted momentarily. The words gave Porter hope.

Murielle returned with the jacket over her arm and held it out to Keiti.

"Givt'im, Muri. Donn't there, Jona'. See how't feetsya."

Porter took the jacket from Murielle.

"Twas me gray gram tha' mek't. Sh' tet meth'waulkin'. Gra' MaClahrn. Twas fer her guidman."

Porter ran his hand across the raw felted wool. It was heavy, with large oak toggles sewn to the front and engraved ivory buttons on the cuffs. It was in remarkably good condition for a one hundred seventy-year-old garment. Porter looked at Murielle for confirmation.

"She wants you to have it. It was her great-grandmother's wedding gift to her husband, passed from father to son until her father, Gille, wore it. Keiti had me, and George and I had Gracie. Gracie and Julian had your mum. You are the next male child in line to wear the jacket. It's a powerful honor," explained Murielle, eyes closed in a reverent nod.

Porter looked at the coat and then again at Keiti. "Gwon, then. Donn't, now. See how't feetsya!"

Porter opened the jacket and swung his arms into the sleeves. He twisted the center toggle into its opposing loop and let it settle onto his shoulders. Keiti held the back of her hand across her mouth as her eyes welled up. Porter turned to look at Murielle, but she wasn't there. He turned back to Keiti to find a beautiful young woman, perhaps twenty-seven years old, with long curly red hair, wearing a dark, full-length wool skirt and a white cable knit sweater. She wiped the tears from her cheeks and spoke to Porter quietly. "Ye ken." She paused. "Ye see me asa weera bairn, doncha now?"

"Keiti?" Porter leaned in to take a closer look at the woman.

"Aye, Jona'. Tis yer Gra'Keiti." Her voice was no longer raspy and strained, but smooth and lilting with the same brogue. "But yees seein me's a bairn." She bobbed her head with more enthusiasm than the woman he first met. "Och, a wee bit elder'n that, now. How ahwas wenna were a mum t'Muri. 'Telseken yesee, lad? Be'her now, howdyee feel?"

Porter looked around the kitchen and through the dirty back windows. That hadn't changed. He felt a sense of belonging, a sense that he was part of something much larger. He saw his relationships with Lilli, Andrew, Glenn, Louisa, Sariah, Amelia, Bants, Taylor, Josh, Mindy, Bram, Sanchez, all at once, all interrelated, all carefully laid out in a pattern that suddenly made so much sense. Everyone was vitally important. Everyone made up a part of the pattern in a unique and essential way. He saw himself as a child lying upon his father on the ice. He saw the thirty-two-skater flock. He saw where Lilli's thread dropped through the fabric and disappeared. He looked further out across what he now understood to be a tapestry. A weaving. Its expanse went further than he could see, but if he chose, he could fly over it in his mind, seeing any part he chose. Eventually, it faded into simple parallel lines stretching far away from him without any color or thread.

He turned back to the younger Keiti, pleasantly baffled. "What is this, Keiti? What am I seeing?"

"The jack't ye donn'd. Essa tweed Gra' M'Clahrn mek't. Lesya see'tall, th'entire werk, lad. Was fer her guidman."

Porter looked carefully at young Keiti and noticed the sweater she was wearing had patterns similar to the tapestry. But the sweater was all of one being. A part of someone's life. But it, too, ran through the tapestry as other parts of people's lives, thoughts, and feelings did.

"Y'seen th'love in the wool now? Ye feel'n' th'lova ye mums?" Keiti's slowly undulating narrative voice was mesmerizing, almost ritual.

"Yes. I do. I see the work. I see the pattern. I can see the love in the sweater you're wearing. Your mother, Andreana. She knit that sweater for you. When you were fifteen. She gave it to you for your birthday. You had a boyfriend. She didn't like him. She made beef stew one night and burned the potatoes. I can see her kitchen! She was so angry about the potatoes." Porter paused, his face mirroring the emotions. "But your dad came in and hugged her. He told her he liked burned potatoes. She looks up from the embrace, slaps him on the chest, and kisses him." Porter stepped back slightly and focused his eyes on hers. "And I can see you."

"Aye, lad. Ye ken. Ye see 'tall. 'snah jess that'n, eeth'r. 'Sallvem. Och, allvem that'r mek'd b'hends. Th'kennin' goes in like thah'." Her face lit up with a smile, radiant with youth.

"All handmade textiles have this in it. They all carry the feelings—the love—of the people who made them. I've known it in sweaters my mom made for me. I see it now as the whole work. I know now what I have to do, Keiti," said Porter with a resolute nod. "I see all the places I have to go." He paused as his focus changed quickly. "You have a huge textile collection right here in Marston's Mills! How long have—never mind." Porter got up from the table, shifting his focus back to the present. He slipped the jacket off and folded it carefully over his arm. "I have to go now. You're right. There isn't much time."

Keiti appeared once again to him as the feisty elderly woman he first met. "Aye. Ye bes' be off. Agaibh mòran obair ri dhèanamh, gille." *You have a lot of work to do, boy.*

27

PLANIFIQUEMOS

"Will he know what to do?" asked Grace, squeezing her daughter's shoulders. "Will he be able to open the portal?" Her weary blue eyes peered into Lilli's. Lilli was acutely aware of the implications of Porter's success for Grace. She was probably just as eager to see those she left behind, including the grandson she had never met and, for that matter, never knew existed until five minutes ago. Lilli realized that Grace hadn't aged well. Her once vibrant blond hair was almost entirely gray. Her face was wrinkled, and the skin on her neck sagged. Perhaps the pain of being long separated from her kin had taken its toll. Nevertheless, Lilli was glad to be in her mother's arms again. *How long has it been?* she wondered as she hugged Grace for the second time. *Too long.* They had a lot of catching up to do.

"I hope so," said Lilli earnestly.

"Jonas is an intelligent boy," assured Grace, stroking her daughter's tear-drenched cheek. "He can take care of himself." Lilli nodded somberly. This meant a lot to her. Her decision to return to the symmetric scale had been rife with doubt. But Porter would have never fulfilled his destiny had Lilli stayed. It had to be done.

"This is a good thing," said Grace, urging Lilli to be optimistic. "You'll see him again."

Lilli only smiled. "There'll be resistance. He'll need help."

"Then he shall have it," assured Grace firmly. "There are like-minded people here who are willing to assist."

"And the elders?" asked Lilli warily.

"Hang the elders," blurted Grace, with something of her old spark. This brought a smile to Lilli's lips. *She hadn't changed one bit*, she thought.

"It's about time we reached out to other scales," said Grace. "Imagine what unlocking full consciousness would be like on an asymmetric scale," mused Grace. "It'll transform their social fabric. Art and music will flourish, and people will be more nurturing and forbearing."

"Yes, yes, and man will finally shed his ego, and war will be a thing of the past," Lilli teased. She was more pragmatic and knew the change would be so gradual that it would take years to make a real difference. "But I want to go back when the portal opens," admitted Lilli with resignation. With all its flaws, it was her home for many years. "We can both go back."

Grace patted her daughter's hand reassuringly. "Then there's much work to be done."

Jonas sat in the white Element—a crew car on loan from the airport manager—and stared out the windshield, trying to wrap his head around what had happened. He dug through his duffle bag and turned on the gondol. "Sariah. Are you there?" There was no answer. He drove north on Route 149 until he came to a large grass field. He pulled the car over and got out. The area was thick with towering trees, which made the open field that much more unusual. A red biplane flew low over his head, banked sharply left, and landed in the field. He'd come back to the airport from a different direction and hadn't recognized it until now. At the far end, he could see Bant's 182 parked next to other small planes. Nearby stood a white windmill and a few hangars. He recognized the scene from his vision when he donned the jacket; this was the place Keiti and Murielle had stored their collection of handmade sweaters, tapestries, and blankets. Jonas got back in the car and drove to the airfield's entrance. Sariah's voice came to him just as he pulled into the parking area.

"Jonas. Can you hear me?"

"I can, and I need your help."

"Are you alright?"

"Yes, I'm fine. I've figured out what I need to do and where I have to go. It might sound crazy, but I think you'll understand." Porter paused. "I need Bahn and his plane, a second plane for myself, four thousand gondols and twenty thousand kilometers of steel cable. I need to know if you and Bahn can help me get all of these items before we go any further."

"Jonas. That's quite an order. I'll do some checking and get back to you. Meanwhile, I've received some concerning Air Force communications coming from Hill AFB in Ogden." Her slightly rattled voice unnerved Porter. *This can't be good.* "They're tracking the signal the gondol emits when it's active. They're tracking you right now."

28

ABRAMOS

Porter switched off the gondol and walked across the field to the windmill. It was clearly once functional, but all that remained were the spars from the windblades and the tie down cables, rendering it no longer operational. Next to the windmill were two old airplane hangars. A faded and illegible sign over the hangar's doors gave a sense of its history. The field had been used in the 1920s as a military base. These were the same hangars he saw through the jacket's vision. The door was unlocked. He struggled to slide it open. The sun shone through dime-sized holes speckled across the corrugated steel roof. Thick dust swirled slowly across the shafts of sunlight. As his eyes adjusted to the darkness, he could see an old airplane without a propeller in the far corner and a Piper Cub near the door. Massive, dust-covered steel warehouse shelves held various aircraft and car parts. Rusty barrels sat in oily puddles covered with sawdust and grime. He was certain this was the place he had seen while wearing the jacket, but he couldn't imagine how anything valuable could be stored here. Porter climbed onto a large wooden crate to see what was behind it when an old man pushed the hangar door fully open. Porter turned, ready to explain himself. The old man finished opening the door. He turned and walked to the other door and opened it as well.

Porter stepped down from the crate to speak with the old man, but he had already walked back outside. Sunlight now illuminated the hangar's interior, and Porter had a better view of what he had been investigating. He started to walk back toward the open doors when the old man came around from the building's side, driving a golf cart. He connected the cart to the Cub's tailwheel and towed it out onto the field. He didn't seem to notice or mind that Porter was there.

The old man proceeded to open the plane's engine compartment to check the oil level. Porter walked out and looked around. There were two or three other people working on planes. A man on a tractor was mowing the airstrips. Still, no one showed any interest in Porter's presence.

Porter went back inside. He stepped back over the crate and noticed a cast iron panel under the shelving units. After removing airplane seats and car tires from the bottom shelf, he was able to lift the shelf itself and expose the panel. He brushed the dust off with his hand and felt distinct embossed lettering in the cast iron. The panel was round, about four feet in diameter, and was bolted to the concrete floor. The concrete was crumbling around the bolt holes. Porter was able to fit his fingers under the panel's edge but was still unable to lift it. He found a steel rod leaning in the corner and used it to pry the panel open. The bolts lifted from the cement with relative ease. He moved the lever to the other side and pried free the remaining bolts. Thick cobwebs rustled as he lifted the panel to expose a dark, damp, undefinable space beneath the floor. He wanted to explore further but was certainly pushing his luck as a trespasser by now. He replaced the panel and found an oil-soaked chamois to cover it. After returning the shelf, seat, and tires to their place, he reluctantly left the hangar. He was certain that he had found where he needed to go, but it would have to wait.

Porter walked along an access road to the parking lot. He saw an old stone wall close to Race Lane, walked over to it, and found it was an entrance to a tunnel that went under the road to another field. The stone walls at both ends of the tunnel were 1920s military vintage. Porter was certain this wasn't the only one.

29

ENCONTREMOS

Cape Cod Airfield was a day-use-only, grass field airstrip, and by nine-thirty, it was completely dark. Porter parked the Element by the golf course opposite the airfield. He brought flashlights, hand tools, and rope in a backpack and crossed the field to the hangars. As he approached, he noticed a light from high in the windmill and decided to change course. He circled through a wooded area and approached the hangars from the northwest, avoiding anyone who might be working in the mill.

The hangar doors were closed but not locked. He had the same trouble opening the door as last time and struggled to keep the rusty corrugated steel from resonating. He slipped through the opening and turned on a headlamp. The Cub was parked where it had been before.

After he cleared the cobwebs from the space he had uncovered, the bottom of a dry well with concrete walls became visible. Rusted rebar rungs, some mangled and bent, protruded from its walls. He climbed down to the bottom and found a lateral tunnel leading southwest. Six feet in diameter, it was constructed with the same corrugated steel as the tunnel under Race Lane. He explored for sixty feet and found another vertical shaft, which undoubtedly accessed the other hangar.

He continued another sixty feet until he came to a cubic concrete vault about ten feet wide. The corrugated tunnel tube mated with a round hole in the vault, and the continuing tunnel connected to the vault's opposite side. He calculated that he was directly beneath the windmill. A round panel, identical to the one he had pried from the hangar floor, was mounted to the wall inside. Porter stepped into the vault. The bolts attaching this wall panel were fast; he unscrewed them with channel lock pliers. As he loosened the final bolt, the panel swiveled to the vault's floor with a resounding thud and thick dust cloud. The matte-black cube in the cavity behind the panel confirmed he had found what he was looking for.

30

EDIFIQUEMOS

Porter awoke to a landscaping crew maneuvering their mowers and weed trimmers around the Element. He had driven a few miles south and found a dark parking lot behind a bar in Mashpee; he was hoping to take a quick nap. Apparently, he needed more sleep than he thought. The sun sparkled through the condensation lining every window, adding to his rude awakening. After visiting the bathroom in the bar, he returned to the car and switched on the gondol.

"Sariah, are you there?"

"Jonas! Where have you been?" Sariah asked, her voice urgent. "Bahn is waiting for you at the airport. He has been there since early this morning. He wants you to meet him there as soon as possible. How soon can you get there?"

Porter was already driving. "Tell him I'll be there in fifteen minutes."

Porter drove slowly past the maintenance hangar and followed the gravel road past the windmill and old storage hangars. Bahn was waiting for him at the end and led him by foot to a small clearing in the woods. The Kartikeya, moored with three ropes to ground stakes, was rocking gently as she hovered above the forest floor. Next to her was a second, very similar airplane.

Bahn introduced his work. "We pulled a continuous Kevlar spar through the halfgate array and reinforced the wing assembly. We wrapped the plane in composite and resin after we reassembled it. She's heavy and we had to go without retractable gear. With a halfgate on board and full fuel, she will only fly inside a gondol field. She's comfortable and capable and will definitely make it to the

South Pole. Lakshmi finished running bleed air through the heating systems. You should be able to stay deiced even at minus eighty degrees Celsius." Porter had specifically requested a pole-worthy plane, and Bahn had not disappointed him.

Porter ran his fingertips across the fuselage. The plane was as rugged as it was beautiful. And, like her sister, the entire craft was painted matte charcoal black; its only visible marking was a green emblem next to the pilot's door.

"She's beautiful, Bahn. What's that mark mean?"

"It's her name in a language I used to speak: Embarquisa. Sariah told me about the equipment list you need," informed Bahn, crossing his arms. "Now, tell me your plan."

31

FALTEMOS

Bahn wiped the polished gear strut with an oil-soaked rag and laid it down carefully among the parts he was reassembling for the Embarquisa. Porter waited for Bahn's reaction. "That's your plan? It's the perfect recipe for an aviation hazard," said Bhan dismissively. "And the media will have a field day."

"Just hear me out," defended Porter, raising his palms. "At max 16,000 feet the whole array will be far below any commercial air traffic. Plus, it'll be strung along the 110th parallel. It's all ocean and Antarctica south of Indonesia, and mostly Siberia, Mongolia, and rural parts of China up north. It's very unlikely to attract much attention."

"And the gondols will repel any craft that gets near the cable," added Bahn thoughtfully, his resolve to shoot down the whole idea as unworkable evidently waning.

"Exactly," said Porter. He knew that everything hinged on Bahn's support.

"Then what? Once all the textiles are cabled and gondol-suspended from pole to pole, how's it going to work?"

"That's the beauty of it!" grinned Porter. "It doesn't have to work. It only has to be there." Porter expected to harness the earth's true energy through the steel and textile array strung from pole to pole. Porter hoped it would allow—at the very least—those willing to embrace change to ease into the tumultuous transition from materialism to consciousness.

"I disagree. You told Keiti that you were going to cover the whole earth. Love it all, Mr. Sherman," said Bahn, pointing a greasy finger at Porter. "This sounds like you're only carrying it across one part."

"You've done this before, haven't you?"

"And failed," Bahn admitted flatly.

If they failed this time, the consequences would be dire. In the throes of transition from materialism to consciousness, the world would plunge into chaos. But Porter also had a vested interest. Although he never admitted it, even to himself, he secretly hoped this would help him find his mother.

"What was wrong? What happened?"

"I'm telling you, it isn't enough to run the cable. The entire assembly has to surround the planet. Otherwise, it's no good," dismissed Bahn, with a shake of his head. "They'll find it and destroy it. If I'm going to help you build the world's longest clothesline, I'll need clothes, don't you think? Where are these textiles you keep talking about?"

"The windmill. They're in the tunnel under the windmill."

"What, on racks? In boxes? How much stuff are we talking about?" asked Bahn skeptically. Bahn felt it was his responsibility to see holes in what he thought was a half-cocked plan. *And by God, he was determined,* thought Porter grudgingly.

"Plenty," assured Porter. "There are some amazing textiles down there. The Yatz Termeh on its own will put us over the top."

Bahn was clearly impressed.

"You'll see. The entrance to the tunnel is under the shelf in the first hangar that you can see there along the road."

32
ARREBATEMOS

Blueye stepped off the ladder's lowest rung into the damp, sandy soil. He shivered and pulled a hood over his head. As the neglected son of an abused Irish Traveller who spent countless nights out in frigid Irish weather, Blueye detested anything cold and damp. It reminded him of the deplorable conditions of the Traveller halting sites. Rejected by his mother, ill-equipped to care for a nonverbal autistic child, Blueye spent the better part of his adolescence being shuffled from one impoverished community to the next. He could never stay in one place long enough to feel a sense of community until he met Bahn:

By the time they met, Blueye had already left the Traveller life to find his own way in the world, with almost fatal results. A street fight with a drunk Dubliner, who took offense to his unintelligible ravings, cost him his eye. Bahn and Yves stumbled upon the hungry and homeless little person while bar hopping in Dublin. Bahn took him on board the Kartikeya, literally taking Blueye under his wing. The unlikely trio hit it off almost immediately. As an Irish Traveller, his nomadic lifestyle with Bahn and the others suited Blueye perfectly.

When Blueye fixed a persistent electrical issue in the Kartikeya that had eluded both Bahn and Yves, they realized that he had a way with machines. They came to understand that what seemed like an affliction was, in fact, a gift. Blueye demonstrated an almost remarkable aptitude for math. It wasn't until their visit to a Cairo bazaar that they recognized his flamboyant fashion sense. He lit up like a Christmas tree when he saw the brightly embroidered satin waistcoats and vibrant cotton pants that would eventually become his signature look.

Although Blueye was incapable of articulating gratitude, it was evident when Bahn and Yves presented him with an entire wardrobe of these eclectic clothes.

Removing a short sledge from a duffle, he drove an eyed stake into the ground. He attached a pulley with a machine bolt to the stake, threaded the rope that he had suspended with a pulley from the storage shelf in the hangar, and tied a knot. He checked that the rope ran smoothly, readjusted his pants, and walked down the tunnel toward the vault.

The panel that Porter had loosened still hung from the wall by a single bolt. Bahn hadn't told Blueye the cavity holding the halfgate was almost twice his height from the vault floor. By replacing the bolts and looping some rope, Blueye was able to reach the vault cavity's top.

He brushed off the cement dust from the halfgate top and saw that the status lights slowly glowed and diminished in a rhythmic pattern. The design was somewhat different from those he had seen on the Kartikeya. He balanced himself against the rope and let one leg penetrate the front intention panel. The warmth inside the halfgate was a welcome change from the tunnel's damp and cold. He removed his leg and set both feet against the cavity's bottom edge. His heels hung over the vault's front wall. Arches forward, his feet disappeared inside the halfgate. He opened his backpack, retrieved two gondols, and attached them to the cube. He adjusted the volumes until he could feel the halfgate start to slide deeper into the cavity. Drawing his feet backward until they were again visible outside the intention panel, he looped another rope around the halfgate and pulled it taut with a knot at the front left corner. He left a lead long enough to reach the floor, adjusted the gondols once again, and finally lowered himself to the vault's floor.

Blueye gathered his tools, scrambled into the corrugated tunnel, and made his way back to the ladder and pulley. The halfgate hovered behind him like an oversized balloon drawn through the breeze by a child. He pulled it gently, giving it enough momentum to move slowly through the tunnel, keenly aware he would have to exert the same amount of force to stop it.

He tied the lead rope to the knot in the pulley system and slowly raised the halfgate through the vertical tunnel until it bumped against the shelf in the hangar. He put the duffle in his backpack and climbed the ladder. The half-gate hovered, slowly oscillating above him. His backpack brushed against the halfgate's bottom as he stepped from the top rung. Before he could slide out from under the halfgate, a muscled and sinewed arm, adorned with red tattoos and leather bands, reached out from the bottom intention panel, grabbed his backpack, and whisked it and Blueye into the halfgate. A dusty cement cloud roiled under the halfgate as it rocked gently, absorbing the sudden transfer's momentum.

33

SECUESTREMOS

The sun was slowly burning off the morning fog. Bahn made his way quietly behind the storage hangar. The sliding door was standing open just enough for someone slight to slip through. He stepped inside and let his eyes adjust to the dark.

Bahn checked the gondols attached to the halfgate. He loosened the lead rope from the pulley knot, moved the halfgate to the floor, and turned off the gondols. His flashlight shone down the vertical shaft, but there was no sign of Blueye. *Where the hell is he?* Bahn climbed down into the shaft and through the tunnel to the vault. Two short rope loops hung from bolts on either side of the now empty cavity.

Bahn returned to the halfgate. He slowly inserted his arm into the top intention panel and then removed it. He shone his flashlight around the hangar. Bahn bit his lip. Process of elimination left few possibilities. He untied the pulley knot, tied the rope around his waist, and secured the other end to the heavy storage shelf. He kneeled beside the halfgate and put one arm and his head into the side panel. Something immediately seized his arm and yanked. Bahn could feel the heat from bright sunlight inside the halfgate. He instinctively swung his arm backward, breaking the grasp. Another grip fastened onto his coat collar. Again, he freed himself, staggering out of the intention panel with a grunt. Still in a half crouch, his hand shot to the status bar. He held his fingers to the two outermost lights until they extinguished. Bahn hung his head, resting a hand on his knee and wiping sweat from his brow with the back of the other. "Phew, that was close," he said to no one in particular. He had little doubt what had happened to Blueye but there was no time to look for him now.

Bahn returned to the Kartikeya, halfgate in tow. "Here you go, Yves. Finish up the mount and get ready to lift off. I want to leave before the fog clears."

"Did you find Monsieur Blue, Capitaine?" asked Yves, as he hefted the halfgate onto the Kartikeya.

"I believe so," grimaced Bahn. "We'll have to address that later. Get us ready to go."

"Oui, Capitaine."

"I'm going to see Porter and Lakshmi off." Bahn cocked a finger at Yves. "Did you finish those last few mods to the Embarquisa?"

"Oui, Capitaine."

Bahn turned to leave but swiveled on his heel to add, "And Yves. Keep the intention panels disabled on that halfgate. That one's live."

34

TARTAMUDEEMOS

Blueye skidded and rolled once before stopping on the soft dusty ground. His backpack, still heavy with rope and the sledge, had slipped above his shoulders. Removing his arms from the straps, he sat up with one leg extended and turned in the direction he had been thrown. His glasses had fallen, but through the blur, he could make out a figure standing ten feet away. Saying nothing, he searched for the glasses in the smooth, dry silt that covered the ground and his body, hair, and clothing.

The lenses felt intact as he pulled the cable temples around his ears. The sun was bright, overhead, and hot, casting a glare in the lenses and dark shadows on the ground. The figure he had seen stood beside a stone altar. The man sifted silt onto the altar's open top and, with considerable effort, slid the stone lid into place. He turned and took two slow steps toward Blueye. Blueye scrambled to his feet and faced him. He looked around for others but could see only low, distant mountains across a vast flat expanse of the same beige silt. Although the breeze was light and the air clear, dusty swirls lifted and dissipated in the dry heat. Dust devils whorled sporadically across the heat-distorted horizon, partially obscuring the mountains. The expanse, the clear, bright air, and intense sunshine gave the stone altar a surreal and startling focus.

The man spoke to him in a language he did not understand or recognize. "Tiachihpil katsuak, noikniu. Uelia mitsnikmana akameh atl?"

He was not particularly tall but nonetheless imposing. His hair, jet-black, thick, and straight, was neatly braided with fibrous leaves and held close to his head with a narrow leather strap. His skin was deeply tanned, dry, and cracked. He was dressed in a cotton embroidered tunic that fell below his waist. His look was completed with baggy cotton pants and a woven sash, dyed with bright emerald and magenta stripes, tied around his waist. A dusty patina from the desert floor partially homogenized any differences in color and texture between his skin and clothing.

Blueye scowled at the man and turned away from the gourd vessel he had extended to him.

"Tikpiah kopa yauilistli. Tiuil moneki atl." The man advanced toward Blueye, extending the gourd. Blueye stepped away.

"I- I- I- augh... d- d- d- don't..." Blueye stuttered painfully. He stopped trying to talk and recomposed himself. He stood taller, removed his glasses, and wiped them off with his shirt tail. He replaced the glasses and approached the man, then accepted the gourd. The water it contained was warm and tasted like gourd but was not altogether unpleasant. Blueye handed it back.

"Matlali," the man pronounced as he held a palm over his heart. "Matlali," he repeated, waiting for Blueye to respond.

Blueye let his arms fall to his sides and looked out across the open desert. Matlali crouched to bring his face level with Blueye's.

"Matlali," he repeated, this time more softly, but with more intent in his gaze.

Blueye pursed his lips but then relaxed. "B- b- blu," he stuttered.

The sun's heat was oppressive. Beads of sweat formed over his lip. He felt short of breath and nauseous. He dropped to one knee and leaned a hand on the dusty desert floor.

"Bubbahblu," Matlali repeated quietly, smiling. Blueye shook his head angrily and waved his free hand vigorously. The mountains in the distance seemed to continue moving after he had stopped shaking his head.

"N- n- n- no! B- b- blu!" he mumbled quietly.

Matlali stood back and wiped the dust from his hands onto his tunic. He looked down at Blueye with resolve and some admiration. "Bubbahblu."

35

LAVEMOS

Blueye awoke to bright sunshine, streaming between the outside trees and then through the open window beside his bed. He had no idea where he was. The heat and dust from the place where he met Matlali were gone. The air was crisp and cool, carrying a subtle yet majestic pine fragrance. He pulled back a heavy blanket and sat on the edge of the bed, dangling his feet above the floor mats. His boots, laced with desert dust, had been neatly placed at the foot. He kneeled on the bed and leaned on the window's adobe sill, looking outward.

It appeared to be a village. Twenty-seven single-level adobe structures with thatched roofs were arranged around a circular pavilion. Outside each building was a stone slab serving table, set concentric to the pavilion. Each table had a recessed area at one end to hold and contain a cooking fire; most of the fires were smoldering.

The village was active with people who looked and dressed much like Matlali, moving trays and baskets from the houses to the serving tables. Fires were stirred and tended. Men, carrying large ceramic water jars on their shoulders, walked from table to table, pouring into smaller containers for those who requested it. Others carried dry split pine bundles, replenishing stockpiles at each table. Everyone moved with timely purpose, yet serenity surrounded each. No one seemed rushed or panicked. An important event requiring preparation appeared imminent.

"Tikpia okatka kochitok uikpa se ueyakauitl. Tikpiah mitsnokpiliua toyuka." *You've been asleep for a long time. We have to get you ready.* Matlali spoke softly as he entered the house. Blueye turned and sat again at the edge of the bed. Matlali's hair was still lightly powdered with the desert silt and the wrinkles in his face were highlighted with sweat-caked dust. He held a tunic over one arm and presented a pair of leather sandals to Blueye. He bowed slightly as he invoked his name.

"Bubbahblu."

Blueye opened his mouth to correct him but realized he would only further confuse Matlali. He followed Matlali outside without protest. Past the circular village, they came to a river which cut a canyon through the granite. Along the water's edge were seven stone structures with similar thatched roofs following the riverbed's fall. The river's flow had been partially diverted into the upstream house. Open granite spillways ran between each house. The flow continued through each and returned to the river after the last.

Despite their language barrier, Blueye made clear to Matlali that relieving himself was first on the list this morning. Matlali offered a gentle acknowledgment and led him down smooth granite steps to the first bathing house.

Each house had a door on the bank side and open windows overlooking the river on the other.

Two men dressed in tunics similar to Matlali's stood next to a table with folded towels, decorated ceramic water jars, and vases holding flowers and pine boughs. One spoke softly to the other, who began removing Blueye's jacket. Blueye jerked away and crossed his jacket lapels over the chest.

"N- n- n- No! I- I- I- c- c- can." He looked to Matlali, hoping for understanding. Matlali smiled and turned to the men in the bath. One gently untied Matlali's tunic and drew it down across his shoulders and arms, hanging it neatly on the wall. Matlali stood shirtless before Blueye with his arms out, peacefully confident. He slipped off his sandals and turned toward the bath attendant, who without pause or ceremony, untied his pants and gently lowered them to the floor, allowing Matlali to step out. Matlali turned, now naked except for his leaf-woven braids, directly toward Blueye, who grunted in discomfort. The attendant carefully folded Matlali's pants and placed them gently on the table. Matlali stepped up to a stone bench with a smoothly polished round hole in it and sat down. He relieved himself while Blueye tried to offer him privacy. The bath attendants reacted with curiosity to Blueye's withdrawal. The attendant poured warm water into Matlali's lap while he washed himself. When he was done, he stood and again faced Blueye with confidence and ease. Matlali nodded to the attendant, who rested his fingers on Blueye's shoulders. Matlali crouched and carefully removed his glasses and unbuttoned his dusty jacket. A stern, commanding look was all Blueye needed to relax.

Once Blueye had finished and washed as Matlali did, he stood and turned back toward the toilet. Underneath the bench, a small door was opened from the outside. Light streamed in, and the ceramic jar under the hole was lidded and removed by someone, presumably another attendant. Uncomfortably aware of his nudity, Blueye stood in the doorway and watched as a young man carried the covered ceramic jar away from the river, disappearing up the hill into the forest.

Matlali gestured toward the next bath house. Inside, a hot fire was burning in a deep ventilated pit. The granite floor was almost uncomfortably warm under his bare feet. Water, diverted from the river, flowed across several flutes carved into the floor and continued into the next bath house. Matlali sat on a low bench along the side wall and invited Blueye to sit. The two men remained until their bodies were hot and dripping with sweat, then they continued to the third house.

The hot water ran across a stepped granite fluting in the floor, bringing warmth and humidity to the room. The steps were uneven in height, offering a tonal harmony as the water fell gently from one to the next. Sunshine streamed through a nautilus mosaic made from transparent glass and prisms, casting brilliant kaleidoscopic colors onto the room's floor and walls. Cushioned chaises were neatly aligned on both sides of the water flute. Matlali lay face up on one, and the attendant gestured for Blueye to do the same. The filtered sunlight was warm and inviting. The light reflected off the attendants' tunics and towels, creating a living projection of the mosaic in the roof. Matlali lay quietly with his eyes closed, and despite his diffidence, Blueye soon did the same.

Blueye awoke to a gentle hand. An attendant silently offered him water in a gourd, which he politely refused. Matlali stood patiently near the door to the fourth bath house as Blueye was escorted out.

They descended granite stairs. Warm steam filled the room. Again, mosaic windows covered the roof, but these were limited to ruby and coral hues. The floor was wet but not slippery. Two parallel flat stone bridges, without handhold or rail, perhaps two feet wide and ten feet across, spanned over the open darkness below. Two smooth and consistent waterfalls dropped from granite slab edges protruding from the third house, splashing onto the spans. Matlali slowly walked across the right side bridge, arms outstretched, with his head directly under the water sheet. The attendant urged Blueye to follow. Blueye cautiously looked over the slab's edge into the darkness and shied back.

Matlali, dripping wet, stood on the opposite quay with attendants who were applying and vigorously scrubbing a substance into his back with what looked like small woven mats. Blueye could see them speaking to each other, but the falling water muffled their voices. As Matlali turned, he saw Blueye still standing on the other side. He motioned to the attendants to suspend their work and walked slowly back across the bridge. Without leaving the waterfall, he extended his hand to Blueye. The attendant motioned with encouragement. Blueye again looked into the darkness apprehensively, then stepped onto the bridge, head down, carefully placing each step. He continued into the water flow. The water was pleasantly warm and created an open umbrella as it struck his head. He continued but tilted his head to the left to try to see the bridge. As he did, the water flow took him off balance, and his leg shot outward. Before he could fall, Matlali gripped him by the wrist and brought him back to center. He shot Blueye a stern look.

They continued to the opposite quay. Two more attendants appeared through a side doorway and began scrubbing Blueye. His relief to be standing on the quay overcame any shyness he might have had from being scrubbed by strangers. The substance felt like wet, salty paste and released pungent pine and eucalyptus vapors. The attendant offered the paste to Blueye to apply to himself as he desired. It made his skin tingle and opened his sinuses. It was so oddly rejuvenating that Blueye smiled with satisfaction despite the strange circumstances. Matlali walked toward the other bridge, stopped and turned, and held his hand out to Blueye. Blueye walked confidently past Matlali without taking his hand and walked into the water sheet, this time remaining centered underneath it. The water was significantly colder than the first, catching him off guard, but he managed to maintain his balance. He continued across the bridge, Matlali following after him.

Entering the next house, attendants offered heavy, absorbent tan robes. The robe's warmth was welcome after the brisk, frigid water awakening. This house was darker than the others. Small fires offering a subdued light burned in recessions in the walls. Sage and lavender incense filled the room. The walls and ceilings reverberated with rich vocal tones, chanting out of unison, repeating the same vowel sound. The effect created a resonant breathing tide. A wooden, rectangular pergola stood in the room's center, surrounded by a step that served as a bench. Matlali stepped down. It was a jump for Blueye, but he proceeded with interest. Matlali closed his eyes and began to chant the same sound as the others but in his own time and timbre. Blueye observed silently, noting the subtle vibrational progressions as they washed across his body and mind. Attendants and bathers came and went.

The next room's focal point was a clear glass sphere suspended over the floor's center. A round skylight, directly above, was covered in a glass mosaic with deep blue and violet hues. Sunlight angled through the sphere and spread onto the room's surfaces. Bathers and attendants sat quietly on cushions facing the sphere, eyes closed. Although he had impatient episodes, Blueye sat quietly for perhaps 20 minutes as he waited for Matlali to complete his meditation. As they left the room, attendants presented them with the clothing with which they had arrived, carefully washed and dried. Blueye's boots were scrubbed and polished. They donned their clothing and left.

The last house was an open-aired platform with a fourteen-column ring. Each column supported one end of a heavy, transparent glass prism, which was positioned horizontally, five meters above the floor of the platform. Each prism radiated concentrically, unsupported, from an imaginary eighteen-foot-diameter circle at the center of the platform. The sun shone through, casting prism-split light spectra across the floor. Matlali paused for a moment. His still wet braids reflected the bright sunlight as Blueye finished tying his boots.

36

ELABOREMOS

Blueye and Matlali emerged from the bungalow. The serving tables in the circle were plentiful with food. Smoke from the cooking fires mixed with a rich warm maize aroma. Water bearers circulated through the village. Baskets and ceramic bowls, colorfully decorated, held varieties of squash, tomatoes, avocados, and peppers. Groups of four to five men attended each table, lifting the lids from ceramic pots, tasting, spicing, and stirring through the rising steam. Each presenter was calm, and yet Blueye sensed the underlying urgency.

A musical band gathered and set their instruments in the village center. A steady beat from a single bass drum underscored the mixed syncopation from five other drummers striking the edges of open gourds and percussionists who embellished the beat with rattles, rasps, and ceramic shakers. String players drew heavy bows over long horizontal leather bands stretched across hollowed tree trunks, resonating deep bass notes. A single ocarinist offered an uplifting melody that danced over the rhythmic waves. Three musicians danced slowly with pairs of decorated ceramic structures. Blueye struggled to identify the source of all the sounds he was hearing.

The procession entered through the open end of the village circle. Perhaps two hundred in number, their regality was surpassed only by a radiant loving eminence. Although the procession's majority was women, there were interspersed perhaps twenty men who exhibited the same nurturing peaceful air. Their individualized dress, decorations in their hair, intricate and intensely hued tattoos—even their facial features and bodies—were endowed by and emanated a relaxed, omnipresent confidence. Although few, if any, could be called physically beautiful, in the classic golden ratio sense, their energies were undeniably attractive. Blueye stepped backward and looked briefly to Matlali for some reaffirmation, but he remained respectfully attentive. The procession spread throughout the village circle as they perused the tables and began sampling the prepared feasts. The men at each table worked with a calm but decisive rhythm, serving each creation with respect and admiration.

"You came through the altar yesterday. Tell me, Blueye. Why are you here?" Despite the large gathering and bustle of service, Blueye didn't see anyone looking directly at him. No one addressed him, and yet he heard and understood the female voice speaking to him and calling him by name.

He responded candidly before full awareness set in. "Well, I didn't come here by choice." Blueye's mind and heart swirled between amazement and a sense of nurture. The thought patterns and reasoning to which he had always been accustomed now formed into complete and concise sentences. To his pleasant confusion, he realized that he no longer stuttered. He heard the words in his own voice, but he did not speak them. He continued, holding his fingers lightly over his mouth, "Matlali pulled me into the halfgate while I was moving it."

The woman's voice affected him from a deep, familiar place. He trusted her as though they had been intimate but knew full well they hadn't. "You knew where we were hidden. You were moving us. What did you intend to do?" Her voice was not reproachful.

Blueye felt a strange soothing unraveling in his gut as his thoughts effortlessly formed into words. His voice, clearly pronouncing his thoughts, came forth with the enthusiasm of an unleashed dog running joyously across a lush, green pasture. "The hand weavings are in here. We're going to hang them on a steel cable from pole to pole. Bahn told me to load the halfgate into the Kartikeya. There isn't much time," urged Blueye.

"How do you know about the weaving collection, Blueye?"

"Bahn told me. The man from Utah told him it was in the halfgate under the windmill."

"That man. The one from Utah. What's his name?"

"Porter. His name's Porter."

37

BUSQUEMOS

Bahn spread four large paper sheets across the parts table, as Porter stood beside him. He pulled a pencil from behind his ear and began sketching. As he drew a rough arc beside a circle representing the earth, Bahn asked, "Have you figured out how much textile we'll need? Do you think we have enough?"

"There is enough under the windmill for the arc's north half," said Porter confidently. "There are two, possibly three, places I'll be stopping on the way south to get the rest.

"I understand you're looking at four thousand gondols," reckoned Bahn, raising a brow.

"I'm still working out the engineering," said Porter, scratching his beard. "I don't have all the information I need to determine what size wire rope will work."

"What do you need to know?" asked Bahn.

"Four thousand gondols over twenty thousand kilometers means each gondol has to support five kilometers each. I'm also wondering about wind and payout resistance, terrain clearance, and the tension closer to the pole anchorages," explained Porter, leaning on the table and peering into Bahn's crude sketch of what would soon become the cable and textile array.

"I'll show you how to network the gondols to compensate for variations in weight. The cable itself can extend the gondol field along its length." Bahn continued doodling on the sketch. "We'll program them to tilt the gravitational field as needed, slipping the string into the wind and maintaining a GPS longitude."

Bahn had experimented with gondols in his home scale, and during his time in this one, he had explored even more options for their use. The opposite asymmetric scale had its share of toxic masculinity. Bahn's confident swagger was a needed cover for his sense of community and care. It was obvious to him that social evolution depended on moving well beyond selfish atavistic attitudes to achieve wholeness and unity. The efficiencies alone made the objective worthwhile. As powerful and enabling as were gondols and halfgates, they were a small sample of a cooperative society's extended benefits.

Conversely, they created opportunity for social divisions and group dominance when their availability was restricted or controlled. Gondol technology had remained a closely guarded secret in Bahn's home scale for decades. A core group gained power and began exploiting it to improve themselves at the majority's expense. As a cocky journalist with his moral compass pointed in the right direction, Bahn resented the increasing politicization of the technology. He believed that real power came not from technological progress but from the equitable dissemination of such technology. His candor on the subject drew unwanted attention.

His engineering background allowed him to experiment with gondol technology, and with the relationships he developed with the symmetric scale, he was able to hit them where it hurt most. He released the technology to the public but at a dire cost to his personal safety. He was labeled a people's enemy and hunted ruthlessly by the core elite. It was during his evasion that Bahn discovered how to tilt the gondol fields relative to gravity. Direct gravitational nullification, or repulsion, was the gondol's primary benefit. Tilting the repulsion added a horizontal vector that made it possible to move laterally or compensate for winds. It was also a handy tool when being pursued by angry hunters. Tilted gondol fields were startlingly effective at altering the course of approaching aircraft or missiles.

Bahn was confident he could supply the gondols that Porter had requested. The more pressing challenge was sourcing and loading the wire rope into the halfgates. Sariah contacted benefactors in Massachusetts who located a supply of thirteen-millimeter wire rope that had been shipped from China to fulfill a Naval purchase order. The rope failed to fulfill the mil spec inspections, and the order was rejected. The supply house in Boston was left warehousing over 400 reels of cable, stuck between the Navy and the Chinese, and was unsure how to resolve the situation without losing valuable business. Sariah's benefactors arranged to purchase the cable at a deep discount from the Chinese manufacturer.

They would divide the cable spools between them equally. Bahn would deploy the north half of the arc in the Kartikeya, and Porter would take the south in the Embarquisa. He and Porter planned to meet in the middle, somewhere over Indonesia. But they still had other logistical problems, including labor and storage. With Blueye still MIA, it was now down to Bahn, Porter, Lakshmi, and Yves. Porter knew that it was not nearly enough manpower to string the world's longest clothesline. Bahn told Porter what he suspected had happened to Blueye. They both agreed that they would have to follow him into the halfgate. Not only were they interested in his welfare, but they also needed to determine if—and how—the cables could be stored inside.

As he crawled through the intention panel, Porter was met immediately with the underside of the altar stone that Matlali had slid back into place. He removed it with a gondol's aid and climbed from the altar into the night desert's dark chill. Porter gently set the altar top in the dust and removed the gondol. Bahn climbed out behind him and dusted his trousers. Two shallow parallel trenches led away from the altar as if a gurney had been dragged, marking the path toward a distant mountain range.

Morning sun streamed over the pine covered mountains as Bahn and Porter entered the village. Smoke from dwindling cooking fires wafted gently upward.

"Jonas. Can you hear me?" She sounded on edge. "You're in a space where our communication could be interfered with. You may hear voices that aren't..."

"Sariah? Are you there?" He turned to Bahn "Could you hear her too?"

"I've found ways to keep her out of my head," said Bahn. Porter realized that Bahn's toneless voice belied the simmering tension between them. "What did she say to you?"

"We got cut off abruptly." Porter felt uneasy. What would happen if they got stranded here? "She said something about our link being interfered with."

Bahn looked around the village. "Strange things can happen in a halfgate. Particularly one that has this much history."

From across the village compound, the sound of breaking pine boughs preceded a man's arrival, shoeless and naked except for weavings in his long, partially matted hair. He stopped, crouched, and swiveled toward the forest, listening. Bahn and Porter could hear his heavy breathing. The man turned quickly, focused his attention on Bahn and Porter and ran full speed directly toward them. A five-man group, clothed but unarmed, emerged from the forest and pursued him with a confidence that didn't seem to require them to run as fast as the man. As the man approached Porter and Bahn, he stumbled, then caught his balance and ran between them. He slowed and turned back to look at Porter, exposing a smile. He then slowly disappeared. Over a three-second period, he continued on, turning his gaze toward Bahn as he became increasingly opaque, mountains and trees in the background interleaving through him until his image and presence were gone. Porter, amazed, looked at Bahn, who appeared more dismayed than surprised. Porter was still trying to process what had happened before he realized that the five men who had come out of the forest stood in a circle surrounding them. Bahn didn't even look up. He spoke quietly into his chest, but enough that Porter could hear.

"We have to go with them. Be as cooperative as possible. Go where they want us to go. Whatever you do, don't resist them."

One of the men extended his arm, indicating the direction from which they had come. The men flanked and escorted Porter and Bahn to the seven bathhouses, leading them through, just as Blueye had been led.

The sun was bright overhead as Porter and Bahn finally stepped out into the prismatic spectrum cast across the seventh platform. An attendant ushered them to the exit where the five men who had met them in the compound were waiting.

The men led them back to the village and escorted Bahn into a house. One man stayed with Bahn, and the other four escorted Porter down a slope and into a clearing with a brook, surrounded by tall pines. *Don't resist*, Porter told himself, against his better judgment. The men stopped their march and one indicated to Porter to continue on the path toward the brook. Porter complied, parting the dense, supple willow leaves that lined the brook, emerging onto a small wooden bridge. He looked back toward the men, but they were obscured by the tree branches. He stopped at the apex and listened to the water gently gurgling over smooth rocks beneath him.

"You are the man from Utah. The one named Porter." By now, Porter had become less astonished by women's voices in his head. But this was not Sariah. And the experience was more intense than hearing a voice. He felt emotional—open and vulnerable in a way he had never been. The words he heard were accompanied by underscoring emotions. He knew they weren't his, but he felt them as though they were.

"Yes. I'm Porter. Who are you?"

"Why are you here, Porter?" She ignored his question. "What do you want?"

"We are looking for our friend. Blueye," said Porter tentatively. "We believe he's in this halfgate."

"This halfgate. Is that what you call our community?"

Tread carefully, Porter told himself. "I do not wish to offend you," pleaded Porter, raising his palms in defense, although he could not see the woman and was unsure whether she could see him. "I'm simply speaking from my own perspective. Have you seen our friend?"

"Blueye is here, safe and well. He and I have discussed the plan to merge our weavings with your scale's energy. If we're to work together, you must convince me that you understand our wholeness." As Porter heard her voice, he felt the emotions of unity and completeness that accompanied it. "That our halfgate, as you call it, is no less this existence than any other you perceive. We are not your perception's subset. We flow with unified intention and work together to accomplish it."

Porter realized that honesty would be the best policy here. "I know that in my heart. One of my personal challenges is fixating on a purpose at the expense of maintaining a holistic vision," he spoke in earnest. "So, you understand what we're trying to do?"

"Blueye told us enough. We've been waiting a long time for you to come."

"I wasn't sure he could talk at all," said Porter with some surprise. "You will help us, then?"

"The challenge has always been how to surround the earth with the energy in the weavings. How do you plan on accomplishing that?" Porter could feel her turning from confrontational to compassionate.

"With twenty million meters of steel cable."

38
MEDITEMOS

The four men led Porter back to the house where Bahn was waiting.

"What'd you find out?" asked Bahn.

"Well, I think Blueye is going to stay here for a while. I spoke with their leader. She's gentle but very powerful. Wow!" said Porter running his fingers through his long hair. "The more I think about that experience—" Porter paused and smiled. "She said they are going to help us deploy the textiles."

"What do you mean by a while?" Bahn cocked his head.

"You are going to have to pilot the Kartikeya yourself. They want Blueye to stay here and lead the textile deployment on the north arc."

"They've met him, right?" Bahn asked sardonically.

"Yeah, they have. And they're impressed."

"You're kidding me." Bahn got up from the chair and looked out at the waiting men.

"They are going to let us see for ourselves."

The men led Porter and Bahn through the pine forest to a red rock canyon's edge. A thick granite slab structure, perhaps two cubic meters in size, was open on the side facing the canyon. The men brought Porter and Bahn fifty meters from the structure and indicated they should continue. Seated cross-legged on a woven cushion in the floor's center was Blueye, dressed as always but without the eye patch. His eyes were closed, and his body faced the canyon. Though they could see the opposite cliffs, the canyon's scale was mysteriously vast.

"I've solved the cable transfer and storage problem."

Both Bahn and Porter looked at each other and then back at Blueye who had neither moved, spoken nor opened his eyes.

Bahn spoke first. "You're not stuttering. That's interesting, at the very least. I've got an idea, Blueye," he said, crouching next to him. "Let's get out of here and fly to the world's end. We've got work to do."

Porter turned back toward the canyon. The sunlight's angle had changed only slightly, but the canyon appeared to be a completely different place. Shadows were longer, relief was deeper, and certain aspects of the bluff were only now discernible. The red rocks' colors merged into mauve and black.

"Your plan is beautiful, Jonas." It was definitely Blueye's voice, but his lips never moved. "Your intention comes from a place of love. I know it, and so do the Nahua. It resonates with their communal purpose and intent. That is why I need to stay here." Blueye continued. "The Nahua will move with us. But the timing and sequence are critical. I can resolve the differences."

Porter brought the conversation back around, "You said you resolved the cable transfer problem."

"It's simple, really. It's all in managing twist."

"Twist?" Porter knitted his brow.

"Ten million meters of cable. It's not going to be on one big spool. Too awkward. There have to be many. An array."

Porter got down on one knee and faced Blueye. This diminutive telepathic meditator was a far cry from the fidgety, nervous wreck he remembered. Blueye's face was devoid of emotion, yet Porter could tell that he was at peace. "The cables get twisted up unless all the spools move in unison," added Porter.

"Or you manage the twist." They heard Blueye say.

"How?" asked Bahn.

"Swivels."

39

CARGEMOS

The cable supplier was near the old Boston Naval Shipyards. Bahn and Porter had arranged to meet the supervisor at the beginning of the graveyard shift. The warehouse was immense. 28 inch diameter cable reels were stacked in heavy industrial racks, and the warehouse was fully automated. Hydraulic robots mounted on overhead tracks could locate a specific set of reels, retrieve them from the rack, and move each loaded reel set from rack to loading area with mass-defying agility. The supplier had been stuck with twenty thousand reels of the 13-millimeter cable Porter needed.

The longshoreman walked over to Porter and Bahn with his clipboard.

Porter extended his hand. "You must be Lenny."

"I thought we'd never see the end of it," said the pudgy longshoreman. "Glad they'll work for ya. Figure it's going to take about a week to get these moved out. A flatbed semi can take ten at a time. How many trucks do you have coming?"

Porter and Bahn exchanged knowing glances. The Element and a borrowed pickup were parked just outside with a halfgate loaded in the back of each.

"Actually, Lenny, we've brought our own transport. If you could have the reels brought out to the loading dock, we will load them as fast as you can bring them. You wouldn't happen to have a shallow ramp that we could use to get them rolling a bit, would you? I figure we can get this done by morning."

Lenny looked at them incredulously. "Hold on. My paperwork here says you guys are taking 11,400 number 65 cable reels. We use this ramp to roll them onto the flatbeds but even with that how's this gonna work?"

Porter pointed to the overhead loader and asked, "How many reels can that loader carry at a time?"

"Well we don't usually do it, but it can retrieve ten at once. What a flatbed can carry." replied Lenny.

Porter stood next to the robotic warehouse crane which towered over them. "Let's try loading ten and see how it goes. Then we can figure out what it will take to load the rest."

Lenny shook his head slightly and wandered into the control booth to issue the retrieval instruction to the loader. Porter gondoled the halfgate out of the Element and set it on the dock and the end of the shallow steel ramp Lenny used to load the reels. Within a minute the robotic crane had returned with ten reels. Much like a giant Pez dispenser, the robot spit a 4000 pound reel onto the ramp and it rolled slowly toward the halfgate. Porter let his hand slowly brush over the reel as it rolled and intended it inside. Bahn signaled to Lenny to keep them coming and the robot spit out the remaining nine reels one at a time, all of which rolled easily into the empty halfgate. Lenny, still somewhat perplexed by the unorthodox procedure, lumbered out from his control booth, pulling his pants back up as he did. He knew better than to question what happens at a Naval shipyard, particularly when the opportunity to move these reels was looking like it might work. He issued the same instruction and ten more reels disappeared from the warehouse. Bahn got him to bring out a second ramp and engage the second robotic crane and started loading his halfgate in the same manner.

Lenny left the control booth and walked over to the warehouse door. He scratched his head under the hard hat. The Element and pickup were still parked as before. There wasn't any sign of a dockside mess. Despite his surprise at being able to fit all the reels into the two small vehicles, he was all too glad to get this inventory off his hands and he wasn't asking any questions. As Porter had predicted, they were finished loading by morning.

40

GIREMOS

Blueye had always felt as if his brain was locked in a perpetual battle with his body. He was in a constant state of heightened awareness and sensitivity. It was as if he had night vision goggles on and lived in perpetual fear of someone shining a bright light on him, rendering him momentarily blind. But this sensory overload was not merely visual. Autism affected all of his senses. He was relentlessly bombarded by sensory input with no way to articulate it. Those around him felt the need to rectify or fix him, along with the communication deficiencies and social awkwardness associated with autism.

Unfettered by such biases that closed their minds to the limitless potential of those on the spectrum, the Nahua saw Blueye's true potential. They saw him for what he was: someone intrinsically attuned to consciousness and a potential asset during the paradigm shift. They understood that while other so-called "normal" people, oblivious to their own autistic traits, struggled to find their footing in the new world order of the consciousness paradigm, those like Blueye would lead. Through guided meditation, Blueye discovered that what was perceived as a handicap in the materialistic paradigm is, in fact, a superpower in the paradigm of consciousness. Because they appreciated the power of this heightened physical and social sensitivity, Blueye thrived among the Nahua.

Blueye's Nahua education progressed rapidly when he opened himself up to the consciousness paradigm. He was able to manipulate energy and matter inside the halfgate and had even assembled a massive array in the desert, 300-wood-en-cable reels strong. Each spool was mounted on a steel base holding an axle that ran through the spool's barrel. He had designed a cable swivel to allow the spooled cable ends to be linked while still enabling one reel to payout its load. As the cables fed in from Lenny's warehouse, the Nahua wound them onto their wooden spools and began weaving, pulling eyes and swivels into each cable end. By the time morning had come in Boston, 271 reels of cable wire were mounted on vertical axles and assembled around the intention panel in 15 concentric circles on the flat, dusty desert floor.

Blueye had assembled a modest Nahua army, who were busy transporting hundreds of carts filled with hand-woven textiles, some over fourteen hundred years old. The challenge now was to attach the gondols and textiles to the cable as the Kartikeya pulled the halfgate toward the meeting point at almost nine-tenths Mach.

41

COQUETEEMOS

Porter and Lakshmi arrived in Tooele about three and a half hours after they left Cape Cod. Lakshmi calibrated the gondols to direct their fields within a narrow range in order to support their own assigned weight and limit the signature signal. Sariah was monitoring the military communication during their flight, prepared to warn them of any activity. Amelia met them later with a cotton tarp and two ladders to cover the Embarquisa.

Lakshmi climbed down from the ladder after helping Amelia pull the tarp over the Embarquisa. Lakshmi stood away from the aircraft, looking for anything that might attract any especially curious onlookers. She wondered about Amelia. She seemed intelligent and was actually quite attractive. Lakshmi tilted her perfectly round face and regarded Amelia with fascination. Why would such a woman be flying skydivers in Utah? They ended up talking for a while under the evening light. Lakshmi even dared to ask some probing questions, which caught Amelia a bit off guard, but she quickly regained her composure.

Amelia's father owned a hay farm in Milford, Utah. Lakshmi loved the way Amelia rolled her big blue eyes as she related how she and her sister were raised like boys to make up for the sons her father never had. Amelia had blossomed into a free-spirited tomboy, whereas her younger sister, a girl through and through, as Amelia put it, grew up in her shadow. Amelia was to inherit the family farm—that is, until she discovered flying. She cut her teeth in aviation on an Air Tractor AT-500, helping an AG pilot crop dust her father's farm.

"The first time I flew, I was 13," reminisced Amelia wistfully. "And I've never looked back. I just knew I'd never want to do anything else."

Lakshmi watched Amelia's eyes light up as she recounted her unsanctioned flying lessons. After a failed romance with the AG pilot's son, Amelia discovered her sexual orientation.

"I knew I was attracted to girls, but I was just confused. It took me a long time to come to terms with it, you know..." faltered Amelia, looking into Lakshmi's eyes. "...to realize that there was nothing wrong with me."

Lakshmi nodded her understanding. Coming from a conservative background herself, she could relate to Amelia's struggles.

By the time Amelia was 17, it was obvious her passion for flying overshadowed any interest she had in the family farm. Amelia's relationship with her father was already strained when her younger sister decided to make the best of a bad situation by telling him about Amelia's "deviant behavior." It drove a formidable wedge between them. Amelia eventually went off to college at the University of Utah, the relatively liberal alternative to Brigham Young University, and her father was less than pleased.

"Long story short, my sister got the farm, and I got to live my dream. It was a win-win," Amelia laughed. "I wasn't cut out for the family business anyway." She had since made peace with her family but hardly visited.

"Your turn," said Amelia, playfully jabbing Lakshmi with her elbow.

It was not that Lakshmi didn't trust Amelia. On the contrary, she was surprised at how easy it was to open up to her. Rather, Lakshmi didn't feel like revisiting her past, so she stuck to the basics: She was from an equally conservative background, and her family disapproved of her sexual orientation. However, Lakshmi knew that no two people could be more different as far as upbringing was concerned. Whereas Amelia was encouraged to exercise her independence at an early age, Lakshmi's migrant parents raised her to be demure and submissive. It took her personality years to shine through these firm traits that were instilled through years of conditioning.

Lakshmi was groomed to secure what her mother liked to call a "decent" job, marry a "respectable" Indian man of her mother's choosing and, as soon as possible, give her—preferably male—grandchildren. This was to be the sole purpose of Lakshmi's existence, and she was content with her lot until she matured enough to realize that her and her mother's ideologies diverged considerably. She was in her mid-teens when she began to understand herself and was so overcome by shame and guilt that she vowed never to tell a soul.

Much to her mother's chagrin, Lakshmi enrolled in flight school. While training as a navigator, she met Nikhil, who she felt was a kindred spirit. Despite an obvious lack of physical attraction, Lakshmi reciprocated his advances because Nikhil was considerate, caring, and respected her independence. Lakshmi was stunned when her mother consented to their marriage. It seemed easy, too easy.

Just days before the much-publicized wedding, Lakshmi learned that her and Nikhil's apparently serendipitous meeting was, in fact, staged by her mother. She had coaxed Nikhil into courting her with the promise of a considerable dowry. It was the ultimate betrayal, and something in Lakshmi snapped. Outraged at being sold to the highest bidder, in a moment of weakness, she came out to her parents.

Disowned by her family for disgracing them, Lakshmi juggled multiple jobs to pay for her tuition. Out of desperation, she replied to a job posting for a navigator at a shady company, which turned out to be a front for Bahn's operations. In a way, Bahn saved her from a past she preferred to forget.

Amelia could almost feel the anguish of Lakshmi's untold story, but she did not press her. Instead of reliving her past, Lakshmi continued to explore Amelia's aspirations. Their conversation turned lively. Lakshmi enjoyed making Amelia laugh.

"Come with us. We need you." It was Lakshmi with her big grin this time.

"So, where are you going?" asked Amelia playfully.

"You mean, where are *we* going? You're coming with us," Lakshmi stood closer now.

"Don't I get to know before I decide?" Amelia asked quietly.

42

AYUDEMOS

Everyone had a job to do. Porter inspected the cargo nets securing the halfgate to the Embarquisa's deck. Amelia switched on the runway lights and taxied to runway 17. The cold autumn night caused the windscreens to fog. Lakshmi, in the copilot seat, adjusted the defrost fan and began to program the GPS. Porter had a plan for the first destination, fully expecting there to be welcome detours along the way. The first was Chilchinbito, 267 nautical miles southeast. Although they hadn't tried it yet, they were confident that they could land the Embarquisa vertically on any stable, level surface. Still, they opted to land at the closest airport to remain inconspicuous. Lakshmi set Kayenta as the destination.

The Nahua, with Blueye's insight, solved Bahn's labor problem. He and Yves were well along their way to the North Pole. Porter sensed that Sariah had a trick up her sleeve when she urged him to set off for the South Pole and leave his own manpower issue to her. He knew that another halfgate full of people would be too good to be true. The best thing he could hope for was that Sariah would come up with some revolutionary apparatus, like the gondol, that would allow them to pay out the cable to match the Embarquisa's airspeed.

The structural and wing shape improvements Bahn made to the Embarquisa, combined with the almost negligible induced drag—Bahn had equipped the Embarquisa with four integrated gondols, negating any need for the wings to create lift—endowed the aircraft with a maximum forward airspeed of 530 knots. However, until they were outside US airspace, if they were going to remain undetected, they would keep their airspeed under 250 knots. They knew the Air Force could detect the gondol's interference, so every precaution was crucial. Porter had distorted the gondol radiation to make it more difficult to locate, but they all agreed the less time they were active in US airspace, the better.

The cloud ceiling was high enough for the dawn sun's disk to cast its orange glow through the fog. Amelia adjusted her headset, looking out the pilot side cockpit window. Staying low and under the cover of darkness, they had so far escaped scrutiny from the radar crews at Hill AFB. They were about to cross into Arizona.

The Navajo Nation had produced the world's largest woven carpet, and they stored it in Chilchinbito. Although that initially attracted Porter, it was impractical to try to use such a large textile for their purposes. Keiti's gift showed him that the Navajo serapes and saddle blankets were some of the finest handmade textiles. Chilchinbito was a logical place to start.

Porter could see a subtle silhouette of Amelia and Lakshmi's headphones backlit by the dimmed cockpit lights. They were alternating between pressing buttons on the dash and animatedly chatting and smiling. The cabin was dark. Porter leaned against woolen blankets and drifted off under the engine's drone.

Sariah called Porter's name and he woke with a start. She had made contact with the Diné, who asked if the Embarquisa could be brought to Chi'ini'li instead. They had collected textiles from across the Nation and assembled them inside the mouth of a nearby canyon. Porter relayed the coordinates to Lakshmi.

The shades of the horizon were beginning to change as they arrived. The canyon forked multiple times as it extended east from Chi'inil'i. The southerly winds were constant, though thankfully light, and allowed Amelia to slow the plane to a stop, with the propeller barely biting the air. Bahn had equipped the Embarquisa with supplemental gondols mounted in the nose, wingtips, and tail. Lakshmi used a side-mounted joystick to keep the craft level as she slowly reduced the primary gondol's field volume. As the Embarquisa descended slowly into the canyon, the deep walls protected them from the wind. Amelia shut down the engine. The waning night's stars were visible above them. Two natural spires stood against the glowing backdrop of the eastern saffron sky. Amelia shut down the remaining electrical systems except for the exterior lights, which were beginning to illuminate the sandy floor. Lakshmi slowly and silently brought the Embarquisa to a soft touchdown. Pickup trucks filled with folded textiles were parked around the perimeter of their landing site. Lakshmi opened the cockpit door and cool morning air filtered through the cabin. Amelia shut off the exterior lights. Navajos from every truck began walking toward them, each shouldering a heavy bundle of handwoven textiles.

Sariah continued her conversation with Porter on how the symmetric scales were governed. Porter wanted to know who decided who could go there and, in particular, who decided if they had to leave and transfer back. Sariah explained that symmetric cultures are built upon two primary principles: individual agency and love for community. Symmetric beings, separated from the distractions of toxic egos and chaos, were powerful creators and exceedingly adept at the science, maths, and logistics of manifesting their creations.

She asked Porter if he had noticed anything about the Nahua. He told her they all seemed happy and were almost always busy. She asked again if he saw their light. She asked him to think back about the procession that he had witnessed. Porter told her that he could sense both the women and men had a power about them but that he believed he felt the reverence from the men preparing the meals. Sariah asked about the man they saw being pursued when they first arrived. Porter recalled that although he was startled by his sudden arrival and subsequent disappearance, he also remembered a feeling of emptiness and darkness that surrounded his body as he disappeared. As Porter recalled that event in comparison to the procession, he began to understand what Sariah was describing.

"The Nahua have explored and expanded the science of intention," Sariah continued. "Each individual has the freedom to choose what they do and the intentions that found their actions. If you were to visit them again, it would be plain to you that those who choose to regularly practice the intention of nurturing themselves to love their community have a visible light that surrounds their body. It's visible to everyone there and grows in intensity according to how expansive their communal love becomes."

"So, what happened to that guy we saw disappear? Why were those men chasing after him?" Porter asked.

Sariah explained that new arrivals to the symmetric scale are washed and nurtured as he had been in the baths. The intention is to imbue the arrived with enough light to hold them there until they can begin to progress on their own. The Nahua had adopted the symmetric practice into their community inside the halfgate. Progress continues as the recently arrived learn to choose to serve themselves and the community with love. Each may choose to serve as they wish. As long as their intention is to build the community as a whole, and it is reflected in their actions, their light continues to grow. One of the best ways to accelerate that growth and light is to teach others.

"Teaching from a place of universal love is, perhaps, the most powerful way to brighten your light. But that community-centered life isn't for everyone. Some reject it. The man that you saw disappear had chosen to return to the asymmetric scale. The men who pursued him were reminding him that he was wanted, cared for deeply, and would be missed." *They have a funny way of showing it,* thought Porter. As if reading his mind, Sariah smiled audibly. "Although it was not what it looked like and they were unsuccessful, their intentions were honorable, and in the end, everyone, including the man who transferred, was exercising individual agency."

"What about people who are secretive? Aren't there people who try to subvert their culture and take it for themselves?" asked Porter. "Who decides if they have to leave if no one knows their intention?"

"Everyone makes their own decision to stay or leave, Porter. It is impossible for someone who holds purely selfish intentions, even if they are secret, to hold the light and show it to others. They would simply slip back to the asymmetric scale. There is no judgment," said Sariah matter-of-factly. "Everyone does what they want. But if they choose to be one with the community, they also choose to love it actively. It's a simple matter of the integrity of existence. In the same way, our bodies are whole according to a specified pattern, the Nahua culture and other symmetric scale communities are too."

Standing on the Embarquisa's raised deck, Porter could see across the canyon floor. Sariah hadn't been entirely forthcoming about how she communicated with the Navajos, but their preparation was evident. Over 200 pickup trucks and SUVs with trailers were heavily laden with hand-woven blankets and rugs. The group was surprisingly unfazed that an airplane had landed vertically in this narrow canyon and that the textiles they gathered far outweighed what even a fleet like it should be able to carry. They were pleasant, unassuming, and clearly ready to work. Matt and Darrell came forward and introduced themselves to Lakshmi and Amelia as the organizers. The two women turned and pointed toward Porter as he dropped down from the cargo deck. Matt extended his hand to greet Porter as Darrell stood beside him.

"Mr. Porter. I'm Matt Begay, and this is my cousin Darrell." Apart from their physiognomy, nothing hinted at their Native American heritage. With their faded jeans, button-down shirts, and sneakers, the Navajo would have passed for typical non-native Americans. Porter shook hands with the cousins as their people moved in closer to listen.

Porter cut to the chase. "I'm not sure how much you know about what we're doing. It looks like you have quite a bit of material gathered."

"Well, Mr. Porter. This is unusual for us but not surprising. Typically, our Nation is led by our chapter government in Window Rock. On rare occasions, though..." Matt and Darrell exchanged looks, "...we receive direction from our Nation's matriarch, and this is one of them. She told us to gather as many hand-woven rugs and blankets as we could find. The Diné people hold sacred the matriarch's word, and these weavings you see come from families across the Nation."

"I can't pay you for them," Porter replied.

Darrell spoke for the first time. "We understand. We're not expecting money. The weavings and the members of our tribe who will accompany you bring hope to our Nation in ways you may not fully understand."

Porter reacted with some surprise. "I'm only picking up the textiles. I have no intention of taking any of you with me."

Matt stepped closer. "Mr. Porter, there are 6,400 bales in these trucks, each weighing about 125 pounds. That's 800 tons of blankets and rugs. Even if we helped you load them, you will have to unload them, and our understanding is it's going to be done piece by piece. You need our help."

"Matt. This mission is risky and dangerous," Porter shook his head. "I can't accept responsibility for these people's safety."

"Mr. Porter, we have volunteered to go because we know there is an opportunity to lift our people out of the risk and danger we face every day. The land and water here were poisoned by uranium mining years ago." Matt spoke earnestly as he turned the brim of his cowboy hat between his fingers. "Our daughters develop uterine cancer at a rate far higher than the rest of the country. Over forty percent of our families don't have access to clean water. This desert is beautiful and has a strong spirit, but the land is harsh, dry, and difficult to farm." He stopped fiddling with his hat and looked Porter in the eye. "Not wanting to put too fine a point on it, Mr. Porter, these weavings aren't going with you unless you accept our help and bring the men and women who have volunteered to go. We've been entrusted with these weavings, and we want to support your effort to endow the earth and our Nation."

Effort to endow the earth and our Nation, his words seared into Porter's mind as he was reminded of what was expected of him. "I do need help, you're right about that," confessed Porter, looking down as he kicked up dust with his shoe. "How much do you know about what we intend to do with the weavings?"

"We know that our matriarch, Delphine, speaks with the woman who is never seen. She told us to gather the weavings, assemble 108 strong volunteers, 54 women and 54 men, and meet you here. We know she loves and nurtures our Nation. That's all we need to make the choice. We had over 1,400 tribal members volunteer."

"The woman who is never seen. That is interesting," replied Porter.

After Porter reluctantly agreed to let the volunteers join, they built a wooden platform with stairs beside the Embarquisa's cargo door. A pickup pulled up to the platform, and two older men emerged from the cab. They unloaded a rug bale and carried it up the stairs. The bale's height and width would allow it to pass through the intention panel, but its length was twice that. Porter slid the bale into the halfgate. The men exchanged knowing glances, acknowledging the greater powers at play. Another bale was brought, and the older man slid it into the halfgate himself. The process accelerated quickly. After four trucks had loaded their cargo into the halfgate, Porter suggested it may be a good time for some volunteers to pass through the halfgate to organize the bales inside. Without a word, the man who had been sliding the bales through disappeared behind the intention panel.

Matt stepped up to the halfgate, inserted his arm up to the elbow, and ran it around the perimeter of the intention panel as though he were checking to see if a clear glass window was actually open. He turned an open, upward-facing palm to half the group that had been segregated for this part of the mission. They came forward purposefully and crawled into the halfgate one by one. Family members who witnessed the passage were supportive but stoic. No tears or extended goodbyes accompanied their pride for these brave men and women. The excitement among the remaining Navajos was evident in their vigor to load the remaining bales. In addition to the textiles, they loaded supplies, including food staples, insulated coolers, cooking equipment, water, and propane. By the time they finished loading, the spires' shadows were crisp against the red canyon floor. Matt ushered the group's second half into the halfgate, then followed his cousin through the portal. The hot desert silt from their hair and clothing swirled in toroid vortices around the cube's edges as they slipped with hope into a space hundreds of zeroes to the right of a decimal.

43

PELEEMOS

Colonel Fowler answered the phone at his desk.

"Colonel Fowler, this is Major Rice. I have another sighting of the radar anomaly we reported in the Sevier MOA near Tooele week before last. This time, it's approximately 100 nautical miles southwest of Holloman about to cross into Mexican airspace. Moving at 250 knots."

Fowler leaned forward in his eagerness. "You have it on radar, now?"

"Affirmative, sir. I have Major Dawson of the 49th standing ready to deploy two Nighthawks. Awaiting your orders, Colonel."

"Tell Dawson to scramble the Goblins with strict orders to monitor and report, remain stealthy, and do not intercept," emphasized Fowler. "I want to know what it is and where it's going. Feed the data directly into OASIS."

"Yes, sir, Colonel."

Fowler switched to a secure line and dialed two digits. After two rings, it was answered. No one spoke but Fowler knew he was there. He dialed four more digits and hung up.

44

NAVEGUEMOS

Amelia reset the autopilot to hold as low an altitude as she could. Lakshmi pulled one headphone behind her ear and turned to Porter as she refolded a navigation map. "We've crossed into Mexico. We can stay low until we're south of San Luis Potosi. Are we going to Mexico City?"

Porter wrapped a heavy blanket around his shoulders and crouched between the cockpit seats. "Our first stop is near Lake Titicaca in western Bolivia. We'll pick up more textiles there."

"Going direct takes us out over the Pacific, near the Galapagos," said Lakshmi.

Porter watched the desert slide by underneath them. "We're a bit less conspicuous and hopefully safer if we stay low and increase our speed over the water."

"Safer from what?" Amelia shrugged. "No one's following us."

Porter took the map from Lakshmi and opened it to show the route to La Paz. He reached forward to the traffic radar screen and expanded its range. "The only thing more unnerving to me than knowing they're following us is not knowing where they are." He paused to calculate the best move. "Bring us to a southwest heading toward Mazatlán. Once we get over the water, set us on course toward La Paz. The textiles are in a place called Lukurmata about eighty kilometers west of La Paz."

Porter had spent most of the flight from Tooele wrapped in the jacket Keiti gave him. He'd been drifting in and out of sleep adding dream qualities to some of the visions. He experienced conscious and subconscious thoughts, emotions ranging from joy to anguish, and time becoming fluid rather than referenceable—all reticulating into an understanding of the unity of everything. As he explored the fabric's extent and paid closer attention to areas that attracted him, his appreciation of its wholeness continued to blossom. It had a unique and readily recognizable shape.

As he explored it, the fabric displayed repetitive patterns interspersed with such staggering degrees of chaos that resolutions into known repeated patterns became increasingly remarkable. The time and space between distinguishable patterns appeared to increase with each repetition, leading Porter to the understanding that the only real chaos was his ignorance and fear that the familiar theme may have played for the last time. He held close the images of young Keiti's tears, her mother's kitchen, and his own mother's encouraging calls on the Minnetonka ice. He'd traveled further than his faith would support. Everything he could experience was in varying degrees, like something he had seen before but always different—always changing. He let go of the theme. He no longer expected the initial image that had repeated with comfort and familiarity. What he once considered chaos was now innately beautiful. He marveled at the increased intricacy and varying rates of change. Pattern granularity refined into what he could only perceive as variations in hues and color.

A black void appeared as a pinprick at the center of a brilliant, fully circular rainbow. As Porter continued toward the center, the void grew in size while the rainbow's inner circumference divided and fringed into such fine detail that it could no longer be distinguished from the growing darkness. At the center of the void, defined by a thin, white rim of light, the initial theme's image appeared once again.

Porter woke as the Embarquisa encountered rough turbulence. Still groggy from sleep, he rolled onto his knees, removed the jacket, and folded it into his knapsack. The cabin and windows were dark except for the instrument panel's dimmed illumination. Lakshmi and Amelia were focused, intent, and proactively calm. Porter donned his headphones.

45

COMPREMOS

Following the money to Quinto Condottiero was all but impossible. The group was loosely organized somewhere in South America, probably Colombia. The vibrant cocaine trade provided ample opportunity for clandestine military and intelligence agencies from any government to fund their activity and take advantage of their services. Colonel Fowler had very little information on who was behind QC. The only link he had was through OASIS. QC was given access to a more-than-generous database quota, and they reported back using the same system. Fowler would have to answer to his superiors when the always substantial wire transfer requests came due. The results were typically justified despite their expense.

The Nighthawks reached their range limit as the suspect craft flew over the Pacific south of Mazatlán. They uploaded their reconnaissance data and returned to Halloran. They had gathered infrared photographs of a small high-wing aircraft as the source of the anomalous signal affecting the radar at Hill. The aircraft's last monitored trajectory showed it 500 feet AGL, traveling at 0.8 Mach on a 124-degree track. QC monitored the target with satellite and radar and alerted their counterparts in Peru.

It took three hours to fly from Mazatlán to Peru's northern shores. Amelia maneuvered the Embarquisa across the beaches south of Ecuador at 4 a.m. Lima time. They agreed that avoiding the weather, rising from the ocean to the Andes Cordillera, would be the best route toward La Paz. She flew inland. The tops of the canyon walls began reflecting the sun as she dropped in low over the Ucayali River to follow it south.

Prior to La Paz, Porter asked Lakshmi to turn southwest and climb into the mountains. After crossing a range at 5,000 meters, they landed in the hills overlooking Chahuaytire. Porter asked Lakshmi and Amelia to stay with the Embarquisa as he hiked down the hill into town. There were cultivated fields and animals in the farms surrounding it. At 4,200 meters, even descending the hill's slopes winded him. He used a gondol to ease the descent. Almost immediately, Sariah's voice resonated within him.

"Jonas, we haven't spoken for a while. Why are you stopping there?"

Porter stopped hiking and steadied himself against a rock. "While I had the jacket on, I found a pattern showing an extensive collection. It should be enough to finish the southern arc. I'm not exactly sure where it is or how it's stored. I'm hoping to find someone in town who can help."

"Most of the people there speak Quechua, some speak Spanish. Let me know if you need help translating," offered Sariah. Porter remembered that, as a research scientist, communication was Sariah's forte. "What do you plan to exchange with them if they let you take the textiles?"

"What you're saying is I shouldn't expect to be lucky enough to find a hidden and unclaimed resource like I did on the Cape?" asked Porter. He hadn't thought that far.

"Or a fantastically generous tribe of Diné either," said Sariah. "Do you have anything you can give them in return?"

"If they have the trove of textiles I think they do, even my last paycheck from the drop zone would be a paltry excuse, and I've barely got that."

It took Porter under an hour to hike down the hill into town. He stepped up from the sandy road onto the cobblestone plaza. Well-established shrubs, about a meter high, were planted in a diagonal pattern subdividing the square. Benches and tables roughly followed the pattern set by the shrubs. The morning plaza was busy with vendors setting up stalls to market their goods. Porter strolled along the plaza's front row. He didn't want to draw attention to himself, but he soon realized that was going to be difficult. His beard and dark hair pulled into an elastic band may have helped, but his dark tactical pants and hoodie stood in stark contrast to the multicolored ponchos and chullos worn by the town's folk.

An older woman was seated on a blanket laid out on the cobblestones. Her bare feet held one end of a backstrap loom as she methodically wove a smooth wooden needle between tightly stretched alpaca. Arrayed beside her outstretched legs was an assortment of dyed yarn balls that she pulled through with the needle and tamped into place with a smooth wooden dowel. The emerging pattern was intricate. She stopped and held out her finished works toward Porter. With a gentle insistence and words he did not understand, she invited him to hold her weavings. Porter knelt beside her, laying the textiles across his thighs as he paged through them. The woman kept speaking to him as she went back to her work. As she switched her weave from one color to another, she routinely let a yarn ball roll from her hand onto the blanket. A ball left her hand and arced above the loom a little too slowly. Porter stepped back and turned the volume down on his gondol. He looked back at the woman, but she didn't seem to have noticed. The yarn rolled to the blanket. A young man in the adjacent stall said something to her in Quechua.

The woman stopped her work, looked at the floor, and shifted away from Porter. He sensed her discomfort, laid her products back on the blanket, and shifted backward into a standing crouch with his arms crossed over his knees. The woman spoke quietly into her chest, keeping her eyes averted from his. Porter looked down the plaza across a line of weavers. They were keenly aware of the foreigner's presence and respected the opportunity of the woman before him.

"I don't know what you're saying. I'm sorry if I made you uncomfortable," Porter told the woman, not expecting her to understand. He stood slowly, bidding her a good-day hand gesture. She again picked up her works and offered them to him, this time holding her gaze. She untied the loom from her waist and gently made her way to stand. She spoke rapidly, held the weavings out to him, and stepped toward him. Porter knew what she wanted.

Sariah's voice, quieter than usual, came to him as the woman continued to speak. "She wants you to buy her textiles, Jonas. Her two daughters and four grandchildren live with her. The 200 nuevo sols she is asking for would support them for a month."

The woman looked directly into Porter's eyes. She was weeping.

Porter took the bundle from the woman again and selected a weaving depicting a thunderbird in purple and black. He handed her fifty US dollars. She rubbed her fingers across the bills and looked at them closely, speaking rapidly again. She motioned to the young man who had spoken to her. She showed him the bills, and he again spoke to her quietly. Her eyes welled with tears as she turned to Porter. Her gratitude was clear. Porter bowed slightly to the woman and the boy. He turned and walked back toward the hill where the Embarquisa was moored.

"The difference you made in that woman's life is immeasurable, Jonas." Sariah's voice was laden with emotion.

"I get that, Sariah. But that fifty bucks was the last I had. How do I tell her I need to find thousands more like these..." pleaded Porter, waving the weaving he had just bought. "...but I have no way to pay for them?"

46

ASPIREMOS

F ive and a half hours after the Kartikeya left Cape Cod it was approaching the north pole. Yves would have followed Bahn to the ends of the
earth. He owed Bahn that much for springing him out of Senegalese police
custody after he became an unwitting accomplice to a drug smuggling
operation that went south. In his defense, he was young, naïve, and a
hopeless romantic—a dangerous combination. He was a rookie pilot, fresh
out of flight school, smitten with an American woman who didn't turn out
to be who she said she was. If it weren't for Bahn, who knew the right palms
to grease, Yves would still be in a Senegalese prison serving ten to twenty
years of hard labor. Or worse, he would have been hunted down and killed
like a dog by the Tabasco Cartel for losing their "precious" cargo after it
mysteriously disappeared along with his American girlfriend.

He could never go back to Senegal, but he escaped with his life. The least
Yves could do was help Bahn one last time. That was what Bahn had
promised both Yves and himself, that it would be the "last time." Over the
years Bahn had tried everything to get back home, including something
similar to what they were doing right now. Yves had no idea where "home"
was for Bahn, and out of respect, he never asked, but Bahn didn't get far
on any of their previous attempts. Though their alliance was fraught with
its own dangers, Yves was almost sorry to see an end to their exploits. Bahn
was putting all his eggs in one basket, and if things went south, Yves feared
that Bahn would never recover emotionally and would simply give up. *If it
fails, especially if it fails, I need to be with Bahn to pick up the pieces,* decided
Yves.

"Yves," called Bahn, jarring Yves out of his thoughts. "I want to drop at least three anchorages from the halfgate about one nautical mile apart along an arc around the pole. Bring us down close to the sea ice. Hover above the anchor sites before we drop them." Yves was already descending, intently watching his instruments. "You'll have to shut the turbine down for the first drop, or you'll never get us still, without any airspeed. Once the first cable is away you can start it back up and balance against the anchor cable's drag. I'll get the anchors ready to drop." Bahn inserted a hand crank into a socket in the floor of the Kartikeya and turned it, opening a mechanical iris door underneath the halfgate mount. The frigid, rushing arctic air once again pulled the heat from the cabin. Bahn passed his hand over the halfgate's front corner, revealing a set of illuminated buttons. Bahn retrieved two richly colored cable knit sweaters from the halfgate. He held them for a moment, raising them to his face with gloved hands. He pushed his face into the wool and inhaled deeply.

Yves studied the GPS intently. Finding the precise moment, he held up two fingers to Bahn. When he didn't acknowledge, Yves reached back and touched him. Bahn turned to him with the wool's aroma wafting through his head. Yves held up two fingers, and Bahn nodded as he wrapped the sweater's sleeves around the halfgate's bottom edge to keep out the cold. The blustering wind was muffled by the sweaters. Bahn pressed a button on the halfgate to release a five-meter stainless steel rod toward the ice-covered sea below. The rod resembled a train car axle with a point on its end. A section of 13 millimeter stainless steel cable was welded to the top of the rod and payed from the halfgate fast enough to let it fall unimpeded.

Bahn turned to Yves. "How deep is the ocean floor right here?"

Yves called back. "About 4,000 meters." The cable oscillated as the payout rate suddenly slowed. Again, Yves held out two fingers, and Bahn acknowledged. Before the rod hit the ice, three spiked arms exploded from the cylinder at 45-degree angles, creating a tripod to hold the rod perpendicular to the ice surface. Immediately after the tripod was embedded into the ice, the head of the rod began to glow white hot. The ice squealed, and steam billowed as the rod slipped through. The rod descended through the water beneath, and the cable whined in response. In one minute, the cable relaxed and slowed its payout as the rod embedded itself deep into the ocean floor. Yves dialed the onboard gondols into repel and restarted the turbine. The Kartikeya accelerated, then lunged against the drag of the anchorage cable. Bahn adjusted the halfgate to increase the payout rate. Yves signaled for the second anchorage to drop, and Bahn hit the button. A second rod, weighing slightly over 12,000 kilos, dropped away toward the ocean, paying out its own cable. The Kartikeya's prop audibly struggled against the cables' drag. At Yves' signal, Bahn slowed the payout rate, and Yves gently increased the throttle until the aircraft was stretched to a stop above the third anchor site. He confirmed the coordinates, and Bahn dropped the third anchor.

47

ESPIEMOS

The lone Quinto Condottiero mercenary operated out of Cuzco. Comandancia QC in Medellin knew him only as Chacalito, but they had employed him previously with excellent results. They activated him early that morning when the target signal stopped near Chahuaytire. His jeep took him only as far as the town. The satellite tracker indicated the target was still ten kilometers east. He hiked the remainder, turning the tracker off as he crested a hill, and the target aircraft came into view. He took photographs from a distance, then proceeded quietly toward the Embarquisa. His deceptively squat form often worked to his advantage; he looked nothing like a seasoned assassin. He was armed and equipped but dressed in local indigenous attire, a poncho concealing his equipment.

Chacalito's native tongue was Quechua, but he spoke fluent Spanish and German. He approached the craft, seemingly unfazed that it was moored with ropes to the hillside and floating above the earth. He took more photographs. Seeing no one in the area, he boarded the plane. The status lights in the halfgate's corner blinked dully. He felt gravitation fall away from him as he approached the gondol supporting the halfgate. More photos. He made a cursory review of the aircraft's instrument panel. When he dropped back to the ground, the craft oscillated gently in response. He opened the engine compartment cowling and attached an inconspicuous magnetic box to the Embarquisa's firewall. Then, he removed the ceramic oil dipstick, inserted a cylindrical object into the oil filler tube, and replaced the dipstick. He slowly lowered the cowling; Before he could secure the latches, he heard voices from inside the airplane. He retreated from the craft and dropped over the hillcrest undetected where he lay prone beside a shrub to take more photographs.

Chacalito took pride in his work, particularly his ability to remain stealthy. The voices from inside the plane took him by surprise. One person, likely a woman, emerged from the craft and lifted the cowling he had opened. She looked around suspiciously for a moment, then secured it and returned inside. The woman wore a baseball cap that partially concealed her face, which kept Chacalito from getting any decent identifying photos. A man emerged from the plane and walked around it. Chacalito continued taking photos and video. The man climbed into the cargo door and closed it behind him. The engine started, and the plane left in a manner that clearly defied gravity.

Chacalito's dark lips curled into a crooked smile as he saw the opportunity for another contract. He withheld a few points of key information from his report to the Comandancia, including most of the photographs and all of the video.

48

FILTREMOS

With civilian consulting assistance from their database software vendor, NAVSOC at Point Mugu wrote and installed a data search protocol using the signal data they received from Hill. NAVSOC managed the raw data received from all active Naval satellites and an unspecified number of similar satellites from intelligence agencies. Aerial photography was their forte, searching for a previously unknown transmission without knowing its location was not. Nevertheless, they filtered the satellite data feeds to find signal patterns that matched or were closely similar. The orbital passes covering South America were prioritized. It wasn't until the consultants included the NASA SARSAT search and rescue data that they discovered a match. SARSAT was designed to pick up distress signals, so it was better suited for the job at hand. It was also one of the few active polar orbiting satellites.

49

PAGUEMOS

Colonel Fowler's administrative lieutenant laid a file in front of him for signature. The document authorized a wire transfer of $450,000 in support of Operation Pica Suave.

Later the same afternoon, Fowler received notification that there was new information in OASIS, accessible only with his encryption key. Fowler's brow furrowed in consternation as he went over Comandancia QC's thorough report. The photos were unnerving. There was only one person photographed from a distance, and the face was obscured. Fowler authorized an extension to QC's contract: Follow, surveil, and report in a timely manner, without being detected. Before he ran this up the chain, he needed clear evidence to support any claims made—especially if they involved defying gravity.

50

DOSIFIQUEMOS

Considering the relatively low risk of exposing gondols in use, they flew for about thirty minutes under the midday sun, down the Cordillera's eastern slopes to the Amazon plain. Amelia settled the Embarquisa into a narrow clearing among lush greenery. Mosses and vines wrapped the rainforest's trees. Moisture dripped from the leaves without pause, and steam rose from the deep grasses covering the sunlit clearing. Lakshmi dropped from the cargo door into the clearing to moor the craft. The air was still, and a wave of jungle sounds came alive when the engine noise subsided.

Porter and Amelia drove stakes into the ground and secured the mooring ropes to the plane as Lakshmi held another to keep the plane from yawing.

"So, what are we looking for? Did Sariah describe the plants to you?" Amelia wiped her hands on her pant legs and pulled a cap down to shade the sun from her eyes.

Porter didn't ask how she knew about Sariah. He hadn't even noticed when Amelia started calling him Porter instead of Badger. Lakshmi likely filled her in, and ever the diplomat, Amelia chose not to question Porter. The chemistry between her and Lakshmi was hard to miss, and if Lakshmi could trust her with the information, so could he.

"She did. They are three relatively distinctive plants that I'm hoping won't be too hard to find. There's a dark brown moss with purple blooms growing on the finned trunks of the kapok trees," explained Porter, recalling his earlier conversation with Sariah. "There's a small, orange fruit, with a nut inside, that grows on the ujushte tree. And a mushroom, with a round red bowl on top, that looks like an empty eye socket with long lashes around it. We'll likely find that one growing on decomposing logs and stumps."

"And how much of each do you need?" A voice came from inside the airplane. All three of them turned to see Darrell sticking his head out of the halfgate with an inquisitive look.

"Actually, yeah, we could use your help with this, Darrell," admitted Porter. "We only need a couple of kilos each of the mushrooms and moss, but we'll need about 300 kilos of the ujushte fruits. If you could spare a few folks to help with that, it would be great."

Darrell pulled himself out of the halfgate and sat with his legs inside the intention panel. He wiped inky grease from his hands with a rag. "We're done assembling the spool arrays and the swivel blocks. I'm sure I can get a few volunteers to climb some trees. Everybody is eating now. Are you guys hungry? We've got some pork chops on fry bread with tomatoes and onions if you're interested."

"I am literally starving. That sounds amazing. I didn't realize how hungry I was until now." Amelia set the small sledgehammer on the cargo floor of the Embarquisa.

"We need a break, Porter. We've been at it for almost eighteen hours," pleaded Lakshmi before following Amelia into the plane.

Darrell slipped back into the halfgate and Amelia slid in right behind him. Lakshmi swung her legs into the panel and held on to the halfgate's corners, ready to continue. "Join us, Porter. We all need some food and rest."

Porter looked around the clearing and checked the mooring ropes again. "Yeah. That does sound good. I'll be right there."

For centuries, female Clerics of Ankara have been entrusted with the fabrication of halfgates. Although they share the scale with Sariah's people, Ankarans are a breed apart. Despite the religious connotations of their name, Ankaran Clerics are a secular community and are completely self-sufficient with unparalleled technical skills. They are also intelligent, creative, and intuitive.

Handpicked initiates receive rigorous training that ranges from physics and calculus to Creative Manifestation. The training culminates in a form of communal existential sharing. Practitioners of this rare discipline can commune with each other in groups of as few as three and as many as the entire Ankaran cohort. Rather than relying on the cerebral cortex, they lay bare their limbic system to communicate emotions for which there exist no words in any spoken language. At the height of this *evolution*, practitioners achieve something resembling a hive mind, a communal neural network that allows them to parallel process ideas, emotions, and social paradigms. Halfgates were first conceived through this elaborate coalescence and the craft was perfected through the generations.

The fabrication of halfgates became so skill-intensive that the craft turned almost artisanal in nature. And like most vocations in any scale, the craft defined the worker. Ankaran's cloistered existence, requisite to their demanding training, evoked obsolete spiritual imagery even in a people like Sariah's, who had long escaped the shackles of religion. Ankaran women were consequently often referred to as the clerics of Ankara. The motivation behind the fabrication of halfgates, to expose beings within and across scales to the harmony of unified existence, adds to their mystery.

Creative Manifestation, CM for short, was not only integral to the early development of halfgates, but also to their maintenance. Halfgates are all delivered empty from Ankara. When materials and beings enter, the excess matter, representing the difference in scale, is converted into energy and stored inside. When anything leaves a halfgate, that energy is used to re-establish its original scale. What became apparent after their development was the impracticality of introducing everything through the intention panels. The halfgate Porter brought to Chi'ini'li was empty. When the Diné boarded it with their belongings and supplies, they found themselves in an empty plane. Gravity held them to it as it would in their original scale, but the plane, and everything around them, were a mildly iridescent fog. Although they could clearly see and interact with one another and with their equipment, everywhere else was a gently morphing color cloud.

Creative Manifestation linked the intentions of the occupants to the excess energy available. Using the same technology in the intention panels, CM made possible the physical, interactable manifestation of any non-organic element or compound in any imaginable form. Although foliage could not be directly manifested, if seeds and small plants were introduced to the system through the intention panel, soil, water, and fertilizer could be manifested for their planting with temporarily accelerated metabolic rates allowing full-grown trees, shrubs, and agricultural fields to develop in a matter of days. Once mature, the plants were able to reproduce as they would in other scales. Ethical factors led the Ankarans to restrict the use of CM on non-plant biologicals. Humans and animals would still have to come through the intention panels but could only grow and reproduce organically.

Intentional capability varied among individuals. Some could create in a focused area for short periods of time. Others may or may not practice enough to manifest. A few—typically artists and artisans who had made it their work to design and build, imagine and paint, wonder and write—were able to manifest forests, jungles, meadows, fields, mountains, lakes, streams, rivers, oceans, and even weather. They were also adept at coalescing and maintaining their creation's integrity so it would function autonomously. CM was not mutually exclusive. Even within a manifested desert or meadow, separate manifestations could coexist. Others, less interested in manifesting for themselves, were free to roam among and interact with multiple overlapping manifestations. Walking among them would be akin to perusing a visual art museum. The infrastructure is available for all to enjoy, and each visitor can freely pass from one piece of art to the next or even observe many at once. All manifestations created inside a halfgate stayed in the halfgate. The only beings or things that could exit were those that entered through the panels.

Porter entered and found himself at the corner of a large steel structure similar to an aircraft hangar. Amelia, Lakshmi, and Matt stood beside the closest cable reel as he described how they were interconnected. Matt walked toward Porter and beamed with enthusiasm, "There is a way to attach the textiles and keep up with Embarquisa's airspeed."

This was a logistical problem Porter had been working on since Chi'ini'li. He had discussed the challenge with Matt and Darrell, but until now, the solution had eluded them. If the Embarquisa was traveling at 530 knots, paying out the cable by itself at that same speed was certainly manageable. Concatenating the reels with swivels solved the continuity problem. The question was how to attach the textiles and gondols to the cable between the time it left the reel and exited the halfgate. The cable would have to stop or at least slow down to a manageable speed to allow the Diné to attach each item, but it also had to continuously exit the halfgate at Embarquisa's ground speed.

"What'd you come up with, guys?" asked Porter as he rotated a swivel between two cable reels.

The aircraft hangar, housing the cable reel array, retained its structure momentarily, but its surface morphed into a mosaic of circular convex mirrors of varied circumferences. The concrete floor disappeared underneath a lush, misty meadow replete with prairie grass, wildflowers, dewdrops, and honeybees. The air chilled a few degrees as the now orange morning sunlight rose over soft green hills, casting a dramatic shadow upon the cable reels. The mirrors that covered the aircraft hangar pixelated into a fine granularity and then resolved into a deep steely blue sky filled with stars, galaxies, and multicolored nebulae, still bright despite the rising sun. Standing thirty meters away from the first cable reel was a heavy granite stair-stepped pyramid about three meters tall. An object, its shape somewhat undefinable, rested upon the platform at the top.

Matt gazed at the sky's beauty. "It wasn't us, Porter. She's going to show it to you herself."

A woman in her early teens walked toward them from the pyramid. She wore a full-length tiered dress with an embroidered bodice. Her arms were bare. Her dark, black hair was loose around her shoulders, and she wore a broad-rimmed woven hat. Her dress was textured with rusty orange tulle. As she walked toward them, the dress's fabric skimmed over the grasses and wildflowers, taking on their colors. She moved with serenity, and as she bent to smell the flowers, the hat's weave brushed against them. When she straightened, it was subtly adorned with wildflowers.

The young woman approached Amelia and Lakshmi and extended her hands to them. "Lakshmi, Amelia, welcome!" She smiled youthfully. "We are so grateful for your contributions and loving intentions toward our efforts. I'm Haseya. It is an honor to meet you both."

Lakshmi and Amelia each clasped Haseya's hands, and for a moment, the three were one. Haseya nodded politely to Matt and Darrell, then turned to Porter. Lakshmi, uncharacteristically overcome with emotion, wiped tears from her eyes as Amelia drew an arm around her and pulled her close.

Haseya addressed Porter with unexpected familiarity. "It wasn't hard, Jonas. It's like a nested 'for-next' loop. You'll love it!" She sauntered toward the pyramid, motioning for the group to follow. Matt approached Porter and spoke as they followed her.

"Haseya's always been a bright, happy, and intelligent child. She's been studying computer coding at the technical college, and she's only fourteen. We celebrated her *kinaalda* recently." Matt explained that the kinaalda represents a coming of age. "Her mother and grandmother are here with us. They washed her and tied and wrapped her hair. We all shared an *alkaan* they baked in a buried earth oven. In the morning, she ran toward the rising sun as we cheered for her. Others have learned to manifest in the halfgate. But something happened to Haseya after her kinaalda," he said, knitting his brow. "Her surroundings have become one with her imagination. Her power to manifest is unusually strong." Matt beamed proudly, stretching an arm out over the undulating grass with patches of wildflowers. "We stand among her creativity. Let her show you what she's done."

Porter stood at the pyramid's base. The stone foundation steps radiated the lights from what he realized was a cube. Now that he was closer, the cube's definition was distinct from the light it cast. Bright pastel colors filled the changing geometric outlines on the six panels, which faded in and out continuously but without repetition.

"I love finding an elegant solution to a problem. Pretty cool, isn't it?" asked Haseya.

"It's beautiful, yes," said Porter, mesmerized by the vibrant display. "You have a knack for manifestation, that's for sure."

"You don't see it yet, do you Jonas?" she asked, playfully cocking her head.

"How can I not?" said Porter, arching his brows. "Your artwork is as inspiring as your ability to manifest."

"It's only arty 'cause I thought the black cubes were so boring." She rolled her eyes, which reminded Porter that despite her mastery of Creative Manifestation, she was essentially still a teenager. "They needed some color. It works the same."

"What black cubes?" Porter asked. "What works the same?"

"Jonas! It's a halfgate," chirped Haseya, a crooked smile playing on her lips. "Inside this halfgate."

"No. You can't do that!" protested Porter in awe.

"Oh, there's a lot we can do!" promised Haseya confidently. "This is just the start. The crews and all the textiles go inside. The cable passes through this panel and out the other side at the same speed as the Embarquisa."

Porter finally saw what she had done. The meadows, celestia, and lights were her artistic expression surrounding the engineering elegance. She had manifested a fully-functional nested halfgate. "And the scale compression will slow the cable. They might actually have to wait between pieces," realized Porter, regarding the nested halfgate with something like reverence.

"The compression factor is adjustable. We can match your groundspeed while maintaining attachment quality, spacing, and deployment efficiency," assured Haseya, sounding uncharacteristically mature for her age.

The Diné rallied and split into teams to gather the botanicals. Two smaller groups went out to find the mushrooms and moss while the rest began harvesting ujushte fruits and leaves. The older women, including the matriarch Delphine, who speaks with "she who is never seen," gathered wood and water and started a fire to prepare the paste. Ujushte had to be harvested young and unripe: not yet orange.

After the harvest, the Diné sat around the fire to prepare the ujushte by carefully slicing open the fruits to remove the nut inside. They boiled the nuts into a watery mash. While still hot, they folded the brown moss into the mash and simmered the mixture for about four hours. Once the mash had cooled, they macerated the mushrooms and folded them in gently. They poured the mixture into wide-mouthed bowls and covered them with linen cloths. A vigorous fermentation process began almost immediately. The cloths billowed above the bowls as pink foam seeped over the rims to the dark forest floor.

Once the fermentation was complete, some three hours later, they turned over the mash loaves into the linen cloths to wring out any remaining liquid. Gathering in cross-legged circles, they laid the cloths out in the centers and began spreading a gram or two of the sticky tan paste onto individual ujushte leaves, and then folded them into little books. They stacked the folded leaves and tied them in small bundles with twine that was spun from mature kapok seed pods.

When the work was complete, the Diné matriarch stood, took a folded leaflet, and placed it under her tongue. After holding it there for a minute, she spit onto her finger, applied the saliva to the inside of her lower eyelids, and blinked rapidly. As she reapplied it, she encouraged the others to do the same, and they followed suit. As Porter placed a leaf into his mouth, Amelia and Lakshmi confronted him.

"Okay, we've been watching this and listening to them speak Navajo all day, but what is this stuff? Does it get you high?" Amelia made a face. "I still have to fly the plane."

"No, it isn't anything like that," assured Porter. "What it does is soften the lenses in your eyes and invigorate the muscles that adjust focus. Do you remember looking at something small like an ant when you were a kid and being able to look up across a field and instantly see something far away with the same clarity?"

Amelia shot Lakshmi an inquisitive look. "What do you mean when I was a kid? I can do that now. Can't everybody?"

Lakshmi replied, "Actually, I can't. My vision isn't as good as yours. I can see well up close, but far away, it gets blurry."

"We're still pretty young," Porter chimed in. "It affects people as they age, and by the time they're about forty or fifty, their lenses harden, which limits their focal range. But sometimes it happens sooner, as in Lakshmi's case. The eye's ability to change focus based on what we look at is called accommodation. So far, the only remedy has been glasses or contact lenses, but those don't really restore it. This stuff does," said Porter, pointing at the pile of bundled leaves.

Amelia picked up a folded leaf and sniffed it. "That's actually pretty cool. Certainly, something every pilot could get excited about. Not to seem ungrateful, but why are we doing this? I mean, aren't we on a schedule? Shouldn't we be picking up some ponchos and blankets or something?"

Porter swabbed his eyelids again and removed the leaf from his mouth so he could speak more clearly. "Not *some* ponchos and blankets. A lot of them. And some other really fine textiles which many consider works of art. They represent hours of fine workmanship, and I had to find something to trade for them. I don't have any money. I know it won't directly feed their families, but it will definitely improve their lives and their ability to provide."

"So, you're going to trade fine textiles for these little goober leaf sandwiches?" asked Lakshmi dismissively.

Porter riposted cockily, "Try one. By tomorrow, you'll be enjoying the views from the plane as you never have. Perhaps then you won't be so sassy."

"We'll have to see about that, Porter." Lakshmi slipped the leaf under her tongue.

51

NEGOCIEEMOS

Porter waited until early morning to return to the plaza in Chahuaytire. The woman who sold him the tapestry wasn't there, but the boy who translated for her was. Porter tried communicating with him, gesturing to the place where the woman had set up yesterday. The boy stayed seated and shook his head silently.

"He won't know," said a voice behind him.

Delphine, accompanied by a young woman wearing sunglasses and dressed in shorts and a black KISS t-shirt, stood a few meters away. Delphine motioned to Porter. "We followed you into town. Sariah said you might need some help. Let's walk down a little further." She gestured toward a man in the crowd. "That man in the bowler hat."

As they started walking, the young woman grinned. "What, Jonas? Is your Quechua rusty? Couldn't you get anything out of that kid?"

"Sorry, do we know each other?" Porter eyed the young woman as he followed Delphine, through the market crowd.

"They told me you were a bright engineer," said the woman, smugly. "This is the second time today you've failed to impress." She smiled and lifted her sunglasses.

"Haseya? Wow!" exclaimed Porter, looking her over. "I would've never guessed. This is what you look like normally? You were so..."

"I was going for a touristy look." She shrugged. "But yeah, these are my regular clothes."

"I've been meaning to ask how you keep that halfgate going when you aren't…"

"How do you want to handle this?" Delphine interrupted him as they approached the man in the bowler hat. "What we have to offer isn't exactly accepted currency. This man is influential in the community. If we can sell him on the idea, it'll be a good start."

"Let's show him what we've got," said Porter. "Can you talk to him?"

"I only speak English and Navajo. Sariah is going to help. You talk to him. I'll relay Sariah's translation."

Porter gestured to a woman who was inspecting her work and bending uncomfortably over her loom. "Ask about her," he said, leaning over to Delphine.

Between hand gestures, Haseya's demonstrations, and Delphine's best shot at imitating Sariah's Quechua, they were able to convince the marketing man and his four manufacturers to dose themselves with the accommodation serum. Delphine told them it would take four to twelve hours for the effects to show, and the change would be lifelong. Porter didn't want to start any negotiations until they knew it worked. They left to peruse the market and the town. When they returned, a throng had gathered. As they approached, the man in the bowler hat called out to them and pointed excitedly. Porter and his companions were suddenly engulfed by a Quechua cacophony.

It took the entire Diné crew to pack and port the weavings back to the Embarquisa. Still, it was clear to Porter and Delphine that they hadn't yet found what they were looking for. The first woman Porter had met walked up behind him and touched his arm. Delphine saw her face before Porter turned toward her. She did not speak at first but looked directly into their eyes. Both knew she could see them clearly and confidently. She spoke softly to Delphine, who translated for Porter.

"Her name is K'antu. She wants to take us to her mother. She hasn't seen her in over thirty years."

Porter turned to Delphine. "We have to be careful here. I'm grateful for what we've found, but it's not nearly enough, and we need to keep looking. I'd love to do more for them, but we don't have much time."

As if sensing his reluctance, the woman said something to Delphine, still holding onto Porter's arm.

"She says we need to help her mother to see," Delphine translated.

Porter smiled at the woman and looked at Delphine without speaking. K'antu looked at them as though she was a teacher, patiently waiting for them to understand.

"Tell her we're sorry. We have to go, Delphine." But the woman would not take no for an answer.

"She says her mother lives by the sacred lake. Something about cats, I think, but I'm not sure."

Porter gestured a goodbye and started to walk away.

"Porter, she says she knows we need more. Her mother is a guardian of a vault that holds ancient garments."

52

TRANSFORMEMOS

Orange and blue seeped from the eastern horizon, but the sun hadn't yet risen as the Embarquisa slipped gracefully close to Titiqaqacucha's still and glassy surface. A few birds along the shoreline had begun to stir. K'antu stood behind the copilot seat, gripping it tightly as she searched through the windows. She grew up on the lake but had never seen it from the air. She recognized the mountains east of the lake and knew that she had walked the shoreline at their base many times.

K'antu's mother wept gently and spoke softly to her daughter when they embraced. She held K'antu's cheeks with her palms as they silently held their faces close. K'antu buried her teary face in her mother's blouse and inhaled deeply. Porter shifted his weight and leaned over to look through the window. Sheets on the backyard clothesline gently billowed and unraveled in the breeze. Lakshmi caressed Amelia's two-handed grip on her bicep and released a barely audible shush through her lips. K'antu's mother slipped from her embrace and toddled slowly toward the home's back wall, which cut into an adjacent hill. K'antu gazed lovingly into Porter's face, took his hand, and motioned for him to follow her mother. Along the windowless wall was a solid earthen shelf, waist-high to the diminutive woman. Air cooled by the moist earth flowed over the wall as she set aside clay jars and pulled down a tapestry covering the shelf. She turned, bent slightly forward, to look into Porter's face and smiled.

Porter's eyes were still adjusting to the darkness away from the windows. He looked back at K'antu, who again gestured toward her mother. Lakshmi and Amelia drew closer. K'antu's mother had turned toward the exposed shelf wall and lowered to her knees. She brushed the earth from a section of the wall with her open palm, side to side, then top to bottom. She turned toward Porter, still on her knees. This time, she glanced with a knowledge that, up until now, hadn't yet illuminated her face, and promptly disappeared through the intention panel. The sunlight that angled across K'antu's face only half illustrated the love she had for her mother. Porter, Lakshmi, and Amelia followed her into the halfgate. K'antu remained in the kitchen, found her mother's concha and bombilla, and sat down at the table to enjoy a hot yerba mate.

Porter had to catch his balance. He was seated in the back of a reed canoe that tipped with each stroke of the oar by a shirtless man kneeling at the front. Three colorfully dressed women, wearing black bowler hats, sat in the middle between him and the rower. Each held wrapped bundles on their laps. *Where am I? Who are these people?* wondered Porter. The man faced forward, intent on his task. The women spoke softly to each other in a language Porter did not comprehend. The canoe was well away from the shoreline, but Porter recognized the terrain they had seen upon arrival. They were on Lake Titiqaqacucha. Neither Lakshmi nor Amelia was there. Porter, too, had a wrapped bundle on his lap, which he set aside. His feet, or what seemed to be his feet, were small, dark, and sandaled. He wore the same vibrant tunic he saw on the other women. He reached for his head and took off a hat that was a bowler like the others'. His hands weren't his, but they moved at his command. *What's going on?* He felt a sudden urge to escape. He stood too hastily, lost his balance, and as the canoe rocked, fell into the water. He struggled to come to the surface, but the wet poncho's weight dragged him under. Panic shot through him as he realized he could not swim as well as he had thought. All his Navy training went out the window. Trying to convince himself that none of this was real didn't keep the fear at bay. He was drowning. He removed the shawl and worked toward the surface. He broke surface and found himself being pulled back into the canoe. The young man scowled at him briefly, then returned to his oar.

The women rushed to his side, talking excitedly, smiling and laughing. One removed her shawl and wrapped it around him. All three asked questions, but he could not understand or answer them. They continued speaking and laughing for a short while, looking back at Porter on occasion to see how he was doing. The near-fatal experience left Porter drained. He was too exhausted to think and curled up on the canoe floor, not trusting himself to move. He closed his eyes briefly and took a deep breath. When he opened his eyes, he was thankfully seated on the kitchen floor, dry and dressed as he was when he arrived. He looked up at K'antu, who smiled at him, sipping her mate. Lakshmi and Amelia weren't there.

Porter pulled a gondol from his pack to contact Sariah. He explained his experience to her, and she taught him how to ask K'antu what she knew. K'antu relayed the garment vault's history as Sariah translated for Porter.

K'antu's mother was the sixth generation to guard the vault. Inside were textiles, garments, and weavings from various cultures around the world, the oldest dating back more than 1,400 years. Not only were they superior handicrafts, but the quantity was equally astonishing. K'antu's reunion was emotional, not only because she had returned to see her mother after twenty-three years of absence, but also because she knew the time had come for her to take her mother's place as the vault's guardian.

K'antu has long had the vault's inventory committed to her memory—ever since her mother taught it to her as a child: 1,256 Indian Megh veils and saris, 808 meters of Ghanan nwentoma—cotton and silk kente cloths—1,475 meters of Lakiyan Bedouin weavings, 2,221 meters of Mongolian Kasakh carpets, two types of Indonesian ikat—108 meters of blurry and 227 meters of double—1,798 Malay songkets, 1,715 meters of Turkish headscarves, 998 Palawan grass weavings, 2,440 meters of Yogyakartan silk batik, 702 formal Nipponese kimonos, and 312 meters of finely embroidered Yazd termeh.

Porter didn't have to ask Sariah the question. She was as curious about how refined textiles from Southeast Asia, the Middle East, and Western Africa would be found in the Bolivian Andes. Even more curious was how long they'd been there. K'antu explained that a large part of her taking the guardian role involved learning the secrets of the vault that her mother *hadn't* shared with her. She didn't have a good answer. She could, however, explain Porter's experience in the canoe.

Guarding the vault and its contents was a privilege that K'antu's mother and their mothers before them enjoyed and held sacred. Over generations, their manifestations within the vault had evolved into their own thoughts and memories. They had moved beyond physical manifestations. Although those flourished, the guardians' dynamic thoughts and memories were the architecture defining the experience. K'antu related a story her grandmother told her when she was a child. *She* was the woman who fell into the water and was pulled back into the boat. It was her friends who tried to comfort her, but she only felt embarrassed. In the fullness of the guardian's manifestation, her physical sensations, thoughts, and emotions were imparted to anyone who entered the vault. This was the manner in which the textiles were kept safe until it was time for their employment. K'antu knew that the time had come to accept her role. She also knew that the time to let them go was fast approaching.

Porter leaned against the window, listening intently as Sariah translated K'antu's story. K'antu turned reflexively as a shadow moved swiftly across the window behind Porter. The door to the kitchen burst open, revealing an armed man. Her heart pounding, K'antu slid slowly from the kitchen chair and pressed her back against the wall. Porter instinctively lunged at the man and grabbed his arm to gain control of the weapon. He dropped the weapon as Porter tumbled behind him, arresting his lunge. Porter scrambled to his feet, ready to fight. The man glanced at K'antu, her eyes as wide as her body was still. Porter leaped, but the man evaded him and ran toward the back wall. Porter's miss was no accident. He dove, arms stretched in front of him. In one sleek movement, Chacalito flew into the halfgate, leaving his gun on the floor. Porter followed immediately after. K'antu's eyes, still wide, thoughtfully shifted. It was all over in a matter of seconds. In the silent kitchen, she sat back down. Cradling the warm mate between her trembling hands, she stared across the room toward the window.

Lakshmi and Amelia, both barefoot and dressed in bright sarapes and bowler hats, followed a boy across a damp grassy meadow. The two women accepted the manifestation far more easily than Porter had. It helped that they could communicate with one another in English even though they couldn't speak with the boy. It was evident, however, that he was there to lead them. His youthful eleven-year-old smile was comfortably innocent. Assuming the other women's bodies with acceptance was stimulating. In one sense, they had to give themselves over to another's feelings, thoughts, and emotions. At the same time, walking barefoot over warm alpaca dung was somehow less disturbing if they maintained their new sense of self.

The boy led them up a steep hill to a plaza that was cut into the earth, some fifty meters wide, and perhaps two kilometers long. It was more a canal than a plaza except for the tightly fitting granite blocks that covered the floor and the walls, cut eight meters into the earth. Sturdy wooden posts, mounted at regular intervals into the wall's parapet, suspended hempen ropes, which in turn supported translucent tangerine fabric covering the plaza. The breeze lifted and furled the orange cloth causing the diffused sunlight passing through it to warp onto the plaza floor. Nine rectangular openings, trimmed with bold reveal in solid granite, were spaced evenly along the walls on each side. The boy ran ahead of them in a wide arc. He began dancing gracefully as he ran, his arms outstretched and his face and heart lifted to the oscillating glow above. Lakshmi and Amelia held hands, admiring the effect the billowing fabric cast upon the scene. The boy circled back and slowed his pace at the first opening. Continuing his graceful motion, he invited the women to enter.

The granite openings were adorned with simple carvings symbolizing animals, birds, ferns, and waterfalls. Moon carvings, depicted in eighteen different phases, arced across each opening. Upon entry, they were confronted by darkness and cool, dry, subterranean air. As their eyes adjusted, delicate sparkles appeared above them. Lakshmi's waist bumped into something. She turned to feel a table, strong and sturdy but still flexible. The light around them did not increase, but their ability to perceive their surroundings did. The table she stood by was one of many arrayed in a sinuous pattern across the cavern. Each table supported half-meter stacks of meticulously folded fabric pieces. The treasures were bathed in the entrance's warm glow. Lakshmi and Amelia, still unaccustomed to their renewed visual acuity, accepted the revelation as part of their journey. Amelia let a garment unfold before her. She held the kimono to her body, modeling it for Lakshmi.

Porter hesitated for less than a beat as he eased into rowing the canoe. He took a few strokes on each side to acclimate to this new body's strength and resilience. He had a feeling one of the passengers behind him was also a visitor. A smooth sweep of his head told him everything. The same three women were seated in the center, chatting and laughing as they had been previously. The woman in the back tightly gripped the canoe, searching desperately for understanding. The three women spoke to her. She observed pale-faced but did not answer. The canoe was headed toward floating reed islands when Porter entered. He continued in the same direction. When they approached, one woman tapped him on the leg and pointed toward a structure. He adjusted his rowing. The woman in the back relaxed and folded her hands on her lap, keenly observing everything. When they reached the island, Porter stepped off the canoe first and held it close as the women disembarked. He did his best to remain in character as the third woman passed him. The first three chatted as they approached the structure. The third followed awkwardly, clutching her bag. Porter kneeled on the reeds and secured the canoe with a rope. As he turned back toward the women, he again found himself seated on the kitchen floor.

Amelia helped him up. "We saw the handiwork. They're absolutely beautiful!"

Lakshmi pushed away from the windowsill. She finished the mate and passed it back to K'antu to refill. She squared her shoulders, addressing Porter, "We didn't see you in there. What were you doing?"

Porter ran his palms against his trouser legs. His eyes met K'antu's momentarily. She had obviously not told the others what transpired in their absence. "We're not alone."

53

HELEMOS

With Sariah's help, K'antu told them that her mother could keep the uninvited man distracted with a memory, but he was clever, and she wasn't certain she could continue for long. Porter and Amelia hired a pedicab to take them back to the Embarquisa. Lakshmi stayed with K'antu. Porter asked the pedicab driver to wait near the town's edge. They returned with the halfgate and rode back to K'antu's mother's house. They set their halfgate on the kitchen floor opposite the one set in the wall. Matt and Darrell crawled out, and K'antu served them mate.

"Where are we?" Matt looked through the window and then, with a hint of social discomfort, at K'antu.

Porter answered, "We're in northwestern Bolivia, not far from Lake Titicaca. We found some textiles and need help moving them into the halfgate."

Amelia cut in. "Some? Try a lot! There's a lot of really cool stuff in there."

Porter continued. "If you wouldn't mind having half your crew follow Amelia and Lakshmi into this halfgate, they'll show you where the textiles are. We'll need about ten people here in the kitchen making the transfer from one gate to the other. The rest can stay inside and receive."

Matt and Darrell slipped back into the Diné halfgate and organized their tribe. By the time they returned, K'antu had prepared empanadas and chimichurri. The Diné graciously accepted her offer as they passed through into her mother's halfgate. Lakshmi and Amelia led the procession into the orange courtyard, and the tribe began collecting, baling, and carrying the textiles back through the intention panel and into the kitchen. Ten Diné took turns lifting the bales from the halfgate and transferring them across the kitchen. When Porter felt confident that the textile fire brigade was operating smoothly, he followed a bale into the Diné halfgate.

After transferring close to three hundred 70-kilogram bales, the Navajos in the kitchen made efforts to improve their efficiency by moving the Diné halfgate closer to the one in the wall. At first, it was a repositioning that allowed the team to work better. As the bales started arriving with greater frequency, the kitchen began filling faster than they could transfer them. Logically, the best placement for the Diné halfgate was directly in front of the other. This seemed to work well. As a bale came through the wall, they could simply take turns pushing it into the Diné halfgate.

Due to a holdup on the receiving end, the kitchen team was able to move one of the bales only halfway through the intention panel, and it became stuck. The next bale came through the wall and ran into the caught bale. At this moment, when both intention panels were open, a three-second rush of what looked and felt like cloud vapor surged out of the Diné halfgate and into the other. The team withdrew, momentarily startled, then tried to dislodge the bale. A similar rush of vapor billowed forth, this time from the wall into the Diné halfgate. The team members who were attempting to knock loose the bale quickly stepped back, their arms and facial hair thick with frost. They danced around the kitchen, brushing their arms and faces to melt the frost. The rush came again into the wall, then back into the halfgate. As the frequency increased, the team reset the gondols and moved the halfgate away from the wall, where it was originally set, and the stream stopped. As they moved the halfgate, the bale that had been stuck stayed where it was. Half of it appeared normal, and the half that had been exposed to the rush was frozen solid and was now conjoined in ice to the next bale that came out of the wall.

Porter exited the Diné halfgate into the kitchen. The kitchen team explained what had happened. He wondered about it for a moment but let it go. He decided to ask Sariah about it later. He cautioned the team to keep the halfgate where it was and continue working.

Once all the textiles were transferred to the Diné halfgate, the loading teams returned through the kitchen. Porter, Amelia, and Lakshmi prepared the halfgate and called the pedicab. As they did, K'antu's mother emerged from the wall and K'antu helped her to her feet. She spoke rapidly but softly to K'antu and appeared concerned.

Porter switched on the gondol attached to the halfgate. "Sariah? Are you there? What is K'antu's mother saying?"

"She says she was unable to detain the man who entered. She says he was drawn away."

"What does she *mean drawn away*?"

"She is certain he isn't inside her vault. If he didn't come back into the kitchen, there is only one other place he could be."

Matt and Darrell enlisted their entire tribe to search for anyone outside of their group, but they found no one. Sariah had not been in contact with Bahn, but Porter knew him well enough to feel confident that he had established his anchorage and had started south from the pole. Time was short, and even if they left immediately, they were still at least twelve hours from the South Pole. Porter asked Matt and Darrell to stay alert for anything unusual but that they were heading south as soon as they returned to the Embarquisa.

There were about twenty-nine hundred nautical miles between them and the Antarctic peninsula and another eighteen hundred from there to the pole. With the gondols set efficiently and considering the mods Bahn made to the Embarquisa, Porter and Amelia calculated they could arrive at the South Pole in a little over eight hours. That was if everything went smoothly and they didn't run into any weather, which was highly unlikely. Their flight path took them across the Salar de Uyuni and south across the Andes ridge. The range that included Aconcagua was higher than they wanted to fly. Amelia recommended heading east first and flying low over the Patagonian plains, but Porter disagreed. They were already attracting attention, and the man that infiltrated the halfgates was likely on board their aircraft. Staying over the Andes as long as possible would keep them away from western Argentina's urban areas.

54

ATRAVESEMOS

It was not at all lost on Bahn, Yves, and Blueye that they were about to transition to Russian and Chinese airspace in an unidentifiable aircraft anchored to the earth with a steel cable one year after the World Trade Center's destruction. Although their path took them over mostly remote terrain, they would pass within three hundred nautical miles of Beijing. It was very unlikely that any US military command would share their intel about the gondol signature interference with either country. Yves calculated their flight time; if uninterrupted, from the Siberian coast to the equator, it would take about twenty hours.

When her grandmother's spirit told Irina Brynner about the imminent union, she had only a precious few hours to prepare to intercept Father Sky's creation. Although the Buryat shamaness was technically Russian, her almond-shaped eyes, jet-black hair, and yellow complexion betrayed a Mongolian ancestry. She wore her finest azure silk *degel*, a long robe, accessorized with a black cap featuring a blue peaked top. *It's only fitting,* she thought as she smoothed out the creases of her *degel*. It was no coincidence that the Buryat favored blue. The color symbolized Father Sky.

Irina looked at the deflated, albeit vibrant, balloon that cut a sharp contrast against the dark blue of Lake Baikal. Shamanistic text, snaking across its still shriveled surface, would ward off any evil spirits that intended harm to Father Sky's work. Now Irina understood why her Shaman ancestors insisted they keep hot air balloons. *They knew this day would come,* she reflected. Every year, the Buryat would take to the Lake to test the airworthiness of their balloons and to gain energy from the spirit of her ancestors. They would pitch their *gers*, tents insulated with skin and felt, on its shores and grill Omul fish over coal fires.

This year, however, the revelries were somewhat muted. Irina knew that the chances of the thirty Buryat, including herself, returning home from this expedition were slim. But Irina had no regrets. She was honored to make any sacrifice required of her to protect the work of the Sky Father. She took comfort in knowing that she was not alone in her devotion. Her grandmother's spirit assured her that similar balloons would soon lift off from Sainshand and Ordos. They would carry shamans, shamanesses, büges, idugans, and initiates of multiple shamanistic tribes across both hot and cold deserts, willing to offer their lives for the protection of Father Sky's work.

55

DESEEMOS

Bahn could hear the textiles apparating from the halfgate and whisking away into the arctic darkness. He'd studied the handwoven works' intricate beauty and wished he could witness their furling glory in the crisp, cold air. But the darkness forbade him. He recalled the times he had attempted this in the past and asked himself why he put himself through this consistently disappointing exercise.

He closed the anchor deployment panel, gathered the two wool sweaters to his chest, and climbed into his seat. The Kartikeya had settled into the flight as Yves balanced the forces to compensate for the cable tension. Despite his familiar face, they were startled to find Blueye standing between them. He turned to them individually with silent acknowledgment, both eyes uncovered and whole, returning a confidence that they each found unsettling.

He spoke using his mouth with the same fluency Bahn had heard in the Nahua halfgate. "It will work out this time, Bahn. It's different. The required elements are present. The texture is right. The energy is balanced. Both queens are free to act as they will."

"There's no way you can know that's true. You may have the Nahua's ear, but you don't know the Diné," said Bahn skeptically.

"It's understandable that you'd settle into complacency after so many disappointments," Blueye smiled knowingly. I've experienced merges with Cihuāt-lahtoāni and Na'ashjé'íí. We know the union is imminent. Your work isn't yet done, but following the current path will bring success. A path home will open to you, my friend. All beings will be free to create and manifest at their will.

Love will be released to entwine those who open their hearts to it. Those who choose to destroy will destroy one another. A place for every desire and every desire in its place. It's cosmically elegant."

Bahn climbed out of the co-pilot seat and sat cross-legged on the floor to give his full attention to Blueye. "What happened to you in there?" Bahn furrowed his brow. "And those names, I'm not familiar with them. Who or what are you talking about?"

"There is unfathomable abundance available to us, Bahn. So much room to grow and learn. All we have to do is accept it," he said with monk-like calmness. "The Cihuātlahtoāni taught me to open my heart, intend my desires, and manifest them in intellectual and physical forms. When you met me at the meditation lintel, she had only begun teaching me. There is so much, Bahn."

"This she you're talking about. Is she the Cihuātlahtoāni?"

"The Cihuātlahtoāni is the Nahua's leader. The day you and Porter came to see me in the lintel, she spoke with Porter. He told you he had."

"He didn't mention her name, but I do remember the conversation. You said a second name. Again, I can't repeat it, but who is the other one?"

"Na'ashjé'íí. She aligned herself with the halfgate on the Embarquisa when it landed in Chi'ini'li. She is more than the Diné leader. She's taught and guided them for centuries. She's studied and practiced loving intention and creative manifestation until, well, the best way to describe her is..." Blueye paused as he fished for the most appropriate word. "...next level. Maybe even a few notches above that. The Diné call her Spider Woman because she taught their ancestors how to spindle and weave. She's known and taught the power in handmade textiles for a very long time. She is personally guiding the Diné in their catalytic work along the southern arc. She and Cihuātlahtoāni work together to complete the arc from the north.

Yves posed a question as he adjusted the engine power. "Ze madame Cihuātlah-toāni—she is here with us, no? In zees 'alf-gate? Mais la madame araignée—she ride en L'Embarquise? Comment parles-tu avec les deux femmes?

"Yves, it's not difficult to do once you understand. Although my practice is limited, I learned it in less than a day. Sariah can do it with her radio equipment. These women have transcended the need for equipment and exercise their practice, their craft, to accomplish broader intentions. Differences in time and space aren't challenging to them."

Bahn sat up taller and addressed Blueye, who, standing and barefoot, was still a bit taller than the seated Bahn Waclire. "You didn't come out of your meditation lintel to tell us about these teachers. Why are you here?"

"Quite true. You need to make a few adjustments. The Russians and Chinese aren't as infused with arrogance as the Americans. They're going to present a challenge."

110.0 degrees east, 66.57 degrees north

Arctic Circle

Central Siberian Plateau

September 23, 2002, 03:48

<u>LAND</u>

Deep within the earth, our roots anchor

The blissful fragrance of a tubor rose.

Supported by a steady foundation,

From earth to sky we find our grounding force.

Beautiful orb of crimson energy;

A secure place where we are rooted strong.

Strength and resilience are grounded here.

56
ROMPAMOS

A little over an hour after leaving Titicaca, they crossed the Andes crest into Argentina. Amelia reminded Porter that not only was this unfamiliar terrain and airspace, but it was also some of the most dangerous in the world. The Cordillera Andes was subject to extreme weather conditions and the winds were particularly unpredictable during the September spring. The mid-afternoon sunlight strobed in their view; the rays alternated between shining through and being shadowed from the peaks to their west as they passed by. The sky was clear, and there was only occasional light turbulence. Porter asked Amelia and Lakshmi to hold their course south.

Haseya emerged from the halfgate and knelt between the cockpit seats looking through the front windscreen, the expression on her face resembling concern. Lakshmi and Amelia acknowledged her, but she remained focused and did not reply.

"What is it, Haseya? Is everything okay in there?" asked Lakshmi.

"Oh yeah. It's all good," she said dismissively. "We're almost ready to deploy."

Amelia scanned the horizon, trying to figure out what had Haseya so preoccupied. "What's up? What are you looking for?"

"That." Haseya pointed toward a tall mountain peak ahead and right of their course. Cresting thousands of feet above the peak hung a cleanly-defined, rounded cloud surrounded by an iridescent sun dog, shaped much like a mushroom top. There were no billows or texture. The backlighting from the western sun added a dramatic effect to it.

That does not look good, thought Porter as Lakshmi looked on with concern. Amelia studied the aeronautical charts. The peak was Aconcagua. The cloud was much larger than others she had seen, but she recognized it as lenticular. Haseya started shaking her head, repeatedly saying, "No." Without warning, the plane jolted violently and dipped sharply left. Amelia asked Porter to adjust the gondols to lighten the plane, but even that didn't arrest their descent. Amelia took the flight controls and, with intense focus, steered into a canyon, avoiding the rising terrain as they dove sharply east. Porter and Haseya braced themselves while Amelia fought to hold the airspeed under the maximum. The vertical speed indicator was pegged at 4,000 feet per minute but she could see, by the rate the altimeter was spinning, they were dropping faster than that. At the base of the narrowing canyon stood a sharp outcropping. Amelia slowly pulled the yoke all the way back, but the plane continued to dive perilously close to the rocks.

"I need more, Jonas! It's too heavy! I can't pull up!" she cried through clenched teeth.

Porter scrambled to readjust the gondols that were supporting the halfgates. He set them into the negative, and they lifted off the deck, straining the tie-down straps. Amelia remained intensely concentrated. The canyon walls were above them—and they were narrowing. Turning was not an option. She held the yoke full back. The airspeed slowly began bleeding off. The rock outcropping was still higher than their flight path, and it was coming at them fast. The nose began lifting. Amelia banked slightly right as they passed the outcropping, hoping to create a little more room. A deafening sound tore through the cabin. Porter grabbed hold of the tie-downs while Haseya gripped the pilot seats as the plane lurched to the left. After what seemed like an eternity, it settled into a level glide, and the slope opened up into the farmland plains below them.

The plane slowed considerably as the nose came almost vertical. Amelia called out to Porter. "Is everybody okay?" The others, still dazed, muttered their affirmations. "Can you slowly increase the gondols back to cruise?" Amelia called out to Porter. "We need to get the airspeed back up so I can control her."

Once the plane leveled out and was flying normally, Porter assessed the damage. There weren't any open holes, but there was some buckling in the floor decking near the left wall. He looked through the side window and saw that the left main landing gear was gone. He looked through the right window. The gear was still attached but hanging loosely and swinging wildly in the wind. He was unable to see if the nose gear had been damaged.

Porter reported back to Amelia. "The main landing gear is shot. The right side is still attached, but barely. I can't see the nose gear."

"We have to set her down, Porter," decided Amelia, her forehead crinkled in concern. "We've gotta make repairs before we keep going. We'll have to bring her down slowly and find a way to protect the prop. Keep the gondols on."

Lakshmi looked up from the map. "There's an airport about forty kilometers north. If we're putting down during the day, it's going to be the least conspicuous place."

The Sarmiento airport in San Juan seemed pretty quiet. Amelia did her best to simulate a regular landing and taxied while hovering to a corner of the airfield between two hangars. Matt and Darrell helped Porter collect some old tires to place under the fuselage to make it look supported if anyone came by. They reduced the gondols enough to depress the tires.

A teenage boy, dressed in coveralls, came running around the corner. Speaking excitedly in Spanish and gesturing at the aircraft, he paused, apparently awaiting a response. Matt asked Haseya to translate for them. He was a student at the technical college studying for his maintenance certificate. He augmented his studies by volunteering to work on aircraft at the airport and asked if he could help with any repairs. The damage to the Embarquisa was evident. Porter, Lakshmi, Amelia, and Matt walked around the plane, assessing the damage. The left main landing gear and the nose gear had been completely sheared off. The strut that connected the two main gear wheels had come unfastened, which explained the loose and swinging right main. They all knew there weren't going to be any parts available to replace these.

The young man spoke again, and Haseya told the others that he and his friends were willing to help with the fuselage repairs. He pointed out the buckling in the frame and skin around the gear attachment points.

Lakshmi turned to Porter and whispered discretely, "Once we leave here, I don't see any reason for us to land until after we meet up with the Kartikeya."

"What's your point?" Porter asked.

"We don't need landing gear. Let's cut it off and repair the dents and bends. We'll need some sheet aluminum and rivets to smooth over the holes where the struts attached."

Amelia added, "Plus, we'll lower the drag considerably. Fuel flow is already low, but this will give us even more range if we need it. We can take these tires, or maybe our bright-eyed friend here could build us a prop cradle in case we do have to put down again."

Porter agreed. He asked Haseya if the young man could help them remove the gear strut and make the other repairs. He obliged and said he would be back with his tools and his friends in two hours.

With their help and as many hands as they needed from the crew inside the halfgate, they made the repairs and refilled the fuel tanks. By eleven o'clock, the students were finished and packing tools into their truck. The main gear and strut lay to the side. They offered to return as soon as the new gear assembly got there. Haseya thanked them and offered pork chops in fry bread, which they all heartily enjoyed. As soon as the boys left, the Embarquisa gently and quietly lifted off and continued south unnoticed.

The Tengrist wore a leather belt with a silver buckle, a Toortsog, a round conical leather hat with a wide upturned yak-fur brim, and Gutals, ornate yet sturdy boots. His brown *deel*, a loose calf-length tunic with long sleeves, accentuated his yoga-like movements. Under normal circumstances, the prayer ceremony used natural light to cure physical and psychological maladies. Tengrist Anarbek Tezekbaev hoped that today, the ceremony would bless the still-inflating balloon, enabling it to protect the work of the mighty sky deity, *Kök Tengri*.

Anarbek's prominent cheekbones, flat forehead, narrow eyes, and thin lips set him apart from Asians of other regions. Environmental factors molded his people into the unique race they are, characterized by physical features such as a stocky build, healthy tan, and sun-blushed cheeks. Life in the Eurasian steppe had always been harsh, and the Tengrists of Sainshand, like Anarbek, developed a delicate and intricate relationship with the animals and their habitat.

Their *gers,* large and round, semi-permanent tents, had vertical walls and a conical roof. Herds of semi-wild Khangai yak and camel roamed the grasslands. Anarbek fondly watched his two children chase after a baby yak that had yet to grow its winter coat. When it came time for them to shed their luscious pelts, herders would hand-comb the baby yaks and manually sort the fur into natural colors: cocoa, tan, silver, and platinum. These were traded for essential goods. There were no luxuries here; the Tengrists were a minimalist people who lived in harmony with the universe.

Anarbek burned juniper leaves from a hand-held container to remove negative energy and bad spirits from the balloon and then blessed it with sacred water from the Disappeared Spring. Five balloons would set off from Sainshand, and he would board this one with five others. *In service of* Tengri, reflected Anarbek. He was honored to serve *Tengri*, the infinite and timeless deity who created the universe.

57

EMPOTREMOS

By dawn, the Embarquisa reached Tierra del Fuego. Rain fell from a six-thousand-foot cloud ceiling. The temperature was above freezing, and the winds were westerly at 30 knots. As unforgiving as it seemed—compared to crossing the Drake Passage only to be welcomed by 2,600 nautical miles across Antarctica followed by another 5,600 miles before they were once again over land—this historically deadly archipelago felt like the warm fires of home. They continued out across the steely-gray arctic ocean.

Antarctica began abruptly. Vertical black rock cliffs, detailed with encrusted snow, stood stalwart against the dark green sea. Ice floes blurred beneath whirling snow and swayed gracefully in the slushy South Pacific. As they approached the coastline, the cloud ceiling parted. Lofty, orange cumulus rose into the periwinkle sky. Amelia lifted the Embarquisa's nose to climb above the cliff line and between the clouds.

Light and darkness during the equinox are as much about space as they are about time. Seen from above, Antarctica appears as a rotating disk evenly and sharply split between dark and light. Near the pole, both night and day can appear, even when traveling very short distances. The duration of darkness or light is directly proportional to the distance from the pole. Day and night are increasingly subjective. South of the Antarctic circle, day is a visible solar disk hovering a few degrees above the horizon, appearing to orbit counterclockwise. Anything rising above the ground plane casts long, rotating shadows. At night the disk dips those same few degrees below the horizon into twilight. Flying across the continent via the South Pole means the aircraft's changing position is added to the equation.

Antarctica presents a vertical challenge. Unlike the Arctic, which is oceanic, Antarctica is a continental landmass. A mountain range dividing east and west runs along the peninsula to the Ross Archipelago. Vinson Massif, rising more than 16,000 feet above the sea, lay abeam to the Embarquisa's path to the Pole. The land elevation at the South Pole is close to sea level. The actual elevation is considerably higher because it is covered with 9,000 feet of ice.

Amelia started a long slow climb to clear the mountain range. The sun hung low on the horizon. Despite it being day, the outside air temperature was ninety degrees below zero. It wasn't possible to maintain a sealed, pressurized cabin while also paying out steel cable, adorned with hand-woven textiles, interspersed with gondols. Bahn and Yves equipped the Embarquisa with a heating system that tapped into the turbine engine's compressor section. Although the aircraft's interior was reasonably comfortable if one wore winter clothing, the heat from the engine met the outside chill somewhere in the middle. Riding across Antarctica in the Embarquisa was somewhat akin to driving in a car with the windows down on a cold night with the heater going full blast.

The cable anchors inside the Embarquisa's halfgate were similar to the Kartikeya's, except they were designed to embed into ice rather than the ocean floor. Amelia and Lakshmi masterfully navigated their craft past the black dome of the Amundsen-Scott station using a clock, the position of Acrux, and the sun's azimuth. Their compass and GPS had become increasingly unreliable as they crossed onto the continent.

The Diné had been attaching textiles and fixing gondols to the cable since they left Titicaca and had a 1,500-kilometer lead on the deployment. Three special cables had been swaged, swiveled, and attached to the thermal anchorages.

"First anchor, ready!" Lakshmi called. "Now!" Porter responded by pressing the release. Amelia banked the plane toward the next anchor point. The anchor fell away from the Embarquisa and embedded into the ice surface. The cable continued to reel from the halfgate and through the open hatch in the aft fuselage. The cable followed the anchor as it slid quickly through the melted ice, exhausting a steamy geyser from the entry point. When the thermal fuel expended, the ice quickly froze, cementing the anchor 200 meters beneath the surface. Soon the second and third anchors were secured. The main cable's first lengths slipped through the hatch. Every direction from the pole was north. Amelia and Lakshmi expanded their sextant craft to follow a course along the 110th east parallel.

Lakshmi leaned against the copilot window and looked outside. "This is all so beautiful. It's so clear and crisp. Even when the sun comes up the little bit it does, you can still see stars."

Amelia readjusted their heading. "It is as long as this plane keeps up to the task. It's minus eighty out there. No one else knows where we are, which, by the way, is somewhere between the South Pole and the ocean, and we're towing an unknown weight of textiles and steel cable. We are way, *way* out there in so many ways."

"And that makes it all the more beautiful because we're so present. So vulnerable. We're flying really fast. This will all be over in a few hours. We likely only have another hour to see Antarctica," said Lakshmi, transfixed. "I can't soak it in fast enough, Am."

"I hope you're right," answered Amelia, trying to be pragmatic. "I can imagine at least one or two scenarios where we would have a lot longer to enjoy Antarctica, and I don't think it would be much fun."

"We're at our planet's top. A hundred and eight of the dearest, sweetest people I've ever met are adorning the world's longest clothesline with the finest handmade textiles. We're flying the plane. We *are* the flow of this abundant effort. We're *here* right *now*. I'm not talking about the sun and the stars, Am," stressed Lakshmi, locking eyes with Amelia. "I'm talking about *us*."

"No, I get it. It is incredibly beautiful and equally fleeting. I'm really happy we're together to share it."

110.0 degrees East, 66.57 degrees South

Antarctic Circle

Vanderford Valley

September 23, 2002, 04:27

<u>SKY</u>

Transcendence and peace dwell within this space.

Stars join with earth, as we surrender

With gratitude to the universal flow.

Violet hues connect us to the divine,

Edifying the matter-energy conduit.

Pure love, in deference to the whole,

Opens the crown to the infinite and sacred.

58

ATAJEMOS

For a community that was so spiritually advanced, the White Buddhist shamans on the outskirts of Ordos appeared deceptively primitive. Their pastoral lifestyle was minimalist and one with the desert. They were shepherds and followed where their flock led. Except for the fact that he was shorter in stature compared to his Sainshand counterparts, Ayunga looked more Mongolian than Chinese.

Richly colored strips and lengths of braided fabric were tied to the White Buddhist shaman's loose-fitting, rust-colored robe and fluttered in the breeze. His elaborate headdress was trimmed with feathers. He lit joss sticks over an *Ovoo*, a cairn of rocks and branches with *khadags*, ceremonial scarves, stuck into it. He chanted a shamanistic mantra and accompanied it with the rhythmic beating of his drum, invoking the blessings of benevolent deities of the White Side.

Soon, thirty-six from his community, including him, would set off in six hot air balloons adorned by giant, intricate, multicolored spiritual motifs. Shamans and shamanesses would act as mediators between the human and spirit worlds during the much-awaited union. Then they would become human sacrifices.

The Russian air defense system detected the Kartikeya well before it crossed into their sovereign airspace. They were not yet aware of the gondol signature frequencies. They detected a single-engine aircraft entering Siberian airspace from Arctic waters. Its lack of identification left them no choice but to consider it suspect. The Kartikeya passed less than 150 nautical miles from Sredny Ostrov Airfield. Shortly after dawn, Sredny launched a single AN-26 turboprop with orders to surveil and report.

Intercept protocol dictated approaching an unidentified aircraft from six o'clock and slightly high to mitigate detection and improve surveillance opportunity. The AN-26 crew thought it over for a few minutes before radioing Sredny with their report. They were quite certain they'd be called in for a stern questioning if their report was anything like what they saw. From a distance, they were unable to appreciate the garments' subtle designs. All they could really say was a small, single-engine turboprop moving at 530 knots was deploying a clothesline replete with, well, clothes, which continued as far north as they could see. They started about five nautical miles behind the Kartikeya and followed the clothesline south. Wanting to defend their report with photographs, they descended directly above and within thirty meters of the clothesline. As the aircraft approached one of the gondols attached to the line, it began to climb. Contrary to everything an aviator is taught to balance gravity, thrust, drag and lift to keep an aircraft aloft, this pilot found it increasingly difficult to hold his altitude *down*.

The reconnaissance engineer became increasingly frustrated with the pilot's poor technique. He had requested a stable altitude and airspeed to take photos and videos. After the third altitude swing, he keyed the radio to the flight deck.

"Что ты делаешь? Сделайте этот самолет стабильным сейчас же! Если у нас не будет четких фотографий, они никогда в это не поверят."

What are you doing? Make this plane stable now! If we don't have clear photos, they'll never believe it.

The pilot and copilot agreed with him. The small aircraft was 200 knots faster than the AN-26. If they didn't return with—at least—a clear reconnaissance of this *clothesline*, they were going to be either reassigned or disciplined. The pilot decided to slip to the side and descend to the same altitude. As he did so, the left wing exited the gondol field while the right side remained within it. The aircraft abruptly lost its lateral stability and rolled over. The large transport plane went into an inverted nosedive. It lost almost 4,000 feet during the recovery. After possible structural integrity loss, protocols dictated an immediate return to base. The engineer obtained blurry infrared photos that showed the clothesline. He was quite sure they wouldn't be sufficient for their report. The crew radioed Sredny, reported the inverted maneuver, and returned to base to accept their fate. The information that Sredny command did find interesting was that this small single-engine plane had evaded the AN-26 with an airspeed close to 530 knots.

Sredny alerted Dzhida Air Base. Located 32 kilometers from the Mongolian border, it was south of the Kartikeya's position. Dzhida scrambled two SU-27 Flankers to intercept the unidentified aircraft.

Bahn woke to the sunlight streaming in from the pilot side window casting Yves' figure into a silhouette. He leaned his head against the copilot side window and marveled at Lake Baikal's beauty, stretching long and narrow to the southwest. At times like these Bahn almost didn't mind getting stranded in this god forsaken scale. *I have Sariah to thank for that,* he mused.

"Bahn," Yves called, jolting him out of his reverie. When Bahn followed his gaze, he saw a blur drop vertically through their altitude less than a quarter mile away. They watched as a second interceptor slowed and settled uncomfortably close into a four o'clock position. The SU-27 was camouflaged in royal and sky blue and pewter. Bahn briefly reflected on how deceivingly cheerful their livery was for such a deadly craft. Bahn turned to Yves for his reaction and saw the other interceptor level off smartly from its climb at their ten o'clock.

Bahn held fast as the Kartikeya began to shudder in the SU-27's wake turbulence. Bahn and Yves exchanged glances; they both knew this was a warning. They were likely attempting to contact them by radio, but Bahn hadn't turned one on since they left the Cape, and he wasn't about to now. The cable now extended almost 2,400 nautical miles behind them. Though it was gloriously adorned with fine handicrafts borne up by regularly spaced gondols, it ultimately rendered them vulnerable. Unless they abandoned their mission and cut the Kartikeya loose, they were unable to comply with the interceptors' presumed directive to follow them to their base. The SU-27 pilots had clear photos of the aircraft and cable deployment that they could share with their command. The SU-27, at ten o'clock, aggressively closed ranks with the Kartikeya, creating a moment of severe turbulence in its powerful wake. As it entered the gondol sphere, it rolled sharply left multiple times and dove away. The interceptor to their right dropped under the Kartikeya in pursuit of their comrades. Bahn and Yves could only hold course, airspeed, and altitude. They were quite certain whatever was coming next would be dispatched promptly.

"Turn off the engine," Bahn said to Yves.

"Pardon moi, Capitaine?"

"Yeah, Yves. Shut it down," ordered Bahn, slipping out of his seatbelt. "I'm gonna tell Blue to stop the cable. I want to hold steady here at 17,000." He crawled into the halfgate.

59

APRENDAMOS

Darkness covered the dusty, desert ground. The Nahua had relocated their feasting, music, and promenades to the area surrounding the cable and textile deployment. The deployment had to match the aircraft's ground speed, and the solution to this problem—in both the Embarquisa and Kartikeya—reflected the respective inventors' personalities. Haseya's solution was defined by her need for creative expression, whereas Blueye took a more no-frills approach that befitted his pragmatic personality. Crude yet effective, his contraption got the job done equally efficiently.

Gondols and textiles, fitted with attachment clips, were fed into a hundred-meter-long slotted track that ran underneath the running cable. The track extended further into the Nahua territory to accommodate multiple assemblies. Wheels mounted below the cable rotated at increasing speeds, accelerating the clip through the track until it reached the same velocity as the cable. The final wheel, with a matching wheel on top of the cable, crimped the clip to the cable as it exited through the intention panel.

Those feeding the track with gondols and clip-fitted textiles numbered in the hundreds. Many more Nahua, however, were dancing, eating, and enjoying the deep beats of the bass-driven music from the artists.

What appeared to Bahn to be thin, luminous geometric planes, each perhaps three centimeters square, floated through the air in patterns that he could only describe as mimicking starling flocks. The planes phased through all tints and hues, sometimes collectively expressing a single color, others creating mixed hues by some carrying colors complementary to others. The values and brightness also varied. In areas where the attachments took place, the squares offered sufficient light to allow the work to be done efficiently. In places reserved for dancing, music, and procession, the squares pranced harmoniously to the music in more subdued hues, but their movement and color phasing expressed a distinct creative force.

"Again, you seek your friend Jackson."

Bahn, until then sufficiently distracted by the colorful display, responded to the woman standing next to him. He recognized her voice. "I am. Do you know where I can find him?"

"He's busy, Bahn, directing the work's expansion," said the woman. Her waist-length *huipil*, hand embroidered with vibrant thread, was tucked under an *enagua*, a wrap-around skirt with a white lace flounce. She wore a necklace and hoops in her ears, embroidered with matching floral patterns. She looked to be in her late 50s, but judging by her salt-and-pepper hair, Bahn suspected that she was older. *Must be one of those women who aged like fine wine,* he reflected.

"You must be the Cihuātlahtoāni." Bahn struggled to pronounce her title and hastily added, "Please forgive me if I'm not addressing you appropriately. We are grateful and respectful for all you are doing for us."

"Bahn. This work's most precious and powerful aspect is the collective love behind it. We're all working together to manifest the softening between scales. Call me Quetzal, it's much easier." The Nahua leader's firm lips curved into a subtle smile, accentuating her charisma.

"Quetzal. I need to find Blueye because we've stopped the plane, and we have to stop the deployment. We don't have much time," he urged.

The work and revelry continued. A wave of pixelated hues shimmered over them, washing Quetzal's sunbaked face in a kaleidoscope of color as she gazed into the sky. Without looking away, she replied. "Be at peace, Bahn. Sometimes coming from a place of love means letting go of what you can't control and allowing the flower to unfold as it was designed."

"We're being attacked by Russian fighter jets," said Bahn, perhaps too emphatically. He furtively looked about for anyone who may have overheard his inadvertent outburst and then continued in a calmer tone. "If we stop the plane, they'll have a harder time intercepting us."

"There are strong, resilient, and long-prepared spirits along your route: The Buryat near Lake Baikal, Tengrists near Sainshand, and White Buddhist shamans on the outskirts of Ordos. Each of these tribes is remarkably advanced in the shamanic arts. They celebrate our work as a significant offering to the Sky Father," said Quetzal, smiling at the heavens. "They've assembled sixteen balloons and are mobilizing as we speak. They'll rise to the textile array and offer their devotion and protection. The governments of Russia, Mongolia, and China will not violate the work of these sacred historic tribes. Well, not within the next five hours you'll need to meet the Embarquisa."

"Quetzal, forgive me, but I feel like I'm living in some kind of fairy tale. Shamans? Balloons? Father Sky?" He grinned, dismissively shaking his head. Then his countenance turned grave. "We've got two Russian SU-27s ready to vaporize us. Is that the best you can do?"

Although Bahn was much taller, and Quetzal had to look up to make eye contact, she smiled at him as if out of compassion for a child's naïveté. "You've been disappointed. I understand why your heart is closed."

Bahn looked crestfallen. He wondered how she knew and then remembered his conversation with Blueye about how differences in time and space did not pose a challenge to her. In a desperate attempt to get back to his home scale, he had tried this before, only to fail miserably, time and time again.

Quetzal continued, "Being a warrior means opening your heart when you feel most vulnerable and finding there's more to you than you knew. We need that strength now, Bahn. Go back to the Kartikeya," she urged him, touching him on his shoulder. "Start the engine and continue your work. Tell Monsieur Muladet what you have learned here."

"What have I learned?" he asked flatly.

"Everything will unfold as intended even if it appears to wax into hopelessness along the way," reassured Quetzal, with that knowing smile.

60

RETENGAMOS

The Russian VVS had been suffering from poor resources and pilot training for almost a decade. The pilots who intercepted the Kartikeya were the best Dzhida had to offer. The SU-27s were the most advanced aircraft based there. Intercepting a small high-wing turboprop towing a clothesline piqued their interest, and they dropped their defenses. They were rattled after the SU-27 skittered into multiple rolls while approaching the Kartikeya. They refused to re-engage and returned to base.

The similarity of the incidences between the SU-27s and the AN-26 triggered protocols that alerted VVS command at the Kremlin. The technology employed was evidently powerful, unfamiliar, and currently deployed over sovereign Russian airspace. Orders were issued to withhold any active engagement. *Do nothing to harm the aircraft or its cabled array. Do everything to apprehend the technology in working order.* The aircraft was already passing into Mongolian airspace. The technology was valuable but not worth risking engagement with the PRC. The cabled deployment had the same effect on the AN-26 as the aircraft had on the SU-27. All focus shifted to the anchorage at the North Pole.

61

CAMBIEMOS

Yves, understandably concerned at Bahn's indecision, remained compliant as always. The two men sat motionless as the Kartikeya continued on its journey south. It had been half an hour since Bahn returned from the halfgate. The apprehension was palpable.

"Everything will unfold as intended. That's what she told me," reported Bahn, shaking his head in frustration. "The problem is there are a lot of people with intentions, and they aren't all the same."

Yves knew better than to reply to Bahn while he sorted things out vocally.

"Where are we now?"

Yves pointed to the map. They'd crossed into Mongolia. The Russians had left them alone.

"Maybe she was right about the Russians. If she was, we might be okay crossing this peaceful Buddhist country for the next forty minutes. Then we've got, what, three hours or so crossing mainland China?"

"Peut-être, Capitaine, the Cihuātlahtoāni, elle a raison."

"Right about what?"

"May be is our intentions besoin de changer. Est-il possible que nous ayons l'intention de notre propre succès?"

"You're proposing we *intend* ourselves across the People's Republic of China?" asked Bahn, cocking an eyebrow.

"N'est-ce pas ainsi que nous entrons dans la demi-porte?" shrugged Yves.

"The halfgate is different. It's made by people who care about community."

"Et nous? Ne nous soucions-nous pas de la communauté?"

"Of course, we do, Yves," scoffed Bahn, taken aback. "You know how I feel about that."

"Alors pourquoi, Capitaine, we not intend it now?"

110.0 degrees east, 45.0 degrees north

Sainshand, Dornogovi Province, Mongolia

Eastern Gobi Desert steppe

September 23, 2002, 07:21

BERTH

Passion weaves through our humble essence

As desire mingles with the soft currents of joy.

A dance of pleasure, washed in tints of tangerine,

Each movement reflecting our inner truth.

Hearts so swell and gently reverberate.

Peace, prosperity and knowledge will spring

From this emotionally sacred sacral space.

62

IMAGINEMOS

The full moon rose above the horizon while the sun dropped below. Continuous twilight soothed any distinction between day and night. The Embarquisa, now 1,400 nautical miles from the South Pole, let the last sharp cliff of reflective Antarctic ice pass beneath her, giving way to the Antarctic Ocean's dark expanse. Although their intended course would pass within 180 nautical miles of Australia's west coast, they wouldn't see land again until they crossed over Yogyakarta, in southern Indonesia, some thirty-five hundred miles farther.

Porter held the fur-lined hood close to his face, enough to allow a hole to peek through without freezing his eyes. He maneuvered his body around the bulkhead to glimpse the blurred cable stream, lined with textiles and gondols, discharging at 530 knots. The moon illuminated the cable. Through the rear hatch, he had a better perspective of their lofted product. Beyond the plane's wake, the textiles hung from the cable and furled gently in the cold. Resembling a regular pattern but otherwise indistinguishable in the subdued light, he could see the gondols' bumps fixed to the cable between long, textile sections. He retreated into the cabin's warmth, removed his winter coat, folded the jacket from Keiti close to his chest, and slipped through the halfgate's front panel.

Freshly plowed rows of peaty, dark earth absorbed his fall. The sky was overcast with exaggerated lowlights, promising moisture. Porter gathered his footing on a row top and brushed the soil from Keiti's jacket. He stood up within a concentric array of spools, deep and close enough to hide the outermost rings. Each spool was mounted two meters above the plowed field on sturdy posts and appeared to be about four times taller than the reels he and Bahn had picked up at Lenny's warehouse. Each one glowed with vertical stripes of cyan, magenta, and emerald. At the center of the circle stood a steep, wooden open-structure pyramid, straddling a halfgate that was set upon a red, sandstone platform. Overhead, the cable sang as it payed from an unseen spool toward the pyramid. A swiveling pulley, mounted at the structure's top, shuddered as it redirected the naked, steel cable downward into the cube. Moving just as rapidly, the dressed and gondoled cable drew away taught from the halfgate's side and disappeared into the shadows under the spools' illuminated majesty.

"Those dusty spools were a bit too boring for me. I had to dress them up a bit. What do you think?"

Porter started at Haseya's abrupt appearance. "I know better than to appreciate you for a colorful dressing up. You know what I came to see."

"Come on. Mind the cables. They'll wreck your day if you get anywhere near them. Follow me through the front panel." Haseya lifted her knee to the top of the sandstone platform and crawled through the panel. Porter donned the jacket as he observed the cable whining through the pulley above Haseya's halfgate. He felt the oscillating wind snap around the cube as each textile exploded through the intention panel on the other side. He placed his palms on the platform edge, lifted himself, and entered with grace.

Porter and Haseya walked together at a relaxed pace on a well-worn path. From a distance, the landscape appeared to be a gentle slope, free from any significant features. Further afield, two snow-dusted parallel mountain ranges defined their space hundreds of meters into the periwinkle sky. They stepped around oak brush, sage, and granite boulders in various degrees of degeneration. They straddled fast-flowing clear-water creeks destined to settle elsewhere. Haseya let her hands brush against sage leaves and brought her gently oiled fingertips to her nose.

"Maybe I should take the jacket off," Porter said softly, almost under his breath.

Haseya replied clearly, without turning away from the bright purple thistle she was admiring. "Were you expecting to see something different? I thought you wanted to understand the progress."

"I do. I knew you had nested a halfgate, but I still haven't been able to resolve how a scale change would allow the Diné to attach the textiles and gondols to the cable while it's moving," Porter admitted, throwing his hand up. He had been racking his brain about the problem ever since he first saw the nested halfgate. "Even if you change the scale relative to the surrounding halfgate, the Diné would still have to be in here, and their scale would remain the same relative to the cable. It wouldn't slow it down enough to allow them to attach anything."

Haseya stopped walking and sat against a smooth granite rock in the semi-shade of a manzanita. "Stop here for a minute. Sit down. Tell me what you see."

Porter sat down cross-legged in the degenerated granite covering the path. He placed his open palm on the ground behind him and leaned into his arms. He felt the warm sunshine trickle through the dark, red bark of the manzanita. A lone black crow lazily hovered in the breeze and disappeared below the sagebrush. His eye caught the quick dart of a lizard behind a rock. The narrow creek burbled gently behind them. "I see the desert. I appreciate the details, but I still don't understand. This is all your manifestation. Can't you tell me how you're doing it?"

"Maybe you should take the jacket off, Jonas."

Porter removed the jacket and laid it on the rock. He stood inside a steel-gray void. His eyes perceived a homogenous, muted gray all around him, but it may as well have been black because it lacked any definition. All the sounds ceased. Haseya was gone. He reached back for the jacket. It and the rock he laid it on were gone. The only sensation he could perceive was gravity holding his body to a solid, leaden floor. He felt an emptiness. Haseya wasn't only invisible to him, she and everything else he had been experiencing, was gone in a way that instilled a foreboding sense of isolation. He walked forward. He could feel his weight against the ground and the motion of walking, but absolutely nothing changed. He spoke as though she were near him. His voice was unaccompanied by any space-defining reflection or echo. He called out to her, conceding that she had made her point, but there was no reply. After thirty minutes, he decided to try dead reckoning his way back to the intention panel they had entered from. He thought backward through what had happened since he came in, pacing as best he could to the start. The cable spools, still mounted above the ground but without any of the colors Haseya had added, began to fade in and out. Their circular mounting pattern helped him orient.

He heard Haseya's voice as he had heard Sariah's. "See, you can do it too, Jonas. Halfgates are truly beautiful works of creation. There aren't many limitations in here. Anything that goes in can come back out."

"And pretty much anything you can imagine can happen while you're in here."

Haseya held the jacket out to Jonas, who folded it over his arm. She waved her hand gracefully to her left, bidding Jonas to look. The entire company of Diné stood by the cable, pulled tight across the plain, each smiling and talking with ease to their neighboring laborer as they attached truly remarkable pieces of clothing. At the line's end, four of them passed and attached gondols. Once the entire line was adorned, the Diné stepped away by only a single stride, and the entire line of clothing and gondols faded into transparency. The cable remained but did not appear to move. They each picked up the next piece from their stack and attached it. This cycle continued at an almost lazy pace, certainly nothing compared to what he witnessed rushing from the Embarquisa's back door. He smiled and sighed gently as he turned to Haseya.

"You don't need to slow the cable at all, do you?" he beamed.

Haseya smiled at his enlightenment. "Nope."

63

RESONEMOS

The Bryansk's Kapitan stood on the conning tower deck to observe the equipment being offloaded. Eight sailors, dressed in full arctic gear, loaded two sleds with equipment and began hiking away from the submarine. The sonar officer had determined the coordinates of what they suspected were three anchor cables strung tightly between the ice ceiling and the sea floor. The unusual sonar returns had piqued his interest because they resonated with the sonar pings, each at slightly different frequencies. One of the cables had been selected as their primary target. The surface crews were ordered to locate the other two and sever those cables. The Bryansk submerged under the broken ice as the surface crews contemplated their fate.

The crew used the coordinates from the sonar officer to locate the anchor cables as they protruded from the ice and extended into the sky. Each cable was covered in ice and frosted with delicate crystals. The surface crew gathered at the southernmost cable and began unloading equipment from their sleds. Within fifty minutes, they had installed a heated, cast-iron bushing around the cable, which insulated and separated it from the nine feet of ice between the surface and the Arctic Sea. They filled the collar with white lithium grease. The crew split into two groups, each departing for the other two anchor cables. Beneath the ice, the Bryansk's scuba squadron had bound one of their own cables unwound from a heavy duty winch inside the submarine to the collared anchor cable. The cable fed through a gasketed portal in the Bryansk's hull, which allowed the cable to pass through it while mitigating blow-by, as long as the ambient pressure remained below two atmospheres.

Once the winch had taken up the slack in the cable, the surface crews severed the other two cables with acetylene torches, and the dive crews did the same to the one extending below the Bryansk. The added lift from the cable flowing through the greased collar oscillated through the Bryansk, which eventually began surfacing. The captain ordered the dive officers to flood the ballast tanks to compensate and hold depth. Once stabilized, the Bryansk began slowly winching the cable attached to the Kartikeya into its shallow arctic ocean depth. The surface crews returned to the bushing and waited for the four-way link between the three anchors and the main cable to descend to the ice surface. They radioed the Bryansk directly below them to hold the winch while they disconnected the two severed anchor cables from the main one. The winch was then re-engaged.

64

RECONVENGAMOS

Quinto Condottiero received a coded message from their contact in the United States. Their communications were strictly scope and time limited. The code asked for a status report on Pica Suave. QC anticipated this request. They, too, were displeased that so much time had passed since they last heard from their contact in Peru. He was overdue by three days. QC deployed a team of five mercenaries tasked with finding Chacalito and obtaining any and all intelligence that he had collected regarding the anomalous signal he'd been tracking.

The team flew by helicopter from a QC base at Aeropuerto Cobo across Amazonas and Acre to Chahaytire. As much as Chacalito thought he was independent and autonomous, it simply wasn't true. QC had tracking devices installed in his jeep, and they found it—and him—easily. The team of professionally trained soldiers dressed indigenously and avoided speaking to anyone unless absolutely necessary. They spread out to look for him. One walked through the plaza in town. He didn't speak Quechua but recognized that the townsfolk did. The gente, now endowed en masse with superior vision, were well aware of an outsider's presence. He tried asking some questions in Spanish about their weavings but was met with questioning looks and a feigned lack of understanding by those who understood him. He reconvened with the group at the jeep. They searched it thoroughly and found two memory cards under the front seat. In addition to photographs of a man and a woman standing near an aircraft, it included a video of the Embarquisa lifting vertically, with a motionless propeller, and then heading southeast after the engine started. They uploaded the cards' contents to OASIS and advised QC. They departed southeast in the helicopter with their sensors set to find the anomalous signal.

110.0 degrees east, 45.0 degrees south

765nm SSW of Perth, Australia

The Austral Ocean

September 23, 2002, 06:58

<u>VISION</u>

The eye of the mind sees the unseen links,

Sharpening perception of the divine.

Iridescent indigo reveals hidden truth.

Transcendental understanding bursts forth

As wisdom parts the veil of illusion.

May you, best beloved, adore the creative,

As she emerges clear and foresightful.

65

COINCIDAMOS

"Colonel Fowler, sir!" boomed his aide over the intercom. "NAVSOC Point Mugu is on the phone for you sir!"

"Fowler here."

"Colonel. Lieutenant Commander Jeffries, NAVSOC reconnaissance, sir," came the voice on the other end of the line. "We found an 85% match to your sample data."

"Nice work, Lt. Commander," praised Fowler. *We're finally getting somewhere.* "Where is the plane now? Is it moving?"

"One end is, Colonel, bearing 360 at 530 knots, sir."

"What do you mean one end, Lt. Commander?" queried Fowler.

"Sir, the source of the signal is along a line. It starts at the South Pole and extends northward along the 110th East parallel. Current location of the end—did you say it was a plane, sir? The end is extending northward at 530 knots and is currently 260 nautical miles west of Australia. Twenty-three degrees, thirty-one minutes south latitude, sir."

"Lt. Commander, how can it be a line you are picking up?" asked Fowler rubbing his brow, bemused. "The signal only comes from the aircraft."

"Negative, Colonel. The signal is strong along the entire line just described. The whole line is an 85% match to the signal you gave us, sir."

66

INTERPONGAMOS

Captain Dylan and Colonel Fowler had assembled in an inter-service command and communications center at Eglin to video conference with General Rappar. "How did we lose him, Colonel?" demanded Rappar. His enlarged image on the monitor was more intimidating than he was in person. "One day we have photos and video, and the next we discover they've traversed Antarctica and are well on their way north."

Fowler shifted uncomfortably in his seat as he replied. "One of our primary assets—we believe he took those photos—went missing three days ago. A backup team found data cards in his jeep and uploaded the media. We can only assume he has been captured or compromised, General."

"Considering the target's present position, your asset is no longer our concern," said Rappar acidly. "It's less than three hours from Kalimantan in Indonesia. What assets do we have in that area to intercept and destroy?"

"The Stennis carrier group is in the Bay of Bengal," reported Dylan promptly. "If the target continues on current course and speed, it will come within Super Hornet range in four hours. They could intercept and perform reconnaissance but not for long."

Rappar leaned into the camera. "Clearly, that's insufficient. This is a strategic military operation. I want valid recommendations. Now, officers!" Dylan's desperation to control the situation within the Navy was eroding his focus.

Fowler interjected, interrupting Dylan's response. "The data cards from the jeep in Chahuaytire had more than photographs and videos."

Dylan turned toward Fowler with suppressed contempt at his competitiveness. He did his best to compose himself in front of Rappar, increasingly aware of his vulnerability.

Rappar cocked his head with a Darwinistic sneer. "Apparently, we don't have all the cards on the table, Captain. Explain yourself, Colonel."

"Sir, we found a schematic diagram of a device designed to remotely disable a turbine aircraft engine," said Fowler. "The schematic included the codes to activate it. We have reason to conclude our Columbian asset had opportunity to plant the device into the aircraft engine before he went MIA. If we can approach within three nautical miles of the aircraft, we can activate it."

"What do we know about the device? What damage will it inflict?"

"We can't be certain of its destructive capacity. It will, at a minimum, disable the engine. I believe it's our best strategic option, General." Fowler's eyes shifted. He was uncomfortably aware of Dylan's anxiety.

Rappar considered this new piece of information. "Transmit the activation codes to the Stennis, Captain Dylan. We have open clearance from the RAAF to land and refuel at Learmonth as needed. Scramble the Super Hornets now. Orders are weapons free." Dylan's relief was palpable. "And Colonel, I want whoever we have at Amundsen-Scott to find where this thing starts. I want answers and I want them fast."

67

MIREMOS

The sun shone brightly and hot that morning. The sky was hazy. The Zurihe air base, mainland China's largest, a mere 125 nautical miles distant, responded as the Kartikeya crossed, unidentified, into Chinese airspace. Four Shenyang J-11s departed Zurihezhen and flanked the Kartikeya in loose formation within seven minutes. At this point, *intention* was easy. Bahn and Yves had little choice. They did not make any attempt to communicate. Their sole intention was to continue south on course and altitude, deploying their elegantly adorned cable.

The lead J-11 pilot, confident the situation was easily contained with one warplane, ordered his tongzhi to disperse and return to base. He very slowly brought his jet into a tighter formation with the Kartikeya until he felt his jet begin to roll. Baffled, he backed away gently and held that formation. He experimented three more times, from slightly different altitudes and relative positions, each time as carefully as the first. He slowed his airspeed to surveil the cable behind them. When he had fallen behind enough to escape the Kartikeya's wake, he had a clear view of the garments and textiles. As he did with the aircraft, he approached the cable until he could feel the roll initiating and then backed away. He brought his jet forward again and held a three o'clock position to the Kartikeya. Bahn lifted his sunglasses. The J-11 pilot lifted his glare shield. For a moment, the pilot and Bahn looked into each other's eyes.

The Kremlin, concerned that Beijing might interpret the Kartikeya and its deployment to be of Russian origin, made diplomatic contact. The communiqué offered assurances that the unusual deployment originated north of Russian airspace and was currently holding altitude at 5,200 meters aligned with the 110th meridian. It presented no threat other than being unidentified and unauthorized. The communiqué indicated, with appropriate reservation, that the deployment included various garments and textiles attached to a steel cable. The Kremlin conveyed its respect and recognition of the PRC's sovereignty and offered support for any decisions Beijing might make to defend its airspace. It also implied that the aircraft and its deployment may be employing technology that could be beneficial to both countries and that capturing it, rather than destroying it, may be preferable. Beijing acknowledged the communiqué and began its own investigation.

68

GUIÑEMOS

Colonel Fowler was pleased to see a new incoming post from QC. He dismissed the gathered officers. Logging into his laptop, he began perusing the photographs and videos. He didn't recognize the people photographed, but the Embarquisa slipping from her mooring ropes and slowly lifting into the air grabbed his full attention. The crew in the cockpit seemed to be as attentive as any pilot would be during liftoff. The Embarquisa gracefully yawed left as her wings rocked, restraining her urge to fly. The white, spring wheat furled beneath her and fell away as she rose skyward. A starter motor's whine preceded the rotation of the propeller. The primary fuel injection lit in a puff of smoke as the turbine speed surpassed the need for the starter motor. When the compressor developed eighty percent of its rotational torque, the secondary fuel valves opened, surging the turbine to ground idle. Even in its slowest functioning state, the propeller bit and whorled thousands of cubic meters of humid air, propelling the wishful curves of the Embarquisa's wings upward. Fowler opened the door to his office. Knob in hand, he asked his secretary to get Captain Dylan on the phone.

69

LEVANTEMOS

S ixteen hot air balloons launched, each carrying a büge and an idugan, supported by four initiates. There were five balloons from Baikal, five from Sainshand, and six from Ordos. Each balloon carried one hundred meters of braided rope, woven from various plant and animal fibers, with a strong metal triple hook lashed to its end. The ropes were secured to the balloon basket's structural members. After attaining sufficient altitude, the hooks and ropes were extended over the basket's side. The Kartikeya had passed Baikal and Sainshand and was 150 nautical miles north of Ordos. Winds from the west drove the balloons toward the textile array. By adjusting the heat in the envelopes, the initiates guided the balloons until their ropes slid against the cable array and the hooks engaged the cable. The initiates drew the ropes in hand-over-hand, docking the baskets. Their intention was to spread themselves along the cable as far apart as possible to create an obviously visible support array against any aggressive black shaman encroachment.

As the initiates closed the gap between the basket and the cable, they entered the gondol cylinder surrounding it. The reduced counterbalance between their weight and the envelope's buoyancy made it increasingly difficult to pull the basket down to the cable. They concluded that there was a repulsive force keeping them from approaching this Sky Father's work. The initiates pulled the balloon as close as they could, then tied the rope off to the basket. The büge picked up a separate, shorter rope length and tied one end to the basket. He lifted his leg over the side and instinctively shimmied down the rope to the cable. He was surprised to find himself weightless, and within a few meters, he was able to descend easily hand-over-hand without entwining his feet. The idugan witnessed his graceful movements with reverence. The büge tied the shorter rope to the cable with a slip knot and tossed the loose end of the knot to the initiate.

He signaled to the initiates to let the long rope go. They did so and then watched in awe as he picked up the hook lashed to the rope and began walking gingerly along the cable top, weighted only by the section of rope below the gondol cylinder, and stepping over the textiles and gondols attached to it. When he had extended the hooked rope to its full hundred-meter length, he reattached the hook to the cable and signaled the initiates to tug the end of the slip knot. Once the knot untied, the balloon rapidly accelerated in a ninety-degree arc, tethered to its radius, until it was hovering directly above the büge who had temporarily secured himself to the cable. They repeated this process, soon coming to the understanding that the work was far less laborious if they let heat out of the envelope. In this manner, they swung along the cable away from their original attachment point. The other balloons followed suit until the idugan declared they were sufficiently distributed along the cable. The five balloon groups from Sainshand attached and distributed themselves the same way.

The six balloons in Ordos benefitted from a light north wind. Anticipating the Kartikeya's passage, they launched before its arrival to travel south before gaining altitude and attaching themselves. By staggering their departure times and varying their ascent rates, the Ordos shamans were able to distribute themselves from Ordos to as far south as the Guangxi province. By the time the Kartikeya crossed the Xan Jiang River, the distance from Lake Baikal to Guiping was dotted every hundred nautical miles with a shaman, a shamaness, four initiates, and a colorful hot air balloon. Being that they were enveloped in one extended gondol field, they were communicating with each other through a linguistically gifted explorer from an adjacent symmetric scale. She respectfully played Mother Sky's role. The büges and idugans chanted ancient mantras in unison. That song, duly broadcast on encrypted military frequencies, moved the not-quite-hardened pilots' hearts to allow the Kartikeya to pass unrestricted across Hainan Island into the airspace above the South China Sea. Sixteen colorful balloons shone gloriously in the mid-morning sun, standing watch over handcrafted legacies emerging from richly overdue cocoons.

110 degrees east, 23.5 degrees north

Tropic of Cancer

Guiping, Guangxi, PRC
September 23, 2002, 10:01

POWER

Warmth, brilliance and abundant solar flame

Breathe confident resilience to the core.

The radiant self actuates and asserts.

Energy radiates, progressing forward

With purpose, action and strength.

Feathers shed that golden alkaline ash.

Power and will arise from within.

70

CRISPEMOS

Dylan never saw the Embarquisa's video. The moment he recognized Porter in the photograph, his gut twitched with anxiety. Dylan's mind was replaying the Trade Center briefing as he strategically processed a rapid thought and question cascade: *How is he possibly alive? He knows. He must know. Not acceptable. The condition magnifies the possibility of undermining the entire operation. Leadership is exposed and vulnerable. What was Fowler blabbering about? Anomalous signal? Nothing else mattered. Porter needs to be dead. Every second he's alive is dangerous. Where is he? What's the fastest and most effective event set? Which is the most acute asset?*

Rear Admiral Sutton, Captain Dylan's commanding officer, had been summoned to Washington along with Dylan. He stood by quite uncomfortably as Rappar addressed Dylan directly. "Your operation is deeply compromised, Captain, and you've been unaware for over a year," bellowed Rappar. "Give me even one good reason I shouldn't have you relieved immediately." Rappar paced slowly behind Captain Dylan, who stood uneasily at attention.

"Sir!" Dylan replied. "I know Porter better than anyone. He isn't married and has no children. Both parents are dead. I groomed him during ordnance training. I can anticipate his next moves, sir!"

"You expect me to believe that, Captain, when your asset has not only been alive but rogue and active for over a year without your knowledge?" Rappar thundered.

"Sir, Porter was on the third floor of the south tower when it came down. I confirmed that his tracking device detonated and remained inside during the collapse." He almost winced at how inadequate he must sound. "His being alive defies all probability."

Rappar brought his face within three inches of Dylan's and lowered his voice to a menacing grumble. "So, what's his next move, then Captain? If I don't court martial and charge you with treason tomorrow morning, what will your orders be?"

Perhaps there's hope for me yet, thought Dylan, continuing with renewed vigor. "Sir! He was last seen heading south toward Argentina. We don't have his current location, but we do know his activities are associated with an interference signal that was first identified near Hill Air Force base. My orders, sir, will be to relay that signature to Naval intelligence and have every satellite available looking for it. We will find him sir."

"I hope I don't have to explain that merely finding him is insufficient, Captain."

It was Dylan who lowered his voice this time. "Sir! I'll finish the job as it was intended, sir."

"I'll advise Colonel Fowler," said Rappar after pausing to stare into Dylan's face. Rappar glanced briefly at Rear Admiral Sutton to convey his intent. "You'll report to Colonel Fowler and proceed under his direct command. Don't disappoint me again, Captain."

"Sir! Yes, Sir!"

71

ABSORBAMOS

Hine's facial muscles were mortared with stoicism as he processed the news. He had already begun to absorb the gravity of his decisions. He felt isolated and detached. It was his responsibility alone to address the full repercussions, and he was certain it was more punitive than his comprehension would allow. It was too late to feel, but an indispensable part of him still did. He wondered what his daughter would think if she knew. Was there any opportunity to redeem himself? None of this could come back to him. He'd been careful to stay inculpable. Ironically, that truth, for him, was the least desirable outcome. He would carry alone, from that day forward, the complete and cancerous truth entwined with his heart. No one could help or truly care. No one.

72

MOSTREMOS

The outside air temperature at 16,000 feet had risen to minus seventeen centigrade, a welcome sign that they were making progress toward warmth. Still, the Embarquisa was over ocean, with no land in sight. In an hour, they would be 240 nautical miles from Margaret River, and an hour after that, they would be able to see Coral Bay's surf and imagine themselves sunbathing on western Australia's warm beaches. Inside the nested halfgate, a conversation also began to thaw.

Escuchó nuevamente la voz tranquila pero firme de Sariah. "Porque decidiste ir al dentro?"

"Quien eres? Como estas hablando conmigo? Donde estas?" Chacalito buscó frenéticamente la voz.

"No es importante. No debes estar alli. Contésteme. Porque entraste a la media puerta? Que quieres?" Ella sabía que tenía que superar su resolución.

"No te puedo ver. Pero siento su voz en el corazon. Como lo puedes hacer?" La paciencia del Chacalito se agotó. "Es tu que tienes que contestar, mujer." Chacalito tomó su arma, olvidando que la había perdido en la cocina.

"Ya se quien eres. Eres un artesano del conocimiento." El tono de Sariah se volvió casi tranquilizador. "Tambien conozco su corazon y es simpatico."

"No sabes nada. No me conoces," dijo Chacalito indignado.

"Si se cuantas veces te han lastimado, Chacalito. Se cuantas veces lo has intentado. Sé lo mucho que te preocupas por otras personas. Pero vendes tu trabajo a aquellos que sabes que causará dolor. Tus intenciones son buenas pero tus acciones no están de acuerdo."

La respuesta de Chacalito fue inexpresiva. "Lo hago por el dinero."

"Y sin embargo sé que tus intereses están mucho más vivos que eso. Creo que estés aqui por otras razones," sondeada Sariah.

"Están construyendo algo profundamente hermoso." A pesar de sus reservas, había una nota de optimismo en su voz "Quiero ser parte de esto. Quiero que mi mano esté en ella."

"Claramente ya lo eres. Todo lo que tienes que hacer para profundizar es comprometer tu intención con alguien que ama la vida," Sariah engatusada.

Chacalito se burló, "No hay dinero en eso."

"Claro que si. Si quieres ser parte de la vida, si quieres amar la vida, debes dejar atrás esas cosas que no están vivas."

"Muéstrame cómo," Chacalito suplicó.

"Os muestra. Muéstranos con las manos. Muéstranos el trabajo que pueden hacer las manos para que podamos confiar en ti," Saríah lo animó. "Demuestre con su trabajo que sus intenciones son sustentar y nutrir la vida. Inserta la mano, Chacalito."

73

DESENMARAÑEMOS

David Brockman, the Vice President's Chief of Staff, ushered General Rappar into the office and closed the door behind them. Hine was finishing a phone call and motioned for Rappar to come in.

"I'm meeting with Rappar now. I'll call them when we're finished. Yes, yes. I understand, Fisher. I told you I'd call them." Hine hung up abruptly and leaned into the cradled receiver. The beads of sweat on his brow betrayed him. Without looking up, he said, "Tell me what you know, Rappar."

"We found a match to the signal that was identified near Hill," said Rappar flatly.

"Shoot it down. Shoot it down! Like you did to that airliner a year ago," Hine barked. "Is that so hard, General?"

Rappar paused. The muscles around his closed jaw flexed. "Don't you put any of this on me, Hine. This was your idea, and it's unraveling now."

Hine launched the receiver into a credenza and stepped formidably around the desk. Rappar leaned slightly backward as Hine delivered full-volume fury into his face. "Who do you think they'll believe when I pin this on you, Rappar? A rogue general commits treason against his president and country? You'll fry, Rappar! You'll go down as an icon of infamy! I'll see to it personally. I strongly suggest you get some perspective, General! Find a solution to this problem. Do it now!"

Rappar said nothing as he held the Vice President's stare. Hine relaxed slightly and turned toward the window. "Tell me why you haven't shot the plane down."

"First of all, the signal isn't only coming from the plane. It's being emitted along a line starting at the South Pole and, as of thirty minutes ago, extending northward along the 110th east parallel to 23 degrees south latitude," Rappar rattled off mechanically.

"What? I'm not a human globe, Rappar," fumed Hine, throwing his hands up in frustration. "Where is that in terms normal people can understand?"

"It's off the west coast of Australia," scoffed Rappar.

The jab was lost on Hine. "You're telling me there's a continuous line, not an airplane, a line—from the South Pole—to Australia? And this kid, Porter, who escaped from the Twin Towers is alive?"

"We have evidence to suggest he's flying the plane, and it's moving north at 530 knots."

"Where's he going?" asked Hine.

"What we know is the line, as it currently exists, remains remarkably steady along the 110th east parallel. We can only assume it will continue on course."

"You said 530 knots? How fast is that?"

"If they continue, they'll cross the equator in a little less than two hours," explained Rappar, matter-of-factly.

"And if they keep going? Where will they go?"

"They'll fly over Indonesia, then into China, and eventually cross into Russian airspace."

"Rappar. This needs to end. Now! I want all resources on this. Find out where it starts in Antarctica. Get the Australian Air Force out there to investigate the plane. And Rappar," said Hine, pointing a threatening finger at Rappar. "That kid. Porter? He needs to be dead. Yesterday. Do you understand?"

"I'll do what I can. This is outside our jurisdiction." Rappar buttoned his coat and turned toward the door.

"You know very well that jurisdiction has little to do with what has to happen here, Rappar. I want another report in an hour. Get out of here."

The Chief of Staff stood in the doorway as Rappar opened the door and stood aside. Hine barked around him. "Brockman! Get them on the line. I need to make that call right now."

74

AHORREMOS

Of the 71 people who wintered over at the Amundsen-Scott geodesic dome that winter, not one was military. Communications had improved greatly with the TDRS relay, but it was still slow, intermittent, prioritized, and less than reliable. The incoming message from NAVSOC was marked "high priority" and for the station director, Caitlyn Ekstrom's eyes only. Although she was contracted as a civilian, as director, she had top-secret clearance, and part of her role was to ensure that any defense directives were given the highest priority. Ekstrom downloaded the encrypted message onto a data card and took it to her quarters to review. The message included the gondol's radio interference pattern. She was directed to scan a ten-mile radius around the station using whatever means available and/or necessary and report her findings immediately.

The station used a nine-meter radio antenna for local communications. She programmed the com system to scan through the frequency range, looking for incoming signals. It was too early in the season for any outside transports. Any crack of light that may have preceded the equinox was blotted out by cloud cover from the blizzard that had been battering the station for weeks. The outside temperature was minus sixty-two centigrade. If there were a signal from the outside, it would be cleanly unaccompanied. And it was. The frequency scan stopped and identified a signal. It was faint but clear. What Ekstrom *couldn't* do with the station's equipment, however, was identify the bearing or distance to the source.

She asked the station's logistical engineers, Brandin and Monte, to take the Spryte snowcat to locate the source with their onboard radio. It would be a trial-and-error excursion. If the signal became stronger, they'd continue. If it did not, they would have to choose a different course. They both had formal search and rescue training and employed those skills to follow and record a grid pattern extending outward from the station. The Spryte was equipped with bright headlights and a rotating beacon, but the blizzard afforded them little forward visibility. Within 20 minutes, they'd triangulated the general direction of the source and continued toward it, verifying the increasing signal strength. About three miles north of the station, the left side of the Spryte suddenly lifted and came to a halt, almost rolling onto its side. Monte slowly reversed the tractor and it came back level to the ice surface. Both engineers alighted from the Spryte and into the blizzard to investigate what they ran into.

Back on the Spryte, Brandin keyed the radio. "Scott base. Excursion team one." The radio in the base command center crackled to life.

Ekstrom replied, "Base here. Go ahead."

"We found the source. It's a guy wire. It's not located where we have any scheduled antennas. We almost rolled the Spryte when we ran into it."

"And you've confirmed it's the transmission source?"

"That's affirm, boss lady. What do you want us to do now?"

"Is it steel? How thick is it, Brandin?" she asked.

"It's covered in ice. We have the acetylene torch kit in the Spryte. If you'd like us to clear off the ice, we could tell you."

"Can you wait there for a few minutes until I get some answers?" Ekstrom asked.

"No problem. The heater in the Spryte is nice and cozy. Standing by."

Five minutes later, Ekstrom contacted the excursion crew. "Base to excursion team one."

"We're here, boss lady. What's up?"

"You have the acetylene kit?" she questioned.

"That's affirm," Brandin replied.

"I want you to sever the cable. Cut through it if you can. Let me know what happens."

"Roger that, boss lady. Hold on one."

Despite the howling blizzard, the crew was able to melt the ice within minutes. The cable whined as Monte held the torch. When it severed, it whip-snapped into the darkness.

"All done, boss lady. What now?"

"Are you still receiving the signal?"

"That's affirm. Not as strong, but it's still there."

"Mark the coordinates where you found it, Brandin. We may need to go back later."

"Roger that."

"Get back here. Be careful guys. The storm is getting worse."

Monte keyed the mic from the left side of the Spryte. "Tell Mr. Chef to save us some of that meatloaf. We'll be home in thirty."

110 degrees east, 23.5 degrees south

Tropic of Capricorn

203 nm due west of Coral Bay Australia

September 23, 2002, 09:34

<u>BEACON</u>

Above our hearts we sing, dancing with fire.

Voices set free in the azure river's flow

Express a place of love with inner truth,

Bridging nature and nurture with genuine ease.

The throat finds form within authentic speech,

Each word a product of our soul's bleeding.

Communication is our foundation.

75

SOPORTEMOS

Fowler and Dylan conferenced with Rappar. "Let's hear your report, Captain," insisted Rappar, his image filling the big screen.

"The Super Hornets are deployed. The Stennis was 2,600 nautical miles from the target when they departed. They'll be almost out of range when they intercept. If they have sufficient endurance, they will engage. If not, they'll refuel at Learmonth and re-engage," reported Dylan, his darkened eyes exposing his lack of sleep.

Rappar turned his attention to Fowler. "And the anchorage, Colonel? What's the report from the South Pole?"

"Amundsen-Scott located the anchorage. They found an unscheduled thirteen-millimeter wire rope cable that was transmitting the interference signal. The cable anchorage has been severed, sir." Fowler wanted nothing more than to disassociate himself from Dylan's train wreck.

"Where are they going, Captain?" Rappar was tag-teaming them relentlessly.

"Sir, I ordered my team at Point Mugu to extrapolate their trajectory. They employed the SAR scans along their extended path, and well..." Captain Dylan paused uneasily, "...sir, we have another situation."

"Captain?" responded Rappar with a puzzled expression.

"Sir, there's another line extending the same signature signal along the 110th east parallel from the *North* Pole," Dylan paused to let this sink in. Rappar remained poker-faced, and Dylan continued. "Last known position is 21 degrees

54 minutes north latitude. At their current closure rate, they'll converge at or near the equator within two hours, sir."

Rappar's bald head gleamed with sweat in the room's stark light as he leaned into the camera. "Has either array presented a threat, Captain?"

Fowler interjected. "Other than our assumption that Lieutenant Commander Porter is rogue and possibly hostile, no sir."

Fowler paused briefly before continuing. "We can also expect that both the Russian and Chinese governments will be doing more than asking questions, especially if the source of this extension from the north originated from US airspace, sir. There is potential for conflict. We also have to assume that when the planes meet, we must be prepared to escalate."

"How has the transmission line been affected by the severing of the south anchorage, Colonel?"

"Sir, our last scan shows it's still in place."

"Colonel, I've read the file on Porter. Whatever he's doing, he's clever, mindful, and resourceful. Do you think he'd be so short-sighted as to plan for only one anchor point for a project like this?" Rappar scoffed.

Fowler ignored the jibe. "No, sir General. I'll dispatch the Amundsen team again at once."

"Finish the job this time, Colonel," sneered Rappar. "We should also assume a similar anchorage exists at the North Pole. What assets do we have in that region now?"

Dylan's anxiety was clouding his resolve. "Unfortunately, the Connecticut finished its latest Arctic tour, sir. The Russians moved in right after us. NAVSOC identified the Bryansk surfacing through the ice within two klicks of the pole yesterday, sir."

"Clearly, they're aware their airspace has been traversed," said Rappar thought-fully. "This is going to have to go up the chain."

"They may do the job for us, General," suggested Fowler optimistically.

Rappar leaned menacingly close to the camera, and Fowler involuntarily drew back. "The job, Colonel, has become much more strategic than severing the anchorages," he barked. "We can't allow the Russians to secure the technology Porter is using. You saw the video from Chahuaytire, Colonel. At the very least, we have to gain it for ourselves as a countermeasure. We have to contain this situation now," he spat, pressing his index finger firmly against the table. "Amend the Super Hornets' orders: surveil and report; do not engage. Extend the same orders to Amundsen-Scott. Direct NAVSOC to extend their surveil-lance to include the signal coming from the north." Rappar leaned back with an exasperated sigh. "And now we have to consider what Beijing is doing."

Dylan's mind was in overdrive, just about to redline.

76
ENCANTEMOS

T he Embarquisa was 1,400 nautical miles from their agreed-upon meeting point with the Kartikeya, which was still some three hours farther north. Porter emerged from the halfgate to check in with Amelia and Lakshmi.

"What do you think?" he asked them.

"I think I'm in love," replied Amelia.

"Are you now?" he remarked with a grin.

Amelia replied to Porter with tears in her eyes. "This regal being knows how to make me happier than I could ever imagine." Amelia turned to Lakshmi. "And I've known you less than a week. Yes, Jonas, I am. I'm in love with Lakshmi."

"Apparently, I've missed some of the conversation you two have been having up here," he said, still grinning. "I'll have to hear more."

A large gray blur hurtled downward, only meters from the windscreen, causing the Embarquisa to buck through its turbulence wake.

"That was a military jet." Porter leaned forward between the two flight deck seats, scanning the sky ahead. "Hold your course and altitude, Am. All we can do is watch."

"And hope," Amelia said as she scanned for the jet.

"You'll need more than hope, senorita," came an unfamiliar voice behind Porter, who immediately went tactical. Chacalito expected the reaction and did nothing to resist Porter's attack.

"We were wondering when you'd show up. Who are you? What do you want?" Porter asked him through the half-nelson.

"I work for an organization that sells information to your government," grunted Chacalito, still pinned down. "I photographed you and the aircraft in Chahaytire. I've been gone long enough now that the protocols have been engaged."

"What protocols?" asked Lakshmi, warily.

"They will come looking for me. Actually, they're more interested in anything they can use."

"What will they find?" demanded Porter.

"I left two data cards with photographs and other valuable information under the floor mats in my jeep." Chacalito panted under Porter's weight. "I know these guys. By now, your government already has them. They know who you are, and they want whatever you have that makes gravity go away."

"You still haven't told me what you want."

"I had a long conversation with the woman who speaks through your heart. I believe you know her. She showed me what you're doing. I want to help."

"Well, thank you very much, but we've got this covered. We don't need your help." Porter tightened his hold. Lakshmi unfastened her belt and twisted around toward the men.

"There's more," Chacalito said through gritted teeth. "Ask your pilot to check the oil pressure."

Lakshmi grabbed Porter by his shoulder. "Porter, we have to shut the engine down. And we have F-18s on both sides."

"You're going to have to trust me," Chacalito rasped. "You can't keep holding me here. I know how to fix your plane because I'm the one who sabotaged it."

"Tell him what you did to the plane, Chacalito," Sariah's voice rang through both men's souls, causing Porter to loosen his hold on Chacalito.

"I inserted a device into the oil filler tube," Chacalito admitted hurriedly. "It impedes the oil flow when it receives a set radio frequency. Those F-18 pilots know what it is because it was on that data card too."

Sariah let Haseya know the situation, and she suspended the cable deployment. Amelia shut the engine down. The cabin became eerily quiet, 800 miles south of Yogyakarta and 17,000 feet over nothing but ocean. Chacalito brought a rope with him from the halfgate. He tied it around his waist and opened the copilot side door. He threw the rope across the windscreen and asked Amelia to pull it through her door. Porter offered a parachute, but it didn't take much explanation to see the futility, given their position. Porter tied the rope around his own waist as Chacalito climbed out the copilot door onto the engine cowling. Riding the airplane's nose much like a horse, he held himself upright with his legs gripping the fuselage. He unlatched the cowling door and lifted it carefully, setting the strut in place to hold it open. He balanced himself with one hand on an engine mount tube and removed the oil dipstick. Bending about a centimeter of the end of the dipstick into a hook, he reached into the oil filler tube, removed the device he had inserted in Chahuaytire, and replaced the dipstick.

An F-18 crossed closely underneath them at high speed. The reaction from the gondols and the wake turbulence threw the Embarquisa into a partial nose-up roll. Chacalito held tight to the engine mount, but the cowling cover came down sharply on his arm. In a moment of excruciating pain, he let go of the aircraft. Porter, off-balance from the turbulence, was pulled tightly against the pilot seat as the rope tied to Chacalito yanked him toward the pilot door. The gondols did their job to right the Embarquisa. Amelia held open the pilot door and helped Porter pull Chacalito back into the plane. His arm was broken and bleeding. Lakshmi and Porter carried him across the pilot seat and laid him on the deck floor.

Chacalito took a deep breath and winced through the pain as he tried to lift his arm. "Help me back into the halfgate. I've seen what the Diné can do. I'm certain Haseya can help me. Besides, you have work to do. The engine should start and run normally now. I'll let them know they can run the cable again."

Porter glanced at Lakshmi and Amelia, who both nodded their approval. Again, the F-18 passed beneath them, throwing the group and any loose equipment about the cabin. Chacalito cried aloud in agony. Within seconds, another jet passed above them from the other direction, rocking them with an even greater force. Chacalito gritted his teeth against the pain. His injury was now fully compounded and bleeding profusely. Porter and Lakshmi quickly lifted him and slid him through the halfgate panel. They briefly looked at one another. All their doubts about his welfare and how they put a potentially untrustworthy element back into the halfgate flashed between them for only a second.

Lakshmi jumped back into the copilot seat and fastened her belts. Amelia already had the engine started. Through the right-side window, Porter could clearly see two F-18s in formation, flying in a slow circular pattern about two miles away. Amelia brought the plane back to cruising speed. The Super Hornets, still in tight formation, came within two wingspans of the Embarquisa and held speed and altitude. Porter knew they were gathering massive amounts of data in addition to clear, high-definition video images. With yet another turbulence wake, this time less severe, both jets briefly displayed their weapon-laden underbellies as they peeled off into steep, diving turns.

Porter, Lakshmi, and a good part of the cabin were covered in blood. Porter lifted himself with shaking arms to crouch between the flight deck seats, staring through the windscreen deep in thought. Lakshmi was pale, and Amelia openly wept as she reached out to ask her bloody-faced companions if they were okay.

Sariah spoke to Jonas. She had been able to intercept and alter the communications between the Stennis and the Super Hornets. She knew they would reassess their situation as soon as the jets that had intercepted them returned to refuel in Australia. She hoped it would buy them enough time to rendezvous with the Kartikeya.

77

JUNTEMOS

Amelia spotted the Kartikeya four kilometers ahead, slightly below their altitude, as the Embarquisa crossed the Kapuas River. She tapped Porter on the shoulder and pointed toward it. His wide-eyed smile was contagious. Amelia slowed the plane while Porter dipped his head into the halfgate to advise Matt and Darrell to slow the cable. When they came closer, it became apparent that their closure rate was about equal to the Embarquisa's forward speed. Amelia increased their airspeed slightly, but they were making little progress. Porter suggested coming up to them faster with a small course offset to the west. Amelia increased the power and brought the Embarquisa within 20 meters abeam the Kartikeya.

Sariah had been communicating with Porter occasionally during the trip. When the Kartikeya crossed into Indonesian airspace, Bahn relented, and allowed her to contact him to help coordinate the joining. Each crew securely attached a 50-meter cable to the main cable behind the halfgates and linked the other end to the aircraft's structure. They unfastened the halfgates from the aircraft decks and let them float through the open tail doors. Amelia diverged slightly northeast as Yves did the same to the southwest until the aircraft had passed one another but the extended halfgates had not. The intent was to converge the two cables, link the extensions together, then sever the cable ends from the halfgates. The north and south arcs of the cable would be spliced together and the halfgates could be restowed in their respective aircraft. That proved more difficult than they had anticipated. The convergence of both cables, both gondol-supported halfgates, and their associated aircraft was lighting up radar screens from the Stennis to Point Mugu. The fighter jets were back with new strategies and tactics on how to disrupt Porter's efforts without sacrificing control.

Porter put on his tweed jacket. Equipped with heavy leather gloves, a sport parachute and a gondol, he shimmied across the extension cable and climbed onto the halfgate that was being towed behind the Embarquisa. Gripping the extension cable with one hand, he ducked his head and other arm through the rear intention panel. An F-18 flew under and perpendicular to the main cable, tossing Porter out and away from the halfgate. He grabbed the extension cable with both hands and waited for the wake turbulence to subside. As he worked his way down the cable toward the halfgate, Matt's head and shoulders emerged from the rear intention panel. The Diné had fastened another 50-meter length of wire rope to the main cable inside the halfgate. Matt held out the loose end of this cable to Porter. This cable, when reattached to the Embarquisa, would become the retrieval leash to rejoin the halfgate with the aircraft after the cables were spliced.

Amelia, watching his progress with bated breath, knew exactly what he was trying to do. Adjusting her airspeed slightly, she brought the cables to cross again, bringing the halfgates closer together. Porter, again mounted on the back of the Embarquisa's halfgate, was intently focused on the other. As they approached, Matlali's naked and tattooed upper body emerged from the front panel of the Kartikeya's halfgate. He reached toward Porter, who extended the cable Matt had given him as far as he could. Suddenly Matlali ducked back into the halfgate as two F-18's passed, one over them, one under them while inverted. The resulting compression jolted both halfgates violently and threw Porter into a tumbling arc high above the cable. Miraculously, he was able to hold on to the cable Matt had given him. He turned down the gondol's volume and straightened into a tracking dive back, aiming for the Embarquisa's halfgate. After he reestablished himself, Matlali cautiously reemerged. The main cables were holding shape and placement, but the two halfgates were diverging. All of them were battling their opposition: a winch in a Russian submarine.

The Diné quickly realized that the southern anchors were also working against them. Porter, still straddling the southern halfgate, called for Matt to release more adorned cable to provide additional slack. Blueye asked the same of the Nahua. Their combined release was enough to temporarily overcome the Bryansk's draw, but it also pulled the two 50-meter cable extensions out of range from each other. They could no longer be used to splice the cable. Whether what he was 'hearing' was propagated by one of Sariah's transmitters or the result of deeply ingrained childhood memories wasn't important right now. The Hornets were already inbound for another concussive pass. Lilli's voice resonated through Porter's entire being: *Go the way the flock wants to go. Feel the whole group as one.* Porter, eyes focused on the Kartikeya's halfgate, readjusted the gondol settings carrying the halfgate. The training Bahn had given him about tilting the gondol fields shone brightly, present in his consciousness. There was no doubt, rethinking, or fear. Porter was one with the moment, contributing his verse to the play. The Embarquisa's halfgate, with Porter astraddle, smartly banked left, trailing its adorned cable in a smooth lissajous while bearing directly toward the Kartikeya's halfgate. As the halfgates approached each other, the same cryogenic frost they witnessed in K'antu's mother's kitchen jetted between them. Porter's brilliant maneuver brought the cubes together with a blinding flash and a concussive crack that rolled both aircraft inverted. Yves and Amelia righted their planes by offsetting their wingtip gondol settings. The cable from pole to pole was complete. The two halfgates were sealed together, and the now rectangular double cube was layered over with three centimeters of ice. Yves and Amelia shut down their engines, both aircraft still tethered to the cable with the extensions. Yves, Bahn, Amelia, and Lakshmi desperately searched the sky and the airspace below the planes. Porter was gone.

110 degrees east longitude, 0.00 degrees latitude

Equator

Sosok, West Kalimantan, Indonesia

12:00 Noon, September 23, 2002

<u>HEART CENTER</u>

Empathy bridges hearts in tender ways,

Which the timid and ignorant ridicule

With boasting, and bullying aspersions.

A subtle emerald band 'tween sunset and stars

Where love and compassion flow through our core.

Strength lies in our vulnerability:

In the heart's embrace, we find our true self.

78

ABRACEMOS

Where Bahn's years of careful planning failed, Porter's daredevil scheme to harness the Earth's energy through the steel and textile array succeeded. The right combination of factors contributed to the success of Porter's plan, and this made all the difference. In his hubris, Bahn was blind to this.

The cable, no matter how firmly anchored, and the handmade, love-infused textiles, regardless of their elegance or intricacy, would have been reduced to a glorified clothesline, had it not been for the human factor. To weaken the barrier between scales, all the array needed was a healthy dose of positive, human energy that only those involved in the process could inject. Porter, Bahn, Blueye, Lakshmi, Amelia, Yves, the Diné, and the Nahua were all a part of the equation. The büges, idugans, and shamanic initiates who sacrificed their lives were also integral to the plan's success.

When the two halfgates merged, the intense energies at play rendered the Earth momentarily vulnerable. Much like two people laying their souls bare to each other, surrendering to the vulnerability of true love, for a split second, Mother Earth let her guard down. The barriers between scales weakened and finally relented. In this moment, the collective wisdom of all those who helped weave the tapestry of the universe, before and since Andreana, pulsed through the cable and textile array in the form of pure electromagnetic energy.

The structure served as a beacon of understanding and acceptance to all scales of humanity. It demonstrated that cooperation, harmony, love, selflessness, and a sense of community are integral to achieving heightened consciousness.

Porter was awakened to this truth, just as those who produced the textiles were awakened to the interconnectedness, patterns, balance, complexity, and evolution of the tapestry of the universe. However, he was enlightened enough to realize that even the union, like all things in life, was fleeting. It was brief as it was fragile, but Porter persevered because he wholeheartedly embraced change.

79

AFERREMOS

Dylan, in his frenzied state, determined he had to take control of the situation or he would be buried so deep in the military justice system no one would ever know he was gone. Fowler, following Rappar's orders, was going to stop the southern anchorages from being severed. Dylan needed Porter to be dead and he wasn't going to let anyone stand in his way.

Although the NOAA-G polar-orbiting weather satellite had been "officially" deactivated over a year ago, the military still had access to what was ostensibly a fully functioning DMSP Block 5 communications unit in polar orbit. It also had the advantage of enabling untraceable voice transmission. It ellipsed the earth once every hour-and-a-half, and during 11 minutes per orbit, it was within contact range of the Amundsen-Scott station. Dylan knew the timing would be critical, considering how much time was left before Porter could hook up with whatever was coming from the north. Fowler and Rappar might have wanted whatever technology Porter had developed, but it was his ass on the line. If Porter was alive, he could expose the entire operation, and Dylan's career would be over. Porter was hooked to this cable from the South Pole, and Dylan was going to cut it.

Director Ekstrom was in her pajamas wearing fuzzy slippers and bundled into a fur-lined parka. Her disheveled hair reflected how relaxed life can become in extreme isolation. She'd awakened a bit later than usual because she'd been monitoring geomagnetic experiments well past her normal bedtime. From the galley, over the coffee maker's gurgling, she heard static coming from the comm and control room down the hall. By the time she had shuffled curiously into the room, the radio had gone silent. She engaged the frequency scanner, and it stopped within seconds on an encrypted military carrier signal transmitting static. She fine-tuned the signal and picked up a faint voice transmission. She set her coffee mug on the counter, put on her reading glasses, and sat down at the workstation. She pulled on a pair of headphones and turned up the volume. It was then she heard a loud static band and a chopped and intermittent voice. She pulled out a reference binder to look up the transmission source and found the NOAA-G listed as being decommissioned.

Suddenly, the voice came through clearly, and the static subsided. "Amundsen-Scott. This is Point Mugu SATCOM. How do you read?"

Ekstrom pulled the desk mic closer and keyed it. "Point Mugu, this is Director Ekstrom at Amundsen-Scott. Loud and clear. How me?"

Dylan keyed his mic. "Five by five, director. This is Colonel Michael Fowler, United States Air Force. This is a top priority DoD order."

Ekstrom replied, "Reading you loud and clear. Ready to copy, Colonel."

"Director, we have reason to believe the cable you located and severed yesterday is only one of possibly multiple such cables. Your orders are to find and sever any and all cables until the signature signal is no longer detectable at your location. Confirm receipt."

"Confirmed, Colonel. How soon do you need this done?"

Dylan came back, but his transmission was beginning to weaken. "This is a matter of national security. Time is a critical factor. No delay."

"Confirmed, no delay. Do you want me to report on this frequency when we've cut the cables?" Ekstrom lifted the mic key but heard only static, which was increasing in volume.

Ekstrom found Brandin and Monte in the music room. Brandin's blues guitar riffs were unmistakable, and he rarely practiced without Monte on stand-up bass. Ekstrom opened the door during Brandin's bend and grind up-the-neck solo. Monte waved at Brandin for him to stop and pointed at the door. They both switched off their amplifiers and turned toward her. "I need you guys. Right now."

The winds were still strong, and the September twilight offered little through the blowing snow. Monte and Brandin started their search from the first cable's coordinates, which they found within half an hour without incident. They radioed their position to Ekstrom and let her know the SAR pattern they intended to follow to locate more cables.

Ekstrom was curious why Fowler had used the decommissioned NOAA satellite rather than the TDRS relay. She had little reason to doubt the transmission's validity, considering the military frequency it came in on. Still, she could see no reason why a confirmation message over the TDRS would hurt, especially since the comm was lost before she could get a mutual sign-off.

Within minutes, Point Mugu replied to Ekstrom that Colonel Fowler was off base and had been for two days. Mugu informed her that they had forwarded her message to Fowler and that he would be able to reply directly. Still curious, but not alarmed, Ekstrom checked in with the Spryte crew.

"How's it going boys? Any luck yet?"

Brandin came back. "We have a signal, but it's a bit elusive. Now that we know there may be multiple cables, we're rethinking our triangulations to account for multiple transmission points. We'll get 'em, Boss Lady!"

"Sounds good, Brandin. Sorry I had to interrupt your session. You guys sound great."

"We've got an awesome set ready for the party on Saturday. Wait until…" Brandin's voice was abruptly cut off before he finished his sentence.

Ekstrom replied, accustomed to wavering signal strengths from the storms. "I'm looking forward to it, guys. Six o'clock, right?"

There was no reply from the Spryte. Maybe they found a cable and were investigating, she thought.

"You wanna know what I think?" Monte asked Brandin.

"Not really, but go ahead," he said with a grin.

"We know there's probably more than one of these things, right? What if we're between two of them? Let's stop trying to define a point and instead find a line between two signals. Once we're on the line, we can follow it to one and then reverse course to find the other."

"Not bad for a guy who likes meatloaf!"

"Brandin, listen. Everyone likes meatloaf. What's the matter with you?"

Monte turned the Spryte hard left and tracked toward one of the signals. As they approached, the signal became stronger. They located the ice-covered cable. Monte stayed in the driver's seat while Brandin got out and severed the cable with the torch. Again, but this time with even more force, the cable whip-snapped into the darkness. Monte checked the SAR locator. There was only one signal on the screen, and it was clear and strong. Brandin climbed back in covered in snow, his facial hairs dappled with frost.

"Hooooooo!" Brandin howled. "It's really cold out there."

"You know what fixes that, right?" Monte asked with a smirk.

"We're not having this discussion anymore." Brandin looked at the SAR scanner as he pulled off his gloves. "Well, would you look at that? There can't be more than one now."

Ekstrom finally received a reply from the real Colonel Fowler. "Confirm. Locate and investigate possible sources of specified signal. Report coordinates only. Do not modify or disrupt. Repeat. Report coordinates and await further directives."

Ekstrom went immediately to the radio to contact the Spryte, but Brandin and Monte didn't reply. She continued trying to hail them without success. She replied to Fowler. "Confirm change in orders. Crew is already following prior directive to find and sever any and all cables. It may be too late to stop." Fowler, now with a clear view to Dylan's mutiny, wrote back immediately. "Do not cut the cables. Do not even touch them."

Ekstrom ran straight to the Spryte bay and started the second one. She had been trained to drive it, but it had been a while and she typically had someone on staff who was better qualified to drive. She lit up the SAR scanner and the signal location came through brightly on the screen. She jerked the cat a couple of times before she got the feel for the clutch again. Once she was going smoothly and headed toward the signal, she tried raising the guys again. Still no reply.

It only took about ten minutes for Brandin and Monte to arrive at the signal site. They found the ice-covered cable reflecting the lights from the Spryte. As Monte pulled closer, the Spryte began to lose traction. He shifted to a lower gear and revved the engine as the cat drifted slowly toward the cable. Cluttered manuals, pens, and old protein bars on the dash started floating in the cab. They were both buckled into their seats. The Spryte, reacting to the tracks' rotation, lifted into the air in a long, slow backflip as it passed the cable. Monte and Brandin, absolutely lost at what to do, held onto the overhead grips. Monte shut the engine down. As the Spryte drifted further from the cable, the clutter in the cab began to settle against the right-side window. The Spryte slowly descended into the snow, skidding to a stop, laying on its right side with the tracks in the air.

"What was that? What happened?" Brandin asked Monte, still unwilling to let go of the grips.

"I don't know. Are you okay? Are you injured?"

"Other than being totally freaked out, I'm fine. What *was* that?"

"I think we need to find out," said Monte, gingerly releasing his seatbelt and climbing up and out through the driver's door. Brandin handed the acetylene kit to him as he climbed over the track and dropped to the snow.

"Get a rope and two headlamps and come with me," Monte shouted over the wind.

Brandin tossed a wound length of climbing rope over the track and climbed out after it. They both stepped toward the cable, the path dimly illuminated by their headlamps.

"You feel that?" Monte shouted.

Brandin held his hand on Monte's shoulder and spoke directly into his ear so he could hear him over the wind. "Yeah. I don't like it. Makes me feel sick. Do you think that thing is radioactive?"

"Radioactivity doesn't make a Spryte fly through the air." Monte took a few more steps toward the cable. As he did, the wind pushed him sideways nearly 50 feet where he landed, tumbling in the snow. Brandin backed away toward the Spryte. Monte circled back toward him, maintaining a distance from the cable.

"That was incredible. I felt completely weightless for a moment," Monte exclaimed. "This has to be some experiment gone wrong. That must be why they want us to cut it. Come on, bring the rope. I've got an idea."

Ekstrom had the Spryte's throttle wide open, trying to reach the guys before they cut the cable. She tried the radio again, which the first Spryte did receive, but they weren't listening to it. She estimated she was a little over five minutes from the signal site.

Monte and Brandin hiked upwind of the cable, keeping their distance. Brandin tied one end of the rope around his waist and dug his heels into the snow and sat down in it. Monte, torch kit in hand, tied the other end around his own waist and walked toward the cable, letting the rope slip through his glove as he did. Again, he felt the weightlessness as he approached the cable. Suddenly, his feet slipped from under him, and he lay prone on the snow, holding the rope against the push of the wind. He slowly let the rope slip through his glove as he hovered across the snow, falling toward the cable. Variations in the wind direction swayed him from side-to-side. Monte timed the sways and let the rope slip in time to grab the cable with the hand he had used to hold the rope. Fully weightless now, he furled like a flag in the wind from the cable's lee side. He tried standing by pulling his legs down toward the cable while attempting to wrap his arms around the cable in order to have both available to operate the torch safely. His hand slipped, and he flew away from the cable until the remaining ten feet of slack in the rope was caught with a grunt by Brandin. Now weightless and crudely aerodynamic, Monte rose about 20 feet into the air, as Brandin struggled against his drag from the wind. Brandin began pulling the rope, hand-over-hand, until Monte was once again able to grasp the cable. Brandin pulled a few more arm-lengths in until Monte was held by the rope around his waist, his feet hooked around the cable, and both arms now free to operate the torch. He lit the torch and began to melt the ice around the cable.

Ekstrom, now less than half a mile from the signal, saw the light of the torch in front of her. She flashed the headlights trying to get their attention, but her course, with the wind behind her, had both men looking away and keenly otherwise occupied.

The torch melted through the ice, and molten steel sparks began to fly in the wind. The cable snapped with a crack, and Monte immediately fell 20 feet into the snow. Brandin, still firmly anchored, felt the sudden slack in the rope and thought it had broken. He got up and ran along the rope on the ground until he found Monte.

"Are you okay?" Brandin asked.

"That was awesome! Did you see that?" Monte tried to stand, but his ankle was broken. He sat up in the snow with a huge grin. Brandin knelt next to him just as Ekstrom parked the Spryte. She knew it was too late.

80

LIBEREMOS

The Bryansk had reeled in enough cable that the northernmost gondol had passed through the greased bushing and was descending through the arctic water toward the sub. The moment it passed through the gasketed opening into the hull, the boat began to surface rapidly toward the ice, which—at this thickness—was beyond the Bryansk's capability to break through. The dive officer called the uncontrolled surfacing out to the captain, who immediately ordered the winch crew to reverse their work. They stopped the winch but were unable to reverse it. The captain, now lividly shouting at them to follow his orders, drove the winch crew to cut the cable. The gondoled cable slipped back through the gasketed portal, through the bushing in the ice, and launched into the sky. The Bryansk settled below the ice to a safe depth. The surface crew, startled by the sound of the whiplashing cable, looked at one another with fearful apprehension.

81

ENROLLEMOS

Much like a warm garden hose carrying a single sharp sinusoidal oscillation from a yet-to-be-enlightened gardener, the cable's release from its northern and southern anchorages took time to traverse its extended state. Four thousand gondols, each set to hold the 110th parallel, accelerated the steel rope's elastic tendency to return to its long, warehoused coiling. The first to experience the wave were the 16 balloon-bearing shamans and their initiates, stalwart in their service to Father and Mother Sky. In addition to the rapid oscillation, the entire assembly was lifting away from the earth. Each balloon, still tethered to the cable, was now free to ascend with its individual buoyancy. Within seconds, the cable was accelerating skyward faster than the balloons' ascent rates. As the baskets began bending upward beside the envelopes, the initiates released the tethers before a potential inversion spilled their heat. The balloons righted themselves, decelerated, and settled into an altitude consistent with their buoyancy. Every büge and idugan, 16 of each—who were previously balancing delicately above the cable's gondol field—floated in suspension within the compressing helical tunnel, accelerating away from the earth into thinner air.

Well before the coiling oscillations reached the halfgate union, it started accelerating upward. The Embarquisa and Kartikeya, still tethered to the cable, were being dragged away from the earth by their tails. Both crews, still wondering what had happened to Porter, had a slowly rotating, receding view of the Indonesian rainforest through their windscreens. Bahn, unfortunately so experienced, had anticipated the cable failure possibility and quickly climbed aft to release the extension cable from the Kartikeya. Yves righted the craft. He reduced the onboard gondol volumes and began a rapid descent from 27,000 feet to thicker air. Bahn slumped back into the copilot seat. With a groan of frustration, he threw his head back and covered his face with both hands. Yves glanced at him, sighed, and quietly continued to fly the airplane.

The Stennis's Super Hornets pursued the rapidly accelerating assembly upward, but approaching the compressed coil of gondols induced uncontrollable rolls during their climbs, deteriorating their speed and disorienting the pilots. They backed away, reconfigured, and reinitiated pursuit at a distance until they reached their 15,000-meter service ceiling. The jets descended and turned their attention to the Kartikeya.

Lakshmi and Amelia hurriedly put on the winter gear that had protected them from the Antarctic cold and donned their supplemental oxygen masks. They climbed aft, attempting to release the extension cable, but the retention bolts were frozen solid, despite their concerted efforts with the wrench. Through the plane's open tail, they could see the halfgate union 50 meters above them, rotating slowly. It was either that, or the Embarquisa may have been rotating; they couldn't be certain. The supplemental oxygen tank was mounted under the deck, and they both knew there wasn't time to remove it. They began hyperventilating the oxygen. Dizzy but determined, they held each other's gaze for a moment. Lakshmi took a gondol that they used to lift the halfgate and zipped it inside her jacket. Both women exited the plane and slid along the extension cable toward the union.

As they approached, they could see the exterior was still covered in ice. Steam began flowing from the surface as the ice shed from one of the ten accessible intention panels. Matlali's head and arms emerged briefly from the panel, but he retreated instinctively from the severe cold and lack of oxygen. It was enough, however, to show the women the panel was open and operative. Lakshmi and Amelia each held the other's jacket in one hand and the extension cable in the other. Arm over alternating arm, they pulled themselves toward the main cable.

Amelia glimpsed downward and saw the Embarquisa repeatedly trying to roll right but was frequently resisted by the twisted wire rope's spring. Behind it, through scattered clouds, she could see Indonesia's lush green separated from the cobalt ocean by a white outline of breaking waves and sandy beaches. *It looks so beautiful, relaxing, and warm down there,* thought Amelia. Lakshmi gave Amelia a shake and quickly returned her hand to the cable. Realizing that she was hypoxic, Amelia shook her head sharply, focused on the cable, and continued upward. Once they reached the still-steaming intention panel, Lakshmi helped Amelia through it. Before following her, Lakshmi looked left into one of the coiled cable tunnels. She was starting to see stars and knew she was close to losing consciousness. In response, she put her head through the intention panel and took deep breaths of warm, dry desert air. Amelia scrambled up from the dusty floor to help Matlali get her inside, but she resisted them.

"You're not thinking straight. What's the matter with you? Come inside now." Amelia was still dizzy, but she persisted with passion.

Lakshmi shook her head. "There are people out there. Floating. Unconscious. I saw them," she wheezed between breaths. "Some closer to the halfgate than others, but there's a line of them inside the coil." She took two more deep breaths and lifted her head and shoulders back out into the cold while holding fast to the intention panel's edge. As she did, one of the idugan floated within her reach. Lakshmi let go with one hand, reaching to grab her robe. At the same moment, Matlali grasped Lakshmi's other wrist and began pulling her back inside. Lakshmi held tight to the robe as Matlali drew her inside. Lakshmi's body had passed through the intention panel, but as she tried to pull the idugan through, she was met with resistance. She asked Matlali and Amelia to help her by pulling on her arm and legs. Her fist, fiercely gripping the idugan's robe, came through the intention panel, but she was unable to pull the shamaness inside. Thinking she was stuck across the opening, Lakshmi broke loose from Matlali's grip and instructed them to hold her legs. She pushed her other arm, shoulders, and head through the panel.

The union had ascended considerably farther upward, and the cold and lack of oxygen were all but stifling. Lakshmi was able to grasp the robe around the idugan's shoulders. She spun her around and saw her frozen face, lifeless and smiling peacefully. Lakshmi could pull the robe's corners through the panel, but her head and any other body part met it as though it was solid. Lakshmi, clearly distraught, pled to Matlali for help, but he kept shaking his head and repeating phrases she didn't understand. Amelia held an open palm to Lakshmi's cheek, gently wrapped her other hand around her wrist, and looked into her eyes. Lakshmi slowly relaxed her grip and let the robe slip from her fingers back through the panel. The three of them dropped to their knees on the warm desert silt.

82

GENEREMOS

U nlike her neighbors, Venus and Mars, Earth is, among other things, a dynamo—a planet-sized, electric DC generator. A molten nickel and iron outer core surrounds an inner core of the same metals, solid beneath the Earth's inherent fifty million pounds per square inch pressure and yet, as hot as the Sun's surface: ten thousand degrees Fahrenheit. The Sun and Moon induce tidal movements in the molten outer core, just as they do in the oceans above. Those movements generate an electromagnetic field surrounding the planet. It does far more than make compass needles point north.

The Sun ejects two million tons of positively and negatively charged particles every second, forming the solar wind. Those particles travel at an average speed of one million miles per hour, reaching Earth about ninety minutes after they leave the Sun's corona. Earth's magnetic field deflects most of the solar wind radiation. If it didn't, the wind would strip away its atmosphere, and the planet's life would cease to exist. What does slip through creates the entrancing beauty of the auroras borealis and australis. What is diverted away from the Earth flows around and behind it in northern and southern tail lobes, extending well beyond her moon's orbit.

Some sixty-seven thousand kilometers from the earth, nestled beneath the bow shock of the magnetosphere, a delicate helical array, bearing shamanic sacrifices and adorned with handiworks, settled into a heliocentric earth-synchronous day-side orbit. Here, four thousand gondols found a stable balance between the weak force of gravity and the strength of electromagnetism. At its core, broadcasting through helical antennae, a community welcomed new members with smiles, warm baths and wisdom beyond language. This sweet energy crystal tuned the sun's wind into an interscale portal enveloping both the Earth and, during periods of fullness, her majestic familiar.

83

TAMICEMOS

Matlali and Blueye had been experiencing the effect for about an hour before Amelia and Lakshmi arrived, but it was far more pronounced in the women. Shifting between shivering, weeping, and laughing, Amelia and Lakshmi, already weary from their journey, were now near exhaustion. Blueye nodded knowingly as Matlali tightly wrapped each woman, arms akimbo, in a woven blanket and laid them gently on the alkaline soil. Amelia's teeth chattered. Her face, wet with muddy tears, beamed both apprehension and joy. Her eyes closed, and her body relaxed within the warmth of the blanket. Matlali was no longer able to pass through the intention panel. He knelt and held Lakshmi close to his body, instinctively wanting to soothe her. She continued to alternate between weeping, shuddering, and laughing uncontrollably, but throughout, she gazed into Matlali's eyes with dignity and compassion.

Blueye knelt next to Lakshmi and laid his open palms on the blanket. He closed his eyes and breathed deeply. Lakshmi turned toward Blueye. She heard his voice as his mouth remained still and smiling compassionately.

"Try to relax. You're shifting between scales. What you know as reality is interleaving with another scale's emotions and intelligence. It can be disorienting and frightening. Believe me, I understand. Take deep breaths," he urged. "Your body is reacting instinctively to control your breathing. Focus on your breath. In and out. In and out. Extend your inhale slowly. Hold it, only for a moment, at the top, then just as slowly, let it out." Lakshmi followed his directions, taking shuddering breaths. "Again. In. Yes. And now out. Slowly, Lakshmi."

Lakshmi's shuddering began to subside, still punctuated with occasional full-body shudders. Tears ran in creeks through the silt covering her face. Her body, emotions, thoughts—her entire being—felt as if they had been sliced and interleaved with a community, a humanity, that was as calming and welcoming as it was foreign. She felt an instinctive urge to protect what her consciousness called familiar. It was not herself so much as it was the world she knew. Her mind and heart moved rapidly between old and new. Images of Amelia flashed before her, welling up deep emotions of protectiveness and love. A woman dressed in a sheer, periwinkle gown stood on a verdant hill with arms outstretched, lifting her heart to the midday sun. Amelia called her name and reached out to her in desperation.

Nine shirtless men carried trays of unfamiliar tropical fruits on a beach at sunset. She saw Porter arranging textiles around the halfgate in the Embarquisa. A four-year-old boy, critically injured in a fall, stood on healed legs for the first time and wept. Her mother scolded her, telling her she would never amount to anything unless she held her posture and pursued her studies. The same nine men she saw previously turned in unison and ran boldly downhill, fruits spilling along their path, into a cresting wave building behind an unusually deeply receding one.

"What's happening, Blueye? Are you there?" said Lakshmi, between quivering lips. "There's so much going on. I'm overwhelmed, scared, and deeply in love all at once."

Blueye's fingers gently wrapped the blanket around her. "You and Amelia were outside the halfgates when they merged, and then you both entered moments before you would have surely died. It's a new feeling for all of us. I feel it. In fact, everyone here does, but nowhere near the extent that the two of you are."

"How can you know what I'm feeling?"

"There are a lot of new things we can discuss later when you're stronger. You should rest now." Blueye pressed her arm gently through the blanket to comfort her.

"Amelia. Where is she? Is she alright?" asked Lakshmi.

"She's right here beside you. Turn your head."

"She's shaking! Is she cold? Put another blanket on her. What's wrong with her?"

"She fell asleep shortly after you entered the union. Her vital signs are elevated but within tolerance. We presume she's having symptoms and experiences similar to yours. Holisticians from both scales are observing and caring for both of you."

"Do you know where Porter is?" asked Lakshmi, her voice trembling.

Blueye and Matlali exchanged looks. "We were about to ask you the same question."

84

EVADAMOS

Yves had rolled the pitch trim as far forward as he dared to hold the Kartikeya in a steep dive toward the islands below. He and Bahn had worked together to install the structural improvements to both aircraft. They knew they were strong but had never actually stress-tested them to find out what their maximum airspeed could be.

The Super Hornets, outmaneuvered by the halfgate union, turned their attention to the Kartikeya, easily surpassing Yves's chosen airspeed. One Hornet dove sharply from above, passing closely underneath the Kartikeya, then abruptly pulled up. The top of the F-18 was all Bahn and Yves could see through the windscreen as the Kartikeya rocked and shuddered in the jet's wake turbulence.

"Faster, Yves. Dive as fast as you can," urged Bahn, hastily unfastening his seatbelt. "I'll collect the gondols."

"Already we are too fast, Capitaine! They cross us again she may not hold," said Yves through gritted teeth. His face was a mask of determination.

"That may be our only chance. Keep your seatbelt tight. I'll be right back."

Yves chose not to argue the logic of his statement. Bahn hurriedly opened inspection panels at both wing roots. He pulled the gondols from the wing tips with the nylon twine he had attached to them during installation. He detached two others from the fuselage, where the halfgate had been, and lowered himself back into the copilot seat. Two Hornets dove toward the Kartikeya in tight formation. The first passed directly above, and the second—only a length behind—passed by underneath. The successive compressions created a sharp downward force, separating both wings from the fuselage. The wings sailed away, spraying fuel from severed hoses as the fuselage dove more precipitously toward the jungle below. Yves shut the engine down to keep it from spinning the fuselage along its axis.

Bahn threw five gondols into a rucksack and gave the last one to Yves. He had to shout over the rushing wind. "You know what to do. Hopefully, we won't be too far from each other. Don't turn it on until you're close to the ground. Stay away from the crash site. They'll be looking for these." Bahn patted the rucksack, then climbed toward the aft opening. The Hornets were circling for another pass, but they were too low for anything but reconnaissance. He clutched the rucksack to his chest and rolled out the door.

The Navy pilots reported the aircraft's disintegration and the crash site coordinates and returned to refuel at Learmonth. Indonesian military search and rescue helicopters were deployed from Berau Regency in East Kalimantan.

Bahn watched the Kartikeya's remnants plummet into the jungle. The remaining fuel had been severed along with the wings, leaving nothing to create fire or smoke at the crash site. He engaged a gondol and arrested his descent above the jungle canopy. Not wanting to attract frequency scanners, he lowered himself to the ground and promptly disengaged it.

Bahn turned to see a middle-aged woman with dark hair and wearing a *batik kebaya* standing beside a supplejack tree.

"If I didn't know better, I'd say you were lost," she said to him.

He knew that voice anywhere. "A face to that voice, and you're still inside me," winced Bahn. He slipped the gondol into the rucksack and slung it over one shoulder.

"I'm not sure what you mean." She pulled her auburn hair into a ponytail and wrapped it three times with an elastic band.

"I've always wondered what you looked like." He leaned over slightly, trying to gain a better perspective through the brush.

"It's strange only communicating audibly, isn't it? I've wondered what my contacts look like, too." *She has the gall to call us contacts,* Bahn scoffed inwardly. She dodged his stare and pulled the kebaya's cuffs gently, straightening the laps in the sheer voile covering her sun-kissed arms.

"How did you find me, Sariah?" He looked into her dark brown eyes for the first time. He didn't know what he had expected. Sariah had always been such a larger-than-life presence that he expected more. Perhaps something other-worldly? But he was not disappointed. She was perhaps a head shorter than him but no less commanding. Yet her delicate features, pert, upturned nose, and softly curved lips were a stark contrast to the powerful voice Bahn was used to. In fact, her petite form was so disarming that he was forced to be civil.

"The portal is wide open. It's much easier to locate anomalies now." The kebaya was quite becoming and accentuated her curves. She swayed back and forth subtly, feeling the give in the garment as it wrapped her hips.

"The kid did it then," said Bahn, smirking. "How is he?"

"We don't know his condition. No one has been able to contact him."

Bahn wondered how she could relay this with so little emotion. Then he remembered the cold pragmatism with which she manipulated him into jumping from his scale to this one. Sariah was not exactly forthcoming about the risks associated with the jump or its irreversibility. It probably saved his life, but he had not quite forgiven her. *Always the unemotional pragmatist,* Bahn reflected.

The sun had fallen from its direct overhead perch enough for him to determine direction. He started to walk north but stopped and turned back to her. "Why are you with me? Surely there are better cases. People you could actually help."

"I'm caring for myself with the intention of serving the universe. After what you did..." Sariah's authoritative voice almost faltered. She smiled. "...helping you find your way out of this jungle seems like a good place to start."

"If all you want to do is get me out of this jungle, I don't need your help," Bahn shot back. He hooked his arm into the rucksack and fell into a steady pace northward.

Sariah raised her voice slightly to be sure she could be heard. "I can help you find your way home if that's what you want."

Bahn stopped, looked down, but did not turn around. "Why do you keep on with me? What do you want? Why do you care?"

"Don't be ridiculous." Her heart was open to him now.

"I've been away so long. I don't know what's there for me anymore," said Bahn, shaking his head. "I'm not sure I can even say I have a home."

"You could stay," ventured Sariah.

Bahn turned to face her. "I can't stay here."

"What makes you think it will be better if you go back?"

"It's taboo here not to honor the killing of our own kind. This branch will be pruned away from the whole. It's sick and self-destructive. Staying here is..."

She interrupted him. "Not all of it. In fact, the majority doesn't hold to that as truth. Only the weak and afraid. Those who refuse to look, let alone try to understand."

"Is that enough reason to stay?"

"They're still looking for you."

"They won't find me." His darting eyes betrayed him.

She stepped smartly into his space. "That may be true. But you won't be doing anything worthwhile because you'll be hiding or running. There's so much opportunity here, especially for someone with your talents and experience. Many hear the voices. Fewer listen to sort the flowers from the weeds. Even fewer choose to act upon that gift to nurture the whole." She peered into his eyes. "You can make a difference in this fabric, Bahn."

He turned away and began hiking into the jungle. Within a few paces, he encountered Yves. "How did you find me?"

"I watch where you go before I leave ze craft. Et, Capitaine, je suis un navigateur par excellence." Yves wiped his Ray Bans with a cloth and held them up to the sun before returning them to his face.

"Come back this way. There's someone you need to meet."

Yves followed him back, but there was no one there.

"She was here."

"Qui, Capitaine?"

"Sariah."

"Vous voulez dire que vous l'avez entendue?"

"She was more than a voice this time." Bahn wondered for a moment. "The river is this way. Let's get going."

"Oui, Capitaine."

85

ENVOLVAMOS

Rappar and Hine stood alone in a situation room buried deep under the Pentagon. Video surveillance from the Super Hornets showed the halfgate union, the inverted Embarquisa in tow, ascending rapidly into a deep blue-to-black, thinning atmosphere. The coiling cable and textile array appeared briefly as an aural blur around the union before the video cut off when the Hornets discontinued their pursuit. The next clip showed the Kartikeya's fuselage plummeting into an Indonesian rainforest, one of the wings spiraling away in the background. Rappar stopped the video and raised the lights with a remote.

"What are they using? How do they move like that?" Hine asked.

"We can't be certain. I have teams studying the video," replied Rappar.

"The video? What about the wreckage? What did you find there?"

"The fuselage and wing were made of a composite material we haven't seen before. It's also in the lab, but we haven't determined how they fly like they do."

"And the signature frequency?" Hine asked, looking at Rappar quizzically. "Are we still receiving it?"

"Not from the wreckage."

"What about that box that evaded your sixty-five-million-dollar toys? Surely that's still humming away." Hine leaned into the table, obviously perturbed.

"It is, but it's not localized anymore. At first it was only the aircraft, then it was a line from pole to pole."

"And now, General? What's happening now?"

"It's everywhere, sir."

Hine cocked his head. "Everywhere?"

Rappar debated on how best to break it to the Vice President. *Give it to him straight,* he thought. "Scanners around the globe, at all hours, are able to pick up the signal with equal strength in all quadrants," he paused. "Essentially, Mr. Vice President, the signal encompasses the earth and extends beyond the orbit of the moon."

"What's it doing? Is it a threat to our national security?"

"Unknown. From a strategic standpoint, it's always a disadvantage to be surrounded, sir," admitted Rappar.

"Surely, we have missiles or rockets that can reach the box with the cables and clothes. What do you recommend, Rappar?"

"As I said before, Mr. Vice President, the signal isn't localized anymore. The only way we have to track the object is with that signal."

"You're telling me you can't find it?" Hine was teetering on the edge of another outburst.

"That's correct, Mr. Vice President."

"We have no way to protect ourselves from whatever this is that surrounds us? We're defenseless against any change it intends to bring?" asked Hine, raising his voice.

"We don't know its intentions, if any, sir," said Rappar evenly. "But the answer to your question is yes."

"Is Porter behind this?" huffed Hine. "Have we verified his execution?

"Also unknown, sir. Porter is a Naval Lieutenant Commander with an impeccable record. He excelled in electrical engineering, and I cannot state conclusively that he is behind it. We also don't know his whereabouts or status."

"So let me sum this up. We're surrounded by something we don't understand and we can't find. We have no idea where Porter is or if he's responsible, and the security of our nation's peace and conservation could be at stake, but we aren't quite sure about that either," bellowed Hine derisively. "Is that pretty much it, Rappar?"

"That's accurate, sir," said Rappar, matter-of-factly.

"And what about that insubordinate Captain?" asked Hine, still seething.

"Captain Dylan has been arrested and charged with insubordination and treason. He'll spend the rest of his life in prison. I'm seeing to that personally."

"What can I tell the President?"

"About this?"

"Yes, Rappar! About this!" snapped Hine.

"Nothing, sir. There's nothing *to* tell."

"Not yet," mumbled Hine.

"No sir. Not yet."

86

ADHIRAMOS

Once Lakshmi's and Amelia's shivering ceased and their emotional states had stabilized, Blueye and Matlali led a small group of Diné, who carried the women, to the Nahua village. Quetzal directed them to the bathhouses. Due to their weakened condition, she was adamant that both women receive their preparations immediately upon arrival. Blueye and Matlali bathed after them. They met Quetzal, standing at the outer edge of a seven-meter round recess under the suspended translucent sphere in the sixth bath house. Violet and blue prismatic colors washed over the room and deflected off the sphere's surface.

Lakshmi and Amelia, rejuvenated from their baths, wet hair carefully combed behind their ears, stood, wrapped in knee-length robes, and were left amazed at the simple majesty of the room. Matlali extended his hand to Amelia and escorted her down two steps into the recess at a right angle to Quetzal. Although his stature didn't offer the same physical support as did Matlali's, Blueye confidently extended his hand to Lakshmi and escorted her into the recess opposite Amelia. Both men respectfully climbed back out and stood quietly. A bathhouse steward brought four folded Navajo blankets and laid them one at a time on the floor before each of the three women and one more across the recess from Quetzal. He gracefully departed. Quetzal motioned to another steward, and he gingerly placed a meter-diameter brass hoop on its edge in the center of the recess. The hoop's flat band was about ten centimeters wide.

Quetzal kneeled on the blanket facing the hoop's opening. She extended her arms to the other two women, bidding them to kneel on their blankets with hips pressed forward and shoulders pulled back as she had. The women followed, arms beside them, fingers extended wide, palms facing the hoop. As though it were bound by an unseen vertical axis, the hoop gently turned counterclockwise without losing contact with the floor. What began as a lenticular curve opened to a full circle, exposing Lakshmi and Amelia to one another through the hoop. The hoop continued rotating slowly and stopped 180 degrees from where it started. Both women silently looked at each other and then to Quetzal, searching for a cue on how to proceed. Quetzal gazed momentarily at each woman. Without a word, an "are you ready?" sense filled the room. The hoop began another slow rotation.

"Why'd you wear a dress, Emily? It's a casual get-together." Amelia held open the door to the flat, stepping aside to invite her friend inside.

"It's not every day I can help my bestie celebrate her fifteenth. I'm getting dressed up, ok? Besides, as you know, I'm fancy!" Emily smiled and sashayed down the hallway runner.

Twenty friends had gathered in the living room. Amelia noticed there were one or two she didn't recognize, but Emily had helped organize and was always on top of keeping their social scene fresh.

"You will watch to be certain your guests do not spill anything on my nice carpet." Amelia tried leaning away from the deeply accented and unfamiliar voice, but her body posture held firm.

"Mami, please." Lakshmi looked uneasily around the room at her friends who were quietly chatting and eating hors d'oeuvres from small glass plates and napkins. "You're embarrassing me. I promise I'll clean up any mess after the party." Her mother pursed her lips and gently ran her right hand over the front of her sari.

Lakshmi gently brushed a tickling lock of long, black hair from the pearl strand strung between her earring and a golden crested nose ring. After a cautious glance toward her mother, she moved into the crowd.

Amelia slapped the sides of her head and ran her open palms over her hair as though she had spiders crawling it. Her hands stopped on her ears, pulling her hair back, slightly distorting her face. She stared bug-eyed at Emily.

"Dude, what is up? Are you okay?" Emily was genuinely concerned. "You want me to change the music? I thought you liked Bowie."

Amelia looked around the room. It was her parents' flat, and all the people were her guests again. That woman was gone. She carefully felt her face for unfamiliar jewelry. One of the guests across the room, who she hadn't recognized before, walked directly up to her. The young dark-skinned Indian woman addressed her far too familiarly, grabbed her arm, and pulled her toward her. Amelia, surprised, stared silently into her big, dark brown eyes. Then she knew her.

As the hoop stopped once again, its edge facing each woman, Amelia's eyes were still locked with Lakshmi's. They were physically farther apart than they had been at the party but newly and more deeply entwined.

Quetzal, holding an open-armed backbend, heart exposed to the suspended sphere, looked upward as she addressed the room. "Inin ka in tenki universotl. In tepitsin iuan ayemo tlatsiski miaktin altepemeh ipan sepa. Tlasemanka sanse. Sekan tlachiuh in universotl."

This is the wholeness of the universe. The small and still hold multiple states at once. Each effect, always unique, serves and nurtures the whole.

Amelia bent and rested her head on the blanket. Lakshmi broke her gaze from Amelia and looked to Quetzal, but her head was still facing the sphere, and her eyes were closed. With silent tears, Lakshmi pleaded to Blueye for understanding. He had his palms pressed together in front of his face. His confident gaze offered encouragement to remain steadfast. It was clear he understood the magnitude of their experience.

Amelia rose still higher on her knees, emotionally unleashed. Her mind struggled to make sense of her inner turmoil. Yet, language often failed miserably when it came to matters of the heart. She realized that the sincerest actions are often driven by emotions for which we have no words.

Her cries filled the room with her anguish. "Why did you let her treat you that way? You were so filled with love. I want that Lakshmi back. I want all of you. I want the love she made you hide."

Lakshmi realized that love often triumphs over the fears instilled through years of parental conditioning. Overcome with compassion, she called back out to her. "Mami only wanted the best for me. I know she was hard on me, Am. But I'm still here. I'm here right now."

Blueye made a half step in her direction but stopped with the subtlest of motions from Quetzal's left hand.

Amelia continued to cry out. Quetzal gently raised her palm to Matlali. "Laks, I thought you were beautiful. You are." Tears were flowing freely now. "But the beauty of your youth takes my breath away. I saw you. I saw her bury you under her insecurities. Why did she treat you like that? Why did she take it all away?" Amelia addressed Quetzal, distraught. "What is this? What are you doing to us? And where are we?" She looked to Blueye and Matlali, hoping for answers. "What is this place?"

Quetzal answered her. "This place is where we've always been. As is every other place."

Amelia calmed upon hearing her voice. "But I don't know where I am. I only know Lakshmi."

Quetzal continued. "Why, if you know her, are you upset about what happened with her mother?"

Amelia raised her wet eyes to Lakshmi. "I didn't know that part."

Quetzal expounded, "You know Lakshmi as one whole being, yet there are aspects of her life you haven't come to know. Your feelings and compassion for her are deep. How is it you can love her, knowing you do not know her completely?"

Amelia spoke softly now. "I feel her. I see her intentions. I know who she is. Sure, there are things I still don't know, but that makes her interesting. It makes me want to know her more and love her more."

Quetzal settled on her haunches and laid her palms on her robe. "So, it is with where we are."

Amelia looked puzzled. "I'm sorry. I don't understand."

Quetzal's voice was warm, and her eyes softened. "Lakshmi is everything to you."

Amelia lifted her eyes to Lakshmi and replied. "Yes, she is."

Quetzal continued. "This place. These manifestations." Her hands gestured to the sphere swathed in deep hues. "This station. The scale you come from. Skydive West. The jungles in Bolivia. The Antarctic expanse. These people. All people. All animals, plants, insects, bacteria, elemental particles, you, Amelia. We are all distinct, unique manifestations of one whole. One universe. Each and every manifestation is both unique and the whole universe simultaneously. We are all one. Every action we take, every intention we hold, affects the entire universe. Every movement of every star, planet, comet, solar system, and galaxy affects everything because it is all one. The same way you know Lakshmi enough to love her, and yet you don't know all of her."

"I still don't really understand. I mean, we didn't fly all the way around the world so I could learn that Lakshmi is my universal love."

"The importance of both of you feeling and understanding this comparison at a deeply emotional level is essential for what we are about to do." Quetzal stood and bid the two women to do the same.

Lilli, Murielle, Sariah, and another woman, who Sariah introduced as Dadirri, were also gathered around the suspended sphere in the bathhouse. Like the others, they had been bathed, robed, and their hair neatly combed.

"Those willing to embrace consciousness are free to do so now that the portal is open," said Sariah while they waited for the ritual to resume.

"Consciousness is a fundamental aspect of the functioning of the cosmos. It complements our understanding of the universe's machinations, without superseding or altering it," explained Dadirri, her ochre-hued robe awash in blues and violets reflected off the sphere. "Much like Calculus to geometry, trigonometry, and algebra. It offers a deeper, more comprehensive perspective of abstract concepts."

Murielle considered this. "A sort of double-slit experiment that offers a glimpse into the profound truth that the conscious observation ironically affects what is observed."

"So you see, Lilli, we owe Porter a great debt of gratitude," said Sariah.

Lilli acknowledged this with a solemn nod.

Despite their failure to locate him, Lilli found solace in knowing that her son had succeeded in his mission. Porter's actions had not altered the cosmos, rather he had succeeded in instilling a conscious understanding that consciousness itself is one of its properties.

Haseya, freshly bathed and robed, entered from the fifth bathhouse, walking silently toward the recess. Following her, all similarly bathed and dressed, were Chacalito, Delphine, and Matt. Darrel stood with the other Diné in the periphery. They distributed themselves outside the recess facing the sphere. Flanked by four bathhouse stewards, a tall forty-something woman, wearing a long white robe, strode confidently, but with the same silent reverence the others demonstrated, toward the recess. Her appearance showed a kinship to the Diné. Her countenance was imposing and somewhat masculine. Her cheekbones were high and wide, jaw prominent and square, and eyes set deep and heavily browed. She wore silver earrings adorned with rough-hewn turquoise arrowheads. Two strands of turquoise beads interspersed with bloodstone, lepidolite, and jasper were draped across her chest. Her long, brown hair was wet and freshly combed as the other women's. Four large white and tan feathers, although clearly adorning her hair, seemed to float effortlessly aside her head as though they were ready to take flight. Her lips were smooth and dark. Her mouth, closed and straight, expressed solemnity.

Two shirtless Nahua stewards stepped down into the recess, turned, and extended their strong, tattooed arms toward the woman. She took their hands and descended gracefully into the recess in position opposite Quetzal. She knelt upon the blanket before releasing the stewards' hands. The stewards pressed their palms together in front of their faces, bowed slightly, and stepped out of the recess. As she knelt, Quetzal did the same and bid Lakshmi and Amelia to follow. Amelia caught Lakshmi's gaze, which was as filled with the same wonder as her own. Both young women raised their eyes to the crowd that had quietly surrounded the recess. One hundred and eight Diné and an even larger contingent of Nahua, all freshly bathed and robed, stood with reverence, facing the center of the recess. The symbolism of the assembly was not lost on Lakshmi. *It's as if their interleaving resembled the mingling of scales and paradigms*, she mused.

Amelia broke the reverence with childlike reason. "Are we going to do that again? I'm not ready to go down that rabbit hole." She gestured politely to the imposing woman. "And pardon me, ma'am. With respect, I don't know who you are or what you want from me." She glanced imploringly at Quetzal and across to Lakshmi for support. "Please, somebody tell us what's going on."

Quetzal stood back up and addressed Amelia. Although it was tender and quiet, Amelia could sense that her voice flowed through the assembly, and they could hear her just as clearly. Quetzal extended her arms gently outward, swept one each past the two young women, then pressed her palms together in front of her heart, and set her gaze upon the woman across the recess. "May I introduce Na'ashjé'íí. She and I have known each other for a very long time." She paused, her eyes offering loving respect. "She does not communicate using language as we do. Instead, through her mastery of manifestation, she will show us our path. She will also touch each of us emotionally at important junctures to underscore the importance and tailor her teachings to each student. The energy field deployed by this halfgate union has opened a gateway between scales. Na'ashjé'íí is one of the architects of the universal fabric. She is here to teach us, as she has many times before, how to weave and maintain.

Lakshmi, Amelia: The way you came into this union was not coincidental. From the very edge of maintaining your existence in the scale you came from, you both entered after the union was made whole. For a brief time, your bodies and your beings straddled both scales. You felt the interleaving. The shuddering in your bodies. The mixing of images and experiences, as I showed you from your fifteenth birthdays. We have the classroom. We have the teacher. We have the students surrounding us ready to learn to teach. You, my dears, are the bridge, the essential catalysts to facilitate the flow of energies, intelligence, emotions, and creativity between these scales."

Lakshmi spoke for the first time. "We don't know what we're doing. What's going on here is pivotal. Are you sure you have the right people?"

Quetzal replied. "Na'ashjé'íí is aware of your youth and experience. You will never be in a position where you aren't ready and prepared. It is the state of your beings, the interleaved energy patterns from both scales infused in your bodies—that cannot be taught. Think of it this way. We can plant a tree and give it soil, water, and sunlight. We can prune it and care for it. But unless there was a seed to start the tree, there is no tree."

"So, we are the seeds that open the portal?" Amelia asked.

Quetzal turned to her. "The portal is already open. It is the energy flow between them that we intend to grow."

"So, what next?" asked Lakshmi.

"Physical dimensions blur with the honing of consciousness," answered Dadirri. "To become fully conscious, we must shed our ego and denounce the last remnants of our matter-centric existence."

As Dadirri spoke, Lakshmi was gripped by an overwhelming sense of fulfillment. She realized that Na'ashje'ii was not the only one with the power to affect someone emotionally. Looking at Amelia's relaxed demeanor, she had a hunch that she was not alone in it.

"Call it an apotheosis," said Dadirri.

Amelia knelt erect, pulled her shoulders and arms back, and extended her hips forward. She gave Lakshmi the game face she was accustomed to making during challenging parts of a flight. Lakshmi mirrored her posture and confidence. Quetzal and Na'ashjé'íí similarly opened their hearts to the sphere. The hoop began a slow rotation, which steadily increased until it appeared as a hazy, translucent sphere, whirling on the ground before them.

87

RECONCILIEMOS

"**A**re you telling me you're responsible for the deaths of thousands of Americans?" Michelle Hine took off her glasses and rubbed the bridge of her nose. The irony of the gesture was not lost on her. Her father did the same thing when he was on edge, and right now, she hated to think that they were anything alike. She didn't know what made her resent her father more, the fact that he gave the orders that led to the deaths of thousands or that, after nearly twenty-three years, he had a sudden pang of conscience that forced him to burden her with the knowledge. Hine had told her everything, from the Twin Tower debacle to the mysterious device, with its textile and cable array in tow, that had so far eluded their most advanced reconnaissance and surveillance technology.

A now much older and wiser Hine averted his gaze. "Our intention..." He stopped short, realizing the hypocrisy of trying to dodge responsibility now. He wanted to come clean with his daughter; he might as well do it right. "*My* intention was to solidify the country's position as *the* global superpower."

"And that justifies such a massacre?" spat Michelle. Her father looked wounded. She knew that she didn't have to rub it in. His part in the scheme had taken its toll on her father. The lines on his forehead were etched deeper, he was balder, and there were bags under his once lively blue eyes. She leaned back in the recliner of her well-appointed office. "And you believe that this could somehow revolutionize conciliation efforts?" she said, incredulous.

"That's my only consolation," admitted Hine. "Our scientists believe that it opened a type of portal."

"A portal to what?"

Hine inhaled deeply. This would take some explaining. "We don't know exactly," he said flatly. "What we *do* know is that only some are susceptible to its effects, those who are inherently predisposed to consciousness. It rewired their brains, altered their brain chemistry." Hine paused to let this information sink in. "We have found that such individuals are now more receptive to the compassion and cooperation that comes with increased consciousness."

Michelle toyed with the three-hundred-something-page report on the findings her father had given her less than an hour ago; most of its physics went right over her head.

"And the evidence is conclusive?" she asked, skeptical.

Hine nodded. Seeing the results, Hine believed he could finally appreciate the role consciousness played in the grand scheme of things. "At the time, I had no idea what I was setting in motion," cringed Hine.

"I think it changed me," said Hine, with a rueful smile. "Let's just say that I now understand the consequences of my actions more than you could ever imagine," he revealed, with unveiled anguish. "And I have come to terms with it. My only hope is that you can look past this."

Michelle realized how hard this must be for such a proud man. "You do realize the position you've put me in," she said bitterly. Following in her father's footsteps, she had taken to politics. She knew that if she had any intention of staying on, her father's involvement could never come to light. And yet he had come to ask for her help to make things right, to implore her to use the information in the report to promote conciliation efforts. "I'll see what I can do without getting your name involved," complied Michelle, with a sigh. "For what it's worth, I'm glad you came to me and had faith in me to use it for the greater good."

Hine mustered the courage to finally look his daughter in the eye, an almost imperceptible smile of relief tugging at the corner of his lips.

88

VAYAMOS

When Andreana entered Mrs. MacLaren's parlor, she found her sitting by the fire. It cast a warm glow over her aging features. On her lap, she had a tweed jacket with large oak toggles sewn to the front and engraved ivory buttons on the cuffs.

"Tha seo airson Gille." "This is for Gille." said Mrs. MacLaren, running her hand over the raw felted wool nostalgically. *"Chaidh a ghluasad bho athair gu mac thar nan ginealaichean. A-nis is e tionndadh Ghille a th' ann."* "It was passed from father to son over the generations. Now it's Gille's turn."

"Tha i breagha!" "It's beautiful!" beamed Andreana, although she puzzled over why Mrs. MacLaren had summoned her instead of Gille if the jacket was meant for him.

"Bidh feum aige air far an tèid e," "He'll need it where he's going," said Mrs. MacLaren, wistfully.

"Gille? Càit a bheil e a' dol?" "Gille? Where is he going?" asked Andreana, confused.

Mrs. MacLaren only smiled knowingly. *"Is dòcha gum bi fir a' caitheamh an seacaid, ach tha e an urra ris na boireannaich dèanamh cinnteach gun tèid a thoirt don ath fhireannach san loidhne."* "The jacket may be worn by men, but it's the women's responsibility to ensure that it's passed on to the next male in line." Mrs. MacLaren added encouragingly, *"Is tu a stiùbhard a-nis."* "You're its steward now."

Andreana nodded with uncertainty.

"Tha a h-uile dad sa bheatha eadar-cheangailte. Thu fhèin, Gille, mi..." "Every-thing in life is interconnected. You, Gille, me..." Mrs. MacLaren smiled radi-antly at Andreanna, *"...agus tha a h-uile duine eile ri thighinn eadar-cheangailte agus deatamach, mar a h-uile snàithlean a nì an seacaid seo."* "...and everyone else to come is interrelated and crucial, like each thread that makes this jacket." She turned to Andreana and peered into her eyes. *"Am faic thu an co-sheirm ann an aodach na cruinne-cè?"* "Can you see the harmony in the fabric of the universe?" She asked this with such uncanny clarity that Andreana knew it was not idle or senile banter. With her fingertips, Andreana felt the tweed of the jacket that Mrs. MacLaren thrust at her. Her eyes welled with tears as she realized that Mrs. MacLaren was right.

He would *need it where he's going.*

Translations

The chapter titles are descriptive verbs in Spanish conjugated into the first person plural present subjunctive. The "we" form choice should be obvious. Present, well, if you know, you know. Subjunctive, through its acknowledgement of doubt, emotion, or being contrary to fact, accepts the infinite possibilities in every moment. English barely scratches the surface of the subjunctive and is seldom recognized or used correctly e.g. "if I was a sculptor." Portuguese does it best and its inherent fluency is reflected in the joyous cultures of Portugal and Brazil. The same is true of Spain and all of Latin America, Spanish being a close second in terms of subjunctive use. The foundational indigenous cultures of Latin America amplify the effects significantly. Love-based subsets of infinity that recognize the wholeness of humanity simply don't roll off the English tongue with much alacrity and that holds those who language-limit themselves from enjoying such rewards. Think again, perhaps, when offered a gourd of sparkling consciousness while dying of thirst in the desert.

Chapter titles

1. Entrelacemos: *Let us intertwine*

2. Caigamos: *Let us fall*

3. Escapemos: *Let us escape*

4. Apuremos: *Let us hurry*

5. Oprimamos: *Let us oppress*

6. Delicemos: *Let us slip*

7. Atragantemos: *Let us gag*

8. Temblemos: *Let us tremble*

9. Discrepemos: *Let us disagree*

10. Afluyamos: *Let us flow*

11. Desayunemos: *Let us break fast*

12. Traslademos: *Let us transfer*

13. Vomitemos: *Let us vomit*

14. Transmitamos: *Let us transmit*

15. Quememos: *Let us burn*

16. Contravengamos: *Let us contravene*

17. Abatamos: *Let us get down*

18. Engañemos: *Let us deceive*

19. Entreguemos: *Let us deliver*

20. Entendamos: *Let us understand*

21. Investigemos: *Let us investigate*

22. Pilotemos: *Let us pilot*

23. Aterrizemos: *Let us land*

24. Distorsionemos: *Let us distort*

25. Golpeemos: *Let us hit*

26. Vistamos: *Let us get dressed*

27. Planifiquemos: *Let us plan*

28. Abramos: *Let us open*

29. Encontremos: *Let us encounter*

30. Edifiquemos: *Let us build*

31. Faltemos: *Let us miss*

32. Arrebatemos: *Let us snatch*

33. Secuestremos: *Let us kidnap*

34. Tartamudeemos: *Let us stutter*

35. Lavemos: *Let us wash*

36. Elaboremos: *Let us elaborate*

37. Busquemos: *Let us seek*

38. Meditemos: *Let us meditate*

39. Cargemos: *Let us load*

40. Giremos: *Let us rotate*

41. Coqueteemos: *Let us flirt*

42. Ayudemos: *Let us help*

43. Peleemos: *Let us fight*

44. Naveguemos: *Let us navigate*

45. Compremos: *Let us purchase*

46. Aspiremos: *Let us aspire*

47. Espiemos: *Let us spy*

48. Filtremos: *Let us filter*

49. Paguemos: *Let us pay*

50. Dosifiquemos: *Let us dose*

51. Negocieemos: *Let us negotiate*

52. Transformemos: *Let us transform*

53. Helemos: *Let us freeze*

54. Atravesemos: *Let us cross*

55. Deseemos: *Let us desire*

56. Rompamos: *Let us break*

57. Empotremos: *Let us embed*

58. Atajemos: *Let us catch*

59. Aprendamos: *Let us learn*

60. Retengamos: *Let us retain*

61. Cambiemos: *Let us change*

62. Imaginemos: *Let us imagine*

63. Resonemos: *Let us resonate*

64. Reconvengamos: *Let us reconvene*

65. Coincidamos: *Let us coincide*

66. Interpongamos: *Let us intervene*

67. Miremos: *Let us look*

68. Guiñemos: *Let us yaw*

69. Levantemos: *Let us get up*

70. Crispemos: *Let us twitch*

71. Absorbamos: *Let us absorb*

72. Mostremos: *Let us show*

73. Desenmarañemos: *Let us unravel*

74. Ahorremos: *Let us save*

75. Soportemos: *Let us support*

76. Encantemos: *Let us enchant*

77. Juntemos: *Let us join*

78. Abracemos: *Let us hug*

79. Aferremos: *Let us grasp*

80. Liberemos: *Let us let go*

81. Enrollemos: *Let us roll*

82. Generemos: *Let us generate*

83. Tamicemos: *Let us sift*

84. Evadamos: *Let us evade*

85. Envolvamos: *Let us envelop*

86. Adhiramos: *Let us adhere*

87. Reconciliemos: *Let us reconcile*

88. Vayamos: *Let us go*

Chapter 15

"Hello. Hola. Bonjour. Bom dia. Ni hao. Hej pa det. Guten tag."

Greetings in: English, French, Portuguese, Mandarin, Swedish and German.

Chapter 26

"Let's set things straight off, shall we? We don't have much time. Laddie, you're about to get the shit kicked right out of you."

"Don't you go underestimating what is about to happen because you think I'm some feeble old lass."

"Your scale is about a half a second from being let go. I'm still here, dammit! I'm still here because I believe in you. I made a promise to the likes of your mother."

"What are you going to do, lad? You found me, yes, but it's you that has to act. Tell me, Jonas. What's your plan?"

"Oh! That's what you call following your intuition, is it? That's the best you know? You can bring a building to its knees but you can't figure out how to address the problem? How to get the men to respect the women? How to get men to respect their own kin? Their own species?"

"How to get them past thinking they're betraying others? It's their greatest flaw. Greatest stopper of the progress."

"A bheil seo mar a dh'fheumas sinn obrachadh, mo nighean?" *Is this how we must work, my daughter?*

"Well then, Jonas. Let's hear it."

"That's a good start. What else do you have?"

"Laddie, if all of them go, why do it at all? There's many who would never go. They wouldn't want it."

"No, it wouldn't be worth a half of a penny to anyone."

"And what about those who take it from others just to serve themselves?"

"Yes, until there's no one left to fight with. So Jonas. I've heard the why. I still haven't heard the how."

Well then! Now you're thinking! Murielle, be a love and fetch the jacket. You know the one."

"I've got a small gift for you, lad. It will help you figure out how to love the earth. You show the earth your love and you will show the men."

"Give it to him, Murielle. Put it on, Jonas. See how it fits you."

"It was my grandmother who made it. She who taught me the waulking. Grandma MacClaren. She made it for her husband."

"Go on, then. Put it on. See how it fits you!"

"You know. You see me as a young child, don't you now?"

"Yes, Jonas. It is your Grandma Keiti. But you're seeing me as a child. Well, a little older than that now. How I was when I was a mother to Murielle. What else can you see, Lad? Better now, how do you feel?"

"The jacket you put on. It's a tweed Grandma MacClaren made. It let's you see the entire work, lad. It was for her husband."

"You've seen the love in the wool, now? Are you feeling the love of your mothers?"

"Yes, lad. You know. You see it all. It's not just that one either. It's all of them. Well, all of them that are hand made. The knowing goes in like that.

"Yes, you best be off."

"Agaibh moran obair ri dheanamh, gille." *"You have a lot of work to do, boy."*

Chapter 34

Ka totonki nikan, noikniu. Teuatlkiya tlasohtla akameh atl? *It is hot here, my friend. May I offer you some water?*

Tikpiah kopa yauilistli. Tiuil moneki atl. *We have a long journey. You will take water.*

Chapter 35

Tikpia okatka kochitok uikpa se ueyakauitl. Tikpiah mitsnokpiliua toyuka. *You have been asleep for a long time. We have to get you ready.*

Chapter 55

Ze madame Cihuātlahtoāni - she is here with us, no? In zees 'alf-gate? Mais la madame araignée - she ride en L'Embarquise? Comment parles-tu avec les deux femmes?

Mme. Cihuātlahtoāni – she is here with us, isn't she? In this halfgate? But the Spider Woman. She is riding in the Embarquisa? How do you speak with the two women?

Chapter 58

Что ты делаешь? Сделайте этот самолет стабильным сейчас же! Если у нас не будет четких фотографий, они никогда в это не поверят.

What are you doing? Make this plane stable now! If we don't have clear photos, they'll never believe it.

Chapter 61

Peut-être, Capitaine, the Cihuātlahtoāni, elle a raison.

Perhaps, Captain, the Cihuātlahtoāni is right.

May be is our intentions besoin de changer. Est-il possible que nous ayons l'intention de notre propre succès."

Perhaps our intentions need to change. Is it possible that we intend to achieve our own success?

N'est-ce pas ainsi que nous entrons dans la demi-porte?

Isn't that how we enter the halfgate?

Et nous? Ne nous soucions-nous pas de la communauté?

And us? Don't we care about the community?

Alors pourquoi, Capitaine, we not intend it now?

Then why, Captain don't we intend it now?

Chapter 71

Escuchó nuevamente la voz tranquila pero firme de Sariah. "Porque decidiste ir al dentro?"

Again he heard Sariah's calm but firm voice. "Why did you decide to go inside?"

"Quien eres? Como estas hablando conmigo? Donde estas?" Chacalito buscó frenéticamente la voz.

"Who are you? How are you speaking with me? Where are you?" Chacalito frantically searched for the source of the voice.

"No es importante. No debes estar alli. Contesteme. Porque entraste a la media puerta? Que quieres?" Ella sabía que tenía que superar su resolución.

That's not important. You shouldn't be here. Answer me! Why did you enter the halfgate? What do you want?" She knew she had to overcome his resolve.

"No te puedo ver. Pero siento su voz en el corazon. Como lo puedes hacer?" La paciencia del Chacalito se agotó. "Es tu que tienes que contestar, mujer." Chacalito tomó su arma, olvidando que la había perdido en la cocina.

"I can't see you. But I feel your voice inside me. How do you do that?" Chacalito's patience had run its course. "It's you that needs to give some answers, woman." Chacalito reached for his weapon, forgetting he had left it in the kitchen.

"Ya se quien eres. Eres un artesano del conocimiento." El tono de Sariah se volvió casi tranquilizador. "Tambien conozco su corazon y es simpatico."

"I already know who you are. You are an artisan of intelligence." Sariah's tone became almost reassuring. "I also know your heart and it's a good one."

"No sabes nada. No me conoces," dijo Chacalito indignado.

"You don't know shit. You don't know me at all." said Chacalito indignantly.

"Si se cuantas veces te han lastimado, Chacalito. Se cuantas veces lo has intentado. Sé lo mucho que te preocupas por otras personas. Pero vendes tu trabajo a aquellos que sabes que causará dolor. Tus intenciones son buenas pero tus acciones no están de acuerdo."

I know how many times they've hurt you, Chacalito. And how many times you've tried. I know enough to know you care about other people. But you sell your works to those you know will use it to cause others pain. Your intentions are good but your actions say something different.

La respuesta de Chacalito fue inexpresiva. "Lo hago por el dinero."

Chacalito's response was expressionless. "I do it for the money."

"Y sin embargo sé que tus intereses están mucho más vivos que eso. Creo que estés aqui por otras razones," sondeada Sariah.

"And yet I know that your interests are far more alive than that. I believe you're here for other reasons." Sariah probed.

"Están construyendo algo profundamente hermoso." A pesar de sus reservas, había una nota de optimismo en su voz "Quiero ser parte de esto. Quiero que mi mano esté en ella."

"What they're building is profoundly beautiful." Despite his reservations, there was a note of optimism in his voice. "I want to be part of it. I want a hand in it."

"Pues claramente ya lo eres. Todo lo que tienes que hacer para profundizar es comprometer tu intención como alguien que ama la vida," Sariah engatusada.

"Well clearly you already are. All you have to do to go deeper is commit to be a person who loves life." She was almost cajoling him.

Chacalito se burló, "No hay dinero en eso."

Chacalito scoffed. "There's no money in that."

"Claro que no! Si quieres ser parte de la vida, si quieres amar la vida, debes dejar atrás esas cosas que no están vivas."

"Of course not! If you really want to be part of life, if you want to love life, you have to let go of the that which isn't alive."

"Muéstrame cómo," Chacalito suplicó.

"Show me how." Chacalito pleaded.

"Os muestra. Muéstranos con las manos. Muéstranos el trabajo que pueden hacer las manos para que podamos confiar en ti," Saríah lo animó. "Demuestre con su trabajo que sus intenciones son sustentar y nutrir la vida. Inserta la mano, Chacalito."

"You show us! Show us with your hands. Show us the works your hands can do so we can trust you." Sariah was encouraging him now. "Show us through your works that you intend to sustain and nurture life. Put that hand in, Chacalito!"

Chapter 84

"Et, Capitaine, je suis un navigateur par excellence."

And, Captain, I'm an excellent navigator.

"Qui, Capitaine?"

Who, Captain?

"Vous voulez dire que vous l'avez entendue."

You mean you heard her, right?

"Oui, Capitaine."

Yes, Captain.

ACKNOWLEDGEMENTS

I offer gratitude for the beings who've shown me their approach to life from a place of love:

Catherine, Duane, Marion, Tony, Jeannie, Larry, Mrs. Mack, Lenore, Reed, Blair, Mr. Smith, Jonathan, Harold, Kingsley, Doug, Wayne, Mark, Donald, Webster, Eames, Chris P., Dr. Bonz, Clara, Helen, Kari, Shelly, Adriana, Stephanie, Eric, Peter, John P., Prudence, Marguerite, Anita, Rhonda, Diane, Malcolm, Craig, Luis, Carl, Maurice, Andrew, Chris S., Marc W., Robert H., Robert F., Mr. Chef, George, Willa, Jami, Dana, Kurt, Sara, Charity, Eileen, Phil, Emilee, Jordan, Gene, Nita, Justian, Jill, Matt, and Kelly. Todd, who on top of all his magic, introduced me to the Mandelbrot set. Adam at MathsTown whose gorgeous renderings of fractal Mandelbrot zooms open a window to infinity. A special thanks to Marc Zegans for nursing this project through its most vulnerable stages.

And to my special someone who makes all the magic become real. You make my world a place of love.

ABOUT THE AUTHOR

"Kamich Aelk" is the pen name of Deaglan Ó Dónaill (also known as Walid Abdel Ismail Ghaffa), a novelist, poet, critic, Egyptologist and trampoline commentator. Mr. Aelk's œuvre, spanning over 37 books, allegorizes the cause of Irish Unification through Nubian folklore.

Long rumored to be a *djinn*, or possibly *faerie* god-king of the Tuatha Dé Dannan, Aelk withdrew from public life in 2017, shortly after being shortlisted for the Booker Prize for his novella *A Shillelagh for Fatima*. "It is high time I returned to the spirit realms," he said, and vanished in a cloud of milkweed.

Reports of shadowy backstage sightings by road crew at the Glastonbury Festival and Mali's Festival in the Desert have gone unconfirmed.

Made in the USA
Las Vegas, NV
01 June 2025

11a38dcd-a80a-415d-8122-1a0694c445cfR01